Every Breath You Take

Center Point
Large Print

Also by M. K. Gilroy and available from
Center Point Large Print:

Cuts Like a Knife

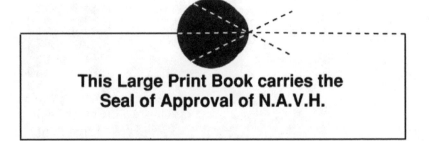

Every Breath You Take

M. K. GILROY

CENTER POINT LARGE PRINT
THORNDIKE, MAINE

This Center Point Large Print edition is published
in the year 2014 by arrangement with Worthy Media, Inc.

The text of this Large Print edition is unabridged.
In other aspects, this book may vary
from the original edition.
Printed in the United States of America
on permanent paper.
Set in 16-point Times New Roman type.

ISBN: 978-1-61173-952-7

Library of Congress Cataloging-in-Publication Data

Gilroy, M. K.
Every breath you take : a Kristen Conner novel / M. K. Gilroy.
pages cm
ISBN 978-1-61173-952-7 (library binding : alk. paper)
1. Policewomen—Fiction. 2. Murder—Investigation—Fiction.
   3. Online dating—Fiction. 4. Chicago (Ill.)—Fiction.
   5. Mystery fiction. 6. Large type books. I. Title.
PS3607.I45525E94 2014
813′.6—dc23
                                                    2013024115

For
Merrick, Bo, and Zach!

PART ONE

Betrayal can only happen if you love.
JOHN LE CARRÉ

1

Tuesday, September 4
9:59 p.m.

No. No! I'm not seeing what I'm seeing. I've never seen so much blood. This can't be him.

What am I doing here? It was so stupid to come over. I just wanted to let him know how he made me feel. He was awful to me. He was awful to everyone. A user and abuser.

To think I thought there might be something real between us. He was too damaged emotionally to have anything real with anybody.

When I didn't hate him, I thought I might love him.

But this was never supposed to happen. I just wanted him to be scared.

Maybe this has nothing to do with me. And I don't think he would have killed him. Just scare him. That's all. Maybe someone else did. There were plenty who wanted him dead.

I need to call the police. But how can I explain why I was here? And how I got in? Will they think I did this? They would have to. Why am I even asking? Of course they'll think I did it. Nothing looks right about me being here. There is no explaining it.

But I can't just leave. What if he's not dead?

I'm sure he is—it looks like his head is caved in. But what if he isn't?

Now my mind is playing tricks on me. He is dead.

There's blood on me. They're going to think I did it.

I can't just leave, can I?

Unable to take in the wound, shattered bone, and blood, she bent over and vomited. She then backed away, closed his bedroom door behind her, and left his apartment quickly. Bypassing the bank of elevators, she took the stairs—all twenty-five flights—two steps at a time and exited the back service entrance. She half stumbled, half jogged two blocks to a public parking garage. Tears streamed down her face as she drove from the area.

2

The Marines have a saying that seems quite apt right now: *Hurry up and wait.* Patience is not my strong suit.

It was ninety-eight degrees in the shade all day here in DC. The sun has set, so the temperature has dropped. Can't be more than ninety-five now. I feel like I'm cooking in the ultra-high-molecular-weight polyethylene jacket I'm wearing. It's state-of-the-art bullet-resistant material —ten times stronger than steel. But that word *resistant* is still bugging me. Why can't the gear be bullet*proof?*

Drops of sweat bead and then fall in rivulets down my forehead and over and around my goggles, some seeping through the rubber ring that fits snugly to my face. When Special Agent Austin Reynolds invited me to participate in an FBI training program designed to help local law enforcement respond to terrorist activities, this wasn't the type of assignment I expected. Sure, I'm way ahead of my rehab schedule from a knee injury I suffered on a murder case I helped bust this past summer. I had a torn ACL and MCL repaired just six weeks ago. The three weeks I've spent running the rolling hills of the FBI training grounds in Quantico, Virginia, every morning have been nothing but wonderful for my recovery —along with daily therapy including electric muscle stimulation, ultrasound treatments, and aggressive stretching and joint manipulation. And glorious massages. Still, I hope I'm ready for this.

We've been poised for the strike for forty-five minutes now. A terrorist cell has been operating within thirty minutes of our nation's capital. The FBI, in its infinite wisdom, has progressed cautiously on this one, letting the group move freely for more than a year in the hopes that members of Allah's Fatwa would make a mistake in the confidence they had not been detected. It wasn't cell chatter intercepted by the super-computers at NEA that made FBI Deputy Director Willingham issue the order for immediate and terminal action. It was the lack of chatter. Change might be good for personal growth and corporate survival, but when it's a homicidal cadre of mad dogs, change should always make you nervous.

Don't use the phrase mad dogs, *Kristen, unless you want to get chewed out again.*

Another bit of data came in from Virgil (real name Operation Vigilance), a computer program developed for Homeland Security that gathers and collates information from federal, state, and local law enforcement agencies. Word from Virgil strongly suggested some bad guys—possibly and probably radical Islamists—had gotten some weapons-grade uranium into the US through the Port of Charleston. Maybe one and one doesn't equal two in this case, but who wants to risk that? Not Willingham. He's a smart guy.

I listen to the transmitter and it sounds like things are a little behind schedule. Four agents have worked themselves to within a few yards of the five-foot chain-link fence in front of the two-thousand-square-foot house with all the blinds pulled and overgrown shrubs nearly enveloping the entire exterior. They popped a manhole cover above the sewer pipe they traversed from a couple streets away. Four more agents are within a few feet of the fence at the rear of the house, having come through the neighbor's backyard. They are the holdup. It's assumed there are trip wires around the perimeter to sound the alarm of an imminent attack.

"Move it," I hear Reynolds say, firm, calm, confident like always. Unlike me, these FBI people are smooth.

Willingham and Reynolds are running the show from a mobile command center a mile away. Although "mobile command center" sounds too sophisticated—no matter how proud Reynolds is of it. Looks like a Winnebago to me. And it's parked at Walmart, not Nordstrom.

But I'll bet they have air-conditioning. We are cooking in here.

My patience is nearly shot. I feel claustrophobic. My outfit itches like crazy. I'm sitting with three other agents in what looks like a converted UPS van about a block away from the house. UPS may have fast service, but their trucks don't have a thousand-horsepower engines and front bumpers with a six-foot-wide cast-iron wedge that can open the side of a house as easily as a bodybuilder hammering a screwdriver through the side of a soup can. As far as I can tell, no one else is sweating and fidgeting like me.

Patience, Kristen.

My cell phone vibrates in four seemingly

endless burrs for a fifth straight time. I can't remember all the specifics of our pre-event instructions (it's the FBI that calls these little assaults "events," not me), but I'm pretty sure we were supposed to leave our Nokias at home. I must have tucked mine in one of the pockets of the Batman-like utility belt that is the final accessory of my chic black-on-black ensemble. I can't actually see anyone else's eyes, but I think my teammates are giving me dirty looks.

I feel a new stream of sweat trace down my back. The inside of my goggles are fogging up. I'm not regular FBI so I didn't get the custom-made outfit and gear the others did. My eyes are watering and I'm desperate to wipe the beads of sweat on my eyebrows. A maddening itch is growing in intensity.

My phone starts a sixth round of low rumbling. I absolutely know better but I can't take it any-more. I snap open the belt pocket and bring the phone to my ear, pushing my goggles and hood back, all in one movement.

"Mom," I hiss in a low whisper that probably isn't nearly as quiet as I want it to be. *Hope they didn't hear that a block away.* "When I don't pick up, it means I'm busy. Stop hitting Redial over and over."

"Kristen, there's no reason for you to talk to me that way," my mother says with her hurt tone, a regular part of her communication repertoire with me. "I just wanted to make sure your flight plans hadn't changed so we can pick you up at Midway on time."

"Mom, same as I told you last night: I'll be there Thursday night at eight—and I've told you ten times I'm flying into O'Hare, not Midway."

"See, it's good I called."

"Mom, I absolutely can't talk right now. This is a bad time."

"Honey, it never seems to be a good time for you to talk to your mom!"

I look at the three sets of buglike eyes that are now staring my direction. Oh, the stories Don Squires, my partner in the Chicago Police Department, could tell them right now. I wonder if it matters whether they write me up, since the CPD has only loaned me to the FBI.

"Mom, I'll call tomorrow. I've got to go. Now."

"You are going to church every Sunday while you're there, aren't you?"

I'm exasperated. "Mom, I already told you—"

A voice barks, "Now! Up position!" as the engine fires into a roar and we are thrown sideways on the uncomfortable benches we've been perched on for what seems like hours. As the turbocharged van powers from zero to at least fifty in about five seconds, I drop my phone and nearly fall completely backward. I hear it bounce against the metal door at the back of the van. I think I can actually hear my mom

15

calling my name above the roar of the engine.

All of us are now standing and have belted ourselves into secure side straps that loop over one shoulder and halfway around the chest so we can enter the theater of conflict from a standing position and without a broken ankle. Still, I can barely keep my balance as we carom forward, drift to the right, and then veer hard to the left. The driver—seems apt that he looks a little like Jeff Gordon—pushes the van up on two wheels in the final turn to storm the fortress while I frantically try to get my goggles situated on my face. The right window is covering my left eye. I can't twist them into position, so I yank my hood off and get the strap over and behind my ponytail. I barely have the goggles centered over my eyes and the hood up when I feel the first shudder of our assault vehicle slicing through the metal chain that serves as a gate. We go through like a hot knife through warm butter.

I'm ready, my Sig Sauer SP2022 double-action in hand, when the bigger impact occurs and we cave in the garage door. Jeff Gordon slams on the brakes. There must have been a vehicle parked in there to help him stop, because all four of us swing forward in the vertical straps, our legs reaching nearly waist level with the final impact. My head is filled with the sound of twisting metal. We were told to expect this and we got it. It's still disorienting.

Our squad leader is first out and unleashes a violent side kick to the entry door. I wince to myself when the door doesn't budge. That had to have hurt. Probably reinforced metal. He's unfazed and quickly reaches into a belt pocket to pull out three MCBs—micro concussion Bombs —that he slaps on the door surrounding the handle. All four of us are out of the truck, crouched with faces to the wall and hands over ears as he wheels from the doorway and positions himself next to me. I think all three MCBs explode at once, and I hear front and back doors blown inward at the same time our side door implodes. I race after my team through the jagged, smoking entrance, my head on a swivel, weapon up and ready to fire.

The architectural drawing of the house indicated a split-level home, with the main level including an enclosed kitchen featuring a shuttered picture window looking into a small dining room and swinging doors leading into the living room. All three attack teams will be entering on this floor. Three tiny bedrooms and one bathroom are up a half staircase on the opposite side of the house. A den or rec room, probably the laundry room, and another full or half bath are underneath the bedrooms a half flight below our entry point. The team coming through the front door is responsible for the upstairs. The team coming through the back door is responsible for the half basement. We are responsible for kitchen, dining room, and living room. My job is to slam through the swinging doors, do a half tumble, and come up firing at anything that doesn't have its hands straight up in the air with a white flag waving. I am then to wait for audio instructions so that I don't get shot by or shoot a team member.

As I emerge through the smoke, ready to turn left and into the living room, I half trip over the heel of my team leader, who I'm following closely. I hear special agent Ted Cane shout an obscenity as he falls against the service island in the kitchen. I hit the side of a cabinet fairly hard with my right shoulder and feel a mild shot of pain course upward, but I instantly regain my balance. I pause and think about checking on Cane, but remember protocol—he's not my problem—and smash through the swinging doors.

I almost feel the sound in every fiber of my body as a thunderous roar explodes from behind me. Someone was waiting. I don't know how he missed me; he had me at point-blank range.

I improvise on the fly, extending my tumble into a full dive and front roll. As I somersault upward to a crouch, I push myself to the side into a half roll to bring my Sig back into firing position. Even as I execute a beautiful sequence of moves, I hear a voice screaming in my brain. A terrified voice. My voice. Even if I can't articulate it in real time, my peripheral vision has already seen I have just one target to put down. My target, however, is in an upright firing position and has a large-bore double-barrel shotgun pressed to his shoulder, one eye gleaming down the length of metal. One barrel spent—but one fully loaded. Even as the voice continues to scream for me to move faster, I know my target isn't going to miss with his second shot, no matter what I do.

As I torque into a crouch, my head cranes as far to the side as it will go as I pray for one shot. *Just one shot.* My target looks relaxed and in charge. Our eyes lock. My arm is swinging forward in the slowest slow motion I have ever experienced in my life. In that nanosecond I feel like I have time to recite Marc Antony's complete speech to the plebeians at Caesar's funeral and maybe a clever limerick about a postman named Chuck that I wrote my first year in middle school. I see my target's eyes narrow and then a streak of blue flame blaze from the end of the barrel, and almost simultaneously I am knocked backward with a violent jolt.

I look upward, knowing that even with the best polyethylene fabric money can buy—it really is bullet resistant, not bulletproof—I am going to bleed to death.

I should have told Mom I love her.

3

"You can stop being dead now," Reynolds says to me. He is standing over me with a half smirk on his face.

I sit up and rub my sternum. When the FBI puts together a terrorist takedown simulation, they go all out. One part mobile PlayStation technology for creating lifelike backdrops; one part movie production with plenty of swarthy villains from the actors guild; one part demolition team to blow the heck out of condemned real estate properties; and one part departmental paintball tournament with ammo heavy enough to leave a black-and-blue reminder that you got killed (unless you were skilled and lucky enough to beat the best of the best to the shot). The ammo isn't live, but that doesn't mean you won't end up with a major purplish-red contusion in this game.

In my short time in northern Virginia, it's become obvious to me that Reynolds is a rising star in the FBI. It doesn't hurt that Robert Willingham, deputy director in charge of operations and a rock star in law enforcement, treats him like a son. That means they can fight all week and go fishing together on the weekend. They're flying up to somewhere in northern

Maine this coming Friday afternoon. Millinocket, I think they said.

Everybody treats Reynolds with respect. He doesn't seem to have a singular job description. One day he lives in front of a computer screen with the analysts. Then he's training field agents at the FBI's national training center (385 wooded acres hidden within a Marine base, complete with dorms, meeting rooms, a state-of-the-art workout and rehab center, a mock town, and a whole lot more). Then Reynolds is meeting with congres-sional aides on Capitol Hill.

The real reason I know he's a rising star is that he seems able to get whatever money he wants to do whatever he wants. Like buying a condemned house in a burned-out, deserted neighborhood in Arlington and basically blowing it to smithereens a couple weeks later in a tactical assault simula-tion.

"How's the knee feel? You holding up okay?" he asks.

I'm massaging my surgically repaired right knee with both hands. My right wrist was recently operated on as well but has healed fast. I stretch my lower back and jump to my feet to show him that I am fully operational.

"Not bad at all," I answer. "I'm actually surprised."

"Why's that?"

"My orthopedic surgeon told me to expect at

least two months of rehab before I could do even medium-paced running and not ever to expect being able to go as hard as I used to."

"He's obviously never heard about our physical therapy staff and facilities in Quantico."

"First of all," I say, "my doctor is a woman. Second, even if she guessed what wonders of science and kinesiology you have at your fingertips, she would never assume I have the pull to get into your country club. I'm just a humble and lowly detective for the CPD. We have lots of weights, treadmills, and rowers in our precinct workout rooms, but nothing fancy like elliptical machines. Sometimes there's even hot water for the shower. But you do have to bring your own towel."

"I do believe you're rubbing off on me the wrong way," he answers. "I used to be so much more politically correct. Here I am assuming that only boys can be doctors. I'm ashamed of myself."

"You better work on that if you want that next promotion."

"Coming from such a savvy politician as yourself, I will."

"So you're working on your next move to the top? Probably doesn't hurt to go fishing with the boss."

He gives me a dirty look. "Being close to Willingham actually cuts both ways. He's made a lot of enemies in his career. Easy to do when you're as successful as he's been."

"People really think that way?"

"You bet they do. No one wants to feel inferior. He can make you feel that way even when he's not trying to. And sometimes he tries."

"Really?"

"Really!" he answers with a laugh. "You've never seen it because (a) you haven't been around him that much, and (b) he does like pretty girls."

"Major, you really are going to lose that promotion. I don't think you're allowed to refer to me as a girl." I make a face at him and add, "I still don't think it's going to hurt your career to be linked so closely with a deputy director."

"Maybe, maybe not. The bigger issue is whether I stay Bureau. If I do, then yes, I'll work on a promotion. If I ever decide to take my economics degree to Wall Street or try to parlay my law degree into a corporate gig, it doesn't much matter."

"You'd consider leaving the FBI?"

"I'm not actively thinking about it, but sure, who wouldn't consider a move if the right opportunity presented itself? Change is good for you, you know. Keeps you fresh."

"So I've heard," I deadpan back to him.

"On the other thing you said a minute ago," he continues, "about you being a humble servant of the CPD." He pauses, looks to the side, and then looks me directly in the eyes with his head tilted down and his eyebrows raised for effect. He really is a good-looking man, but I'm not going to even let myself think that way, much less go there after what happened between us when we recently worked a case in Chicago.

I'm supposed to ask him to continue. "You going to finish what you're saying?" I say, almost smiling.

"Since you're never going to make things easy, I better try and say this just right."

"Are you saying I'm difficult?" I ask innocently.

"Yes, I am," he answers. "But don't change the subject and don't mess up my train of thought. I know I told you this was just a temporary assignment for you. Willingham specifically asked for you, and since he gets what he wants, that was easy to work out with Chicago. But you need to know: if you want in, you're in. I'm authorized to offer you a field agent's job, and if you give me even the slightest indication you'll say yes, I'm going to put the offer packet on the table tomorrow morning. I know your current salary and benefits, and I doubt you're going to argue about the compensation. You might even be able to afford a new car. Not that your Miata isn't a classic."

"What's wrong with my car?"

He doesn't answer. He knows I'm stalling. And

I admit this is a shock. Almost as big a shock as a terrorist blowing me away in a simulation event. I'm suddenly having a little trouble catching my breath. Thoughts fly through my mind. *Would I move away from Chicago, where I've lived my entire life? Away from Mom? Away from my sisters, Klarissa and Kaylen? Especially Klarissa.*

Mom drives me crazy. She drives all of us crazy, even my angelic older sister, Kaylen, who is a pastor's wife and the nicest person in the world. But so what if Mom drives us crazy? We're still crazy about her. We love her. Could I exist without her Sunday-afternoon lunch sermons? Kaylen's husband, Jimmy, may be the preacher, but Mom makes sure we know what's right from wrong. And what about Kendra and James, my niece and nephew? And Kaylen is about to pop a new niece for me. They plan to name her Kelsey—the family obsession with the letter *K* for female names remains intact.

I'm actually dying to get home tomorrow night to see everyone. Even if my mom hit Redial a hundred times while I was on assignment.

I realize Austin is watching me closely and waiting for a response. I don't think his look of amusement is going to last much longer. But I'm not ready to answer. I need to change the subject for at least a minute.

"So did we get the bad guys just now?" Not

a particularly smooth segue, but apparently successful.

"We did," he says with a beam. That was an inspired change of direction; he really is proud of his work and this was his baby all the way, so he wants to talk about it.

"How many did we lose?"

"Just one."

"Dang. You mean I'm the only one that got blown away." I try to correct how that sounded by adding, "Not that I want any of my teammates to die, even if it was a game."

"You're not quite right on that," he says. "We only lost one, but it wasn't you."

"Really?"

"Really."

"Cool."

I did it again. That doesn't sound right.

"Yep, I took a quick peek at the event post-mortem and you're on your way to the emergency room right now for a couple nights' stay—longer if the sternum is cracked. We'll find out later. You got shot with a tungsten-tipped can opener. If he had loaded his shotgun with traditional shells, he wouldn't have missed you coming through the door and you'd be dead. But even though he got you with a body shot, the jacket saved your life. Cane, however, is dead."

"Lieutenant Cane? My group leader? How in the heck did they get him? He's the best."

"That he is. Ex-Rangers tend to be. He took out three bad guys, including the one trying to push the button that blows up the entire house and half the neighborhood. This group wasn't going to allow themselves to be interrogated at Guantanamo and were ready for the shortcut to heaven."

"Is Allah's Fatwa a real group?"

"Not in name, but in makeup and disposition and tactics, yes, it—and a hundred just like it— are real."

"So what happened to Lieutenant Cane? Was it his ankle?"

"Nah. Ted would never let a little sprain slow him down. He did his job, then heard what was happening in the living room. He came in with a smoke grenade and gun blazing, but your bad guy pulled out his Colt 45 and shot him cold dead. No one shoots better with a handgun than a shotgun, but in this little game the bad guy did."

"So I got him killed?"

"Can't look at it that way. But Cane did get blown away trying to save your life."

"Wow," I say with no enthusiasm. I do have a way with words. I wish I hadn't said "Cool" when he told me I didn't die.

"Yeah, wow," Reynolds says. "So you want to talk about that job offer later on? Maybe grab dinner?"

"This somehow reminds me of how you asked

me out for that first date. I'm never quite sure if you want to go out for business or social."

"Not that you make it easy," he says, a twinkle in his eyes.

"Well, after Chicago, I'll make it easier and say yes. But no negotiating—we can have dinner if it's strictly business."

" 'After Chicago'? Don't pin what happened in Chicago on me, Kristen," he says, storm clouds in his eyes, the twinkle instantly gone. He's not playing now. "Besides, I think you're the one who has an obsession about negotiating everything."

"Well, with some people, when you sense they're not telling you the whole truth," I say, even as I wonder why I'm turning this into a fight, "you do have to be a little more careful up front."

"If you're saying what I think you're saying, that I was in some way untruthful with you," he says, "I'll take your obvious but unspoken assessment under advisement and consider the best way to let the next girl I ask out know ahead of time that my wife left me. And that she works for the FBI too. You got any advice on the subject, let me know. In fact, just send me a text."

I think I deserved that. And I would have apologized, but he was already on his way out the door.

If this was part of the job interview, I'm not sure the offer is still on the table. Ditto if he was asking me on a date.

4

Ben Franklin said if you have a tough decision to make, you draw a line down the middle of a piece of paper. On the left side of the line you list all the positives, and on the right side you list all the negatives. Then you see which column is bigger and make your decision.

Actually, I'm not sure Ben said that. My dad said he said it, so there's probably some truth to it. But Dad was known to paraphrase and improvise on the fly.

I look at my yellow sheet of ruled paper again. The line is straight and true. The plus sign and negative sign look just fine. Problem is, I haven't written anything else. I rip the sheet of paper from the pad, crumple it, stand up from my desk, and do a fadeaway jump shot at the wastebasket in the corner. It hits the rims, bounces against the wall, and falls to the floor next to ten other yellow paper wads.

Even if Ben Franklin did come up with the decision tree, it's too simplistic. Not all pluses and minuses are created equal.

Despite getting into it with Reynolds, the package awaited me when I returned to my motel-style room at the FBI national training center in Quantico. I knew the cafeteria would be closed so I talked the shuttle driver into stopping at a Roy Rogers fast-food restaurant as we left DC. Since I was his only passenger, he said fine. I was starved after the simulation and wolfed down three deluxe roast-beef sandwiches, fries, and a water. He must have been hungry too and munched on a couple burgers for our thirty-five-mile drive.

It was close to midnight when we arrived, and I had planned to shower and hit the sack right away so I could get an early start on my final FBI-conducted knee-therapy session in the morning. I took the shower. I got in my jammies. I got under the covers and turned off the light. Then I stared at the ceiling for an hour.

I finally threw off the covers and started scribbling notes on yellow sheets of paper. I didn't have to write down a thing to know what the issues were. Accepting the offer from the FBI would mean more money, the prestige of working for the world's greatest law enforcement agency, and a chance to serve my country. My media-star sister likes to remind me that I'm so old-school I make our dad look like a crazy teenager with acne and hormones. So I wave the flag, and the service-to-country part is a big deal to me.

On the negative side of the sheet is the fact that I already have my dream job. My dad was a detective for the Chicago Police, and as far back as I can remember, it's all I've ever wanted to do. I grew up in Chicago and like it there. Maybe I would like living somewhere else, but why pursue that possibility and give up the sure thing I've got? I don't care what people say about Chicago weather. I don't mind bitter-cold, icy, snowy, windswept winters—at least not theoretically. It's like cheering for the Cubs. Doesn't matter how bad they are in a given year, sitting in Wrigley Field during a ten-game losing streak is proof that you are tougher than the rest of the country. Throwing a nice souvenir ball back onto the field because it was a home run by the other team is part of our DNA as well. That's how we do it in Chicago.

The real two-ton elephant on the right side of the paper—the negative reason that argues against moving—is my family. My mind regrinds those gears.

Could I really live a thousand miles from my mom and sisters?

Who would coach my eight-year-old niece's soccer team, the Snowflakes?

And then there's James, my five-year-old nephew. He will be in kindergarten. I don't like that he has only one volume—yelling—and that he always wants to punch me and sticks his feet in my face when we watch TV, but I do admire his fiery personality. That kid is going to play middle linebacker for the Bears someday. Butkus. Singletary. Urlacher. King. James King—has a ring to it. LeBron is already King James, but my nephew will make a name for himself. I'm not going to tell his dad, Jimmy, that James got his athletic ability from my side of the family. Probably don't have to.

And Jimmy and my big sister, Kaylen, have a third on the way. I think they wanted it to be a surprise whether it's a boy or girl. Mom spilled the beans. Doesn't matter. I found a Manchester United soccer outfit at a baby boutique in Georgetown that will look great on my new niece. My news reporter sister, Klarissa, will be impressed I went shopping. She claims I missed the shopping gene—and usually she's right.

That's another reason to stay in Chicago. I feel responsible for Klarissa. After all, she was held hostage because of a case I was on.

More money and prestige. A new adventure.

Or family.

Where is Ben Franklin when you need to talk to him? I'll have to figure this on my own. My history professor at NIU said Ben wasn't much of a family man anyway.

5

It's not fancy, but it's plenty nice. Open the door and on the right there's a small sitting area with facing loveseats and a coffee table between. On the left is a round table that's not quite big enough for four chairs arranged around it. Behind the table is a kitchenette with a full-size refrigerator, stove, dishwasher, microwave, and a single sink. The bedroom is in the back. This has been my home for the past six weeks.

My black Rollaboard suitcase is packed but still open on the bed. It's too big for the overhead bin on the Airbus A330 I will be on, so I have to check it. I'm dressed comfortably for travel. I'm also dressed like I am every workday. Black slacks and jacket. White blouse. I've put on my Ecco Mary Jane-style shoes that have maybe a quarter-inch heel. That's about as stylish as I'm going to go with footwear. My partner gives me a hard time about my fashion sense, but he's the one that cries when his dress shoes get messed up chasing a punk down the street.

I've opened, closed, and reopened every drawer and closet. I've looked under the edges of the bed twice. I haven't forgotten anything. Satisfied, I zip up the suitcase and move it to the door. My laptop and power cord are in my tattered black carryall.

I have a six o'clock flight back to Chicago from Reagan International tonight. I had my final checkup earlier with the orthopedic doctor that works at the FBI's Rehab and Surgery Center. The majority of FBI agents work in accounting and law, but there is still enough rough fieldwork that they staff their own surgi-center for on-the-job injuries. When Deputy Director Willingham extended the offer for me to participate in TARP—Terrorist Attack Response Program—he added the inducement of the full use of the rehab service to the offer. How do you say no to that? I went in every morning at six o'clock to be put through a torture session. It worked. Even after tearing the ACL and MCL a little over two months ago, my knee feels great. Maybe better than before the injury. And it held up nicely in the terrorist takedown. The doc said I could continue therapy on my own and that I was in great shape.

One more meeting.

"I hope you'll really think this over carefully. I'm leaving the offer packet with you. There is a FedEx envelope already addressed and paid for in the back of it. Even if you say no, I want everything returned. You just sign the first form acknowledging that you're declining our offer of employment. If you do change your mind and decide to accept what I think is a great offer based on where you are now—especially financially—you will need to sign everything in the packet in the presence of a public notary. I would prefer you use the notary in our regional offices in downtown Chicago. I think you're familiar with where they are."

"I am."

I spent a lot of time in the State Building in the Midwest offices of the FBI on my last case.

"Any other questions?"

I'm not sure I had any to begin with. "I'm good. And I really do appreciate this offer. Just not sure I can take it."

"Understood. Each of us has to make the decision that's best for us individually. I'd just encourage you to give it some serious thought."

She's told me that about ten times now. She thinks I'm crazy. If I take the offer, I almost double my salary.

"Okay, your driver should be here now. You better get going for Reagan. You're going against traffic, but you never know how long things will take."

"Thank you," I say as we shake hands.

I walk out into a gloriously sunny late summer day. A black limousine is parked there and the back door opens as I look for the van to take me to the airport.

Deputy Director Robert Willingham—he likes me to call him Bob—jumps out.

"Hop in, Kristen. Your luggage is in the trunk. I'm heading into the city. Let me give you a ride."

He won't get an argument from me.

"I know you aren't going to change your mind, and I respect why you're staying with CPD. You've done well there. You got your detective shield early. I'm sure Deidre made it sound like this will be your one and only chance to come work for us. She does that—especially when we tell her to. But I have to say I was very impressed with your work on the Dean Woods case. We have a great team here at the FBI. The best. But one profile we are not hiring enough is old-fashioned investigators. I believe in the phrase 'follow the money,' so heaven knows we need our forensic accountants. But I'm not sure we focus enough on recruiting tough men and women who can be dropped into dangerous situations. That's why I keep Austin close. He can do it all. And if there's a fight, I'm putting my money on him."

"I appreciate you taking the time to talk with me about this opportunity, sir."

"Bob."

"Yes, sir. Bob."

He laughs. We are parked at the no-parking curb in front of the United terminal at Reagan. A

DC cop walked our way to move us along, but the driver showed him a laminated ID that convinced him to return to his previous spot to monitor traffic flow.

My flight is in forty-five minutes. I don't fly a lot and I'm starting to get nervous. It's all I can do to keep myself from looking at my watch. I will my eyes not to look down.

"I know you're ready to roll, Detective Conner. Don't worry. You're checked in and a friend of mine is going to expedite your passage through security."

"Thank you, sir. Bob."

"You're not asking for advice and don't need advice, but let me leave you with one small word of counsel from an old man."

"I don't see an old man around here, Bob, so who would that be?"

"Nicely played, Detective," he says with a laugh. "And I'm not feeling too bad these days. I'm going to feel even better when I throw a line in the Penobscot River. Austin and I are going fishing up in Millinocket this weekend."

"That's what I heard."

I studied Willingham's career when I was a criminal justice major at Northern Illinois University. I wrote a paper on him. Now I know him on a first-name basis. Bob. And I don't have a clue where he's going with this "word of counsel" stuff.

"Our strengths are usually our weaknesses," he says. "Your strengths are your unbending will, your fierce determination, your lack of guile and political motivation."

"Thank you, Bob."

"Those are also your weaknesses. It's not the right time for you to say yes to us. I understand that and am not pushing anymore. But there are times you need to be a little more open-minded and flexible. Do you know what I'm saying?"

"I think so."

I'm pretty sure not.

"Good. But just in case you don't, I would encourage you to not be too hasty in your judgment of Major Reynolds. He's an awfully fine young man."

Did the deputy director of the FBI just give me advice on my love life?

6

Thursday, September 6
4:55 p.m.

It can't be this easy, can it? Is this over? It's been two days and no one from the police has contacted me. I thought I might be in custody by now. Was I worrying over nothing?

Maybe no one knows I was there. I've thrown

38

away everything I was wearing that night. Not sure how much that helps since I threw up all over the place.

Could I be this lucky? I wasn't hiding my visit from anyone; I didn't go in and leave from the back entrance of his building because I was trying to avoid security cameras. Well, there was one person I didn't want to see who might be there—someone I came to trust but who betrayed me. Again. I wanted to make sure he wasn't listening to her. But it was stupid of me to go over in the first place. That's on me. I can't blame her for everything. Almost. But not everything. She would have made him turn on me. That's why I went over.

Why did she have to stick her nose into things and try to keep us apart?

He was no angel. That's for sure. It's ironic that he told me he loved me but showed me the door by the delivery dock that never shuts all the way. That showed how much love means to him. He wanted to keep me a secret. That was going to have to change. And it would have. But then she stepped between us.

He was definitely no angel, but I could have changed him. He wasn't nice to others, but he was different with me. I think we could have helped each other change for the better.

I still can't believe he's dead. Everywhere I turn and look, I see his face. I don't have to watch news coverage to see him. I think I see him out of the corner of my eye. At a restaurant. At a shop. I turn quickly and he's gone.

Who did kill him? I know who hated him the most—and he gives me the creeps. But I'm not sure he would have done all that.

Could it have been her? Maybe he came to his senses and told her she was out of his life forever. Maybe he let her know he truly loved me and she couldn't take that away. Maybe he had already started to change and she couldn't control him anymore.

Could it have been her?

She's wicked, but she didn't do it.

Doesn't mean she wouldn't make a good suspect.

I need to think. Maybe there is something I can do to point the police in her direction. Even if she didn't do it, she deserves to be as frightened as I've been the last two days.

He was cruel to me the last time we were together. And now he can never make those wrongs right.

7

I could get used to this. I'm thirty-five thousand feet over Dayton, Ohio—that's what the flight map says, anyway—sitting in United Airlines first class. The FBI bought me a regular economy-class ticket but has a deal that if any first-class seats are open, their people get a bump up front.

The flight attendant brought me a bowl of warm mixed nuts while we were still at the gate. Not just peanuts, but the expensive stuff, like walnuts, cashews, and Brazil nuts, and they threw in a few macadamias for good measure. The guy in a business suit next to me was gulping Maker's Mark on the rocks before we were airborne and is fast asleep. His snoring is fairly quiet now but every ten minutes or so he gives a jerk and a loud snort. He'd better get checked for sleep apnea.

I need to invest in a briefcase. My old-fashioned doctor's-style carryall under the seat in front of me is worn out. I don't load up my purse for a trip around the world like my sister does. But I have enough personal stuff to go along with my vintage laptop—a couple generations away from the sleek thin models they are selling now —that when you add papers and reports from my time with the FBI, my purse is stuffed, over-flowing, and straining at the seams. I think the security guy at Reagan International was ready to throw the whole thing away and put it out of its misery. Good for me Willingham called ahead and had an escort smooth the way for me through a crowded security line to make my flight in plenty of time.

My laptop—three years old with a battery that didn't get me out of Pennsylvania—is poking out the top with my FBI training notebook, a couple magazines, and a cardboard envelope that contains the employment offer from the FBI. It's marked *Confidential* and the flight attendant has looked at it with curiosity a couple times.

I told Reynolds and Deidre Cook—the personnel manager who met with me early this afternoon to process my paperwork and review the fine points of the offer—that I had already decided and the answer was no. Cook told me to think about it a couple more days before giving my final answer. The problem is, I don't want to think about it anymore. It's Thursday night. We have an early phone appointment on Monday. I'm not good at the kind of process that prolongs decisions. I want to decide and move on. This lack of closure will probably ruin my whole weekend.

I will be coaching the Snowflakes on Saturday. Tiffany's dad has been running practices for the three weeks before our first game. I talked to him on the phone twice to give him some training ideas and ask how the girls were looking. Both times he hinted that it might be good for us to be co-coaches. I didn't take the bait. The Snowflakes have a head coach: me. Not me and . . . what is Tiffany's dad's first name?

"Anything else to drink?" the flight attendant asks.

I've already had three cups of coffee today and don't need to get any more wired up. I've drunk three glasses of apple juice this flight and visited the bathroom twice already. Even if first class is generous on leg room, I don't want to wake the guy who is contentedly snoring in the aisle seat. It may be good to check if he's alive, however. I haven't heard the guttural rumble of a grizzly in hibernation for at least two minutes.

"I guess one more apple juice," I answer.

Why is it so hard to turn down free stuff?

I should have stopped at a bathroom. I've trekked what felt like a mile from my arrival gate to the escalator that lowers me toward the baggage level where my beat-up suitcase will arrive whenever it decides to get there. I might pee my pants if there isn't a public bathroom down there. I've already passed the point of no return from the terminal and can't go back if there isn't.

I step from the escalator onto solid ground and there is the whole gang.

"Aunt Kristen!" Kendra yells as she bounds forward and gives me a big hug that challenges my bladder control. James, her five-year-old brother, lets out a whoop and leaps in my arms. I bend sideways to put my carryall on the ground, and everything spills all over the floor. I see my tube of red lipstick rolling toward the Wisconsin border. I do know how to make an appearance.

Jimmy and Kaylen are beaming. Mom was right: Kaylen looks ready to pop. Mom didn't say it that way, of course. But wow, is she big!

Note to Kristen: No size references around older sister.

I hustle in her direction to save her the effort of waddling. Mom is holding a sign that says, "Welcome Home, Kristen." Even my drop-dead gorgeous news reporter sister is here. Did she miss me or did Mom wear her down, insisting she come along?

Klarissa beams at me and then sticks out her tongue. Everyone gathers around to give hugs. I stand face-to-face with Kaylen and can't help myself; I have to do it. I put both hands on that belly. I want to connect with Kelsey. But wanting to make sure that bump is real is on my mind too.

It's so wonderful to be home with the people I love, but I'm going to burst if I don't take care of business first. I spot a sign with a stick figure wearing a skirt.

"I'll be right back," I say as Jimmy pushes my

stuff back into my bag. My older sister's husband is a "golly and shucks" nice guy, but he is just savvy enough not to make eye contact with anything in a woman's purse. I notice, however, he gives the FBI envelope a quick and curious glance.

I've decided if I want something to be noticed, I'm going to write "Confidential" on it.

The seven of us are barely legal in Jimmy and Kaylen's minivan. If you count what Kaylen is carrying, we are definitely a seat belt short. James got assigned to the middle of the back row between Kendra and me. He isn't happy and has now yelled, "Not fair! Why does Kendra get a window seat?" four or five times. I've turned sideways a couple times to tickle him, which he likes, but that winds him up and makes him even louder in insisting that life isn't fair. He's already squirming and throwing elbows, so I decide to stop the tickling to save myself from bruised ribs.

Jimmy and Kaylen are sitting up front. Somehow she's twisted around to talk with us without looking too uncomfortable. Her eyes sparkle and she can't help but smile. It's not a big minivan, and her hand has gravitated to rest on Jimmy's shoulder. Familiar affection. She might not even know her hand is there, but that's still where she wants it to be and so does he.

I am not jealous of good things that happen to my family members. Heck, I drive a Mazda Miata that is—what?—fourteen or fifteen years old. Klarissa drives a nearly brand-new Nissan GT-R that I'm quite certain cost more than I make in two years. That doesn't bother me at all. At least it didn't until she let me drive that one time. Wow.

But looking at the affection that flows between Jimmy and Kaylen reminds me that I'm thirty years old and have never had a serious relationship. Never. My last date was with Austin Reynolds—it ended as well as our conversation yesterday. Before that, I sorta dated the brother of a serial killer. Wow. My prospects for finding Mr. Right don't feel real bright. But I am still happy weaving through Chicago highway traffic in a happy little minivan with my happy little family.

I look over at Klarissa. My younger sister has the looks and the highest-paying job in the family—her prospects are much brighter than mine. But she seems a little sad. She looks over at me and then back at Jimmy and Kaylen. I think we just read each other's minds.

I look at her left cheek closely. She was sliced by a knife. Even in a traumatized condition in the back of an ambulance, she opened her eyes, glared at everyone, including me, and demanded that a plastic surgeon be brought to the emergency room.

Smart girl.

8

Two years ago we had the fewest murders in Chicago since 1965. We were back under five hundred. There has been a decade-long decline in violent crime in America and Chicago.

Nationwide and citywide statistics are nice. Doesn't mean every neighborhood benefits in the same way. White, mixed, and Hispanic areas have had about equal drops in murder. Some of our African-American neighborhoods haven't had the same decline rate and, in fact, have had small increases in all varieties of violent crime, from simple mugging to premeditated murder.

I'm not sure why Allen Johnson, the ChiTownVlogger (stupid name) who was in the middle of my last case, was so intent on attacking Commissioner Fergosi for being incompetent. I may not get along with Commander Czaka—my boss's boss—but I think Fergosi has done a great job heading up the Chicago Police Department. When he brought in a consultant from Philadelphia a couple years ago and promised change, everyone moaned and groaned. Consultants don't get paid to tell you everything is okay. They make their big bucks flipping over the apple cart and then telling you they know how to put the apples back in it. But this guy had paid his dues in local enforcement in a couple of big cities and actually had some great, strategic ideas that Fergosi jumped on, particularly on working with the judiciary to be more aggressive with warrants for weapons searches. That may be the biggest reason we have been down almost 20 percent in murders.

But this year murders are back up. *Way up.* Even with more budget cuts and a decade of steady decline, I don't think I have anything to worry about with job security—except for my temper and that running feud with Czaka. Don tells me I need to be patient and Czaka'll give me what I want. Why should I be patient about something as straightforward as having access to the files on my dad's shooting so I can investigate on my own time?

"Would you like to try our new apple strudel coffee cake?"

I look up from the table at a preternaturally happy young man in a green apron carrying a tray with coffee cake samples in little white cups that might be big enough to hold two aspirins. I politely decline. I consider mentioning to him that the fuzzy little goatee he has going probably isn't going to work for another year or two. Unlike Deputy Director Robert Willingham— apparently the Love Doctor—I hold my counsel.

I'm sipping a shot-in-the-dark at JavaStar—a plain cup of coffee with two shots of espresso dumped in—waiting for my younger sister, Klarissa, to show up. In the past year our relationship has been a roller-coaster ride. The first three or four months, we fought at our regular pace. Then we had three or four months where we got along better than at any other time in our lives. Then we had an ugly fight. Then she was taken by a serial killer and I saved her life and she moved into my place because she was afraid of the dark. Then I spent a month and a week in Virginia as part of an FBI training program.

I think saving her life and living together put us back on an upward climb. Saving someone's life can do that. Does it matter we have never talked through our ugly incident?

When I was in high school I went on an overnight trip with my dad for a soccer tournament. I asked him why he and Mom had fought so much lately. He said they'd gone to a marriage enrichment seminar to learn how to communicate better—and now they were arguing about everything. Better to leave some things left unsaid, he told me. He then told me to never lie to my mother but that I didn't need to mention what he just said.

I smile at the memory.

I hear the door and look up. It's Klarissa. A guy two tables away had been looking my way for the last five minutes, trying to make eye contact.

Now I am officially forgotten. Forever. The apple strudel guy makes a beeline in her direction in case the barista behind the counter jumps over and gets to her first to offer a sample of their new blond roast. I laugh. How does Klarissa do it? She doesn't walk into rooms. She makes an entrance.

"Like I said, I don't start until Monday, so I just stopped by the office for ten minutes yesterday. I have no clue what's going on."

I ended up buying a piece of the coffee cake. Klarissa has been sipping on a tall skinny soy latte with nutmeg sprinkles for the last thirty-five minutes and has drained at least an inch and a half off the top. I'm thankful she didn't get the coffee cake. Unlike me, she does share her food. And since she eats slower and less in quantity than any other human being I know, I would have eaten both pieces.

"So you really don't know if the Second got the Durham murder. You're not just holding out on me?"

"I'm not holding out, but even if I knew anything, I'm not feeding you inside information."

"Tell me something I don't already know."

"You'll have to get your scoops the old-fashioned way and bribe somebody else on the force."

"We don't use the word *bribe*," she says primly.

Then we both laugh. We've had this discussion

a couple hundred times. She's in news and I'm in law enforcement. I've let her know that if I was the type of lowlife government employee that broke my vows of confidentiality, she would be the first I would blab and sell my soul to—but not to hold her breath waiting. That's good enough for her. The promise of being first.

She sometimes knows what's going on before I do. I've never had the desire or nerve to ask her if she really is paying CPD officers for news leads. Dad did thirty years on the force before he was shot. When I told him I was applying for a job with CPD after college, the first thing he told me was to keep my nose clean, that there were too many dirty cops. He said the first time you take a favor it will feel innocent, but that's how the bad guys get their hooks in you. I've kept my nose clean—not even a free cup of coffee from the Dunkin' Donuts guy that always offers it.

"So are your Snowflakes gonna stomp somebody today, Coach Butkus?"

I roll my eyes. "Butkus was never a coach. You meant to call me Coach Ditka."

"How could I have messed that up? So are you going to win?"

"With our niece playing, we always have a shot."

"What are you going to do if she loses interest in sports and takes up something foreign to you, like schoolwork or music or boys?"

I look at her in horror and she laughs at me.

"No right-footed kid that can hit a left cross like she can will be allowed to quit," I say. "If I have any say in it."

"I'm sure you will."

I look at my watch, hop up, gather trash, and put it in the receptacle. Klarissa loops an arm in mine and we exit JavaStar like best friends. We didn't talk anything through and we're doing fine. Maybe Dad was at least partially right on not overanalyzing and overtalking everything. Not everything needs to be talked through. We seem to like each other. Good. One less thing to worry about. If I had a list of my unresolved issues in life, I would put a check mark next to this one.

Time to hit the soccer fields.

The tan ragtop is down on my shiny black Miata. I run through the gears fast and hit the first lane of the Crosstown Expressway at seventy. My world is in order and I'm at peace. I'm already unpacked and my laundry is done from my time in DC. Klarissa is on air tonight, my mom is going to an activity with the senior adults at the church, Jimmy and Kaylen have a party at their house with the newlyweds from the church, so I am absolutely a free agent with nothing to do. I might go down to Grant Park for an outdoor concert. I don't know who is playing and don't care. I might window-shop on the Magnificent Mile. I might go to the shooting range and work with the new Sig Sauer the FBI gave me. I might go to a movie or read a book. After five weeks of a strict regimen, it's great having freedom to do anything I want or nothing.

I'm in a great mood even after I get stuck in the middle lane for a couple miles, sandwiched between two drivers intent on obeying the speed limit—and making sure everyone else does too. My Snowflakes won. Tiffany scored two and Kendra scored one—but we actually had three other girls get a goal. I guess Tiffany's dad did okay as assistant coach while I was gone.

About bedtime, I stopped downtown on the way home. Spent an hour buying a new phone at the Apple Store and then jogged down to listen to a group called Salient Scream for five minutes. That made it easy to opt for doing nothing the rest of the evening. I wandered around my little place wearing a T-shirt, battered shorts, and no shoes. At nine, *Jaws* came on WGN and I watched it for maybe the tenth time. Doesn't take much to make me happy.

I watched Klarissa do the news for five minutes on TiVo and wondered what precinct got the Durham case.

9

I've decided I should be more environmentally aware. I do recycle glass and most aluminum and metal—most of the time. I don't pay attention to paper and cardboard like I should. The only time I really notice plastic enough to separate it from the rest of the trash is when it is large enough to hold a gallon of liquid, like milk or distilled water for my steam iron.

Now that my '97 Miata is fixed up inside and out, I've decided to start taking public transportation to work. *Go figure.* But my new commitment makes me feel engaged and green. Don and I are assigned a car from the motor pool each month, so why not? I've downloaded the mobile app that updates the exact location of any bus in the city. *Scary.* I just have to catch a bus outside my apartment complex, jump on the El, and grab another bus that delivers me to the front door of the Second Precinct. If things stay on schedule, I will save five minutes on my commute. I haven't figured the return trip yet.

It's Monday morning. My first day back to work at CPD after a two-month medical leave of absence. I talked to Captain Zaworski on Friday and it's official that Don Squires and I are still partners. I'm relieved. I'm comfortable with Don.

I know his family. He's one of my favorite people to fight with. I'm not sure he reciprocates my level of enjoyment for our nonstop repartee, but it doesn't mean he doesn't give it back to me.

I hit the button to light up the screen on my new iPhone to see what time it is as my bus lurches forward from another stop. My bus is not on schedule and I'm going to miss the Express train on the Purple line. I've been feeling so good about my decision to go green since I watched an episode of *Planet Earth* last night, but now I'm not sure it's going to live to see another day.

"Nice of you to join us, Conner," Zaworski barks.

I'm five minutes late to our morning briefing. I'm definitely done with public transportation. At least once I get home tonight.

Last time I was with everyone in this conference room we were still looking for a serial killer. I was the one who found him. I had a nice stay in the hospital for my efforts. A "Welcome back, we missed you; you're our hero," seems appropriate at the moment.

Ten of us surround the battleship-gray table. A few notes are scribbled on the whiteboard on the wall. Before I can decipher Zaworski's cuneiform, he says, "Squires, hit the lights."

Don is leaning back in his chair and stretches his arm to twist the dimmer knob counter-clockwise.

"Let's go, Randall," he says to a new detective I don't recognize. I look around the room at familiar faces, including Antonio Martinez. We worked with him on the Cutter Shark case. He was partners with Bob Blackshear at the Third Precinct. Don told me he transferred over to Second and was partnering with a new guy. Randall.

Martinez waves and blows me a kiss before the lights are all the way down. Some things haven't changed while I was gone.

Randall clicks the keyboard on an Apple computer that is connected to a projector. They called the sales guy at Apple a genius. Maybe he's a genius too. First image up is a close-up of a man with the left side of his head caved in. The photographer had the place lit up bright as a summer day at the Indiana Dunes, so no details are missing.

"Walk us through it, Jerome," Zaworski orders.

Jerome is a tech nerd from the medical examiner's office. He was the only one besides Martinez who smiled and waved when I made my entrance.

"Multiple blows with a blunt object," he says. "We found a twenty-ounce rip-claw one-piece hammer next to the bed. A pretty common style, but a little heavier than most. The wounds fit the shape and size of the hammer head. It's made by Stanley."

"Thanks for letting us know that," Zaworski growls. "Next."

Someone got up on the wrong side of the bed.

Randall clicks a button and the second image shows the right side of his head. No marks. The blood has been cleaned off. His lifeless right eye is wide open and staring blankly into the camera. The victim was a handsome man. Early forties? Late thirties?

"If he was conscious at the time of the attack, the first blow probably rendered him unconscious or semi-unconscious," Jerome continues. "The position of the body suggests he was already in bed. Blood splatter and pooling tells us he wasn't put there and didn't fall there. The puddle of blood underneath his head suggests he never even turned his head. We can't prove it, but we suspect he was sleeping when he was attacked. The assailant seems to have gone into a frenzy. We think the victim was struck sixteen or seventeen times. The trauma marks start to blend together."

Gross.

"If he had been awake and conscious, he would have tried to turn away and shield the blows with his arms. This side of his face is unmarked. No bruising on his arms."

"That guy is a sound sleeper," Martinez says with a whistle.

"Toxicology reports put him at .23 blood level

content," Jerome adds. "Pretty amazing he was able to put on his pajamas and find his way to bed. Heck, alcohol content was high enough to kill him without help from the Stanley."

"We got it," Zaworski says. "Next."

The third image shows him from head to toe with the covers pulled back. His pajamas consisted of a pair of black boxers and a V-neck T-shirt half soaked in blood. His head is adjusted so he's looking straight up, with both sides of his face visible. What's that guy's name in the Batman movie? Harry Two-Face? Harvey? Our victim makes Harry or Harvey look like a model.

After Jerome finishes describing the body, Randall takes over the narration and describes images of Durham's apartment. Nice place. Scratch that. Real nice place. He had an interior decorator, no doubt. Kind of a blend between contemporary and traditional. The living room was all contemporary, including the artwork—can't tell from a projection but I'm guessing those aren't prints. His study had an old-world European look to it. Dark woods. Leather. Framed antique maps. A big free-standing globe. (I'd bet Don lunch that it opened up and there were bottles of whiskey inside it.) Every other room was a cross between the two extremes of the living room and study.

Randall finishes explaining that the condo has only one entrance door and it does not appear to have been tampered with. There is a manned security desk in the front lobby 24/7. If you are a guest, the guy in an elaborate maroon uniform with lots of gold braids has to press a code for you to use the elevators. He calls up to the owner and gets the thumbs-up or thumbs-down to usher the person into the elevator and key them up.

"Is there a back entrance?" I ask.

"We'll get there," Randall says. "And by the way, nice to meet you, Detective Conner."

"Plenty of time for introductions later," Zaworski says with a scowl. "Conner, you need to get in here early and get caught up so we don't waste our time on remedial work. This case is already almost four days old. Do we have anything to work with, Randall? Anybody?"

Zaworski has only two moods, and both are usually bad. But he's on his A-game today.

"Only thing we got is one of his homeys came over to pick him up for lunch on the day of the murder," says Martinez. He looks at his notes. "Adam Spencer."

I don't think Durham had homeys. And I'm guessing Adam Spencer is rich like Durham.

"He went up to the twenty-fifth floor about one o'clock," Randall continues. "Durham and Spencer were back in the lobby about fifteen minutes later. Spencer's car was parked out front. A Mercedes. It says a CL65 AMG. That's an expensive car."

"Only if two hundred and twenty grand is expensive," Don says.

Martinez looks at him like Don just told him he's married to a space alien and is moving to Pluto next month.

"No way, *amigo*," Antonio says.

"Ladies, keep on task," says Zaworski.

"They took it over to Vines on Clark next to Wrigley," Randall continues. "They ate burgers and drank wine for a couple hours."

"Burgers and wine? What is this city coming to?" Zaworski asks.

That's actually funny. We make eye contact and as a group decide not to laugh.

"Credit card records and the day manager verify the story. Spencer dropped him off at three o'clock," Martinez adds.

I think Randall assumes he will be spokesman of the two, only Martinez hasn't agreed yet. Don is spokesman for the two of us. He gives a better talk than I do.

"Durham went upstairs alone," Randall says, jumping in. Martinez is going to have to get quicker.

"That seemed like a big deal to the security dude," Martinez interjects. "Apparently Durham has a revolving door of ladies who visit him."

"The life of the idle rich," Randall says.

Zaworski glares at him and Randall looks back down at his notebook.

"Anyone else check in the front door to see him?" Don asks.

"Nope," Martinez answers sharply. "We did think to check, Squires," he says sarcastically.

"No offense intended, Antonio."

"*Sonaba como a mí, mi amigo.*"

"Can it, you two," Zaworski snarls. "So who killed him? The Stanley Hammer fairy?"

That's actually pretty funny too, if you ask me. But no one is laughing. The boss is a bear today. *Is it because I'm back?*

"We spent the weekend following up on family members and calling his contacts," Don answers. "We don't have a suspect identified, but we've got some interesting leads."

"Let's hear it," Zaworski mutters.

"When Randall said 'the life of the idle rich,' he wasn't kidding," Don continues. "Durham is thirty-eight years old and never worked a day in his life. He's a caricature of a trust fund baby."

"I don't know what 'caricature' means, so save the big words," Zaworski snaps without looking up from a paper he's reading.

Unruffled, Don says, "He and some pals from high school and college run around and party like they're still twenty-one-year-olds. There's at least five of them that never work, and another four or five that work but like to try keeping up with an unreal social schedule. A few are married, but they all like to date hot young ladies—and

61

apparently going out and meeting them is too much trouble so they use a very exclusive and discreet dating service to set up their girls."

"What's it called?" Zaworski asks.

"Doesn't have a name. Like I said, it's discreet."

"Something can be discreet and have a name," Zaworski growls.

Even the unflappable Don backs off.

"Prostitutes?" Zaworski asks.

"More or less," Don responds cautiously. "But impossible to prove. Apparently Vice has tried. But the owner has built a pretty slick and careful operation. No website, no business card, no brochures. All her business is word of mouth. Her name is Barbara Ferguson. She's been looked at and leaned on hard by Vice through the years. But she has never been charged with a crime. She charges a monthly 'matchmaker' fee for female companionship only. If anything else happens, it's between her clients and the girls she provides for them. Randall talked to Conroy over in Vice and she has apparently insulated herself from criminal activity and has an expensive lawyer on retainer to guard her little black book. But Randall discovered something real interesting from Conroy."

He stops and nods at Randall to take over. Randall hesitates and clears his throat.

"Our body is getting cold," Zaworski snaps.

"You gonna tell us what you got or do we have to play Twenty Questions?"

Zaworski has always been gruff, though I actually thought we started getting along in my last case. *I thought.* Something is eating at him. Probably heat from above.

"Sorry," Randall says quickly. "What Conroy told me is that City Finance has her dead to rights on tax evasion. They think they have a case against her that could result in a serious prison sentence and some enormous fines. Conroy hooked me up with the director of revenue at city hall. He's working with the IRS, county, and state agencies. I explained what we have going with Director Stevens. He wasn't sure they could help us but he agreed to make a call. I was barely out of his office when he called my cell and told me to come back upstairs. Whoever he called—it was the mayor, though we're not supposed to repeat that—told him to say they would offer us whatever we need to leverage her to help us clear the Durham murder."

"If we're not supposed to say it, don't say it," Zaworski says. "So what do we have to offer her?"

"Full immunity from prosecution if she helps us find the killer. She does have to pay back taxes but the fines will be waived."

"We got that in writing?"

"I'm supposed to call back this morning, and if

I give them this"—he hands Zaworski a sheet of paper—"with your John Hancock on it, they'll have Legal draft a contract to present her. If she signs and cooperates fully, we are off to the races."

Zaworski takes thirty seconds to read it. He pulls a fancy ballpoint pen—might be a Montblanc—out of his suit coat, unscrews the cap, and scribbles his name at the bottom.

"Make sure Shelly makes a copy and puts it in the file," he says, sliding it to Randall. He turns to Don. "Squires, are you sure this is the route the investigation needs to take?"

"Absolutely, sir. Whoever killed Jack Durham had free access to his place. Durham was a player and not real nice about it. Lots of people—including those closest to him—disliked him. So one of those friends or working girls did it or can give us an idea on who did it."

"How'd the killer get past security in the lobby?" Zaworski backtracks.

"When we leaned on him a little," Martinez jumps in, "the security guard admitted that Durham had enough comings and goings at his apartment that he had some of his visitors use the back service entrance. We took a look back there. One of the doors was locked but hadn't shut all the way. We think the killer got into the building that way and then walked up the stairs."

"Someone walked up twenty-five flights of stairs?" I ask.

"You aren't the only one who likes to exercise," Zaworski says, cutting me off. "Randall, Martinez —get moving. Get the document down to city hall and tell them we need the Legal offer ready yesterday."

They get up to leave.

"Randall," he nearly yells, "don't forget to have Shelly make a copy and put it in the file."

They nod and head out the door, pronto.

"Jerome, you can scram," he says. "This case is priority. Go over the blood and the tissue results again. Let us know if you find anything else. Most of all, make sure the evidence is righteous enough to convict whoever it is that did this."

Jerome gathers his papers and quickly beelines for the door.

"Squires and Konkade, I want you two to sit down together and write up a plan of action. Keep it to two pages."

They nod.

"What about me, sir?" I ask.

"You got to go down to Personnel and sign a bunch of papers saying you're back on the job. I think they have a physical scheduled for you."

"My knee is fine."

"It's fine when the doc says it's fine. We need all the bodies we can muster on this case. The heat from up high is blazing hot. The dead kid's dad is a billionaire who's contributed big-time to

Mayor Daniels and anyone else Daniels has wanted elected. Daddy wants something for his investment now. The mayor and Commissioner Fergosi are happy to oblige. They don't want another media circus like we had with Woods this year."

"I do have a complete medical report from the FBI," I say, wanting in on the action from the start.

"Good for you. But your knee and wrist aren't okay until our doc says they're okay. I hear that's not the only thing they gave you."

Does he know they offered me a job?

"You got to get that Sig Sauer cleared with the armory."

Maybe not.

He rolls his eyes. What's wrong with carrying a Sig?

"We won't be getting much out of you today. So why don't you hoof it down to Personnel and get things rolling so you can actually get back to work at some point? And don't be late tomorrow."

I'm ready to fight back. I have a couple names I want to call him. But discretion is often the greater part of valor, so I take a deep breath and just nod and stand to go. Then I freeze at a sudden thought.

"What, Conner?" Zaworski demands impatiently.

"Nothing, sir."

I turn quickly and head for the door. I can't believe I don't have my car. I wonder how much cash I have in my purse. If I have to go to a doctor's office from Personnel and then out to the armory to get my new gun properly registered, I'm going to be forking out tens and twenties all day for a couple of cab rides. My green commitment to public transportation is officially over. I walk to the door.

"Conner," Zaworski says.

I stop and turn. What now?

"Welcome back."

I would have said thanks, but he's already huddled with Don and Konkade again.

10

I thought I looked pretty good this morning. I spent some time getting myself ready. At least *some* time for me. I actually blow-dried my hair and must have spent all of two minutes with the curling iron. (I think that two minutes made me miss the first bus outside my apartment complex.) I gave my coif a couple shots of hair spray. I didn't recognize the bright red metallic can that's about as big as a scuba diving air tank, so it must be something Klarissa left behind after spending a couple weeks at my place. That means it's a lot better than anything I buy. I'll tell her she left it, but she'll have moved on to the next product, so I now probably have enough hair spray to last me a year.

So I got off to a great start on my first official day back in the office until I missed the bus and was late for briefing.

My first stop after getting chewed on by Zaworski was Personnel. Claudia Jones has got to be pushing seventy years old, and I've known her since I was ten or maybe younger. She and my dad kidded each other a lot, so that means she likes me. She worked me through the paperwork in thirty minutes. I'm not sure of everything I signed, but she assured me that if I ever were to have a baby, I hadn't given rights to my firstborn to CPD.

The doctor's office was when my carefully coiffed hair and makeup started going south. He asked where my workout clothes were. I could have told him I had some in the trunk of my car, but with my car back home, it didn't seem pertinent. I explained that I didn't know we would be doing this today and he said fine, we could do it later in the week. The thought of explaining that to Zaworski helped me improvise. I put on the baggy shorts and T-shirt they supplied and went through the exam. I had to sign an extra waiver when I told them I was happy to run the treadmill in bare feet. I think I have a blister for my commitment. There was no shower room at the doctor's office, so I put my clothes back on over a sweaty body.

The armory was a hassle. The guy in charge of inventory had never seen paperwork from the FBI transferring ownership of a handgun to a Chicago police officer. He went to show it to his boss, but his boss was already at lunch and apparently very hungry. It took him a full two hours to return. He still wasn't in a hurry to move me through the grinder. I was about to go through the roof with impatience. The only thing that settled my nerves was the thought of punching his lights out.

How old are you, Kristen?

I did use the time to shoot four rounds of twenty-five shells from thirty, sixty, ninety, and 120 feet. I wanted to shoot with my new Sig, but since it wasn't registered with CPD, the guy in charge of the range wouldn't let me bring it in. I used the standard Glock 9mm and did okay. Not great, but better than usual. This has now planted doubts in my mind whether I should have ever switched from the Glock to the Beretta and now over to the Sig. All I want is to improve my handgun score to better than average. I might be able to live with that.

I walked down the street from there and got the Happy Meal at McDonald's. The grandma serving me kept looking around with narrowed eyes to see if I really had a kid. I don't know what the rules are on age, but I may be banned from at least one Chicagoland McDonald's. I did get a miniature Barbie. I'm no fan of the doll, but I may keep this one for myself. When I bought Kendra a Sporty Barbie soccer star for her eighth birthday, I got in trouble with my sister for giving her a toy that might permanently twist her perception of the appropriate female body. I think Kendra is okay so far.

I finally got back to the office at four o'clock, legal and ready to get busy. I might have detected a slight case of body odor when I lifted my arms to stretch my back. Didn't matter. The place was nearly a ghost town.

"Where is everybody?" I asked Shelly.

"The captain took everybody to serve a warrant on someone who might have information on the Durham murder."

Since I'm here, he obviously didn't take *everybody*. I am tempted to point that out but hold my tongue.

"He leave any instructions what he wants me to get started on?"

"Not a thing."

Thanks, Shelly. For nothing.

I decided to brave Chicago's public transportation system and head home early to regroup. Everyone knows I put in long hours, so I'm not too worried anyone will think I'm a slacker—and there's no one around but Shelly to think that anyway.

I cleared e-mail for twenty minutes, walked the stairs down to the lobby, caught the bus almost immediately in front of our building. I hopped off at Walsh and Van Buren, walked a long half block to the LaSalle station, and jumped on the northwest Blue Line. We crossed Western and I was one stop from my exit when I saw Zaworski's name pop up on my screen.

"Yes, sir?"

"Where you at, Conner?"

"I'm just about home, sir. When I got back to the office, it was after four and I didn't see anything on my desk."

The silence at the end of the line is palpable. I guess I could have told him I was still straightening things up, but I'm not going to lie to the boss.

"I'll head right back in, sir."

"You do that, Conner. Turn your car around and be here in thirty. Straight to my office."

He saved me from explaining that I'm not in my car because the line went dead.

I get off on California. It takes me ten minutes to find an ATM and then another fifteen minutes to flag a cab. We're in the middle of rush hour, so the drive to the precinct is about thirty minutes. I run up the five flights of steps to Homicide and head straight for the captain's office. Three quick raps on the door and I open it slowly and poke my head in. He is huddled with Commander Czaka and Sergeant Konkade at a small meeting table.

"Not now, Conner," Zaworski says. "Go find Squires and get up to speed."

I shut the door quietly and head over to the cubicle farm where Don and I and the other detectives are lined up. He's not in his cube. I walk out front and Shelly has just picked up her purse to leave.

"Thought you scrammed," she says.

"I did but the captain called me back in."

"Yeah, he had all the detectives in the conference room to go over new developments on the Durham case."

Not *all*, Shelly.

"Squires and the others hiding somewhere around here?"

"No. That meeting ended fifteen minutes ago. Captain told everyone to go home because tomorrow is a big day. You probably need to get home too."

"Captain didn't leave a message for me to wait around to talk to him?"

"Not with me. He's got a big dinner tonight. When he's done with the commander, he'll be out of here in a hurry."

While she heads for the elevator bank, I blow hair off my face in exasperation.

● ● ●

I turn sideways and kick ten times as hard as I can with my right knee. A quick hop to my right and I kick ten times with my left. I square up and punch left, right, left, right as hard as I can for ninety seconds.

"Time!" Gary calls.

"Not bad, not bad."

I start to lean down and put my hands on my knees, but straighten up and get my hands over my head to open my lungs. No doubt. My deodorant gave up the fight hours ago. My thighs and everything else on me are burning and complaining from the past thirty minutes of kicking and punching. Not sure there's a better singular workout program than fighting.

I waited twenty more minutes at the office for Zaworski to finish meeting with Czaka and Konkade. No way was I leaving the office without checking in with him. I did have to go the bathroom, though, and when I came out, he was gone. Shelly was right; he was out in a flash.

It took me ninety minutes to navigate the route to my house. The El was packed. The guy standing next to me for a couple stops, who looked like he was homeless, kept wrinkling his nose and giving me dirty looks when I held onto the overhead straps. I finally gave him a dirty look back and won a stare down. He moved farther down the car. Glad I got one victory today.

I was steaming when I got home. I threw on workout clothes and headed to the Planet Fitness about ten minutes from my apartment. I don't know what's going on tonight but the traffic was so heavy it took me twenty minutes. I didn't have a game plan and was thinking maybe weight machines and then the elliptical. A guy was shadow-boxing on one of the mats. He had the punching paddles there, so I asked if he wanted me to hold for him.

Gary decided to get cute and flirt a little until he saw the expression on my face was all business. When he started his punching routine and I didn't budge an inch holding the paddles, he got down to business too. He came in fast and furious to show off. I still held my ground. After he was all punched out, we talked a few minutes and he ended up being a nice guy. He told me he was a baggage handler for American out at O'Hare and had been in the Marines—two tours in Iraq. He boxed while he was in the service, and before that, did some Golden Gloves. He definitely had fast hands. When I told him that, he started flirting again. I cut him off, telling him to give me the gloves and to pick up the paddles.

I did offend him when I asked, "So you're an ex-Marine?"

"No true Marine ever stops being a Marine. *Semper fi.*"

Okay. Dramatic. But I like the loyalty.

I started out slow and steady but picked up the pace. I started mixing speed and power and then switched to kicks and karate chops with hands and elbows. I ended with a speed routine that is designed to take the muscles to absolute failure. It worked. I am shaky. The only reason I keep moving is to do an appropriate cooldown and save myself from lactic acid buildup.

"Let's work out again sometime. You punch great."

I think he wanted to add, "for a girl," but caught himself.

"Give me your number so I can put it in my phone," Gary continues.

I hesitate. I give out my number all day every day, but usually to witnesses and suspects.

"I promise I won't bug you," he says. "I have a girlfriend already and I'm loyal like a Marine. I'll just call if none of my workout partners wants to punch."

I give him my number with a trace of uneasiness.

"So what do you do?" he asks.

"I'm a cop. Detective first class, Chicago Police Department."

"I for sure won't bug you, Detective Kristen."

"Good workout, and thanks," I say as I make my typical graceful exit, stepping on a fat rope someone left at the edge of the mat and nearly biting the dust. I look back and he's watching me and laughing. I give a curtsy and head for the door.

You better be loyal to your girl and not bug me, Gary.

I put a towel on my seat and sink into my Miata. The ride home takes the customary ten minutes. I plan to take a quick shower but the water feels too good and I empty my water heater. My green consciousness is definitely reeling with all the water and electricity I just wasted.

I flip on ESPN to *Monday Night Football* and watch Cincinnati versus Baltimore for twenty minutes. Ray Lewis has definitely slowed down, and the Bengals are a lot better than I ever remember them being.

First day back in the office. What a disaster. And what's with no real welcome home? I wasn't expecting a brass band to play "Seventy-Six Trombones" from *The Music Man*. But a little recognition within my department might have been nice. What's up with Zaworski anyway?

So much for easing back into things. We're on a full-blown high-profile murder case. Well, the others are, and I plan to be tomorrow. I don't need to ease back in anyway. I've had an all-expense vacation in Quantico, Virginia. My knee feels great. I'm ready to go.

11

"Okay, let's see what we can do with you."

Why do I feel like a bug under a microscope? I got called into Zaworski's office this morning within five minutes of arriving at the precinct. I was actually twenty-five minutes early.

Sergeant Konkade and Bob Blackshear were in the office with him. Blackshear works at the Third Precinct, so I wonder what he's doing over here.

"Sit down, Conner," Zaworski orders with his patented charm and courtesy.

I smile at Konkade, who ignores me while he smooths the three strands of hair on his bald dome. Blackshear and I nod to each other and both of us have a little smirk on our faces. I like Blackshear a lot. He's a rung or two above me on the detective ladder. I can see him getting a big-time promotion in the near future.

"Blackshear is here because he is going to run Homicide in the Second for a month or so."

Apparently I am a prophet. Okay. That's a surprise.

"And in case you're wondering where I'll be and what I'll be doing, don't ask, because I'm not saying right now."

"Yes, sir."

"I like that, Conner. Just keep saying 'yes, sir' and don't ask any. . . darn questions."

"Yes, sir."

He looks up to see if I'm being a smart aleck. I am. But I think I've emptied my face of even the hint of a smile or any other sign of emotion.

"In the big scheme of life, I'm not sure if our new case really matters," he presses on. "All murders are wrong and a tragedy. Some are just a little less of a tragedy. If you or Blackshear quote me on this, I'll swear you are lying, but sometimes when the herd gets thinned a little, everybody gets along a little better."

Where is he going with this?

"This Jack Durham may have had a boatload of money but he was a lowlife if ever there was one. My wife is very enlightened, so I don't talk this way at home. But I'm not crying in my beer that we lost Durham.

"Doesn't mean this isn't a huge case, however. It's still wrong and it's still a tragedy, and we got everyone from the mayor's office to every hack writer with a blog watching us like a hawk. I think I saw your sister waxing eloquent about it on the late news."

He pauses and looks at me intently. He better not be implying I feed her information or this meeting is going to get heated. *Sir*.

"If we break the case this afternoon it won't be

soon enough," he sighs. "According to the news, we'll still have moved too slow and botched everything we did along the way. Fine. We know better. Bottom line, I want this one cleared fast. Preferably before I get back."

"Yes, sir."

"Good memory, Conner. You're still doing well. Don't mess it up now."

Uh-oh. Something's coming. My magical detective antennae trembles all around me.

"You did good work undercover with Alcoholics Anonymous earlier this year. Well, you mostly did good work. We met with the lady who we think is our leverage in this case. We told her what we had on her, what we planned to do to her, but what she could do for herself if she decided to help us. She folded like a cheap tent. Didn't she, Bob?"

"Yes, sir, she—"

"That's right, she did," Zaworski interrupts. "Well, Bob and the sergeant here and even Commander Czaka and I had a late-night powwow to think through how to play this. Randall and Squires wrote a nice two-page strategy report. It was good but not inspired. We wanted it to be inspired. And despite Czaka's objections we got inspired late last night. I thought about it all morning driving into the office and I'm still inspired. So we have a little something we want you to do on this case."

● ● ●

I didn't do quite as well on the "yes, sir" as I had earlier. I had a lot of questions and a few out-and-out objections. We argued. Zaworski stopped being a bear—wonder what the heck is wrong with him to be taking a month or two off—and was his usual stern self, but had a lot more patience and a lot less sarcasm. He could afford to be patient because he'd already won. At the end of the day, Zaworski wasn't putting in a request with me. He was giving me an assignment and was happy to help me think it through strategically.

At the end of the meeting he actually smiled, shook my hand, and said, "Glad you're back, Conner. We're a lot more fun than the FBI anyway. When's the last time you saw an FBI agent smile?"

So he knows I got a job offer from the FBI. I haven't told a soul, including my family. How did he know? It would have to be Willingham or Reynolds, the two fishing buddies. Maybe they called from a fishing boat on the Penobscot River.

So here I am with Barbara Ferguson in an apartment on Chicago's Gold Coast that makes the stuff Klarissa had in her townhome seem Spartan. And Klarissa's place was never Spartan. I think Don's wife, the ace realtor who keeps her detective husband happy in expensive shoes and clothes, had an offer on it in less than a week.

Klarissa took it. No way was she going to live there again after being taken hostage by Dean Woods.

Barbara's place is pure luxury, from the art on the walls to the rugs on the floor to the furniture to the view of Lake Michigan. A fog is rolling in to match my mood, but it really isn't doing too much damage to the ambience.

Not sure what's new and what's antique, but as much as I hate to admit it, it blends together and looks fabulous.

"Nice place, Barbara," I say.

"Call me Bobbie. And yeah, it'll do."

I'm not good at guessing ages but I'm thinking she's fifty years old, give or take a few either way. A very well-preserved and attractive fifty, I would add. Her hair is pulled back and up to show a nice neckline—no wrinkles—and a lot of casual bling disappearing into a low-cut that my mom would not approve of and cascading from her ears. I've been telling myself I have to upgrade my wardrobe and accessories. She's not my style but seeing her dressed for success reminds me of that.

"We've got our work cut out for us, Detective Conner," she says with the same tone you'd use to explain an outdoor project to the landscaping guy.

"Call me Kristen."

"I'm so pleased to meet you, Kristen," she

responds, looking me in the eyes with all the warmth and earnestness possible from a truly caring person—or someone who is just good at introductions and first impressions. My antennae are still up from this morning's meeting with Zaworski and I suspect the latter.

"Let's go sit down," she says. "Something to drink? I have a bottle of white chilled."

"No, thanks," I answer.

"That won't do," she says with a grimace. "In my line of work the answer is always yes."

"In my line of work the answer is almost always no."

"And that's why we are meeting here," she says. "Because you are about to enter my world."

We stare each other down. She is a cool customer. She looks unfazed, maybe slightly amused.

"Your charming captain said you might be difficult."

"No doubt he's a charmer," I say with a snort of laughter.

She looks at me blankly. Apparently Ferguson wasn't making a joke. "I found Captain Zaworski to be very charming. Perhaps I am more attuned to noticing the good in people."

"Are you judging me?"

"Are you judging *me*?"

"I asked first."

I'm not sure we're off to a great start.

Zaworski ordered me to behave myself. He had a list of words and phrases I was not to use with Ferguson, including *prostitution, madam, pimp, call girls,* and words I didn't know the meaning of. If at some point I needed to acknowledge Ferguson's role, it was that she had been hired by the CPD to serve as a *consultant* on the Jack Durham murder case.

"I don't like her and what she does any better than you, Conner," he had said, "but we got to keep her on our side. You grind on her and she clams up and it isn't going to help us nail a killer."

I get that. Still doesn't mean I have to like that she's coaching me to pose as one of her escorts to get close to the friends Durham ran around with.

"How long is this going to go on, sir?" I asked.

"As long as it takes to catch a murderer—or until our list of suspects figure out you aren't legitimate."

"First time someone thinks something's going to happen that isn't going to happen, my cover will be blown, sir."

I wondered if he understood what I was saying.

"Talk to Barbara. She'll help you work through all that. They have procedures and exit strategies they learn."

I wondered if I knew what *he* was saying. Exit strategies? Procedures? I think that was the first time I'd heard Zaworski not sound too sure of himself.

I pointed out to Zaworski that my real-world dating life isn't doing so well and there might be better candidates than me.

"Not inside my department," he said. "Unless you want me to put a skirt on Squires, I think you're the man for the job."

That actually sounded like a better plan to me, but I should have kept my mouth shut. He wasn't amused.

In a follow-up meeting with Don, Martinez, and Randall, I got more details than I ever wanted to have on Barbara Ferguson's high-class (*high-class* is Don's phrase, not mine) escort service for the rich and famous. Beautiful girls. Discreet arrangements.

Ferguson gets paid to set up dates but nothing more. The costs for illegal "benefits" are somehow magically understood but not stated or in writing. It is paid directly to the girls, cash only. The men know to refer to the cash as a gift, not payment for a service. Everyone knows the rules and thus it is very hard to charge or convict Bobbie Ferguson for running a prostitution ring.

I didn't start out in Homicide—my first gig with the CPD was routine patrol. I was fortunate to avoid working in Vice, a pretty disgusting work environment where the women officers often have to play dress-up. It ends up causing problems with real-life relationships, and the internal mocking is brutal. I let Don know that if he turns this into a joke—or if he lets others in the department turn it into a joke—it is not going to be received well by me.

Bobbie is returning to the room with a glass of white wine for her and a cup of tea for me. I can't argue with her beauty. I am reminded that my first objection to Zaworski was based on my personality; I'm no shrinking violet, so there's a good chance I'd let someone have it before dinner.

Then he and Konkade showed me a portfolio of Ferguson's "girls" and *wow* was all I could think. That led to my second objection: I'm not in the same zip code in the looks department.

I think that's why Bobbie has two furrows in the middle of her forehead as she looks me over.

"Hmmm," she says.

"You know you could save us both a lot of trouble if you just tell the captain this isn't going to work."

"I agree," she says. "But your captain is pretty adamant that I need to make it work. And I am very motivated to do whatever your captain deems is right." She pauses. "And based on your looks, I think it could."

"I saw the pictures of your girls, Bobbie. No need to flatter me. I'm not high enough in the food chain to sweeten your deal."

"I have a hair stylist and a makeup artist who can work miracles."

She gives a triumphant smirk. So much for flattery. I do agree a miracle is required.

"But it's still going to take all my considerable abilities and savvy," she continues. "Because with your attitude and mouth, I don't care what we make you look like, it's not going to play well with my clients. I should say ex-clients. Even if I avoid charges and possible jail time for misunderstandings on my taxes, I'm not going to have any clients left."

We narrow our eyes in unison and give each other a hard stare. I am not breaking eye contact first. I can do this all day.

After ten seconds she gives a laugh—*Hah! You lost that one, Bobbie!*—and claps her hands. "Let's get started."

I think the enthusiasm is faked.

I leave Bobbie's condo a block off Lake Shore Drive a little after two, but rush hour has started early. Back to the office or head home? I can make calls and type reports just as easily there. So I continue north.

Mom and Kaylen loved the movie *My Fair Lady*. I can't remember watching it all the way through, but I've seen enough to know I have the Audrey Hepburn role as Eliza Doolittle and Bobbie has the Rex Harrison role of Professor Henry Higgins. I bet she's a better actor.

We ate a two-hour lunch with the sole purpose of refining my table manners, which I think were just fine to begin with. She didn't correct my work with knife and fork, but I got hammered by her on my inconsistent eye contact and my inability to keep my opinions to myself.

I'm thirty years old and single. No regular beau. But I've assumed I want to get married someday. After listening to Bobbie's jaundiced view of what men want, I'm not so sure. I definitely prefer single to the kind of client she takes care of.

I stay out of politics. But with all the debates about the 1 percent—her clientele is the 1 percent of the 1 percent, I think—there is no denying there's a privileged class that is too lazy to even ask a girl for a date.

What in the world have I gotten into?

12

I don't recognize the number.

"Conner."

"Hi, Kristen, it's been a long time since we've talked."

Dell Woods. No way. I guess you could say we dated at one time. I think we showed up at places together out of convenience, but I never had romantic feelings for him. He wanted to marry me. He wormed his way into the middle of my family, and all of them thought he was a super guy. He courted me with the gusto of a stark-raving-mad stalker. Other than that—and me telling him that there was no hope for us and that I didn't want to ever talk to him again, and the fact that his brother was the serial killer that tried to kill my sister and me—I am delighted he is calling me. *Not*.

"Dell, why are you calling me?"

"Kristen, I just wanted to tell you—"

"Dell, I've already told you I don't want any apologies and I don't want communication between us."

"Kristen, all I wanted to do is—"

"Dell, I'm not going to meet you one more time to rehash things so you can find some kind of closure and let me know that if I change my mind you are there for me. The book on us is closed."

"Kristen, it's not that. I just want to—"

"Stop now, Dell. Nothing is going to change between us. It's not healthy for you or for me for you to call me. And you are making me mad."

"Would you just listen for a second? All I want to do is tell you I'm engaged and I want to introduce you to my fiancée. She knows all we've been through in the past year and wanted to say hi to you."

Okay. That's unexpected. But not bad unexpected. This is good. At least I hope it is for her sake.

"Then put her on."

"We actually wanted to take you out for a bite to eat."

Always another meeting.

"Nope. Not going to happen. If she wants to meet me, it's going to be through the miracle of technology. So put her on the phone. Now."

"Kristen, she's not here right now."

"Then why are you calling me without her if that's the reason you called me?"

"To set things up."

"Or to reengage."

"I'm engaged. Stop being so suspicious of my motives."

"If she was standing next to you and talking to me, I wouldn't be suspicious. It's strange for you to be calling me."

"Well, don't you think it's strange that, after all we've been through, we have never talked about it?"

Here it comes. Dell is still Dell. I may meet with his fiancée so I can warn her to run the other way.

"Maybe if I thought about it at all, I would. But I don't think about it. And I've let you do exactly what you set out to do and what I've told you countless times I don't want: I've let you start a conversation. You are not a part of my life, including my family's."

"I thought you were supposed to be a Christian. You don't sound very Christian to me."

I was wondering when that would come up. If one angle doesn't work, he tries another. Why not false religious guilt?

"And so are you. So do the honorable thing: focus on your wife-to-be. Build a life with her. Stop giving me even a single thought. And that's all I have to say."

"Can we talk about it?"

I'm not going to answer that. He's just looking for yet another way to engage. This guy is good-looking, very successful in business, and seemingly has the world by the tail. But there's something very wrong with him, particularly when it comes to me. I guess that last part isn't so unusual.

"You there?"

"Good-bye, Dell."

"Wait! Kristen, don't hang up! I had one other question for you. It's not about us."

"Make it quick."

"Do you know where they're keeping Dean? I can't get any information from anyone. I'm not sure that what they're doing is legal. I know what he did was horrific. But he's my brother and I should be allowed to visit him."

"Dell, you know as much as I do. The CPD is

no longer involved in his incarceration, questioning, or prosecution. You need to take it up with the FBI."

"They won't return my calls. Someone even mentioned that this might be a national security issue."

"You're not the only one calling them. All I can say is keep trying."

"I've called every business day for two months now. They're threatening to press charges of harassment if I call again."

They might not be the only ones. But I have to admit, this doesn't sound quite right. Two months and no answer? I think the feds have gone the wrong direction at times by sweeping everything under the national security rug.

"Dell, I'll call a friend and see if they can get someone to call you. I'll call now. But don't call me back to see how it's going. It will happen when it happens. Might take a couple weeks. So don't call me back. You focus on that pretty fiancée of yours."

"She is pretty."

"I knew she would be. And Dell—congratulations. I wish you the best."

"Thanks, Kristen. That means a lot to me."

He starts to say something else but I hit the Off button.

"I thought you were a Christian."

I have enough feelings of guilt and don't need

91

that added jab. I'm happy to help people where and how I can. As a cop, I am in the service industry—and there's a reason for that. I'm willing to serve. But even if you say you love the world, it doesn't mean you are suited or able to help every single individual in every situation, does it? I know a lot of people would say yes because they think that's the right answer. I'm not so sure. And when it comes to someone who has a strange obsession toward you, I don't think they're really coming to you for help anyway.

Dell's engaged? I hope he knows what he's doing. I hope she knows what she's getting into. I'm not sure I agree with how the FBI has handled his brother. But as long as he's locked up somewhere far away I'm not going to lose any sleep over it.

I'll call Reynolds and see if he can get someone to visit with Dell.

13

"So what have I gotten myself into?" I ask Don.

I'm eating lunch at the Billy Goat Tavern, a long flight of steps below street level on Michigan Avenue. The Wrigley Building and, across the street, the glorious neo-gothic Tribune Tower make this one of Chicago's grandest architectural crossroads. The art-deco NBC building a block closer to the lake isn't bad either. The Billy Goat is a hole in the wall that didn't get the memo on grandeur. It does serve great burgers, and if you're feeling daring they'll put a slice of cheese on for variety.

"Seems to me your love life is about to take off," Don answers, mayonnaise overflowing to the corner of his overstuffed mouth. "About time," he adds, wiping his face with a napkin and taking a big gulp of Diet Coke.

I think he's lost a few pounds while I was in DC. Don is never going to look thin. Too wide in the shoulders. He was a college running back, with the short muscular physique that goes with the position. He says he played for Ball State at five-eleven and 225 pounds. Guys do like to exaggerate their height. I've known a lot of six-foot men that were only five-ten. I'm five-seven. I don't wear anything more than a half-inch heel, tops, and usually stick to flats. He's five-nine if my eyeball test is right.

"Must be nice to get paid to go out on dates," he says.

He's going to keep pushing this. I decide to play innocent.

"Right," I answer with a roll of my eyes. "I'm not real good at dating guys I know. I can't imagine how bad it's going to be dating strangers."

"Might make things go better."

I've had enough. I wad up the napkin on my plate and throw it at him.

"Hey, watch the shirt," he says in horror. Don is a sissy when it comes to clothes. He might be the best dresser in the Chicago Police Department. His silky purple tie is slung back over his shoulder so he doesn't get food on it. Smart move.

"I'm not the one who uses half a bottle of Heinz," I say. "And you deserve a ketchup stain for not supporting your partner. We've covered this. I don't want my assignment turned into a joke."

"Yeah, yeah." He shrugs dismissively. "I've got your back. My wife likes you and has given me strict orders you aren't to get hurt again while under my watch. She won't even listen to me when I explain that you make that an impossible task. For one thing, you never listen."

"Under your watch?"

He smiles and shrugs. "Take it up with Vanessa."

"So I'm still waiting for your words of wisdom."

"I can't remember what we were talking about."

I sigh. "There is no way in the world I can do undercover on this case."

"You did okay working Alcoholics Anonymous."

"Even if that's partially true, it had nothing to do with us catching Dean Woods."

"I don't know. We might not have connected the dots otherwise."

We? It's funny how time blurs memories. I was the one who connected the dots. Now anyone in law enforcement within a three-hundred-mile radius of Chicago is taking credit. Including Don.

Drop it, Kristen. Be a good sport. Everyone pulled their weight.

"I now have a dating coach."

"Is that what she is? My momma had another name for ladies in her line of work."

I roll my eyes. "You were there when Zaworski said we play nice with Bobbie. No name calling."

"I don't think she eats cheeseburgers at the Billy Goat. So since neither she nor the captain are around, I'll say what I feel. I want to catch Durham's killer and close this case as much as the captain does. But I think everyone involved with Durham is the scum of the earth. If I need to apologize, I apologize to scum everywhere. These people aren't right."

Prostitution is a tricky business—no pun intended. If CPD runs an undercover sting where an officer poses as a call girl, once money is mentioned and agreed to, a bust can be made. However, a sting is considered entrapment if presented in such a way that it would lure somebody into doing something they wouldn't normally do. Most successful stings are run in settings where there's no question what the customer has come to buy. Or, if the sting is designed to get hookers off the street, there will be little question what is being sold.

Bobbie Ferguson is running a service that caters to wealthy men who want someone on their arm in a social setting and then extra benefits later. Jack Durham and about ten of his buddies are some of her biggest customers. What a sleazy business.

"So Durham and his rich friends set up their dates through Bobbie," I say, thinking out loud. "Why don't they just hit bars and health clubs like normal immoral sleazebags?"

"You know how they say some guys are interested in the hunt and then lose interest when they land the girl they're chasing?"

"Yeah," I answer.

"Apparently these guys are so jaded they don't want to even pretend to like or pursue a woman. They plan a party to hang out with each other—and let Bobbie take care of the eye candy."

"And these guys are grown-ups?"

"I would call them adult adolescents, but that wouldn't be fair to adolescents."

"Did you know guys like that in college?"

"Heck, yes. Our football coach wouldn't let us join a frat, but the football team was a fraternity just the same. Parties and girls. We were the campus stars, so there were plenty of girls."

"Tell me you weren't like that."

"I absolutely—"

Don's phone vibrates on the table with enough vigor to spill Diet Coke on his plate. He pushes it in my direction to make sure nothing spills on his clothes.

"Yeah?" he answers, a finger stuck in his free ear as he listens. "Thanks, Shelly. Can you text me the address so I don't have to put it in my GPS?" A short pause. "We're on our way."

"Where we heading?"

"A condo about seven or eight blocks from here. Blackshear wants us to talk to one of Bobbie's girls who knew Durham well. She's been told to sit tight until we arrive. I think it's better to walk than move the car."

"So what's up with Zaworski? He never even told anyone ahead of time that yesterday was his last day before his leave of absence."

"Yeah, it's real hush-hush."

"So what do you know?"

"Nothing."

"Any guesses?"

"Gotta be health. But I've not been speculating because the boss has been shooting at anything that moves."

I don't have any singles and leave a pile of change beside my empty water glass as a token tip. Don looks at that and shakes his head. He leaves two crisp one-dollar bills.

We weave through heavy pedestrian traffic on

Chicago and cut over on Erie. I realize I never got a chance to ask Don to clarify if he was like the other guys on the football team back in his college days. I know he's a good husband and father. He's a good cop too. I hope he wasn't a jerk like Durham and his buddies.

Why is Don giving me a hard time about this assignment? Maybe I'll talk to Vanessa.

14

"Do you know anyone who would want Jack Durham dead? Did he have any enemies?" Don asks Penny Martin.

Looking at the blonde sitting on a white leather sofa across from us, all I can think is, *Double wow*. She has her legs tucked beneath her. She is leaning against the armrest, her body slightly turned from us. Is that a comfortable position, or is her body language suggesting she doesn't want to be too open in what she shares with us? I suspect both. She is wearing white slacks and a black top that is much tighter and lower than I would wear. Actually, I could wear her light-weight pullover—cashmere?—and it would look like a sweatshirt on me.

I can't help notice that Don is being very formal and very careful to maintain eye contact. I'll give him a hard time about it later.

"Detective . . ." she says with a long pause.

"Detective Squires," Don answers.

"Yes, Squires, thank you," she says. "Well, Detective Squires, the better question might be, who wouldn't want him dead?"

"What does that mean?" I ask.

She doesn't look my direction as she answers my question to Don.

"Jack had a lot of friends because he had a lot of money. Not because he was pleasant to be around. But he did know how to throw a fabulous party. So we all showed up."

"Does that mean you would have liked to see him dead?" Don asks.

She laughs. "Of course. You just don't know Jack. But not enough to kill him. And I definitely wouldn't kill someone who invited me to most of his parties, even when they were on an exotic island or his dad's yacht and he would charter a couple of jets for his favorite people, of which I was one."

"So you traveled with him internationally?" I ask.

"Kos, Ios, and Mykonos last month," she says to Don. *I am obviously not present.* "His dad's yacht was our ferry. It's only a hundred and sixty feet long, but sometimes you have to settle for what you can get."

The way she says it reminds me of Barbara Ferguson saying her condo "will do."

Does Penny understand this is a murder investigation? Even if she's losing a ride on the Jack Durham gravy train, she doesn't seem too upset with Durham's brutal murder. She is not a suspect—yet—so we do not have to give her any warnings that anything she says can be used against her in a court of law. Once she moves to a person-of-interest status, it's usually time to suggest she consider the counsel of an attorney, even if full Miranda Rights aren't required. If she was ever charged with the murder her defense team would try to have any previous testimony thrown out.

I don't think she killed Durham—she looks way too cool to have beaten his brains in with a hammer while he lay on his bed asleep or in a drunken stupor—but if she did do it, she wouldn't be the first murderer to draw attention to him- or herself as a ploy to allay suspicion.

"When was the last time you saw him alive?" Don asks.

"I saw him the Sunday before last, at the Bears' preseason game," she answers. "He has a private suite at Soldier Field. Strike that. His *dad* has a private suite at Soldier Field that he uses. So probably thirty of us watched the game together."

"Did he fight with anyone at the game?" Don asks.

"Of course he did," she answers with a snort. "He always picked fights. Drunk or sober, didn't matter. He was an equal-opportunity jerk."

"Did you know everyone who was there?" Don asks.

"Not everyone. He always invited fresh meat to his parties. But probably twenty or twenty-five were regulars."

"Fresh meat?" I ask.

"I'm old at twenty-five. Jack likes pretty young things," she says with a laugh, but maybe a hint of resentment. "I guess I should say Jack *liked* pretty young things," she corrects herself and for the first time a shadow passes across her eyes. She shudders.

"We're going to need you to make a list of everyone you saw there," I say.

I have a lousy feeling that we are going to interview a yacht-load of arrogant, dismissive, full-of-themselves jerks (*jerk* is her word, not mine) before this case is solved.

She finally looks at me and rolls her eyes. She has recognized my existence, for which I am sure I should be grateful.

We ask Penny questions for another twenty minutes. If I had a buck for every time she rolled her eyes or looked at her jewel-encrusted watch I might be able to afford a cashmere sweater for myself. If I had to give a buck for every time I wanted to knock that haughty smirk off her face, I might not break even.

We thank her for her time and help. She

promises to have her list of Bears-game attendees faxed to us by Friday. I'm not sure why it's going to take her all day Thursday to make the list, but arguing with her will be counterproductive.

"So I'm going to date guys that date girls like Penny?" I say to Don as we get into our mud-brown Chevy Malibu. He was quicker to the parking spot so the keys stay with him. Both of us prefer to drive so our standing rule is first one to the car drives. There's a reason after partnering two years with me that Don doesn't hold doors open for me anymore. If we don't think anyone is watching, we've sprinted to get to the car first.

He pulls the shift into Reverse. "I'll pay good money to see that."

I punch him in the shoulder and he laughs at me. My phone rings. Tchaikovsky's *1812 Overture*. I assigned the ring tone to the boss, Zaworski.

"Yes, sir?" I ask after swiping the arrows on my new iPhone about three times. My old Nokia just had a button to push.

"You and Squires close to the shop?"

"Thirty minutes, sir."

"Good. Come on back. I sat down for a final planning meeting with Konkade and Blackshear. With you going undercover to meet Durham's friends and Ferguson's girls, we don't want you on any of the interviews."

Ruh-roh.

"I thought you had already left the office, sir."

"Why would that be your concern, Conner? You trying to get rid of me?"

"No, sir."

"Good. You and Squires hustle on in."

"Why do I get the feeling I don't want to hear this?" Don asks as he mashes the accelerator and darts into a gap in heavy midday traffic.

15

"Okay, here's what we're going to do," Zaworski says.

So much for being gone. Seven of us are crammed into his office for a "stand-up" meeting.

"I'm not supposed to be here but I had to pick up some stuff I forgot," Zaworski started things as we all trooped in. He was picking at a stain—probably mustard—on his white shirt. Not going to come out, I wanted to tell him. His jacket was back off. He had dark sweat circles under his arms. Must be heavy stuff he forgot.

"I gotta get out of here in ten minutes, so we're not sitting down. We sit down we get comfortable and the meeting will go forever. Konkade, watch the clock for me."

Konkade nodded and pushed some buttons on his wristwatch. Ten minutes later an alarm went off. Another forty-five minutes have gone by since then and we're still meeting and standing. I'm switching from one foot to the other and counting to sixty while I exercise my calves by going up and down from flatfooted to tippy toes.

"Stop fidgeting, Conner. Here's what we're going to do," he repeats. "We're going to stay the course. I'll call Ferguson myself and let her know that Conner has been seen as a cop by that Penny girl. I'm taking blame for that one. We were moving too fast and didn't establish the correct protocol."

"We need to talk to Penny again," Martinez says. "Maybe I could go over and talk to her."

He's got a little smile, so he's already heard she's a knockout of all knockouts. *Don*.

"Not now, Martinez. I have to get out of here. What you say, Squires? We tell Penny too? Your call."

"How about when you talk to Ferguson, you tell her not to schedule Penny for any place she knows KC is going to be," Squires says.

"Detective Conner, not KC," I say.

"Right, Detective Conner," he corrects. "I know she said the boys call the girls directly after they've been introduced, but this cuts chances they'll run into each other."

"Okay. That's what we do. No one figures Conner is going to be undercover long anyway. She mingles with the crowd a time or two, listens, only asks questions if it won't throw suspicion on her, and writes down impressions to see if we can narrow our field of suspects down a little.

"Anyone disagree?"

Twelve stoic eyes look solemnly at him.

"Okay, folks, Blackshear is running the show starting now. Not sure when I'll be back. Just so you know and can stop speculating, I went in for my routine annual checkup. My PSA count in the prostate was fine last year. Not fine this year. Cancer has metastasized, so they're going after it hard. Chemo and then surgery. I've been doing the chemo treatments for a month. Time for me to take a little time off before I kill somebody and youse have to investigate me."

I think six jaws just dropped to the floor.

"*Santa madre de Dios, apiadate de nosotros,*" Martinez says and crosses himself.

"Thanks, Anthony," Zaworski says and does the same crossing motion. He then holds up his hand. "No one else say anything. I know you want to say something encouraging and I know Squires will want to lead a prayer meeting and lay hands on me. Believe me, I'm not knocking any man's faith. I appreciate it and know what's in your hearts already. If you all pray and want to say a prayer for me when you're going about your business, I won't complain. Put in a good word for me. I'd love to tell you that this is nothing and I'm going to beat it no problem. But that's not the way it is and I don't lie. It's hell. Men, get your exam. Conner, do whatever women are supposed to do."

He gives a quick nod, slings his coat over his shoulder, picks up a heavy airline pilot's case, and is out of the office in a flash.

I don't cry but I do have some moisture around my eyes. We all just stand there for a moment and breathe.

Konkade breaks the silence. "Blackshear, you maybe want to give Barbara Ferguson a call to update her. You might want to go over with Squires so she knows you're running the show now."

"Captain is calling her," Blackshear says.

"Captain has been forgetting things," Konkade says. "I'll call him in an hour and tell him we already got Ferguson covered. He'll gripe and complain a little. He might chew me out a little. But he'll know we did the right thing. Sends him the message he can stop worrying about things."

"When's his surgery?" I ask.

"Your guess is as good as mine," Konkade answers me.

I feel a little guilty going home at six o'clock. Don is already driving with Blackshear to meet with Bobbie personally. I wasn't invited. They want to keep my complicated relationship with Ferguson as simple as possible.

Traffic is at a crawl. Maybe I should give public transportation another shot. Not. I have a lot of time to think. I've really not prayed like I should lately and it seems like the right time.

Dear God, I'm putting in a good word for the captain . . .

16

The waitress brings the check and puts it next to Kevin. He looks at her and looks at me. "We can split this."

"I don't think so," I quickly interject. "Bring two checks."

Did I just say that out loud? I did. *You are so bad, Kristen.* We are at a high-priced restaurant called Tru on St. Clair, just off the Magnificent Mile. The menu features French and global fusion. *Okay.* I don't know exactly what that means but everything I ate was very tasty. And small. I'm not antisophistication, I just like bigger portions.

Other than the food tasting so good, my first date under Bobbie's direction and tutelage has gone from bad to worse. I know CPD is going to reimburse me for anything I have to pick up since this is on assignment. I don't care if it's not money out of my pocket. No way am I going to let CPD pay for Kevin's drinks. I'm just not able to escape my habit of adding up the prices on a menu in my head and staying on a budget. I grew up in a working-class home.

I ate plenty of different things—celery soup that tasted like potato soup to me, a beet salad, butternut squash ravioli, and an awesome black-and-white crème brûlée that will probably bring me back here with Klarissa for a dessert night, which my budget might be able to handle. All I drank was water. Nothing I ordered was labeled as a "large plate" on the menu, though I saw the larger portion of the ravioli go by on its way to another table and it might almost qualify as big. I'm still not sure it would fill me up.

Kevin—who specifically said, "Let me take you to dinner," which I assumed was the same as saying, "Let me buy you dinner"—started off with a twelve-dollar martini, consumed an entire bottle of wine that probably cost as much as my weekly grocery bill, added two Irish coffees for dessert, and ordered just about every small, medium, and large plate on the menu, including the most expensive item, some kind of pan-seared duck. This is a French restaurant so I still haven't figured out why there is Amish chicken on the menu. Are there Amish in France?

"We can split this." I don't think so, Kevvy.

The waitress lets a shadow cross her face at my outburst and then cheerfully picks up the black leather booklet and says she'll be right back. It's just me and Kevin again. He is pleasant enough but far from the sharpest knife in the cutlery drawer. He doesn't run with the same crowd that Durham was part of. That was part of the point. Bobbie said I needed a trial run. So she and I went through profiles on a couple of local dating services.

In addition to posting a picture of himself that was probably snapped five years ago, I suspect Kevin told a few fibs on his dating profile. If he's six-two then I've grown from five-seven to five-ten in the past week. For someone who loves the opera and reading about the Civil War, he knows nothing about Verdi or Stonewall Jackson. I asked questions about both because the prep Ferguson gave me said I need to ask him about things he is conversant on. Make him look and feel smart.

What Kevin loves to talk about is da Bears. I don't mind guys loving their sports. Heck, I love my sports and I am definitely a Bears fan. They won the Super Bowl when I was in kindergarten and even if I didn't know what was going on at the time I could still feel the euphoria emanating from all the grown-ups. It was contagious. Talking about the Bears was probably the only other okay part of the date next to the crème brûlée. I do wish he would have saved me from having to study the Civil War and recent operas that have played in Chicago. I went to Barnes and Noble and found the Dummies books on the topics. I need to remember to turn in the receipt tomorrow.

Most of all I think Kevin lied about his mid-range six-figure income. I got to the near north side restaurant before he did so I could watch him show up. The car wasn't nice enough; I don't know makes and models well enough to say what he dropped off with the valet, but it wasn't close to what Durham and his friends drive. His clothes don't look like Saks or Macy's either. I could honestly care less what the guy drove or wore. But wouldn't you figure if you exaggerate every-thing about yourself on the profile the person you go out with would figure it pretty fast? There is that concept of truth in advertising and Kevvy flunked.

Bobbie said ChiTownSingles.com is owned by someone she knows and is legitimate in every way. It's the best online dating service in Chicago and the go-to site for up-and-coming young professionals.

Well, Kevin may be up-and-coming but he still has a long way to go. Does he use this dating site as a scam to get half of real expensive meals paid for?

"Is this Cutler's year?" he asks.

"Might be," I answer.

"We have a great defense but the Bears will only go as far in the playoffs as Cutler takes them."

"I hadn't thought of that. I think you're right."

Now this is painful. *"I hadn't thought of that."* Bobbie told me twenty times to let him think he's the smart one at the table, so I've stayed away from talking about whether Lovie Smith's cover two defense is still effective in the NFL.

The waitress returns with two checks. Mine is a little over sixty bucks. I don't want to think about how much his cost. We both pull out our plastic and slap it down on our checks before she can get away. I'm relieved he feels the same way I do about ending the evening.

"Want to come to my place?" he blurts out. "Maybe we could get to know each other better."

Where did that come from? I think his Irish whiskey is talking.

"I'm going to head to the office real early in the morning," I say. "So I'm going to have to call it an early night. Sorry."

He doesn't look too disappointed. His offer was made with the enthusiasm of telling someone you picked up clothes from the dry cleaner the day before.

I studied Civil War and opera last night and shopped with Bobbie today. Everyone on the task force agreed that my wardrobe wasn't going to pass the "look test" for Durham's crowd. Bobbie said it wasn't going to pass the "look test" for CTS—ChiTownSingles.com—either. If the site is all Bobbie says it is, Kevin could use some remedial work as well.

We add tip and sign the checks. Don thinks I am a miser when I tip. I bet my 15 percent beat Kevin even if Don would have rolled his eyes and told me 20 percent is the bare minimum.

We exit the restaurant. I tell him my car is close—close being a relative term, so I didn't lie to him. It's about six blocks away as I refuse to pay twenty-five dollars to put my car in a garage for two hours even if the office will reimburse it. I tell him I can get there myself and no need for him to walk me. Despite some dramatic protestations, he looks relieved again. Then he gets a feigned look of shock and surprise on his face and slaps the middle of his forehead.

"I think I left my keys inside on the table," he says. "If you think you're okay walking on your own, I need to go look for them."

"No problem," I say, and give him a thumbs-up. He scurries back into the restaurant like his hair is on fire. Since I saw him use valet parking I know he's lying about his keys. They are on a portable pegboard at the valet stand. I walk twenty feet down the sidewalk but, curious, retrace my steps back to the picture window to look inside. Kevvy has already elbowed his way to the front of the bar and is ordering a drink. He turns to a woman and says something that is obviously very funny. He and Bobbie Ferguson touch glasses, take a swallow of whatever they're having, and laugh their heads off.

I actually agreed with Ferguson that I needed a test run before going out socially with one of her clients. But I don't like being played for a fool.

Nice, Bobbie. Not sure I will visit you when you rot in prison for tax evasion.

I get home and hit "Cancel account" on ChiTownSingles.com. A message tells me it can take up to one month for this action to take effect. A month? Are you kidding me? They next offer me a fifty-dollar coupon toward their video service to reconsider parting ways. I hit no. They ask me to fill out a survey. I say no. They tell me more people have looked at my profile and messaged me. *Help.* Can someone stop this thing? It's alive.

Bobbie had hovered over me as I filled out the ChiTownSingles profile at her condo a couple days ago. I thought she seemed a little too enthusiastic at the time. Now I know why.

I thank God over and over that I didn't use my real name. Bobbie assured me I could take my profile down immediately after my evening with Kevin. She may still be laughing. I bet she picked up his tab.

Bobbie's crew truly are miracle workers. We did use my picture. But after her makeup artist, Tracy, finished with me and George the photographer took a few hundred shots, what we posted didn't look like me. I have to admit they made me look great—even if I don't recognize the person smiling back at me. When Bobbie gave the green light and I hit Upload, within five minutes of my account going live I got an e-mail expressing interest in meeting me. It has been pinging like a pinball machine ever since.

I'm thirty. Single. Haven't been in a relationship longer than six months since my first year at NIU. I was on the soccer team and he was on the basketball team. Neither of us had time to see each other, so it lasted almost the entire school year. We actually went out on real dates a couple nights a week the last month of spring semester when he got some time off after the basketball team lost in the opening round of the NIT. That let both of us take a look at the other more closely and say no.

I'm tired and need to hit the sack. Time to shut the computer down. I look back at my account again. I may not have this relationship thing figured out, but watching my inbox pile up I realize I'm not the only one that has problems connecting.

The thing is, Bobbie didn't even need to go to the trouble of setting up a lousy date for me. I've usually been able to do that myself.

I did like going out with Reynolds, but that's water under the bridge. Probably on the Penobscot River.

17

No way.

"I told your captain this was a bad idea," Bobbie says, arms crossed, a furrow between her neatly plucked eyebrows.

"So you've told me about a thousand times now."

She rolls her eyes and sighs in exasperation. People close to me tend to do that.

I wear a size 2 long jeans. I think that's plenty form-fitting and my mom believes it's too tight. Bobbie and I are in the dressing room of Bloomingdale's on Michigan Avenue, across from Water Tower Place. She has handed me a pair of size 0 long to try on. The last time I wore a size 0, I was a sophomore in high school. Maybe a freshman.

"Just do it," she says.

"Even if I could pull these over my butt, no way can I get them buttoned."

"Trust me. They'll fit. They are the perfect size for you."

Maybe for Klarissa. Not for me.

When she handed me these to try on I don't know if my eyes got wider at the size on the label or the price tag. More than one thousand dollars for a pair of jeans? Really? *Really?* I already helped bust the department's budget on my last case—serial killers are expensive to find—and I don't want to go through another round of glares and mutters from Zaworski when he gets back to the office and has to look at his financial reports.

"Take your time. I have nothing else to do. You people have seen to that."

Her tone on *people* was not affectionate. The fact that she has nothing else to do wakes me up. I do. I need to do a little grocery shopping and I want to work out. We couldn't meet until one o'clock because I had an eleven o'clock game with my Snowflakes. (We won 5-3 and Kendra was a beast with four goals.) I've been back in Chicago for nine days and I've barely caught my breath. I've coached two games and been assigned to the high-profile murder case of a prominent socialite who dates girls from a less-than-savory service provided by Bobbie Ferguson.

To hear her explain and defend, I should say "Saint Barbara Ferguson, the Martyr of the Gold Coast." Her clients are gracious, kind-hearted, generous gentlemen. Her independent contractors are angels with nothing on their minds but the betterment of mankind. The evil Chicago Police Department is a bunch of bullies who love to persecute law-abiding and tax-paying citizens.

I only met her at the beginning of this week. She was much more composed in our first few meetings. I don't think it's all me—despite what

Don said about my effect on people—but she seems to be unraveling a lot easier than I thought someone with her poise would. She's preoccupied. I nailed her hard on the set-up date with Kevin and she mumbled an apology. I've never heard the queen of elocution mumble.

It probably didn't help that Squires, Martinez, and Randall paid her a visit last night to question her on whether she had ever visited Jack Durham in his condo. The Martin girl told Don she thought Barbara and he spent some time together. That got everyone buzzing for a second—but her alibi was rock solid.

"Is there a secret to pulling these things on? Like Vaseline on my hips?"

"You'll figure it out."

She slings something over the door.

"Try this top with the jeans."

No way. *No way.*

Bam. Bam. Bam. I'm pounding up the steps of Section 1. I've hit every step from A to Z and am working on the double letters. DD, EE, FF, GG . . . *Bam. Bam. Bam.* I am at the local high school football stadium. One of my favorite workouts is running every step on the home side of the field. Sometimes two or three times.

I am wearing an old pair of my NIU soccer shorts and a sleeveless Under Armour sport top. It's form-fitting but feels wonderful after my ordeal of pulling on a pair of Dolce & Gabbana jeans that cost more than a thousand bucks along with a maddening array of tops and heels so high that I can barely stand, much less walk in them. On the Dolce & Gabbanas I thought the butterfly embroidery was cute and the pink-leather patch with their gold logo on the back pocket was a nice touch, but twelve hundred bucks with tax? People can afford this?

"You'll probably get to keep everything we buy for you," Bobbie said. "Except for the jewelry," she added. "We're borrowing that. But someone is getting a wardrobe upgrade."

But is that what I want? Take the jeans, for instance. I'll have to admit, they looked unbelievable on me, but dressing to wow people is not what I've been about. That's my sister Klarissa's department. Even if she wasn't a media star, she's always been a girlie girl. Dolls and dressing up like Ariel from *The Little Mermaid*, while I got in dirt-clod battles with the guys and held my own.

Klarissa has been after me to dress up my wardrobe. Heck, Don, the most nattily dressed detective on the CPD, lets me know my taste in clothes could be better. Much better. Then he starts on my shoes. He wears only Allen Edmonds, which cost at least 350 dollars a pair. He loves to let us know that. But even if I wanted to buy expensive shoes—and I don't—let's face it, comfort has never been the priority for women's shoes. Why would I ruin my feet in high heels? If that's what impresses a guy, he probably isn't the guy I want to impress.

Heck, I don't know what I'm talking about. The one constant accompaniment in my wardrobe is a black leather holster that goes over my shoulder and keeps my handgun of the month within easy reach halfway between my side and the middle of my back.

Monday night I am going to a Bears game in four-inch heels—I dug in and refused the six-inch stilettos—and jeans designed to asphyxiate me with all the efficiency of a boa constrictor.

At least I can wear my Urlacher jersey. Bobbie said a fitted jersey completes the ensemble.

I might be done with undercover by the end of the evening. No way will I fit in. Maybe I can take the jeans back to Bloomingdale's and trade them for a number of items. Items that fit me.

Showered, I flip channels. There's Klarissa anchoring the WCI-TV late edition of the evening news. She is incredible. You don't get a gig in Chicago when you're twenty-six—the age she got promoted from a Springfield, Illinois, station to the third-largest market in the US—if you aren't incredible. I know the news business isn't what it used to be (that's what she tells me, anyway) but I could see her having her own show on a network or major cable outlet in the not-too-distant future.

"The brutal slaying of Jack Durham, eldest son of Chicago billionaire businessman and philanthropist Robert Durham Sr., still has Chicago buzzing, in part because there appears to be no progress on the case."

Thanks, Sis.

"In a new development, the elder Durham has issued a press release through his attorney, Stanley McGill, indicating he is disappointed in the lack of progress by the Chicago Police Department and will be offering a reward of one million dollars to anyone who provides information leading to the capture and conviction of his son's murderer.

"For more on that story I send you over to WCI-TV news correspondent Trevor Jenkins . . ."

When a million-bucks reward is attached to a case, you better believe our job just got more difficult. Every con artist and person who thought they saw a shadow in the last month will now be calling it in.

I should listen but I click the Off button. I know my sister has her job to do, but couldn't she sound a little less forceful about our lack of progress? She doesn't know how hard we're working this. Durham's dad doesn't know. And whoever this Trevor guy is who is reporting from city hall, he doesn't know either. But this is the kind of newscast that gets the politicians looking over our shoulders and often does more harm than good to an investigation.

I think we've made some strategic progress. But I guess we have nothing to show for it. Yet. Maybe we'll get a breakthrough from my date on Monday night. Bobbie sent my picture to one of Durham's closest friends who wanted to meet and take someone new to the game. A bunch of Durham's friends are meeting up at Robert Durham's luxury suite at Soldier Field. He e-mailed her back with a yes. Batter up. Kristen to the plate.

I pad back to my bedroom with a notebook that provides biographical background and details on Jack Durham's friends and acquaintances, moving from closest to most casual. Everyone is considered a suspect. I've already gone over a second notebook with pictures and descriptions of Bobbie's independent contractors. All beautiful. Not nearly as much detail. Many of them are doing quite well financially from their line of work. But I can't imagine in a million years that this could make you feel good about yourself.

Just thinking about this crowd makes me feel like taking another shower.

18

Saturday, September 15
7:00 p.m.

I'm on their radar. But a lot of people are on their radar. So I'm not standing out. At least it doesn't appear I am. Or am I?

Despite mentioning to the black detective—Squires—that I thought Barbara would visit Jack at his condo from time to time, they're not looking at her. That would only be a temporary diversion anyway. She didn't kill him.

It had to be him. He's the only one that makes sense. He's not the only one close to him that hated Jack, but who else would have that easy an access? I wish we could talk. But he's not contacting me and I'm not contacting him until this thing is over. That's our deal.

The only question is whether there's anything that ties me to that night, to the scene. I've talked to an attorney. They can't request a DNA test on me unless they can show probable cause. If they can force that, I'm as good as convicted. I vomited in his bedroom. But they need something else before they get to that.

No one has told me I can't leave the state. I'm

wondering if it's time to make a move. Paris. London. Buenos Aires.

I came to Chicago with such high hopes. I accomplished a lot more than I dreamed of. I got close to him, after all. But now I'm not satisfied with what I've got. I feel like there's more reward for me to stay here.

Is it worth the risk?

Sometimes, late at night, I still see his battered head. That open socket just stares at me.

19

I was at church early and helped Kaylen teach Kendra's Sunday school class. Kendra is my buddy. She stayed close to my side the whole hour. She did laugh at me when I got outside the lines on a coloring activity. And I heard her whispering to her friend Holly that I carry a gun. Holly looked over at me with awe and fear. She's probably going to go home and tell her parents that her Sunday school teacher is packing heat.

I am designated as the guardian for James and Kendra if anything were to happen to both Jimmy and Kaylen. I am honored but I will never let myself think of anything bad happening to them. So I've not even asked myself whether I could make a good parent. I'm not sure it's possible for a single parent who is a homicide detective to pull that off.

I am sitting in a pew toward the front with Kaylen and Klarissa. Klarissa was going to another church for a while but has come back to good old Calvary Community Church. I doubt it bothered Jimmy and Kaylen too much, but you never know. Preachers are human, and whether or not they try to hide it, I'm sure they feel pride for their work. Everybody says nobody goes to church anymore, so I guess they have to work hard for their market share.

Kendra used to sit with us and I'd scratch her back until her eyes glazed over, but we started doing a separate church service for kids. I'm sure that's a good idea. I remember how painfully long and boring church was when I was a little kid— though it's crossed my mind that if I had to suffer through that as a kid, why shouldn't she? On another level, I wonder if kids should be with their parents in big-people church and not segregated once again. It's not like families spend too much time together (my family being the exception). But then again, there are a lot more kids than parents here, so if parents are dropping them off and heading to JavaStar for a cup of coffee, then having a separate service for them is probably good.

We sing about twenty-five minutes, standing the whole time. I wonder how the old geezers hold up. I get dirty looks from Kaylen for shifting my weight from foot to foot and generally fidgeting during singing time. Maybe she and Zaworski have been talking.

The words are projected on two screens up front. We have old-fashioned hymnals in racks that are fixed to the back of the pew in front of us; they haven't been opened in years. I guess we don't want to look old-fashioned.

Mom sings in the choir, which I think probably makes us look a little old-fashioned anyway. I never hear her sing anywhere else. I wonder if she's in the choir just so she can be up front and keep an eye on me.

Not that I'm paranoid.

After offering and announcements and a solo that was just a little out of tune, Jimmy gets up to preach. He's thirty minutes on the nose with his sermons, but then he sometimes preaches another sermon before he dismisses us to leave. I don't think he knows how to close. Today he read the story from the Bible about the woman caught in adultery. The Pharisees were going to stone her and Jesus forgave her. He's preaching against judgmentalism. I know I'm supposed to just nod and agree with the preacher, even if he is my brother-in-law and I see him when he's a civilian. But for some reason, I'm not sure I agree with him.

Now I believe in grace and forgiveness and

not holding things that have been forgiven against people. But I can't help thinking that judgmentalism is a little underrated in our society. I think that sometimes the most judgmental people I've run into are the ones who are judging judgmental people.

My line of work will make you judgmental. Every six months we go to a training day and invariably one of the required seminars will be on not judging people based on race, creed, lifestyle, or appearance. In other words, we're not supposed to profile. I mostly agree with all that, but believe me, I and everyone else in my field still profile.

"Jesus judges the self-righteous more than the sinner, it would seem," Jimmy says.

Now I know Jesus is God, and he can do anything he wants. But isn't Jimmy still talking about judging? I'm going to get worked up and start an argument with him at lunch today. Mom won't be happy. She says I argue too much. But it's just too fun to pass up the opportunity. I've watched Jimmy with people after church and he's the most caring person and the best listener I have ever seen. But for some reason he gets a little awkward around his wife's sisters, so we never really engage in important conversations. That's okay with me. I'm not going to judge him.

I smile at that thought. I look up front and I think Mom's eyes narrow a little. I wonder if she's wondering what I'm smiling about. *Wouldn't you like to know?*

The passage Jimmy read said that after Jesus forgave her, he told the woman to go and "sin no more." So if she kept up the adultery stuff after being forgiven could the Pharisees have stoned her then? Forget the stoning. Would they have been okay to judge her?

Based on the way I go about life and interact with others, people don't believe I think about things like this. I guess that makes them judgmental—or at least profilers.

My mind starts to wander. Bears on *Monday Night Football* tomorrow night and I'll be there in a luxury suite. *Cool.*

I feel a hand on my shoulder and someone gives me a little shake. It's Kaylen. Why is she standing? I look around. Everyone is standing. Thankfully their heads are bowed. I wasn't paying attention. I pop out of my seat. Kaylen scowls at me—pretty judgmental if you ask me—then shakes her head and gives a little laugh. Jimmy says "Amen," we open our eyes, sing a song, say a prayer in unison, and head for the exits.

Lunch at Jimmy and Kaylen's as usual. Wonder if Jimmy wants to talk about today's sermon.

20

I'm running as hard as I can. I have to get there before the car door slams shut. I lengthen my stride, grit my teeth, and try to stoke my internal engines to push even harder. My hands pump higher and harder with a mind of their own. I call on all the discipline I have to follow my training from when I ran track back in high school. I loosen my shoulders and lower my hands but continue to pump them as fast as I can, knowing my legs will follow.

She is fighting. She has clawed halfway out of the backseat and onto the street. Her blonde hair is disheveled. He is pushing and she is kicking. I might still have time.

My lungs are screaming for oxygen. Every stride is torture. My legs ache with the exertion. They want to quit, but I can't let them. Why am I not drawing closer? I can't close the gap. My arms start to pump higher again, perhaps reaching to heaven in supplication for more oxygen. I have to have more oxygen.

I'm drawing closer now. *About time.* She gets her hands free from him and scratches jagged lines down both cheeks. He bellows in rage and draws back his fist to hit her. Am I three car lengths away? Two? I am suffocating. I have never in my life run harder and longer than now. What will I do when I get there? Collapse?

He stuffs her back into the rear of the car and slams the door shut. He moves forward a step and slides into the front car seat. Only a few more feet. The door is closing. This is going to hurt like crazy and it might not stop his capture of her. But the only thing I can do is dive forward and hope to get my arm between the door and the body of the car.

I feel a sharp pain in my knuckles. I hear a crash. I am up on my feet, fists up and in fighting position. I am disoriented.

"Kristen, are you okay?" Mom yells from the door to the kitchen, a look of fear in her eyes.

She's the first to arrive at the small sunroom at the back of Jimmy and Kaylen's house. Kaylen, Jimmy, and Klarissa are right behind her. Next to take a look at the commotion is Patricia Williams. She and her husband, Jeff, came over for dinner. I met Patricia through my undercover work with AA. Jeff has headed to the office. She has stuck around. The six of them have been drinking coffee, nibbling on Kaylen's blackberry pie, and chatting around the kitchen table. I couldn't keep my eyes open and decided to take a catnap on their lumpy couch. I think I could still hear their voices while I dozed in and out of my nap. Then I was dreaming. Apparently I came up punching because I've knocked over a floor lamp. The shade is smashed into an oblong shape and the bulbs are shattered.

"Sorry, guys. Weird dream," I say sluggishly, still trying to clear the cobwebs in my head.

"You're weird enough in real life; I'd hate to think what a weird dream for you would be," Klarissa says with a smile.

I barely have the energy to look up and stick my tongue out at her. Mom looks over at her with a frown—a judgmental frown from my angle—but Klarissa just looks angelic.

Kaylen has left the room and is back with a glass of water for me and a small brush and dustpan for the mess. Everyone is gathered around me, just a little too close for my comfort level and space needs.

"Just a dream, guys. I'm fine."

I smooth my hair and the back of my dress and follow everyone back into the small kitchen. Kaylen follows me at a slow waddle. I look back at her. Her lips are pursed. I can tell she isn't convinced I am fine.

Jimmy pulls a sixth chair up and I crowd up to the small round table between Mom and Kaylen.

"So what'd you dream about?" Kaylen asks.

"It was nothing," I say.

"Must not have been 'nothing' or you wouldn't have attacked the back porch and killed the lamp like a ninja warrior," Klarissa snipes.

We really are doing okay and back to normal.

Kaylen puts an arm around my shoulders and pulls me in close. "C'mon, baby sis, what was your dream?"

"I thought I was 'baby sis,' " Klarissa says with a pout.

"You are," Kaylen and I say in unison with a laugh.

Everyone is still looking at me. I'm awake but still feel slow. In my mind I sometimes complain that I can't grab and hold attention like glamorous Klarissa or angelic Kaylen. But when I finally do get attention I don't want it. I feel embarrassed now.

"Let's hear it," Jimmy says.

"A lot of it is a blur," I say. "It started out kind of nice, then it turned scary. I was in a big house and all of you were there—except you, Jimmy. And Patricia."

Mom and my sisters laugh and he just shrugs and makes a face. Patricia just watches me closely.

"There were others there too. I'm not sure who they were, but it was kind of like they were relatives. Maybe cousins."

"You don't have cousins," Mom says.

Do I remind her I am recounting a dream and not a genealogy lesson? Nah. I press on.

"Everyone had their own room, but when it was time to meet for dinner, everyone started yelling because their doors were locked and they were trapped inside."

Okay, this sounds crazy. I'm ready to stop. But everyone is still looking at me. Like they're actually interested.

"Then I heard a scream. I looked out the window and a man was dragging a woman down the street."

"One of us?" Klarissa asks, serious now.

"I don't know. I think for a moment in the dream it was you. Then I think it was Kaylen. Then—and I know this sounds crazy—I think it was me. Then I think it was some girl I interviewed on a case I'm working."

"Her name?" Klarissa asks with a smile.

"Not gonna happen, baby sis. Not allowed to give details to the press."

She makes a face at me and I return the compliment.

"What happened next?" Kaylen asks, her arm still comfortably around my shoulders, her pregnant belly pressed into my side.

"I tried the door but it was locked. I kicked it a couple times."

"Naturally," says Klarissa and we all laugh.

"Then I opened the window and jumped out. I was a couple stories high, but I landed in some soft bushes."

"You jumped out the window?" my mom asks with incredulity.

"Not really, Mom. It was a dream."

I pause and think. Dreams are funny. They are

so clear when you're dreaming them. But when you wake up, they start shifting shapes. You start to confuse what you dreamed and what you think about what you dreamed. You can watch parts of it disappear into forgetfulness.

"And?" Kaylen prods.

"I chased him down the street to save her. He was trying to stuff her into the backseat of a car and drive off. I had to get there before he could get his door shut."

I pause. Kaylen has a half-empty cup of coffee in front of her. I pick it up and take a swallow of lukewarm watery decaf with sugar in it. *Yech*.

"Who did the man look like?" Klarissa asks.

"Do you really want to know?" I ask in response.

"I kind of figured this is where it was going to go," she said.

"Are you talking about that serial killer?" Mom asks with a shudder. She loves his brother, Dell, but can't bring herself to say the name Dean Woods.

"It was," I say. "But not the whole time."

I'm glad no one thinks to ask me who else the mysterious man dragging one of us off looked like. For a fleeting second it was Klarissa's on-again, off-again—now off-again—boyfriend, Warren. Then it was Zaworski. But at the very end, right when I reached the front car door, the

133

kidnapper looked directly at me and smiled. It was Dad.

"I don't want to think about him," Mom says. "I just know my girls are safe and sound now."

She's technically right. But then again, is anyone ever truly safe? I'm a homicide detective. I see the worst of what people do to each other. Most murders are done at the hands of family members or close friends. It's not the stranger from without that is most dangerous, but the one from within that you have to worry about. I think that's a quote from someone famous. I can't remember where I heard or read it or who it was.

"I think your dream means something," Patricia says.

"It might—but what? And how would I or anyone else figure it out?"

"When you say it like that I know you're not going to try and think about it," Patricia says.

She's smart and observant.

"Have you talked to a counselor about your experience with the Cutter Shark?"

I look at her blankly.

"I know you've worried yourself crazy about how Klarissa was doing. And I think she's doing great, by the way," she says, giving Klarissa's hand a squeeze. "But don't you think you might have some post-traumatic issues? I'm surprised Chicago Police doesn't require some form of counseling after being in the middle of something like that."

I think it was suggested. But then I went to Virginia. And why go to counseling? I'm fine. What happened, happened. Talking about it will change nothing. And I'm realistic about life. Sometimes it's great. Sometimes it's tough. A lot of time it's somewhere in the middle. Maybe a deeper understanding can help, but even if you can't figure it out, what are your options? You live. That's my story and I'm sticking to it.

The conversation has ground to a halt. I jump up, now fully awake, and say my good-byes. "Long day tomorrow. I better go."

"Dinner tomorrow night?" Klarissa asks. "I'm off air."

"No can do. I'm working late."

I give hugs all around and save a big one for Patricia. I whisper in her ear, "I'm so proud of you. And I promise, I'm doing fine. Don't worry about me." She pulls me in harder.

My affection quotient has reached its limit, so I break away and beeline for the door. Everyone follows me.

Let it go, folks. It was only a dream.

My family is funny. We talk about almost everything and get in the middle of each others' lives. But then we completely sidestep the two most traumatic moments in our family's history: the death of my dad and the kidnapping of my sister at the hands of a murderer I was hunting down. We probably need to talk sometime.

"Did you save her?" Jimmy asks with all of us standing on the front stoop.

"I don't know. I woke up just as I got there."

21

"What's wrong with what I have on?" I ask Bobbie indignantly. "We're going to a football game."

Apparently she and I have different definitions of a fitted jersey. She shakes her head wearily. I think she's had her fill of me. Get in line, Bobbie. The club is full and there's a waiting list to join.

"When Derrick picks you up he is expecting to be wowed. His friends expect to be wowed. If they aren't wowed you will stick out like a sore thumb."

"So the more you dress me up like a street walker, the less I'll be noticed. Is that what you're saying?"

"I never said anything as coarse as 'street walker,' and I'm frankly quite surprised you, as an officer of the peace, would say such a thing. Very catty. I also did not say you wouldn't be noticed. I said you won't look out of place. You're the detective—or so I've been told. Do you want to fit in so you can observe and learn something or do you want people to avoid you like the plague because they know you don't belong there?"

I hate to admit it, but she makes a great point. Doesn't mean I have to acknowledge it.

"It's just a football game," I say lamely.

Knowing she's won, Bobbie patiently says, "No, it's a major social event in a luxury suite where powerful and beautiful people show up to see and be seen."

"Does anyone watch the game? I was looking forward to seeing how the Bears match up with the Packers this year."

"If Derrick and his friends want to watch the game, then you can watch as well—as long as you are attentive to his needs."

I don't consider myself a feminist. But everything I'm hearing goes against every fiber of my being. A hundred years ago I would have been called a tomboy. But I grew up when girls' sports exploded. Volleyball. Basketball. Softball. Gymnastics. Heck, even the cheerleaders had competitions that highlighted athleticism as much as great looks and huge white teeth. I lived and breathed soccer. Kaylen and Klarissa didn't gravitate toward sports, so they complained about the extra attention I got from our dad. They watched chick flicks, I watched the Bears and Cubbies.

"And his needs are?"

"At the game he has only one need and that is for a beautiful young woman to be at his side and make him think he is the most handsome, charming, and interesting man in the world."

"And with my personality, I do that *how?*"

"You've got the looks—at least you will after I'm done with you—but I've been wondering the same thing myself. I mentioned as much to your boss when he first hatched this crazy plan that I doubt catches a killer but probably puts me out business."

"What did he say?"

"He said you would be the most difficult person I've ever worked with but that you would do your job when it was crunch time."

I ponder that. Am I really that difficult?

"I now know he's right on the first half—you are difficult—but I have no way to assess whether you will come through in crunch time. I do have my doubts on whether you'll be up to the challenge of fitting in with this crowd."

"We'll see about that," I shoot back at her.

We glare at each other. Then her face breaks into a bright smile.

"Your captain also told me that you'd cooperate at least a little bit if I told you that you weren't up to the task at hand."

Am I that predictable?

Duh.

"How is the captain? I heard he took some time off for health reasons."

"Your guess is as good as mine."

"I'll ask around since you haven't bothered to and let you know what I find out," she says.

She really is zinging me this afternoon. She seems to have her focus and poise back.

Bobbie has a bathroom about the same size as my kitchen and living room combined—something you would see in a magazine. Marble floors and countertops. The fixtures are gold plated. (I don't know how real the gold is but nothing would surprise me.) I think the bathroom in my master bedroom would fit in her floor-to-ceiling glass shower.

We've been in this bathroom for hours. I now know what a dog feels like at the Westminster Kennel Club Dog Show. I have been groomed. Bobbie brought in Stefan, a stylist, to work on my hair; a makeup artist (Tracy again) to fix my face; and a third person whose name I couldn't understand and wasn't going to ask for a third time, who did my nails, including tips that make my fingers a half inch longer than normal. I now have on more makeup than I've ever worn in my life.

It didn't take Crisco to get the jeans over my hips, but I squirmed and jumped around enough to get in a good ab workout.

I thought my Brian Urlacher Bears jersey was

just fine, mostly because it covered the skintight jeans. Bobbie already had a Bears jersey waiting for me, but last I checked the Bears don't wear pink. And jerseys are supposed to hang on you. This one is about as fitted as the jeans. I don't know whether to feel embarrassed or relieved that I'm not very big up top. I'm not going to lie and say I've never wondered what it would be like to be a little bigger, but I've never thought about it enough to feel self-conscious about being small. *Until now.* Bobbie put me in a bra designed to push whatever you have up. Since that doesn't amount to much, she's added some padding. I look in the mirror again. Yep. I definitely feel self-conscious now. I might break into laughter.

I've got enough jewelry on my ears, neck, and wrists to set off a metal detector at the airport in Milwaukee without leaving this room. But the real killer is the five-inch heels. Derrick better be taking me up to the luxury suite by elevator because I don't think I can navigate more than a few steps.

I thank God everything is covered. But this is still way over my comfort level—and I think we've reached the edge of what I'm willing to do for the CPD.

"Okay, let's see you walk to the door and back."

I lower my head and arch my plucked eyebrows at Bobbie. She doesn't flinch and returns the stare. I turn and walk toward the door. You win this time, but don't get used to it.

"Slower."

I stop and sigh.

"Shoulders back and glide."

I obey.

"Now turn slowly. Don't even lift your feet. Pivot. Smile. Walk back slowly. Give me a little hip, please."

I'm going to give her something but it won't be hip.

I stop in front of her. Will I qualify for best in show?

"Kristen." She pauses. "All I can say is you are stunning."

My face burns beet red. Might be hot enough to burn off the makeup.

PART TWO

God has given you one face,
and you make yourself another.
WILLIAM SHAKESPEARE

22

"Conner, let's hear your report," Blackshear says matter-of-factly. "When you're ready."

His last phrase disconcerts me for just a second. I'm used to Zaworski's barks to get started now, now, now.

It's Tuesday morning. I'm not as quick on my feet with presentations as many of my colleagues. Most don't prepare comments; they can wing it. I got to the office at six-thirty and tried to type up my notes without messing up the fake nails. I couldn't do it. I went to the bathroom and took twenty-five minutes to get rid of them, then hammered out my report in forty-five minutes. Then I wrote ten sentences on ten note cards by longhand to organize my thoughts.

Don, Martinez, Randall, Konkade, Blackshear, two uniforms—Sawyer and Shane—assigned to help investigate, and the big boss himself, Czaka, are present. There are also a new man and woman that were introduced. Alex and Gretchen. Can't remember their last names but have their business cards. They are from the Department of Revenue at city hall. No one said why they were present, but I think it's obvious they're monitoring what their return on investment will be in letting Bobbie Ferguson cut a deal that forgives a lot of tax penalties. My powers of detecting at work again.

Czaka could be present for any number of reasons. He might want to get a feel for how things are going so he can report more in depth to Commissioner Fergosi and city hall. He might want to observe how Blackshear handles running a meeting.

Czaka might also be here to keep an eye on me. Zaworski said the commander didn't like this plan for me to go undercover, so he might be ready to pull the plug on it now. I'm not sure that would bother me too much. Probably wishful thinking on my part. Once a course of action is begun he might consider a change in direction to be a sign of weakness to colleagues from other city departments.

"I showed up at Bobbie's at three o' clock on Monday, September 17, three hours before I was to meet with Derrick Jensen—the plan being for him to pick me up at Ferguson's place. The preparation for the Bears' game included a facial—"

"We want to hear what happened at the game, not what kind of eyeliner you wore," Czaka interrupts.

I hear some sniggers. Don and Martinez are my two chief suspects and they will pay for it later. Innocent until proven guilty is for a court of law.

"Did I tell a joke?" Czaka demands, cutting off the laughter immediately.

I take the first card and move it to the bottom of the stack, look at the second, and then move that to the back too. I clear my throat. I'm tempted to tell about Cutler's touchdown pass with thirty-seven seconds to go in the game, since Commander Czaka said he wanted to hear what happened at the game. I somehow doubt he or anyone else present would find it very funny.

Focus. Just talk.

"Derrick picked me up at a little after six and we drove south on Lake Shore to Soldier Field. We proceeded to the corporate suite owned by the Durham and Durham Law Firm. Obviously you know that Durham and Durham are the names of the victim's father and uncle. The suite itself was twenty feet by thirty feet with a wet bar, a food counter, and two sitting areas. There are glass doors that provide access to twenty-four standard stadium seats."

"Now you're bragging," Martinez interrupts. "I can't even afford to pay the bucks to get in the nosebleed seats."

"Can it, Martinez," Czaka cuts in. "I'm out of here in fifteen," he says, looking at his watch. "Conner, you can give full details after I'm gone. Just let us know if you found out anything pertinent to the case."

So much for him letting Blackshear run his meeting and so much for me following an outline. I stick my note cards in my black folio.

"There were twenty-one guests in the suite. Eleven men and ten women. The host was Stanley McGill, a senior partner with Durham and Durham. Neither Jack's uncle nor dad were there. His brother didn't attend either. McGill was the only person there without a companion. His wife is in Paris for a fashion show, he told me."

Czaka is trying to hide his impatience.

"I worked the crowd as best I could. Of the ten men present besides McGill, I think only three were with the law firm. Those three were with spouses. I'm not sure any of them—the wives—were that excited to be part of the rest of the group. They stuck together in a small pack. I'm pretty sure they knew the score with the other women present.

"The other seven men were friends of Jack Durham. I've got a report with their names and where they fit in Durham's hierarchy of friendship. I looked back over the notebook of his closest friends, and two of the men present are married, but neither was there with his spouse. In checking Barbara Ferguson's list of independent contractors, I think six of the seven other ladies present work for Ferguson. That number includes me."

I pause and glare in Don and Martinez's direction to warn them no jokes. Czaka looks in their direction too, with a scowl. I don't see even a flicker of amusement in either of their eyes.

"Unfortunately, I talked most to the woman that I finally figured out isn't connected to Ferguson. She was nice and clueless. I said something about how sad it was about what happened to Jack and she said her boyfriend, Donald Jackson, is still pretty broken up about it.

"The other girls were reserved around me and each other. They were on the clock and paying attention to their men. I did meet one named Angie. I said the same thing to her: 'Too bad about Jack.' She laughed. Kind of confirms what Penny said to Detective Squires and myself in an earlier interview. Really, it confirms what everyone but immediate family members have been saying: Durham was the life of the party but not a beloved person."

"Anything else I need to hear from you or anyone else present?" Czaka asks as he rises.

Ten blank sets of eyes stare back at him. I wonder how he'll spin this meeting to Fergosi and Mayor Daniels. My bet is that's exactly who he's headed to see. I would also bet he's decided to leave me in place and sell it as a promising line of inquiry. Derrick was Jack's best friend and a member of the inner circle, so I've hit the jackpot.

The second Czaka exits, Randall, the new guy I still don't know very well, asks, "Ferguson didn't tell you which of her girls would be there? I thought that was part of our deal with her."

"I knew the five working girls from her descriptions and the notebook. Ferguson told me two that would probably be there because they are regulars. But she's never 100 percent positive which of her contractors will be picked. She couldn't even guarantee Penny wouldn't be there, though she was going to try and make sure she wasn't by putting her on another assignment."

"So she doesn't set up all the couples?" one of the uniforms—I think Sawyer—asks.

"Only about half the time. She charges her clients a flat monthly retainer for unlimited assistance in setting up a date. If the client likes one of the contractors he can contact her directly. The contractors are supposed to let her know they went out, though they don't always remember to. I suspect they owe Bobbie a percentage of their additional earnings and some try to hide it. Zaworski thought the same. But no one has come out and said that's the business arrangement."

"So this . . ." Martinez pauses. "I know the Z-Man said we need to avoid using derogatory words when describing our consultant"—he draws quote marks in the air as he says "consultant"—"but he's not here and I so badly want to call her every name in the book. She's skimming the cream every way you look at it."

"I've been in her place. It's incredible. I'm sure she's raking in the dough."

"So is Barbara Ferguson being helpful?" the

lady, Gretchen, asks. "We're giving up a lot of revenue in the fines she owes by letting her cut the deal with you. If she's not keeping her end of the bargain or this isn't going to be a real line of inquiry, we'd like to know now and get Legal involved in breaking the contract."

"We've interviewed more than 80 percent of Bobbie's contractors," Don says. "None of them are very forthcoming. They're afraid or obstinate or both. We've talked to all of Durham's known associates at least once. Most twice. Ditto on not getting anything from them that will help find his murderer.

"Someone we've talked to knows something. We might get lucky and one of them might make a mistake or remember something that will help us focus our investigation on a prime suspect. But everyone has an alibi the night he was killed. And everyone agrees that just about anyone has thought about killing the guy. They all make it into a joke, but you can feel the truth beneath the words.

"So what I'm trying to say in a roundabout way is that I think Detective Conner working with Ferguson is our best hope of getting someone to speak more frankly. I'm just not sure how long she can pull this off before she gets identified as one of us."

"How long can you keep this going?" Blackshear asks.

"Don's right. Not very long. Just in case any of you are wondering—and you better not be wondering—I'm not sleeping with any of these slimeballs. I don't care how many billions their daddies have. And as much as I love the CPD, I've got my boundaries, even on a murder case."

"No one was wondering," Blackshear says.

"I was," Martinez says with a laugh.

"That's my partner speaking, not me," Randall says and gives Martinez a punch.

Good. I like Randall better now and I still don't even know him.

"When Derrick started driving me to his place after the game I told him I ate something bad at the game and needed to be dropped off at Bobbie's. He was very nice about it, but I don't think that he'll accept that a second time. So if my next appointment is with him—which is doubtful—maybe one more date and I'm done."

The two suits nod at each other and stand up.

"We appreciate the briefing and all you are doing to apprehend the murderer of Jack Durham," Alex says. "Keep us informed."

"We will," Blackshear says. "If you don't hear from me you'll hear from Sergeant Konkade."

We stand up and shake hands with the two as they head out the door. Gretchen hands me another business card. She's written on the back: *We need to talk.* I nod at her.

As everyone is sitting back down to continue the conversation I look down at my phone and swipe the touch screen. A text has come in. It's from Bobbie.

Derrick wants to see you Thursday night. Call me.

We go over interview notes for the next two hours.

"I don't want to beat a dead horse," Don says with a groan while rubbing his eyes, "but if Bobbie isn't certain which of her female escorts are working solo or group dates and Penny Martin shows up on Thursday, KC is busted. Are we sure we shouldn't just tell her?"

"So you and Martinez can visit her for a nice little chat?" I ask, giving Don a dirty look. He knows I hate the nickname KC. "She did seem to like *Detective* Squires, if I recall."

He ignores me.

"*Si a él le gusta, yo le encantaré!*" Martinez says.

Don gives him a dirty look. Wish I knew what Martinez was saying half the time.

And you took high school French instead of Spanish because your mom wanted you to take Spanish, Kristen?

"Sounds like if Kristen don't go to bed with this Derrick dude it's over anyway," Martinez says. "So what's the difference? And if Penny is

153

the one with answers, we don't want to tell her nothing."

"In my book, Penny is the prime suspect," I say, looking at each face around the table. "I don't think we should tell her anything. If I see her Thursday night I'll handle it."

"You're right, *amiga*," Martinez says. "But that means I have to wait to meet her another time."

"You know, it's possible this Derrick is the killer and Conner is in harm's way with no backup," Konkade says.

"Good point," Blackshear says. "Do we need to put a wire on her Thursday night?"

"I'm in the room, guys," I say. "You can talk to me. And the answer is no. No wire. First of all, with what they put me in, there's no way to hide a wire."

"And you have no meat on your bones," Martinez interrupts.

"And second," I continue, ignoring him, "I could take Derrick any day in a fight."

"My money is on Kristen," Don says as everyone laughs.

"I've heard what you can do with the fists," Randall says with a serious tone. "Just remember, this group is dangerous even if they don't know how to throw a punch. They fight with money. And when Derrick and some of the others do figure out that Kristen is staking them out as CPD, they aren't going to be very

154

happy. We can't forget this case is about money."

"Good point. I'm gonna call Legal again," Blackshear says, writing a note on a blue index card he always keeps beside him. "The captain vetted the plan with them and they said we have no liability if Conner is exposed. But I want to double-check that."

"Smart move, Bob," Konkade says. "But you don't have to do everything. I can follow up for you with a double-check. I was the one that talked to them the first time."

"Good."

"So he really wants another date?" Don asks me.

"Thursday night," I repeat.

Do I see the trace of a smile in the corners of his mouth? Better not be.

"Who's doing lunch?" Martinez asks as we return to our cubicle farm at noon.

We stop to talk before going our separate ways.

"I'm in," Don says.

Randall sticks an arm into his cubicle and pulls it out holding up a sack lunch. *Nerd.* I shake my head no as well.

"I forgot to make a real important call I promised I'd make and better hit it," I say, realizing I haven't called Reynolds to see if he can help Dell out on seeing his brother.

"Let's go, *amigo*," Martinez says to Don. "Two

of us know that man don't live by work alone."

"Bread alone," Don corrects him.

"You are right on that too," Martinez agrees. "I like some barbecue pulled pork on my bread."

Don looks like he's going to say something but lets it go.

"So you really think Penny needs a closer look, Conner?" Randall asks.

"She did give off the vibe of someone who would kill her grandma if she thought some money was in it," Don interjects.

"No question in my mind," I say. "I'm not saying she's the killer, and she's not the only one who took Durham's murder way too lightly, but she's over-the-top too cool about all this."

Konkade walks up. "I somehow know who you all are talking about. I told Blackshear that after I call Legal I'm going to talk to someone in Financial Forensics about looking at Martin again. Thanks for the idea," he says to Randall.

"Me?"

"Yeah. You're right. This case is going to be solved the old-fashioned way. Follow the money."

"Have at it, *amigo*," Martinez says.

"Conner, you got plenty to do after your call?" Don asks.

"Paperwork is piling up," I say.

"Maybe Antonio and I will go visit Penny. We won't say anything about you. But it might not hurt to turn up the heat a little. Antonio and I can grab a bite up at the Weber Grill on State and then head up to her place."

I scroll down my address book to punch Reynolds' name. After a slight pause the phone starts ringing before it goes into a message. I skip Reynolds' promise to call back as soon as possible and the female voice that explains how to leave a message and hit the number one. There is a beep and I leave my message:

"Austin, Kristen Conner calling. Hope you had a great time fishing with Willingham. Listen, I needed to ask a favor of you—or at least ask a question. I got a call from Dell Woods. Yes, *the* Dell Woods. He's been trying to get information from the regional FBI office as to the where-abouts of his brother. He wants to visit him. No one will talk to him. It would be great if you have a contact here in Chicago that could get back to him and talk things through with him. I think if he gets put off much longer he's going to hire an attorney. I wrote his number down. It's . . ."

I can't find my slip of paper.

"Well, crud. I can't find it. I'll text his number to you. Catchya later."

I swipe the End Call image on my screen.

A text pops up.

You are always on my mind.

No caller ID. Okay, is someone having some

fun at my expense? This better not be Don and Martinez's idea of a joke to play on me in light of my assignment. Might be a wrong number.

"Hey, big sis, I missed having dinner with you last night."

I pick up Klarissa's call while driving home. I crane my neck sideways to hold the phone between my shoulder and ear so I can steer and shift gears. I drop it into fifth to pass a poky driver in the right lane.

"I went to the Bears game."

"Really?" she asks, surprised. "Who with? Oh . . . don't tell me. It was Detective Day at Soldier Field?"

"It was a night game."

"A Detective Night game?"

"Ha-ha," I deadpan at her. "Believe it or not, I had a date."

"And you didn't tell *moi*? Now I'm not going to see if you want to grab a quick dinner. I think I'm going to be mad at you instead."

So what do I tell her about my date? This is the point when things can get tricky. If I tell her nothing, it makes her suspicious. So what I do tell her feels like a lie. I'm sure God understands and approves a little subterfuge when it is done for a good cause like a murder investigation. I know there are lies of omission, but I think he would expect me to follow company rules first—even if my sister doesn't. The ethics course I took for my criminal justice degree at Northern Illinois University certainly absolved me in matters such as this.

"But I'll forgive you if you tell me everything about him," she says. "Meet me at M. K. Restaurant on North Franklin. My treat tonight."

I stifle a groan. I was planning to stop at Planet Fitness on my way home. I'm tired and have had enough people interaction for one day. I just want to work out, eat carryout, take a long shower, and maybe veg out in front of the TV for an hour before bedtime.

"You there?"

"I am," I say quickly. "I was just trying to figure out what the occasion is if you're buying."

"Maybe I have a little secret too," she says coyly.

"I'll see you there in fifteen," I say as I cut back over to the exit lane to make a U-turn and reverse direction.

23

"He's just someone I met through work," I answer truthfully.

Klarissa and I are at M. K. Restaurant on North Franklin. She has told me it is often overlooked. Any restaurant that charges more than thirty

159

dollars a plate is overlooked on my budget. But she's buying.

"So you're dating a cop?" Klarissa asks incredulously.

"Just a reminder, baby sis, your dad was a cop and your sister is a cop. So you might want to watch your tone when you say 'cop.'"

"Well, I didn't mean it as a put-down on officers of the peace," she corrects me primly with a twinkle in her eye. "I just thought you had a thing against dating people you work with, unless he happens to be a handsome FBI agent."

She thinks she's getting my goat and laughs loud enough for someone five feet away to hear her, which is practically shouting in her book. I notice she sets down her fork with a piece of shrimp on it small enough to fit on a microscope slide.

"He's not a cop—and you better not bring up Reynolds," I say.

"So now you're dating the criminals?"

She had started to raise the fork carefully and slowly toward her slightly parted lips again, but she's put it back on the plate so she can politely cover her mouth to protect me from her bellowing laughter. Not. I wish she would eat more. She's the tallest of the Conner sisters. Maybe five-nine. I doubt she weighs 110 pounds.

"Sorry to disappoint you, but I'm currently not dating any criminals."

Is that true? Derrick might not be charged with anything yet, but he's a guy with some illegal habits who is heading for serious trouble.

"How about let's talk about you," I say. "Sounds like you might have some news."

"You are so predictable, Kristen. When you don't want to spill the beans you change the subject."

True.

"So what's happening?"

"Your little Jedi mind game would not work on me normally—except I do have some very big maybe-news."

Maybe-news? She has held her fork with the piece of tined shrimp for a couple of minutes. Even if she takes a bite now, it could be days before she's done chewing. I do have to be in the office early tomorrow. I have a sudden urge to grab the fork out of her hands and stick the food in her mouth for her. It also crosses my mind to just eat it myself.

"Yes?" I prompt. "Full-time anchor of the evening news?"

"I'm still on the short list to get that when Judy retires at the end of the year. But that's not new news."

"How are your chances?"

"I'm anchoring at least once a week. No one else working at WCI is coming close. Doesn't mean they won't find someone from outside to bring in."

161

"Nah. You're a Chicagoland rock star."

She raises the fork back to her lips. When it stops again I finally blurt out, "Put that piece of shrimp in your mouth before I do it for you!"

We both laugh. She stands and walks around the table and gives me a hug around my neck. I reach up and hug her back.

"Okay, enough goo for one night," I say as she sits back down. "Just tell me what's new. Now."

She takes the bite of shrimp. Now I have to wait for her to chew. And chew.

"I'm on another short list but it's not for sure," she finally says.

"WGN?"

She can't answer as she takes a long slow slip of water. I look at my empty plate and her almost full plate. I may eat too fast but she eats slower than anyone I have ever witnessed in my life. When people give up on her ever finishing she just puts her tableware carefully at four o'clock on the dial with her napkin folded neatly on top and pushes the plate away. I want her to eat so I mask my impatience.

"Something juicier. *Chicago* magazine is about to list their top-ten eligible bachelors and bachelorettes and I've been told I'm for sure on the list and even have a good chance of winning."

"Now there's a surprise," I say with a laugh. "Let's see: you're beautiful, on TV every night, pretty well off financially from where I sit, and have that sparkling Conner personality. But I need to tell you something."

"What?"

"I'm in the same issue."

"You are?"

"Yep. I'm just on a different list: the ten most likely bachelorettes to spend New Year's Eve alone or babysitting nieces and nephews."

"Doesn't mean you aren't sizzling hot."

"That's you, baby sis."

She shakes her head. "You're the strong one, Kristen. You can have whatever or whoever you want in life. You leave a trail of broken hearts in your wake and usually don't even know it."

I can't resist. I stab a piece of shrimp off her plate and pop it in my mouth. She rolls her eyes and shakes her head slowly. I just smile.

"There is one other thing."

"What could be bigger than being the most eligible bachelorette in Chicago?"

"Channel 2 in New York City called, so you were on the right track. They want to interview me for their evening news anchor seat."

"I'm assuming Channel 2 is big."

"The biggest local affiliate in the country."

"More money, I assume."

"A lot more even if I landed the anchor seat here."

"Wow. Are you considering it? You wouldn't leave your loser big sister behind, would you?"

"That's why I wanted to have dinner with you, Kristen. I fly to New York tomorrow morning for my official interview. I would have to move. And you're not a loser."

"Wow," is all I can say.

"Okay, not that big of a loser," she says with her radiant smile.

I've never had the desire to move from Chicago. I guess I'm as boring and predictable as people say I am. I was never looking for a job offer from the FBI. Klarissa, on the other hand, has always stated her ambition to move from local to network news. After she graduated from University of Illinois with her communications degree, she landed in Springfield, Illinois, for two years. Then she got bumped up to a top-thirty-five market by landing at the top station in Kansas City, Missouri. That was a quick stop of two more years. She got called to WCI-TV just four years after graduation. She's pined for a promotion from news reporter to anchor in Chicago as her stepping-stone. If she gets a desk job in NYC, she'll definitely have scored a shortcut for her rise to the top.

"You just wouldn't understand what I'm going through, Kristen," she says. "What am I going to do if I get the offer? I'll have to take it, of course. It's what I've wanted. And my business is brutal. You are either moving up or down. There's no standing still. But after being back here in

Chicago with my family and all we've been through together the past two years, now I don't know if I want to leave."

I frown. Why wouldn't I understand? Didn't I just turn down an offer from the FBI? I'm tempted to correct her assumption that I wouldn't understand, but I hold my tongue. This is her moment. And Klarissa and I have had a strained relationship so much of our lives, it's better to keep momentum going when we get along. It does cross my mind to show her pictures of Jack Durham's head caved in so she knows the true meaning of the word *brutal*.

"I'm on in less than an hour," she says with a gasp. "I have to run. Grab the bill and I'll pay you back."

Suddenly alone in a crowded room, I look around. Will anyone notice if I eat her barely touched mixed green salad topped with tiny bay shrimp? I catch the waitress's eye and lift my hand, rubbing my thumb and fingers together to let her know I want the check. I am classy like that. She promptly ignores me for ten minutes. That does give me time to eat Klarissa's salad.

I wonder again if I can keep some of the clothes Bobbie bought me. I also wonder how long it's going to take Klarissa to pay me back for a dinner that was seventy-five dollars. It was easier for her to call out she would pay me back than it will be for me to remind her of that.

● ● ●

I am flat on my back. My arms are straight over my head. I am gripping the underside of my couch to keep my back flat. I slowly raise my legs up, keeping them perfectly straight, until they are at a perfect ninety-degree angle. Then I tilt my hips up so my rear is off the floor. I hold the position for ten Mississippis. I then take another full ten seconds to lower my legs to the floor. My abs are screaming. I'm on number seventeen. My plan is to do twenty.

I didn't have time to hit Planet Fitness on the way to my apartment, so I'm doing one of my floor workouts. I usually do cardio last, but I started with fifteen minutes on the light jump rope. The old man below me complains when I do double leg and eagle jumps, but I'm not too loud with the rope when I jump on the exercise mat I keep rolled up in the corner of my living room. I did five sets of twenty push-ups next. Three sets with my palms on the floor, but two sets using seven-pound medicine balls as my base. All one hundred were boy-style. On the last ten, my arms and shoulders were shaking like a cement mixer. I would have preferred going to the health club, but my heart is pounding and I'm sweating just as hard here. My mat is soaked from the thirty-two ounces of water I drank at M. K., and I know my stomach will be sore all day tomorrow. Sore is good. That means it was a good workout.

Eighteen . . . nineteen . . . and twenty, and I'm done and hitting the shower. Fifteen minutes later I'm in my pajamas looking at myself in the mirror as I brush my teeth with my Braun electric tooth-brush. Beautiful? No. Makeup does miracles. Attractive? Maybe. I do have good skin, if you don't count the scars on my right knee and right wrist. Sports and combat injuries.

I'm thirty years old. I've just turned down a big career move to work with the FBI. I like being a detective for the Chicago Police Department. Klarissa wants more. I'm not sure I do. What's wrong with being satisfied? I adore my nieces and nephew. Kendra is my soul mate, I believe. Do I want kids of my own? I think I do. Do I want to be married? Sure. Do I want to go through the strange rituals of dating and courtship? That's another issue.

I wonder why Reynolds hasn't called back to let me know whether he can help Dell Woods out or not.

Reynolds is the first guy I've been attracted to in forever. He made it clear the feeling was mutual. But we met under pretty intense work circumstances. I think that probably microwaved his emotions a bit. I doubt he's given me much of a thought since returning to his natural habitat.

I don't really know him well enough to give him as much thought as I do. I don't know what makes him tick. I'm pretty sure he's a good citizen and overall honorable—I know the selection process for being an Army Ranger is very exclusive and tough—but that doesn't mean we share the same values and beliefs.

So why am I thinking about him?

24

At the top of the corkboard are two pictures of the victim, Jack Durham. The one on the left shows a handsome man holding a drink and laughing. It has been cropped so whoever else is in the original picture is missing. He looks happy, but if you get right up to the picture and look closely you can see his eyes are red-rimmed and glazed. If he hadn't died young I doubt he was going to age well. I don't think livers are made to sustain the abuse he heaped on his body. Move in closer and you can see broken veins on his cheeks and early wrinkles around his eyes. A hard liver.

The second picture was taken by a techie at the crime scene. Probably Jerome. His head has been straightened on the bed where he died. The right eye is open, but lifeless. Where the left eye should be is a crater. The supraorbital foramen and sphenoid that make up the eye socket are gone. The temporal and zygomatic that form the cheek are destroyed. The parietal is half missing.

Whoever wielded the Stanley got to his brain through there.

Underneath Durham's two pictures is a long row with seven pictures. All males. All handsome. White teeth. Year-round tans. All attended Farnsworth High School in River Forest, Illinois, a western suburb of Chicago. At this small, exclusive, highly ranked university prep school run by the Catholic Dominican Order, the eight boys formed a friendship that endured the separation of six different colleges and three of the eight living out of state for up to five years before returning to Chicago.

We have run through Durham's e-mail and social media accounts. The group has stayed in close touch for years through daily correspondence and in the past year a Circle on Google. He's got a Facebook account but has never used it. The topics the friends cover are male. Sports. Dirty jokes and dirty pictures. Politics. Gossip. Trash talk and personal insults. Memories. Exploits in the bedroom. These are no gentlemen—they kiss and tell.

Two are married. Either both wives come to the get-togethers or neither comes and both are replaced by Bobbie's escorts. These friends have thought through their cheating ways carefully and work as a team. Five have good jobs. Two of those five are in family-owned businesses, so who knows how much they work. Two of the other three are professionals: a lawyer and an accountant. They just don't go into the office. No dummies in this group. The three ringleaders were Jack Durham, Derrick Jensen, and Kelly Granger. They were the three that don't work. All appear to live off family trust funds. Durham's alpha-male status seems to be a function of personality and money. He has the most of both. Based on the e-mail, social media, and phone records, no one seems to have spent close to as much time as Durham keeping the group together. Durham might have been a sleazebag, but he was committed to this group of friends. With a billionaire dad he had means to do so.

I wonder what will happen to the rest of the Lost Boys now that Peter Pan no longer lives in Never Never Land.

On the night Durham was murdered, his father, Robert Durham Sr., had just landed in Chicago from Moscow on a private jet with Robert Jr. The younger Durham hasn't followed in his brother's footsteps. Both brothers are attorneys, but this one seems to work hard at his father's side. He is married with three kids. He is heir apparent to a law firm that seems to mix estate planning, mergers and acquisitions for family-owned companies, private equity, and personal law for a very high-end client list.

I don't know much about planes, but Don and Randall yammered on and on about Durham Sr.

owning a Bombardier Global 5000 like two Georgia teenagers who just saw Dale Earnhardt Jr. drive by at Talladega. I think Talladega is in Georgia. Maybe Alabama. My connection to NASCAR is I think Jeff Gordon is cute. The Global 5000 apparently could make the 5,016 miles between Moscow and Chicago without refueling. Easily. Randall and Don even nodded at each other silently and solemnly on that point. I'm glad I know that now.

Durham was murdered on Thursday night, September 4, a few nights before I flew home to Chicago from Washington, DC. The funeral was held on Tuesday, September 11, the day after I was introduced to the case and the same day I was assigned to work undercover as an independent contractor. The funeral was closed casket, of course. Not sure the guy who did makeup for *Lord of the Rings* could have fixed up Jack for open viewing.

There is a computer monitor with electronic files of the case basketed together. I click on a photo album of the funeral. I look at the Durham family. Mom has her head buried on her husband's shoulder. In the next she has turned to her younger son for comfort. In another it looks like Durham Jr. is trying to wipe a speck from his eye. In the next his expression is stoic but his eyes are shiny. What emotions must be caroming throughout the family?

Durham Sr. was interviewed by officials of the CPD at his offices in the Standard Oil Building. The presence of his attorney, another member of the firm, was not considered suspicious, but standard procedure for a billionaire. Stanley McGill is a partner in Durham and Durham, and Durham Sr. and Jr.'s personal attorney. He was the nice man that kept to himself at the Bears game.

I read the interview transcripts for Senior and Junior carefully. Without ever having seen them together live and before looking at the pictures, I still feel that you could just tell these two think, talk, act, and probably even look alike. They do look alike. Jack, the older son, didn't fit. He was different physically and definitely wired differently than his brother and father. A little like the Jacob and Esau story in the Bible—this elder son appeared to have lost his birthright too, and his father's blessing, as a contributing member to the family's business and fortune.

Senior and Junior answered every question in precise, short responses. No elaboration. *Just the facts, ma'am.* Without listening in or being there I could feel a palpable lack of emotion. What was going through Robert Sr.'s mind? Disappointment in his son? A little bit like another biblical story that starred brothers: the prodigal son. In this case it wasn't the younger but the older that ran off to a far country and slopped with the pigs.

Family members are always persons of interest but with the two of them out of the country on business together, neither has generated any suspicion. Neither had much contact with Jack and both apparently headed straight home after landing.

Still, if this case is about money, wouldn't Junior have to be a big suspect? Half of the family fortune he is working to build and his brother is working to squander would still have gone to Jack upon the father's death. Now it's all his.

I look at my watch. I was in early but Don is uncharacteristically late today. He and Martinez must have had a long, scintillating conversation with Penny.

I run through things in my mind again. The younger brother definitely has a motive, the oldest one in the book: money. I've felt Penny was hiding something from day one. But shouldn't Junior still be looked at closely? It just stands to reason he would have to be frustrated. He is helping create more wealth for the family trust. His older brother was working just as hard to spend it on extravagant parties, trips, and luxury items. Going through the financial reports, I see it was not uncommon for Jack to buy a quarter-million-dollar car, get tired of it, give it away, and buy a new one. The family is loaded and could afford his reckless spending. But wouldn't that be a recipe for disaster over time?

Durham's mother was interviewed at their gated estate in Burr Ridge. Just reading the transcripts I was assaulted with a tsunami of her emotions. Despair. Confusion. Anger. Overwhelming sorrow. Moms don't tend to kill adult children. This case will be no different.

He was such a beautiful little boy, so charming . . . I don't know when I lost him . . . He could be so kind . . . He didn't care about anybody. . . I was invisible to him . . . He didn't like coming to the house and he didn't like Robert and me coming to his apartment . . . I always believed he would settle down and start a family . . . I set him up on a date with one of my best friend's daughters and was humiliated at what he did, how he acted that night . . . I don't know what happened to him . . .

People respond differently to trauma. Mr. and Mrs. Durham are living proof of that.

Underneath the pictures of the seven friends is a bingo board of pictures, mostly female. Connecting lines have been drawn from the guys to the girls and there is enough red crisscrossing that I think everybody in this group has been with everybody. *Gross.* Who are these people?

On the left side of the board is a large photo of Bobbie Ferguson. All lines meet at her. She's considered a key to solving the murder. Has she ever been suspected of being the murderer? Something Penny said made Blackshear and

Zaworski take a closer look at her, but her alibi was too neat.

Any of these people could have hired a killer. But hired killers don't usually use a hammer as a weapon and then vomit at the murder scene.

I'm mostly caught up with the other investigators on the case, but I started a couple days late and have been on an assignment that has isolated me from all but one official interview: the one with Penny Martin.

There are other friends and their pictures are at the bottom of the board. They interacted with Jack and his seven closest friends from time to time. But there were eight who were close as brothers. An octet. Three in the inner circle. The godfather is now dead.

At the Bears game I saw all seven of the survivors. I saw no family members but was told that Durham Sr. and Jr. were at the game together in another suite. Apparently Senior was drinking heavily, which is not common for him. Reports say that Junior and Senior's chauffeur had to help him to the car before the fourth quarter started.

What is going through the mind of a father who has lost his oldest son? What is going on in the mind of a mother who, according to reports, is on a shopping trip in New York City less than a week after her son's funeral?

One parent is chasing thoughts away with drink and the other by buying stuff.

Only one of Bobbie's "girls" is highlighted. Penny. Even Martinez, who worships the ground of about any pretty woman he sees, got a real bad vibe from her. Don told me when he called to update me on his drive home. He also said Konkade has got the Financial Forensics team to make her accounts—from bank statements to PayPal to charge cards and cable bill—top priority.

"How long is it going to take?" I asked him.

"Now that they are focusing on the independent contractors, all of whom do well financially but nothing like Durham and his friends, one of the guys told Konkade it will go much faster. He said looking at their numbers will be like switching from three-dimensional chess to checkers. Accountant humor, I guess."

I am reviewing the board one more time when I realize Martinez is standing next to me. I nod. He doffs his fedora complete with a little feather in the silk ribbon and smiles.

"*Ay, mi chica, eres muy bonita.*"

Antonio is okay. But I know he likes to tease me by flirting with me in Spanish. I give him an angry glare, which is what he was waiting for, and he gives out his loud laugh. As he does, Czaka rounds the corner.

"Glad my homicide detectives find murder to be so amusing," he scowls. "We need a break, folks," he says as he stomps off.

"*El jefe está en muy mal humor hoy,*" Martinez

whispers under his breath. "*Muy mal.* It's like Zaworski never left."

"When is Zaworski coming back?" I ask him.

He just shrugs.

Zaworski was a bear to be around the short time I saw him after my return from DC. But I have a bad relationship with Czaka already, and with him hovering over the case, I have to watch my mouth even more closely. I prefer the other bear.

Shelly walks into the room and comes toward us with a kid who looks like he might be a sophomore in high school.

"Here's Detective Conner now," she says.

The kid looks up at the board, sees the cratered head of Jack Durham, and looks down quickly.

"I got your phone, ma'am."

Ma'am? I know he looks young but just how old do I look?

"Anything I need to know about this?"

"If you've ever had an old text-and-call phone with no bells and whistles you should be fine."

"Then I'm fine," I say.

"I taped the number on the back like you asked," he says.

After dinner with Klarissa last night, I talked with Bobbie and she said Derrick had called her three different times asking for my number. Not sure why we didn't think of that up front, but it makes sense I need a number dedicated to my undercover assignment. We don't need him calling me and hearing me answer it "Detective Conner" or even my usual brisk "Conner." I'm supposed to be breathlessly awaiting his call as if nothing else in the world is more important to me. Bobbie told me to sound enchanted. *Gag me.*

"Could you sign here, ma'am?" the IT newbie says.

"I can, but if you call me 'ma'am' one more time, I'm going to arrest you for assault and battery."

He looks flustered and his eyes dart to the left. I now know what's up. I look over as Don tries to whip his fat head back around the corner.

"How much did he pay you?" I ask.

Now the kid looks real flustered. I look more closely and see the name Kenny on his laminated ID badge.

"I think it was just a little joke, ma—uh, Detective Conner."

"How much, Kenny?"

"Just a five-dollar card for JavaStar."

He has gone white as a ghost. He thinks he's in trouble. Poor kid.

"Make his phone go dead and I'll make it a twenty-dollar gift card," I say.

"I can't do that . . . uh, Detective. What if a call came in for him with a hot crime tip? I could get in a lot of trouble."

I shake my head. "Just kidding, Kenny. Just kidding. Enjoy your coffee."

• • •

"Gretchen," she says brusquely.

"Hi, Gretchen," I say. "This is Detective Conner."

A pause.

"We met on the Durham case at the Second."

"Yes, of course. Sorry, Detective Conner. I've had my head in a project."

Another pause.

"You gave me your card and asked me to call," I prompt her.

"Right. I just need to get focused."

I wait.

"This is a little embarrassing."

Okay.

"But I wanted to ask how Randall is working out."

Huh? Now I'm the one that's tongue-tied. "I've just been back on the job for a couple weeks, so I really don't know Randall that well. But he seems to be on top of things."

What else am I going to say about a colleague?

"I shouldn't have asked that," she says with a sigh, no longer the stern professional I met a couple days ago.

Where is this going?

"Here, I'm just going to say it," she blurts out. "Randall was getting a lot of attention due to his finances maybe six months ago. He may have even been on paid leave. Your IA department came to us for his tax records. I never heard how it turned out. I hadn't given him another thought, and then there he was in the meeting."

"Should I be hearing this?"

"Probably not."

Not *probably*. I shouldn't be hearing this. I've been looked at by Internal Affairs once, and I know I wouldn't want any of that being whispered to the people I work with.

"You're right, and I apologize. Apparently he got cleared. So I'm way out of bounds."

You can't be a detective if you don't have an inquiring mind. But there are also things you don't want to know or think about. It's a hard enough job without getting into a teammate's personal life.

We exchange a few pleasantries and are both relieved to get off the call.

What kind of financial troubles did Randall have?

25

Six of us are doing a stand-up meeting in Zaworski's office. When did stand-up meetings get so popular? I feel like I'm at church during the singing.

It is strange to be in Zaworski's office and see Blackshear behind the desk. Blackshear has been given the title of *acting captain* on a temporary basis. He is carefully navigating the line between making an executive decision when the team hits an impasse and deferring to others' ideas and instincts.

Don and Martinez really like Penny Martin for this murder. I did too. But now something doesn't feel quite right to me. It's probably because I spent so much time in front of the board and my mind is muddled.

"Go down the list for me one more time," Blackshear says. "I meet with Czaka in twenty-five and he wants something. I don't want to force anything, but this actually sounds good."

It's Wednesday afternoon. Don and I spent all morning with Byron Tedford, one of the Financial Forensic investigators assigned to our case. I met him once before on a case where a low-level drug dealer got killed. I thought I remembered his name and called him Bryan. Close but no cigar.

The guy had built an array of charts on everyone who is an independent contractor for Barbara Ferguson. Our reports come in two colors: black and white. He had a color for every factor on his summary sheet.

"Basically I've built an annual and monthly profit-and-loss sheet and then a balance sheet for each of the young ladies," he said. "I've built in cross tabulations based on demographics like age, years of service, debt and assets prior to working with Ferguson, and then the obvious numbers like monthly expenses and earnings.

"This Martin is off the charts on topline income, literally. I had to build her as an inset on Excel before graphing her with the others. She's a little like Alaska or Hawaii on a US map printed in a limited space. She doesn't fit real easy."

I'm not very good with numbers. I was okay in math, but the stats classes I had to take for my criminal justice degree were tough sledding. I didn't take any business courses other than a management of government workers class my senior year. But Tedford was patient when I asked him to repeat things so I could understand. I have a simple mind and he drew the picture simply enough that I could see it.

Penny has a ton more money than the others that work for Bobbie. She had about the same amount of money or even less than the others before she came to work for Bobbie but now makes a ton more than everyone else. A ton. So unless she is working twenty-four hours a day, something doesn't add up.

"She's either blackmailing someone or she's got a sugar daddy somewhere," Tedford said. "Either way, whoever is supplying the monthly nut is being way too careful because I've only been able to track her extra source of income back seven transactions to a bank in Switzerland."

"Name on the account?" I asked.

"None."

"Can we find out?"

"Not a chance. The Swiss have relaxed privacy laws in cases of suspected terrorism and the like, but not for whoever is funding a call girl from Chicago."

"So she could be blackmailing someone?" Don asked.

"That's the first thought that came to my mind," Tedford said.

"Well, if it's someone from Bobbie's client list, she's hit pay dirt," I add.

"Who gives someone a hundred grand a month if it's not blackmail?" Tedford asks rhetorically.

Don is a better presenter than me, so he walks the team through what we got from Tedford.

"Here's the summary," Don says to Blackshear, handing him a couple copies of a three-page report. "Got one for you and one for you to hand off to Czaka."

"Thanks, guys. You're making me look good."

I wonder how long that sense of gratitude will last once he gets a permanent bump in job title.

"Average monthly gross income for contractors working for Ferguson is around twenty thousand bucks. At least that's the average of what they are reporting and what is showing up in accounts we've located. Most use the same CPA. I think Ferguson must set this up for them. Probably insures she gets her cut of their revenue. Based on what they've made, they are all paying their taxes to the IRS, state, and city. Tedford doubts they're depositing all their cash in a bank; they probably have a nice nest egg squirreled away somewhere else. That would fit Ferguson's own profile and even if no one is singing yet, she has obviously mentored all these ladies on what to do and what not to do.

"But look at what Martin is bringing in every month. About the same until you look at the deposit that comes from that bank in Switzerland."

"You sure there's no way to know who's sending it?" Blackshear asks.

"The only way we'll find out is if we stumble on someone who is depositing a hundred thousand a month into that bank from here. Tedford says Swiss laws will make extracting a name next to impossible—and there may not be a name anyway."

"Have we looked at Durham and his buddies?" Konkade asks. "Sounds like how they would do it."

"Now that he's drawn a picture of Martin, that's Tedford's new top priority," Don answers. "But he said the financial transactions for these guys, both automated and human directed, are a labyrinth. And someone may have funded an account in Switzerland or the Cayman Islands or elsewhere years ago that has sufficient money to make the monthly disbursement to Martin."

"According to the note that goes with the asterisk on that input, it says that it has the appearance of a blackmail payment," Blackshear says. "Anything more than speculation?"

"No," Don answers. "Just speculation based on the amount. Tedford says the going rate for mistresses and other kept women is a lot less than an annualized figure of more than a million bucks."

"We just got started on this line of investigation in the last day," I say, "but she is definitely looking better for this."

"I thought she had an alibi," Martinez says.

"That's a funny thing," Don answers. "She says she met a client at Ferguson's place the night of the murder. Ferguson backs her up with her records. But two things. The client who booked her services was new with Ferguson and none of his contact information is real. That by itself is not absolutely suspicious. She has about fifty clients. We know eight of them through Durham. Half don't use a real name and keep a DBA account to handle finances."

"What's 'DBA'?" Blackshear asks.

" 'Doing Business As,' " Konkade answers. We all look at him. "What? My wife has a drapery business and it's too much hassle to set up a company."

"But here's the second thing," Don continues. "Penny Martin didn't make a deposit the day after the murder. Or Saturday. We compared Ferguson's calendar of when Martin was working and she was like clockwork making a deposit the next day. She was the person standing outside a bank at 8:59 waiting for the doors to open."

"You said that Tedford suspects the contractors don't deposit all their earnings," Blackshear says.

"True," I answer. "That's how City Revenue division got Ferguson. That's how Zaworski leveraged Bobbie from day one. We aren't saying we've got Martin or any of the other workers on tax evasion. Everything might be as 100 percent straight as the bank records look. And her alibi might be good. But it looks like a good trail to follow."

"No doubt," Blackshear answers. "I'm just talking to myself because I know what Czaka is going to grill me about. This is good stuff, guys . . . and Kristen. Anything on your line of inquiry?" he asks, looking at me.

"I go out with Derrick tomorrow night. Don't know if any of the other friends or any of the contractors will be there. I'll just find out what I can."

"That's good," he says. "Good to have a fallback angle if this Penny Martin thing doesn't work out." He switches gears. "Randall, you been able to collect all the public camera footage near

Durham's place yet? We're a week in and this delay is getting a little ridiculous."

"Getting close, boss. Not making excuses, but it's been tough. Some guy owns a couple of the garages and he got sued last year after he turned over video files to a private investigator on a divorce case. The guy on film sued for a violation of his privacy. The garage owner won, but it cost him some serious dollars to defend. So he's made us come back three times now with basically the same warrants. Legal finally has everything in order, we think."

"If you're not getting the right kind of cooperation in house or from some jerk with a garage, this is the kind of thing you come to me or Konkade on."

"Sorry, boss. I'm on it."

26

After the meeting to update Blackshear on Penny Martin officially becoming a person of interest I went for a four o'clock training session with Barry Soto. He's been a fight instructor with the CPD for thirty years. He might be over sixty- five years old, but he is still a physical specimen with a tiny waist and lots of chest and arm muscle. He's only five-eight or -nine and has to be around two hundred pounds based on the width of his shoulders. His long black stretch shorts, the white socks and black athletic shoes, and the gray collared workout shirt with CPD embroidered on the chest make him look like a gym teacher from the fifties. The 1850s. He wears heavy black glasses with a ski croaker to hold them on. He's mostly bald with two wild patches of wiry gray hair sprouting above his ears. His nose is another physical marvel, both for its size and for the fact that there might be as much hair coming out of those nostrils as there is on his head. He isn't going to win any beauty contests. As I walked up, he was doing fingertip push-ups. The guy still has a muscle tic that allows him to fire off the floor.

Soto looks sideways, sees me coming, and rips off ten more quick ones before springing to his feet. I think he's showing off now.

"Very impressive, Mr. Barry."

"That?" he declares indignantly. "I used to do one hundred without stopping. Barely got me breathing hard."

"You are one of a kind."

"Who you fighting with these days, Princess Kristen?" he challenges.

"No one. I'm behaving."

"I doubt that. But even so, don't mean the other guy will behave. Always good to be ready. You need to get down here more."

"I'm here now and ready to do some big-time boxing."

"No boxing today."

Rats. I like to box.

"You heard me say it once, you heard me say it a hundred times: all fights end on the ground, Conner. So pay attention and stay alive. You like to kick and punch because it keeps your pretty workout clothes clean. What you gonna do when you get punched and go down and he comes down there after you? You ain't gonna be kicking and punching then, are you? If you do punch, it's gonna be from about three inches away and I don't care what those kung fu movies show—no one can do any real damage from that close. You're gonna fight on the ground today. I hope you're ready."

I'm ready.

Krav Maga was developed by the Israeli Defense. It is a mixed martial-arts approach that includes kicks and punches, but focuses on using hands to defend, grapple, and attack with joint locks and chokes. First time I was introduced to it was a self-defense for women class at NIU. I think it is the best survival program for in-close fighting. I try to combine that with classic men's wrestling when I'm on the ground. Greco-Roman is interesting, but it's all about staying off the back, so I don't think it replicates street condiions well enough to spend too much time on it.

Soto usually has two fight assistants on staff, one male and one female. He knows I like to fight the males. Call it my ego getting the best of me or just being realistic. I've had to break up more than a few female cat fights as a police officer—and I've been scratched, bitten, kicked, and spit on in the process—but the vast majority of fights are started by men against other men. I want to make sure I can fight with the big boys. I bend over and do a slow stretch to my hammies.

"You doing ballet or you gonna fight today?" Soto says. "Stand up and let's get you warmed up."

"Where's the love, Mr. Barry?" I ask.

"I bet when you hammered that Shark guy's nose to a pulp you knew how much I loved you. Enough chitchat. Let's get going."

Chitchat? What chitchat?

For fifteen minutes I do a series of dynamic stretching exercises and then work solo on down-position wrestling moves. I go from flat to getting my knees under my stomach, elbows under chest, pushing up, and kicking either right or left leg out to where I'm on my butt and can throw my opposite elbow back and slide behind the attacker that had me down. That's how it's supposed to work when the attacker is present, anyway.

I've got a sweat going and am breathing medium hard when an athletic gal, maybe twenty-five or so, at least a few years younger than me, joins us to put me through my combat paces. She is probably two inches shorter but at least thirty or more pounds heavier than me. She's not over-weight, but she's thick. Big legs and big butt. It's not fat. I was a middle distance runner in high school. Bet she was a sprinter. She's definitely in shape and has a lot of definition in her arms and shoulders. She's probably a big-time weight lifter.

I am a mass of contradictions when it comes to my body. I want the strength she has, but I don't want the size. I'm in a big club on that one. Pound for pound, Soto says I'm tough as anyone—but that I need more pounds. I am quick and have good leverage. I'm stronger than I look and have a ferocious grip. I'm limber and can fully extend with kicks and chops. I've done enough training that I can maximize my body position and torque to really get some power behind my punches and moves.

But she's going to be a handful.

"On the ground, Conner," Soto says. "Meet Denise. But don't shake hands until you're up on two feet. Denise doesn't want to meet you and she plans to keep you on the ground."

She doesn't smile. Soto knows how to pick 'em. He had a brawler named Timmy that I worked out with a few times earlier in the year. Timmy was a very good fight partner because he loved his work—maybe too much. I suspect he needed a little more law and order to go with his love of a fight. Not sure I could beat him under any circumstances.

I drop to the mat. I'd rather have Denise's role. I think it's harder to keep someone down than to get up. I want a hard workout.

"Flat, Conner," Soto says. "You just got punched from behind and you're completely down. Hope your thinking isn't as fuzzy as usual."

Soto is in fine form this afternoon.

Denise settles in above me and puts her chin in the middle of my upper back, one hand on the outside of my hip, and grabs my left wrist firmly and roughly. I'm not ready when Soto yells "Go" and she digs her chin into a nerve cluster that about paralyzes me in the first second of the drill. I slide forward and squirm left and right to get her chin off me and get a second's respite, but she keeps finding new ways to dig in. As soon as my knee slides forward enough to get my quad off the ground, she brings her knee on top of my hamstrings and then tries to slide that leg forward and hook my right leg. She starts pulling my left wrist down and trying to get my arm behind my back. I crab to the side enough to get her chin back off me, but she's happy to drive it into my right shoulder. Plenty of nerves there too.

I have to tilt my body to get relief from the chin and start getting my legs into a position where I can push from the strongest part of my body. She immediately lets go of my wrist and slides her left arm under mine to leverage my arm and shoulder and flip me over on my back. If this were a real fight, she would do that so she could start punching me in the face from above. If she gets her hand behind my neck into a half nelson, I'm in big trouble.

I leverage everything I have down hard on her left arm, get on an elbow, force both knees under me, and sit out of her hold in a fast, fluid motion. But she's quick and is already back behind me, trying to leverage both of my arms up and behind me in a move called the surfboard.

I repeat what I did before and go the opposite way. I think I might have room to escape and get to my feet. But again she's on top of me, and this time she completes the half nelson and plants her legs off to the side of me to finish flipping me on my back. If she gets me there, she's going to bury an armpit on my face and lock me in a hold around my neck that controls my shoulders so the bottom of my body can flop all over the mat but I can't get loose.

I do an all-or-nothing move and let her flip me but roll hard with it back onto my stomach. I get both knees and elbows up, and this time when I sit out, I give her left arm a nice chop with my elbow. She pursues me like before, but not quite as quickly. I get completely free of her grasp and I'm up on two feet and whirling into a fighting position.

She bull-rushes, then drops low to snag a leg to tackle me. But I throw my long legs back in a sprawl and get over the back of her head and force her down on all fours.

"Break it up!" Soto yells. "I said we start again after Conner escapes and gets on her feet. You two need to listen."

I start to protest that Denise continued to bring the fight to me, but I know Soto will give me a lecture that out in the real world fights are never fought fairly either.

"She had you down over a minute, Conner," Soto says, looking at his stopwatch. "I thought I trained you better. In a minute she would have beat you to a pulp if this was a real fight and we weren't going easy on you."

I roll my eyes.

"Yeah, you cop an attitude and roll your eyes at me, but don't come complaining to me when you get your clock cleaned."

Soto trained my dad when he was on the force. I've known him since I was in elementary school. That's why he's Mr. Barry to me.

He puts me on bottom again, this time on my back. I start in a worse position than the first time but get free in under a minute. Next he has me try to keep Denise down. She was up in fifteen seconds.

Soto sputters and fumes and yells and spends the next thirty minutes putting me through ground drills: "Get your hands free. Get your butt up. Use her momentum against her. Turn into it, away from it, with it. You're getting your clock cleaned, Conner; you're getting your clock cleaned. I told your daddy I'd keep you alive, and you're making me into a liar."

My big sport was soccer. I lettered four years at NIU. I was a starter for three years and was all-conference my junior year. A soccer game goes ninety minutes. It's a grueling sport and demands endurance. But I guarantee you that if you get on a mat and wrestle as hard as you can for five or six minutes, you end up being even more tired.

As I trudge up four long flights of stairs to Homicide after I showered, I look at my iPhone. Three missed calls. Reynolds and Mom. The third is a number I didn't recognize. I then remembered to look at the temp phone to handle calls from Derrick Jensen. A fourth missed call and a text. I look at the text.

Can't wait until tomorrow night.

My stomach crawls.

I'll start listening to messages and returning calls as soon as I get to my desk.

27

Wednesday, September 19
8:00 p.m.

So much for staying off the radar. Two more visitors earlier this week. Second time for the black guy. His partner stared at my chest the whole time. Squires obviously suspects me.

Can you give us the name of who you were with the night of September 4 . . . I want to ask you about your relationship with Jack Durham again . . . You say you were out that night and went to a play and dinner. What was the play again . . . Where was the dinner . . . Did you see anyone you knew . . . Is there anyone that can corroborate you were there . . . What did you have for dinner again . . . What was the play about . . . Have you ever spent the night with Jack Durham?

Do they think I'm stupid? Do they not know I know they're trying to trick me? To get me to slip up? Not going to happen.

This would have nothing to do with me if I hadn't decided to go over there. But I had to go over to confront him. Tell him what he did to me. Tell him what I thought of him and how I never wanted to talk to him again. And then see if he would make amends so we could finally have a real relationship.

I just wanted him to talk to me and get to know me.

And if I'm honest with myself I wanted to make sure she wasn't over there bad-mouthing me.

I knew it was only a matter of time before they turned the spotlight on me—thinking I was home free was wishful thinking. I guess they're into my finances now. That doesn't look good.

I wish I knew for sure who did this. It's got to be one of two people. I don't know who my real friend is.

I've waited too long to face the inevitable decision: time to go. I think I can have everything ready in the morning. There's nothing here for me anyway. Never was. My life is a blank. I'm a zero. He reminded me of that.

She went back to her bedroom and into her walk-in closet. She bent down and pushed a hidden lever underneath three built-in drawers stacked on top of each other. The whole stack moved forward and separated from the wall. In the space behind the drawers was a recessed wall safe. She punched in nine numbers and letters from memory.

She removed a blue passport with her picture and another name in it. She looked through three checkbooks, each with another name at the top.

She had a driver's license for each account. She pulled out a robin's-egg-blue Macy's bag and looked inside at stacks of hundreds, fifties, twenties, and tens held together by rubber bands. Last she'd counted, it was about two hundred grand. Combined with the accounts in other names, it was a sizable number. But if she couldn't access the money in her name, it wasn't nearly as much as she wanted. And she wasn't sure her monthly bonus would continue once she was out of the picture.

Go now? Yes!

She carefully replaced the contents of the safe. She pushed the three drawers back into the wall until there was a *click* that let her know it was latched back in place.

Tomorrow or the next day. Just a few more things to do.

28

Twelve per table. I can't stand up and get an exact count, but based on the number of tables on the front row and along the side, I think there are 148 or so total tables. There is a sound-and-light board in the middle of the room, and I don't know how many tables were left out of that space. Probably six. There are fifteen people on a platform, sitting in a straight line facing us. One of them is the President of the United States. I assume no one up front paid for this event. There are two tables on floor level that seem to be made up of lesser dignitaries and workers. They probably aren't paying either.

For the rest of us present at this presidential reelection fundraiser, the cost is a thousand dollars per plate. Drop eight to ten tables for the sound board and workers and there are probably 138 full tables with twelve people each. One hundred thirty-eight multiplied by ten is 1,380. Two times 138 is 276. That makes 1,656 people. Times one thousand dollars. I think that makes 1.656 million dollars. The chicken is a little dry, so I'm guessing they didn't break the budget on the menu.

I'm on date number two with Derrick Jensen. Bobbie said I must have passed the first test at the Bears game. She sounded surprised. He called and specifically asked for me. I thought our first date was our last date since he never asked for my last name or phone number. She laughed when I told her that. She said not getting my phone number was a negative, but she doubted Derrick would ever want my last name.

"What's your last name?" Derrick asks.

Okay. Take that, Bobbie.

"Andrews."

We decided to stick with my real first and a fake last name. Keep things simple for the simple-minded detective. The extent of my cover story is the same I used on my last case. I am a secretary in an insurance agency. As to why I'm working for an escort service, my answer is to be a demure smile.

Once again Bobbie oversaw every detail of getting me ready. Black dress. Five-inch heels. Translucent white pearl necklace, earrings, bracelet, and ankle bracelet. All traditional and very real. What I'm wearing costs more than my car. Brand new.

She frowned when she saw a bruise on my shoulder.

"I thought you didn't fool around," she said.

I gave her a dirty look and that seemed to mollify her and make her happy. She and my makeup artist, Tracy, murmured in low tones about the best way to hide the bruise.

I thought prepping for the Bears game was torture. Bobbie had Tracy take her plucking to a level sufficient to earn a punch in the nose from me. She rubbed in this, dabbed that, brushed something else, and applied enough layers to my face to peel and create a scary Halloween mask. Tracy could feel my growing impatience as the ordeal stretched interminably long. Several times she looked at Bobbie with nervous eyes. Good. Problem is, Bobbie would make a great bulldozer operator, and the more unhappy I got, the happier her expression. I have a way with people.

We will never be friends. Our relationship is tenuous at best. But Bobbie and I might have a begrudging like for each other, as painful as that is to admit. I still don't respect her. And yes, Jimmy, I am being judgmental.

"I know you don't respect me," Bobbie said.

Perceptive woman.

"I'll admit, meeting someone as . . . different as you are is a bit disconcerting. One minute I'm still grateful that I learned early in life that relationships are best when they are thought of as business arrangements. But there are fleeting moments when you make me wish I had followed a different path. Maybe even someone as cynical as I could have found true love."

"Not sure how you would come up with that idea watching me," I retorted. "If my ship came in, I missed it again."

She laughed. "I can almost guarantee you will find true love. At the right time. Someday you'll let go of whatever is churning inside you."

Okay. She is observant.

"And I suspect you already have someone on your mind."

Has she been talking to Willingham? He's my latest love doctor. Tracy looks uncomfortable. Does she know who I am and what's going on? She shouldn't.

"You are a remarkable young woman, Kristen. And even though I know you will never admire or respect me and what I do—without using words you have made that abundantly clear—for your own good, I would suggest that you might learn a positive thing or two from me about getting along with people."

There are a couple caustic responses I could zing her with. But I can't think of them.

"You look beautiful."

"Aren't you sweet? Thank you, Derrick."

I think I just threw up in my mouth a little saying that.

"So, insurance worker by day and . . . uh, glamorous woman about town at night."

I smile demurely. Or maybe I look like I'm grimacing after sucking on a lemon.

"You don't say much, do you?"

"I'm just taking it all in," I say gracefully and slowly, per Bobbie's instructions.

"You have to cool it on that nasal Chicago cop voice of yours. If you have to have coffee, make sure you don't ask for kaaw-feee. And slow down when you talk. Slow down."

"It's exciting to be so close to the president," I say breathlessly. "And to be out with you again," I add. Clumsily. I could be reading my words to Derrick from a stack of blue note cards.

I would actually prefer to be with my Snowflakes for soccer practice tonight. Tiffany's dad is running it again. He still wants to be named co-head coach. I'm still content to call him assistant coach.

Focus.

"He's just another Chicago hack with his hand out," Derrick says with a derisive snort.

"So you're not a big fan and donor?"

"No fan, but big donor. I actually hate all politicians, but I donate to them all. It's a game, but you have to play it. I haven't voted in an election since the year I turned eighteen. I'm very proud of that."

If Derrick had a descriptive middle name, he would be known as Derrick Cynical Jensen.

"So do you know a lot of people here?"

"You might say that. But not very many I would call friends." He lowers his voice. "I do this crap for my old man. He thinks it's good for business. Who am I to argue? The family business is my inheritance, so if Dad wants me to do tricks at a dog and pony show, I'll jump through hoops and wag my tail with a smile on my face."

"You never said what you do for a living."

"As little as possible," he says with a laugh. "Dad has been into anything and everything. At one point he had more car dealerships in Chicagoland than any other air polluter alive."

"What kind of cars did he sell?"

"What kind didn't he sell? That's the better question. He also had a steel mill and a trash service. At one point we had a trucking company.

We owned radio stations. I don't know all we have now. I have to give the old man credit, his timing is always right. He's known when to dump the losers and pick up other companies on the way up. Our main business now is software. He moved into selling computers back in the late eighties. He sold to corporate accounts just when the industry was exploding. Now he owns a consulting and software programming company —the largest in the Midwest and one of the biggest in the country. Corporate is in the R. R. Donnelly building, but he's got offices in Silicon Valley and Mumbai and London and everywhere else."

"So why don't you enjoy working with him?" I ask. "I shouldn't have asked that," I correct myself, but not as gracefully as Bobbie would like.

"I don't mind you asking at all. If you knew my old man, you'd know the answer, though. Not the most pleasant guy to be around. I actually have an MBA from University of Chicago but no real interest in working with him."

"So what would you like do?"

"Later tonight or for a career?" he asks suggestively, leaning over and putting his hand on the top center of my back.

I wonder if people can feel when your skin crawls.

I blush. "For a career."

I don't think Bobbie would agree with my answer.

He laughs and for just a second I spy a glimpse of a younger, unjaded Derrick. But the cynic instantly returns.

"I don't want to do anything. Why would I? I have plenty of dough."

"You're very fortunate," I say with all the earnestness I can muster.

I don't think I sold it. His eyes narrow and he looks at me more closely. *Ruh-roh*.

"What kind of insurance do you sell?"

"Life, home, auto, everything. We're full service. What do you need?"

That gets a laugh from him.

"So why do you do it?" he asks, his eyes still studying me.

"It's a job."

"You make a whole lot more working for Ferguson."

"Well, I just started. I'm sure I'll be able to quit insurance soon."

"Uh-huh."

Derrick's no dummy. If he wasn't suspicious of me already, he is now. The elderly gentleman next to him leans over and asks him a question. Derrick reluctantly turns toward him and the two engage in a conversation. The elderly gentleman stands up and motions for Derrick to follow him. They walk a table away and a third man stands, shakes hands with Derrick, and joins the discussion. *Whew.*

I am sitting next to another of Jack Durham's friends, Brett Cooper. Not in the inner circle but one of the regulars. Divorced and single. One child. A stunning beauty I recognize from Bobbie's portfolio is next to him. She knows how to play this game. She laughs at the right times. Her eyes sparkle every time Brett speaks. She leans over and squeezes his arm or puts her hand on his hand when he's not eating. She says funny things but not too many funny things. She makes eye contact around the table but always comes back to Brett. I think Derrick tried to flirt with her for a while. She went with the flow but held tightly to Brett's arm to show where her loyalty was. At least tonight.

I could never be like Ferguson's contractors. I don't want to be like them. But Bobbie's right; I could learn a few things about getting along with people from her.

"How long you worked for Bobbie?" Brett asks.

"Just a couple weeks," I say.

"Well, you're going to do good," he says. "Derrick is crazy about you. I don't think that's ever happened before."

"Really?"

"Yes, really. In fact, he's ordered everyone else to stay away from you and he's told Bobbie no one else dates you. I think he's about to offer you a business arrangement. But act surprised. I shouldn't be telling you this."

"I think you're pulling my leg. I'm not sure Derrick has gotten to know me well enough to feel that way."

"That's what we've all told him," the stunning blonde says, leaning over. "But he's got it bad for you. He even liked that you wouldn't go home and sleep with him," she adds with a wink.

"If you tell him I said anything, I'll swear you were lying," Brett says as he smiles and holds up his hands.

A business arrangement? Who are these people? Why are they talking about me?

Derrick disentangles himself from the two men he's been talking to and returns to the table, giving me an exaggerated smile. A waiter appears over my shoulder with a bottle of wine.

"Some more white before dessert is served?"

I still have half a glass left. I was able to dump the other half under the table.

"I'm fine," I answer, covering the mouth of the glass with my hand.

"Yes, you are," Derrick says with a wolfish smile. "What say we get out of here before we have to eat fake chocolate mousse pie and listen to a political speech about lower taxes and no deficits? Actually, tonight might be the higher taxes talk."

"Sure," I say.

We say good-byes around the table and stand. I don't know what I'm going to do to thwart Derrick's plans, but after yesterday's workout, I'm pretty sure he has no chance against me if this turns into a hand-to-hand combat.

"Kristen!" I hear a voice I know very well behind me. "That *is* you, sis!"

I turn and Klarissa gives me a half hug and a quick peck on both cheeks. Very European, I'm sure. My brain has turned to mashed potatoes and my tongue refuses to move. She's supposed to be in New York.

"Hi, I'm Klarissa Conner," she says to Derrick, holding out a delicate hand for him to shake.

"I recognize you from the news," he says with an amused smile, looking from her to me and back. His smile grows wider. *Uh-oh.* "And I'm Derrick Jensen, just a humble citizen of Chicago who has been honored by the presence of the famous Detective Kristen Conner."

The synapses in his brain have fired and made all the connections.

"Where are you two off to?" Klarissa asks. "You're staying for the speech, aren't you?"

My mouth is still frozen in a half grimace, half smile.

"We are indeed going to have to leave as we have something we need to discuss," he says.

"Well, that's too bad. I'm here with Warren"—

she points to Warren and we exchange waves—
"and we wanted you to go out with us after-
ward."

"Not tonight, Klarissa," I say, my voice husky
and strained. "But I'll see you Saturday morning
before soccer, like we planned."

"See you at JavaStar," she says.

I think she's started to pick up the awkward
vibe and her face alternates between a frown
and a smile as she looks at me intently, wide-
eyed.

Derrick bows and then goes over to shake hands
with Brett and hug whoever is with him. I can't
remember her name.

Klarissa hugs me a little tighter this time and
whispers in my ear, "Oh . . . my . . . gosh. You
look fabulous. I am so jealous. You better have a
good explanation as to why I don't have a clue
what's going on with you."

"How'd New York go?" I whisper back.

"Tell you Saturday."

"You know I liked you."

"You met me one time, Derrick."

"I knew you were different the second I laid
eyes on you. I was right." He shakes his head and
laughs.

"Yes, you were right. But everyone knows I'm
different."

"You know, what you said is right: I'm cynical.

But you're cynical in your own way. You don't take things at face value either. You make jokes and deflect."

Derrick is more perceptive than I figured.

"So why can't we start over and just date?" he asks.

"I'm not going to date you, Derrick. I'm investigating the murder of your best friend."

"How about after the case is solved?"

"You don't want to date me, Derrick. You don't know me."

"But I want to get to know you. I would be willing to go slow. Very slow. Shouldn't that count for something? Who's to say I'm not about to become a new man?"

"Not I."

"But your tone bespeaks cynicism. You've judged me."

We are sitting in a Wendy's about five minutes from my apartment. Derrick picked up a bottle of Gentleman Jack and has polished a good portion of it off, along with a double burger and large order of fries. The manager came over and told him no alcohol was allowed in the restaurant. He ordered a Diet Coke, poured all but a little ice in the trash can, emptied the bottle in the cup, and threw the bottle away. That satisfied the night manager and he hasn't come near since.

"To Jack," he said.

"You miss him?" I ask.

"I was talking about my friend Gentleman Jack."

I make a face at him.

"Yes, I do. I miss Jack very much. He was a true friend." He raises his cup in salute and takes a huge swallow. I'm glad his chauffeur is in the parking lot. He is in no shape to drive.

"He wasn't very well liked, you know—and he really didn't like too many people. I think he invited people to spend time with him so that he could watch them demean themselves. He wanted to see how much crap they would put up with but keep showing up to enjoy the splendors of his parties."

"Sounds pathetic," I say.

"You are correct," he says. "But Jack wasn't all bad. He was complicated. Just like most of us. I'm complicated. You're definitely complicated. Right?"

"You would be correct," I say.

"Writer," he says.

"Huh?"

"You asked what I'd really like to do and the answer is write."

Interesting. I get ready to ask if he's ever written anything but he lets out a tremendous belch and lowers his face on the table. I think he was fast asleep before the side of his head hit the wrapper from his burger that is smeared with ketchup.

The chauffeur has done this before and gets him in the back of the car. He drives the couple blocks to my apartment. I would open the door myself but can't find the right handle. He opens the door for me and says he will escort me to my door. I tell him no problem.

"Mr. Derrick has his problems," he says to me, "but he is always a gentlemen. And he would insist."

What an evening.

29

"Sah-weeeeeeet!"

I may be as bad as the other coach, Denny Carpenter (I can't get my nickname for him—Attila the Hun—out of my mind), who screams "Oliviaaaaaaa!" every time his daughter scores a goal. Which is actually quite often. She's a very good player. Maybe the best I've seen out here—except for Kendra, of course. Kendra has just passed the ball beautifully across the mouth of the goal, and Tiffany, the only other girl on our team who scores consistently, finished it with a tap in. We now have a one-goal lead with probably ten minutes left in the game.

What a difference a year makes. Last year we lost our first five games. We ended up winning three, two of them against the team that won the league. The X-FORCE. What kind of name is that for little girls? They are coached by Attila, who I once accused of teaching his girls to play rough and foul, but who actually ended up being a pretty nice guy. So even if I don't call him Denny like he asks, at least I refer to him as "Coach" now. I can be difficult.

But this year we're undefeated. Okay, two games does not a season make. But we're looking good. If we can hold on to this game and go 3-0, we'll be odds-on favorites to win the league. I'm not sure the *Chicago Tribune* is covering us yet, but in my pea brain it's a big deal.

"Mark up! Everyone mark up!" I bark at my eight- and nine-year-old Snowflakes. My middle defender, Torrie, is picking daisies in some enchanted field with a castle and a prince who is always on her mind and doesn't heed my call to mark up. Kendra is so fast she can cover for a lot of team errors, but I have her marking Oliviaaaaaaa, with firm orders to not let her score under any circumstances. So she's out wide with Attila's daughter when the ball gets crossed into the middle of the field and a midfielder for X-FORCE swoops in and nails the tying score in a wide-open net. Our goalie made a charge for the ball, but the scorer got there first.

The action resumes. I look at my watch. Five minutes to go. Maybe less. Olivia charges as one of our girls makes a free kick. Olivia jumps up in the air and swivels. The ball hits her in the butt and rolls out of bounds near me. The girl is a dynamo. She's fearless. It is our ball at midfield with a throw in. I have to figure a way to get Kendra or Tiffany free again. The only problem is Attila is doing the same thing as me. He has Olivia marking Kendra and the two are pretty evenly matched.

I have an idea.

"Good game, coaches," the ref says to us as he hands Attila a clipboard with the game form on it to sign. Attila does so and hands it to me and I put my signature on it. The ref trots off.

"Good game, Kristen," Attila says. "You guys are off to a great start this year."

He thrusts out his hand to shake and smiles magnanimously, which is easy to do when you just won a tight game in dramatic fashion, with under a minute to go, after being a goal down. My idea backfired on us and I'm mad but shake hands, make eye contact, and force a smile.

Why did I think my girls could execute a midfield offside trap? None of them are ten years old. Half the time Torrie doesn't know she's on a soccer field. Even if they had worked it correctly, would a field judge working a game with eight- and nine-year-olds make the right call? I blew it.

"Your team looks as strong as ever, Coach," I

answer back. The words almost catch in my throat.

"Call me Denny."

His wife has wandered to the middle of the field and gives him a hug. The only person louder than Denny the Hun is his wife.

"You've met Angie, right?"

"I think last season," I say, though I'm pretty sure we didn't. "Nice to see you again, Angie."

"You too."

"Good job, baby!" she says to Denny and squeals before she heads back over to her side of the field. If my eyes don't deceive me she is doing a victory dance over there. Could that not have waited? Poor sportsmanship. Probably on my part. I'm just mad we lost.

I turn to join my team that has somehow overcome the anguish of our first defeat quicker than me. They are munching the postgame granola bars someone brought for team snack. A couple girls are running circles squirting water on each other from their half-filled water bottles. I think this is the most Torrie has run in the past hour.

"Hey," Attila calls when I'm about ten feet away. I turn back. "Wanted to give you something to think about for next year. I know it's early, but our girls move up a division and teams have to re-form. I was thinking if we team up on coaching we can put Olivia and Kendra on the same team along with the best girls from both teams and end up being pretty tough to beat. That Tiffany girl is a good player too. Her dad is also a good guy, and could help coach."

"I have to think about that, Coach. I'm not that far ahead in my mind."

Team up with Attila the Hun? Me? What he says actually makes sense. Doesn't mean I'd actually consider it. *Would I?*

"Well, there's plenty of time," he says. "But it's not too early to start planning. Next year competitive-tryout soccer starts and being on a powerhouse team will help the girls sign with one of the best clubs."

Wow. That's a blast from the past. Wasn't Kendra born just yesterday? She seems too young to be approaching tryouts and travel soccer. I still think of those as some of the happiest moments of my life. But Kendra? She's still a little girl. And there's no way I would partner up with Attila. *Is there?*

"Thanks, Coach. I'll give it some thought."

"Do that! And call me Denny!"

I'll do that, Coach.

"Okay, good game, girls. You played great. But I think we can get even better. Don't forget to dribble the ball in your backyard every day. See you Tuesday night at seven o'clock for practice."

I wanted to point out to Torrie that she better

start marking up or I'll have to sit her butt on the bench. But it's rec league and there are rules that all girls have to play at least half the game. So it would be an idle threat. And I'm not sure she'd care anyway. And I'm pretty sure she's a sweet girl who wants to be with her friends and that's all that matters.

Even when I know exactly the right way to think and feel, I struggle to get my competitive impulses and quick temper under control. I will say my anger is a lot more under control than earlier in the year. Maybe I'm growing.

I think about my late-night talk with Derrick. Who's to say he can't grow up? Maybe I should have been more encouraging.

I listened too closely in church last week. Now I'm thinking about my judgmentalism.

30

Saturday, September 22
12:15 p.m.

They're watching my every move. I went for coffee and was followed the whole way. I went to the grocery and there was someone new that always ended up in the same aisle as me. Then the lady that followed me to the coffee shop was in a car outside the grocery store too.

They think it's me. They are going to arrest me.

This is my life in a nutshell. I try as hard as I can to improve it. It looks like things might work too. Then something happens and my plans fall apart.

Getting arrested—and I know they are going to—getting charged, and getting convicted. They will. I will.

I will go to jail. That's my luck. Bad and worse.

I'm supposed to leave on Monday. I wanted to fly to another country, but that is obviously much more dangerous now. So where else would I go? Back to Mansfield, Illinois? Even if that wasn't the first place they'd look, Mom and Dad let me know I'm not welcome at home after what I've gotten into. They're not my real parents anyway.

Leaving is the same as running. And that's the same as confessing I killed him. I've got plenty of IDs. But will they hold up? Can I live the rest of my life looking over my shoulder?

I should have left the night I found his body. I should have left two nights ago. Is it too late now?

I don't know how they haven't arrested me already. I've been lucky. It's time to get out of here.

I better talk to him. I'm not sure I can trust

him. I'm not sure he didn't do it. But he's been my only friend through this ordeal. I wish I could see him.

She sighed and put everything back in the safe. She needed to talk to him face-to-face to find out what he knew and get some advice. Most of all to look in his eyes. He'd always refused to meet with her. Said it wasn't safe with all the suspicion on her. But he had come up with a new way to communicate. Each was to buy new, prepaid cell phones every other week—one week he would, the next week she would. As soon as it was purchased, he or she would send a text to the other. The receiver would memorize the new number but never write it down. They would set up times to talk.

Each time the new phone was purchased, the old one was to be beaten to smithereens with a blunt instrument. Ironically, she had kept a hammer at her house until Durham was murdered. Then it went into a dumpster a couple miles from her house. Even though it wasn't the murder weapon, it felt like bad luck. Now she needed to figure out what to destroy a phone with.

31

"Penny Martin, you are under arrest," I say clearly. "You have the right to remain silent. Anything you say or do can and will be held against you in a court of law. You have the right to speak to an attorney. If you cannot afford an attorney, one will be appointed for you. Do you understand these rights?"

"I will only say one thing before my attorney is present," she says.

We wait.

"You are making a big mistake. I did not kill Jack Durham."

"Good," I say. "You are innocent until proven guilty, so prove to us you are innocent."

She says nothing, just gives a blank stare and then holds her arms out to us, wrists together, offering them to be cuffed.

"We need your hands behind your back," Don says, starting to move behind her. She holds a hand up for him to stop and turns around, putting her hands behind her back. Don snaps the cuffs on her gently. She turns back around and stares at me. I can't read the expression on her face. She might have a *Mona Lisa* half smile going on me. But then I see the cloud and mist form. She holds the stare.

Don and I step back. A female uniform, Madison Lopez, steps forward and leads her out the door of her condo by the elbow. This arrest won't stay a secret very long.

The plan is to use the service elevator, get her out the back door, and drive her in a squad car to booking at the Second. There are five of us from CPD, counting Lopez. The low number was intentional to not draw attention; the media interest has intensified lately, despite no progress to report. Don and I will follow the black-and-white with Officers Anderson and King up front and Martin in the caged backseat. Lopez will jump in the backseat of the blue Chevy Malibu we are driving today.

It's a beautiful Sunday morning. The wind off the lake is refreshing—slightly cool and gentle, not the gusts that buffet you around and wear you out. This morning I drove to the precinct with my convertible roof down. It was cold on Lake Shore Drive but still felt wonderful.

Blackshear and Konkade had made calls Saturday afternoon to get us at the Second that evening for a rare weekend meeting. Martinez was wearing enough cologne to offset a herd of rabid skunks. He sulked and complained about the damage this was causing to his love life. "*¿Por qué nadie se preocupa por mi vida amorosa?*" he asked enough times to be my Spanish pronunciation coach.

We only met an hour. The arrest warrant was being circulated to various departments for review before being couriered to a judge's home to be signed. Not sure we needed to gather for that bit of information. But Blackshear wanted to make sure everyone on the direct investigation team was still on board with the arrest.

"Everyone in the office by seven a.m. sharp," he said. "We need to beat the press out of bed."

I might have grumbled alongside Antonio on that one.

The elevator ride is uneventful. I look at Penny out of the corner of my eye. She is stunningly beautiful—even in the morning with no makeup time. She was asleep when we got there. We gave her time to put on a pair of capri pants and button-up sweater top. She had to change in front of Lopez and me. Procedure didn't even allow her to go to the bathroom by herself. Lopez went in with her.

We exit the elevator and walk down a concrete service hallway that is quiet except for the clomp of our shoes that echoes off the walls. We open the back door. Busted. The full media swarm that covers big Chicago news stories hasn't arrived, but we are ambushed by three video cameras and at least fifteen reporters with mikes or recorders stuck in our direction. The yelling has begun.

Nothing went out over CPD channels so someone inside our department leaked the impending arrest to a contact or two. What is with some people? Isn't the job hard enough as it is? As cynical as I am, I am equally naïve enough not to know who is a dirty cop and who is a righteous cop. Everyone looks the same to me.

"Why did you kill Jack Durham?" the first voice calls out to Penny. It's followed by a cacophony of questions:

"How many times did you hit him with a hammer?"

"Did he attack you first?"

"How much money did you extort from him?"

"Why did you do it?"

"Did you have an accomplice?"

"Is it true you are pregnant?"

If that guy jabs me with a recorder one more time he's going to learn the meaning of police brutality.

We wade through the small throng that is growing by the second. Officers Anderson and King move toward us from the opposite direction, slowly and forcefully parting the sea that will soon be overflowing. They meet us in the middle and flank Lopez and Martin. We obviously don't have a big enough force to handle this smoothly.

I notice Anderson is getting irritated and he has the arms to send people flying. He's showing restraint but better be careful or someone will accuse him of excessive force. I know from experience that isn't a good thing to happen.

I look at the parking lot and more cars are zipping up to us. We need to get Penny in that car and out of here. Men and women with cameras and recorders are slamming gear shifts into Park before they're even at a complete stop.

Don moves out front and does some lead blocking to get Martin into the black-and-white. She's tucked into the backseat quickly. Lopez leans in and puts a seat belt on her, then hustles over to our car and jumps in the backseat. Don has driving duties. (He got there first.) The media mob has now doubled in size in less than two minutes. Don is already nosing forward before I am all the way in the passenger seat and have the door shut.

"If we aren't out of this parking lot in thirty seconds we're going to have to call in backup for traffic duty to get us out," he says through clenched teeth. "Who tips the media off anyway? We only got the final green light from the DA an hour ago."

"I'd like to know," I respond. "I'm tired of everyone looking at me like I did it just because my sister works for WCI."

"Come to think of it, you did take a long bathroom break before we left," he says.

I give him a dirty look and he smiles. He didn't even have to turn his head to know what my response would be.

We're tailing the squad car by three feet.

Anderson has finally inched free of shouting reporters that surrounded the cruiser and guns it forward. Four seconds later Don clears the mob and follows suit. We race to the front of the building and turn onto the main drive, to the safety of the street. No one else is exiting, but there is a long line of cars with their right blinkers on to pull into the parking lot. Too late.

It's good to drive against rush hour. I crane my neck and look back—a train of cars is trying to exit the parking lot to chase us. I'm sure they're calling their stations and periodicals to make sure we have a welcoming committee awaiting us.

We turn on Kedzie and complete our escape. Even if there is a herd of reporters awaiting us there we have sufficient troops for easy mob control. The press can make the Occupy Wall Street protesters we had in Grant Park feel like a pack of Girl Scouts. The good thing is even if we don't outnumber them at the precinct, we still have more weapons.

"Well, you were right, KC. You suspected her from the start."

"Everyone suspected her from day one, and my name is Kristen or Detective Conner to you."

He laughs. I look in the backseat. Lopez is stoic.

"How you doing?" I ask.

"Not bad at all. You're the one that busted up the Cutter Shark, aren't you?"

"I am."

"Nice work. I'm hoping I can get my gold shield one of these years and join you on the detective squad."

"I hope it works out."

My phone pings. I swipe it but don't get it right and have to try it three more times. My decision to join a couple billion of my best friends and buy an iPhone is the equivalent of buying my mom a Maserati Diablo. It's shiny and has lots of features, but the operator doesn't know how to fully use them yet.

On the fourth swipe I get the arrow to slide from left to right and turn on the screen. I jab the green bubble showing I have a text.

I can't stop thinking about you.

As before, the number is blocked. Strange. Of course. Derrick? Why me? I sincerely hope someone is sending a text to the wrong number, but I suspect I'm not going to be so lucky. It is definitely possible someone from Homicide is playing a joke on me because of my short-lived dating assignment. Don will give me a hard time but wouldn't go to that much trouble. Not sure who else would either. I suspected Zaworski's assistant, Shelly, was putting yellow Post-it Notes in my cubicle during my last case. But he read the riot act to her and everyone else that he wouldn't put up with such nonsense. I don't know what this is about.

I look back at Lopez. She's back to being stoic.

We get Martin into Booking through the back parking lot. I called ahead to let Konkade know what was going on. He organized a small battalion of uniforms to control media traffic and get us in the building unimpeded.

I'm looking at eggs, bacon, sausage, and a stack of three pancakes smothered in butter and syrup. Six of us have headed to Orange on North Clark for breakfast. Blackshear and Konkade will go back to the precinct and work with the DA's office to supervise the questioning of Martin.

Four of us get to go home and catch some sleep. The temporary boss's orders.

"Nice job, Bob," Don says.

"I didn't do much. It was a team effort."

"I can't believe this thing is already over," I say. "Seems like we just got started."

"We done *muy bien*," Martinez says.

"*Muy*," Don agrees. "And don't forget the Financial Forensics team. Tedford was a stud."

"No doubt," I agree. "We should think of them more than we do."

"Agreed," Don says and everyone nods.

"Any word on Zaworski?" I ask. "Someone needs to let him know we closed it."

"Already done," Konkade says. "I'm going to

stop by and visit him tonight. He's home now."

"How'd surgery go?" Don asks.

"My lips are sealed per the captain's orders," Konkade says.

"Can you give a clue?" Martinez asks.

"I think I can say that prayers and good wishes are still welcome, and anything that's been sent out previously seems to have helped."

"Good," Blackshear says.

We all nod. But the mood at the table has definitely turned somber.

It's almost noon. I'm not going over to Jimmy and Kaylen's for Sunday dinner. I'm going home and taking a long nap. Bears play the 49ers at three. I'll try to wake up to watch the game then.

I can still see Penny holding out her wrists to be handcuffed. A lot happened while I was at the fundraising dinner for the president's reelection. Enough that we busted her.

So why do I feel uneasy?

32

"What have we got?" Don asks.

"Not sure you want to know," the crime scene officer answers. The three of us are about twenty feet inside the perimeter he and first responders have established at the scene of a crime.

"That bad?"

"Real bad."

His badge says *O'Donnell*. He is maybe thirty. Young enough to look shook up over a murder scene. But old enough that he should have seen about everything we have to see by now. If he says it's real bad then it is.

"Twelve-year-old kid."

"Oh, dear God," I say.

"It's about to get worse," O'Donnell says, clearing his throat. "Black kid took a shortcut through the wrong neighborhood. Five Latino kids knocked him off his bike and kicked him to death."

"We know it was other kids?" I ask, bile rising in my throat.

"Yeah. We got three witnesses. We've got 'em inside the church for now," he says, pointing to an art-deco structure that is still impressive even if it has seen better days. The front steps have been patched but are crumbling. Street-level windows are protected with wrought-iron grills that are rusting where the bolts attach to the building. The front is dark gray with black streaks from years of smog and dirt. It probably hasn't been sand-blasted in twenty years. Heck, maybe never. It probably used to be almost white.

The twisted wreck of a cheap bicycle is sprawled by the front door. An EMT van is parked in the middle of the street. A small array of medical and forensic techies have formed a circle and are working like ants carrying crumbs to the opening of an anthill.

If the witnesses are right, kids beat a kid and left him for dead in front of Peace Lutheran Church. I'm too numb to let myself speak the irony of the name, even inside my head.

The three of us walk over to the hub of activity. O'Donnell nods at another uniformed officer who steps forward. I know him. Chuck Gibson. A sergeant, I think. He's got to be around sixty, about the same age my dad would be if he were alive. Gibson worked the Gigi Baker house when I was on the Cutter Shark case.

"Hey, Conner," he says. "And—"

"Squires. Don Squires," my partner says, holding out a paw for a handshake.

"Youse two wanna take a look, I suppose," Gibson says.

"Doesn't sound like we want to," Don says, "but yeah, we better take a look."

Gibson pushes back a sawhorse barricade and we enter the inner sanctum.

"Hey, make some room and let the detectives have a look," he shouts.

Three techies are conferring next to a body covered by a weather tarp. They seem to be comparing notes taken on clipboards. A white-haired gentleman nods to the youngest, who turns to us and gives a hand motion for us to come closer. He doesn't say anything, just kneels down beside the body and draws back the tarp.

Oh, God.

His head is turned at an awkward angle that can only mean his neck was broken. What once might have been a handsome face or an ugly face or a sweet face is bloody purple pulp. His shirt has been cut away. His arms and chest have been savagely kicked as well. One of his ribs pokes from the skin on his side.

"What do we need to hear that we aren't going to read in the reports?" Don asks.

His voice is strained. His eyes have misted over. He might be fighting back a tear. Don has a son. I think Devon is nine or ten. Close enough in age to make the broken body in front of us even more visceral.

The young man straightens up and looks at the white-haired gentleman.

"I'm Lou Fazzoli with the medical examiner's office," he says. "This is my assistant, Kenny

Smith, and April Collins is interning with us from UICCC."

"Kristen Conner," I say with a nod.

"Don Squires." Ditto on the nod.

April Collins is an almost Goth holdover. Jet-black hair. Black nails. Tongue stud. A green dragon tattoo is climbing out of her black shirt and onto her neck. She is pale white. No sun for her. Why do I suspect she read the Stieg Larsson novel or at least saw the movie?

"You two worked the Cutter Shark case, didn't you?" Fazzoli says.

"KC was the hero," Gibson interjects. "She's Mikey Conner's kid. Remember Mikey?"

Mikey? Never heard my dad called Mikey.

"Of course I do," Fazzoli says crossing himself. "Good man. Good cop. And it appears the nut doesn't fall too far from the tree. So that was you that gave that whack job a beat down. I'm impressed, KC."

I hate the nickname KC. I have fought it since grade school. About the time I think I have eradicated it once and for all, it pops back up.

We need to cut the chitchat and look at the body. Fazzoli has been on the job long enough to compartmentalize. All business one minute, *Hey, how is the family?* the next.

"What do we need to know?" Don asks, getting us back on track.

"You're going to get a lot more details from

232

us," Fazzoli says. "We'll tell you how many times he got kicked. We can tell you what blow caused the most damage. But you aren't going to learn anything you don't see with your own eyes. Bad case. Bad. I'm an old geezer and this is as bad as it gets.

"Kid gets pushed sideways right by the curb over there," he says, pointing. "Looks like his attackers were running at him from the other side of the street. We got a lot of cigarette butts and a few blunts over there, so we think they were in the recessed doorway. I'm no detective, but the kid on the bike was probably pedaling as hard as he could and got the bike as close to the curb away from his pursuers as he could. He got flung on the sidewalk a couple feet farther than the bike landed."

"We moved the bike," Gibson interjects. "But we have all the photos to document forensics reports."

"If you look at his right arm closely, you can see it's broken," Fazzoli continues. "Compound fracture. Might be from the fall. Might be from a kick."

"Any ID? We have a name?" I ask.

"No ID, but one of the witnesses thinks she knows the kid," Gibson says. "We've sent a detail over to find a family member and confirm."

"Kids killing kids. What is that about?" April has spoken up. Good for her. But she isn't going to like the answer.

"We're on a dividing line between neighbor-hoods," says Don. "And gangs have staked territories based on race. Blacks don't cross the street and go south. The Hispanics don't cross it and go north."

"But he was on the dividing street," she protests, as if that might change something.

"Might have cut through the alley down there," says Gibson, pointing. "A lot of times no one bothers with turf if it's a kid. But sometimes they do. If I was a betting man I'd say the kids who did this are junior members of Diablos Santos. If youse take someone out, even if it's a kid your age, you're a lot closer to becoming a full member."

April looks like she is going to be sick. Maybe it's her preternaturally white skin and she has a nutritional deficiency. Maybe I'm projecting. I feel sick to my stomach too.

"Noooooo! Not my baby!"

A scream pierces the air and drives like an arrow into the core of my belly.

Two police officers, one female and one male, flank a young woman who doesn't look old enough to be a mother but probably is. She breaks free of their grasp. Gibson steps in front of her as she races toward the broken body. He looks to Fazzoli.

"We got what we need. Let her."

Gibson releases her and then holds her

shoulders from behind to steady her as she begins to wobble. She sinks on all fours. Her face is inches from her son. All crime scene activity has stopped. I think the world has stopped. Her head is rotating slightly. She is looking for a sign of life. Any sign. Her eyes are wide open. She is willing her son to open his. Her lips are moving quickly and silently. I think she is praying.

She looks heavenward. Her eyes clench shut tightly. The night is shrouded in an eerie silence. I realize I am holding my breath and make myself breathe in and out.

I kneel down next to her and put a hand on her shoulder. I hear the softest purr coming from somewhere deep inside of her. Her head arches back fully. Her eyes are still shut. A wail rises from her chest and goes straight to the gates of heaven.

"Noooooooooooo."

She lifts off her hands and turns to me and clutches me ferociously. Her nails dig into the back of my shoulders as her scream continues to pierce the silence. Then her head drops on my shoulder and she begins to sob. I feel her shoulders shake and heave. She is purring again. Faintly I can hear her voice between the sobs. "No, God, no, God, no, God, no, God. Not my baby. Not my baby."

I will not forget this moment for as long as I live.

●●●

I sit listlessly on my couch in the dark. I've been back in Chicago two weeks. Two mothers have lost sons. One was a lost soul; the other was full of promise. Doesn't seem to matter. If you brought a child into the world, how do you cope with the gaping wound in your heart?

I want to be a mother someday. But looking at the broken body of Keshan makes you think.

Dear God, why?

I stare at the blank screen of my television.

33

"You're quiet today," Mom says, leaning over her plate and looking down the table past James and Kendra at me.

We always sit in the same seats. Jimmy gets head of the table. Mom to his left, Kaylen to his right. Klarissa sits to Kaylen's right. Kendra and then James are to the left of Mom. I am the only one who doesn't rule from the head of the table or have someone sitting across from me—unless there is a guest or two. No guests today, so I am not face-to-face with anyone. Suppose they are trying to tell me something?

"Tough week," I answer. "Except for yesterday's soccer game with Kendra."

"My team won too!" five-year-old James

shouts. I think NASA satellites are scanning Chicagoland for earthquake activity after that outburst. Jimmy gives him the parental dirty look—a little judgmental if you ask me—and James immediately returns to his mashed potatoes.

I get lost in the shuffle myself, so I understand wanting attention, James.

"I was at your game, King James, and you were incredible."

He smiles sweetly and then opens his mouth as wide as he can so I can see his mashed-up mashed potatoes. *That's my King James.*

They don't keep score at games for five-year-olds—even though most parents and coaches know exactly what the score is. But by my count, James' team lost about 12-1. It's possible I blocked a few extra goals for the other team out of my mind. But even in loss, James truly was incredible. Just not at soccer. He pushed and shoved. He tackled. He laughed. He cried once. *Big baby.* He even missed scoring three feet away from an open goal. He kicked at the ball hard. He just didn't make contact with it. He ended up on his backside. But the kid bounced right back up and pumped his arms like he got the game winner for the USA in the World Cup.

Your resiliency will take you far, young man.

Age five is too young to separate sheep and goats in sports and life, but there will come a day down the road when I suspect King James will make the switch to American football or something else that requires a spirit of reckless mayhem and not necessarily fine motor skills. His dad is a great guy. I love my brother-in-law. But Jimmy doesn't have a clue about sports. Yours truly will have to break it to him and Kaylen.

I smile at the thought. It is my first smile since I held Keshan's mother in my arms.

I look at Princess Kendra and King James, then down at my sister, their mommy. Kaylen is almost full term with Baby Kelsey. What would I feel, what would I do, if something ever happened to my angels? I shudder.

I look up. Everyone is staring at me expectantly. "Huh?"

"Where's your mind, big sis?" Klarissa asks me. "I just said this should be a good week. You arrested the Durham killer. That's a good thing. You're still Chicago's hottest female crime fighter. I saw you on a date with one of Chicago's wealthiest bachelors. I might be jealous."

"You had a date?" Mom asks.

She didn't have to sound so surprised.

"We arrested the killer but Durham is still dead," I say to Klarissa. "And you already know I didn't have a real date."

That lightens the mood of the table. *Not.* I have a gift.

"You've got a tough job, Kristen," Kaylen says.

"I don't know how you do it. I don't know how Dad did it either."

"You still have to feel at least a little good to wrap up a case and put away a killer—don't you?" Klarissa asks.

Of course I do. Penny Martin is the murderer, after all. Isn't she?

"It does," I answer. "My mind is just wandering. I'm already working another case. Kid got killed. This one punches you in the gut a lot more than Durham."

"What happened?" Jimmy asks.

"I really can't say right now."

"No leads?"

"No, we have plenty of leads and the killers have been taken into custody."

"More than one person killed a twelve-year-old?" he says with surprise.

"We're running with it tonight," Klarissa says, looking troubled. "I didn't know you were working that one. I have to say it does sound awful with kids killing kids."

"Kids present," Kaylen says with a cough and stern look.

"What happened, Aunt Kristen?" Kendra asks innocently.

Too innocently to understand and tell.

"I'll tell you a little bit about it later," I tell her with a hug.

"Me too!" James declares.

"Inside voice," Kaylen says to him.

That gives Jimmy opportunity to change the direction of the conversation.

"How about the Bears? Still undefeated. Can't believe they beat San Francisco in San Francisco last week."

Jimmy doesn't know squat about sports, but he is Chicago born and bred. When in doubt and there's a pregnant pause in the air, all you have to say is, "How's 'bout da Bears" or "dem Cubbies" and the world is set right. Doesn't matter if they are winning or losing. They are yours; you are them. I think Chicago is unique in that we are just as happy losing as winning. Either way, we have something to talk about other than taxes and murder. That's not such a bad thing.

My media-star sister has a good heart. Doesn't mean Keshan's mother has crossed her mind or will ever be the real story on a WCI-TV news report. The media has dealt with the story politically and sensationally—but no one has touched the reality of a grieving mother.

Durham was despicable. Immoral. Amoral. Cruel. Unfeeling. Boring except for his money and outrageous lifestyle. But he's still a feature on the news every night.

"You okay, little sis?" Kaylen asks.

I'm getting ready to hop in my fifteen-year-old Mazda Miata.

"I'm okay."

"You don't look okay," Kaylen says.

Klarissa left thirty minutes ago. She's on air tonight. Mom just left to head back for church. It's missionary night and she's our church's missionary president. That means I'm supposed to be there at six o'clock to hear a doctor who works in an AIDS clinic in Zimbabwe. I know that's important and I should be there to support him—and Mom. I just want to stay home and do a mind- and soul-cleaning workout. My apartment could use some cleaning too. I didn't have time or motivation to vacuum or dust all week. I could clean, put a load in the washer, then run the steps at the Van Buren High School football stadium.

"I'm okay."

Even as I numbly say the words I hear Keshan's mother's screech. I feel her fingernails dig into my shoulders. I see her face. Confusion. Rage. Abject sorrow. Back to rage and sorrow again. Then emptiness.

"I'm okay, Kaylen. It's just what I said—a little kid got killed. Murdered. It's not so easy to put this one out of mind. Don't ask me how I'm doing again. Just give me a hug."

She gives me the best hug she can manage in her current condition. I'm no expert, but I bet she's put on thirty-five pounds and is carrying a nine-plus-pound baby. Maybe another soccer player for Aunt Kristen. I'm the one who usually pulls away from contact. But I squeeze her as hard as I dare with what she has situated in front of her.

"I'm gonna roll," I say.

"You coming tonight? It'll be good."

"I can't do it, Kaylen. Cover for me with Mom if you can."

"No problem," she laughs as she bends over and hugs my neck one more time.

I hope maybe having the convertible top down will blow away the funk I'm in. But it's there the whole drive home. I get some dust in my eyes and they tear up a little. But I don't cry.

34

It's nine o'clock. We're halfway through fall but it's raining like an April shower. No running the stadium steps. Didn't feel like driving over to the 24/7 fitness center where I have a membership either. But I wanted a good workout.

I've got Journey's greatest-hits album on too loud. The old guy that lives below me will hit his ceiling with a broomstick if I'm interrupting whatever it is he does, but I need some energy and will risk it. I've done fifty lunges with a thirty-pound barbell in each hand. I held a facedown plank for five minutes, long enough to hear all five minutes and two seconds of "Who's Crying Now." I can go longer but let's face it: planks are boring. And the song was over.

I then grabbed two twelve-pound weighted gloves and punched air for five minutes and twenty-six seconds. My arms were complaining the whole last minute of "Separate Ways." I moved to the light jump rope for both "Lights" and "Lovin', Touchin', Squeezin'." Big hits, but not my favorite Journey songs.

Steve Perry is almost done singing "Open Arms" (I always thought it was a little sappy but hard not to sing along with) and I'm counting out the push-ups. I'm determined to hit fifty. I ran through the first twenty-five fast and easy. The next ten were slow and hard. Now my arms are shaking as I count forty-one.

I hear a knock on my apartment door. That's strange. I next to never have company. Most of my socializing centers around family and church, so I have a steady stream of invites but don't do a lot of inviting and entertaining. Maybe the old guy below couldn't find his broom.

I'm not going to admit I wasn't going to make it to fifty as I stand up from my exercise mat. I have on compression shorts and a sports bra. My hair is pulled back in a ponytail. I am soaked in sweat. Not sure I want to see anyone or be seen by anyone. All I want to do tonight is take a thirty-minute shower and watch some TV or read a book.

I twist the volume knob to low, pad past my eating area and the opening to my kitchen, and down my short entrance hall to the front door. The security chain is on. I look out the peephole. It's Barbara Ferguson. She looks like a drowned rat. Not as bad as me, but bad for her.

I slide the chain, turn the dead bolt, and open the door. We just look at each other for a couple of seconds.

"You going to invite me in?"

"Wasn't planning to."

Her eyes narrow and she cocks her head. I laugh.

"Come on in and look around while I get a shower. Not quite as nice as your place."

She doesn't bother to disagree.

I've got a towel wrapped around my hair. I have on an NIU sweatshirt and some comfy plaid flannel pajama bottoms. Bobbie is sitting on my couch sipping a cup of hot chocolate.

"You got anything stronger I can put in here?" she asks.

"Nope."

"I suspected not," she says. "So this is *Chez* Kristen?"

"Impressive, huh?"

"Not exactly the word that came to mind."

I raise an eyebrow.

"No offense meant."

"You sure?" I ask.

"Positive. I like it. It suits you. Austere. Simple. But the quality looks good."

"Single white female with not too many expenses. So I've spent a little on my furniture."

"But not on your TV," she says with a laugh. "Anyone tell you about hi-definition and flat-screen technology?"

"Yeah, it's a monstrosity," I respond. "But it's got sentimental value, even if the picture isn't crystal clear."

I brought it over from the basement of my parents' house. It was what Dad watched in his man cave, which was a beat-up desk and couch on a tattered green piece of carpet in the basement.

"But you didn't come over to look at my style sense. I knew you probably missed me since I got busted on my date with Derrick, but I thought you might hold out another week. What's up, Bobbie?"

She looks at me, then closes her eyes. Her lips open to speak, then close again.

My partner claims that no one can do the awkward pause as well as me. It's a great interview technique. Stumble around and look down at your notes like you've forgotten what you were going to say. People are helpful so they say things they wouldn't normally say to fill in the awkward space you've created. I doubt it would work on Bobbie, but there's a time to nudge and push the conversation along. There are also times you let it move on its own pace. This is that time.

I can hear the Seth Thomas antique windup clock on my dresser in the next room tick-tocking away. My kitchen sink has a drip if I don't push the lever down just right. I obviously didn't push it down just right. The fragrance from my green tea tree shampoo permeates the room.

Bobbie finally looks up.

"There's something I should have told you."

"Okay," I say insightfully.

"Your captain okay?"

She's stalling.

"As of Friday he's doing much better."

Another pause. Long enough that I take her cup and pour more hot chocolate into it. I fill my mug up with coffee. I walk over to my stereo system —about the same vintage as my TV—and click the source button until it is on the CD player. There's an old Warren Hill album in the first slot. Great tenor sax player. I saw him in concert on campus when I was at Northern Illinois. Not sure what happened to him. *Truth* is one of his first albums and my favorite. The first song is "Tell Me All Your Secrets." That's a nice coincidence.

C'mon Bobbie. I'm tired. Tell me all your secrets.

A tear runs down her cheek as she starts to speak.

35

"No way. Unbelievable. Tell me you're making this up," Sergeant Konkade says.

"*Qué clase de madre le haría eso a su hija?*" Martinez adds.

We're back in the conference room. The usual suspects. Blackshear and Konkade, Randall and Martinez, Squires and Conner. Zaworski is on the speakerphone. He doesn't sound like the captain I know. I fear someone has kidnapped him. The kidnapper must have a gun pointed at him and has given him orders to be very polite and never interrupt.

"So Barbara employed her own daughter as an escort?" Zaworski asks.

"It's a little more complicated than that," I answer. "But in a word, yes."

"That changes things. I personally presented terms of agreement to her, and not mentioning that one of her workers was her daughter is covered in the full-disclosure clause. That's material to the contract."

He sounds tired.

"Conner?" Zaworski asks.

"Yes, sir?"

"How do you do it?"

Uh-oh.

"Do what, sir?"

"How do you get the people that open up to you to open up to you? There's been days when I almost put you and Shelly in time-out because you two couldn't play nice together. You push people away from you—and I'm not criticizing you on that; it's not a bad habit for a detective—but then serial killers, raging alcoholics, and madams can't help but tell you every last secret they have."

Now the captain is accusing me of pushing people away? Mr. Congeniality? And I don't remember our serial killer telling me any secrets.

"Sir, I thought you said that the word *madam* is off-limits."

He laughs at that. "Sorry, Conner, I shouldn't have said what I just said. Blame it on the painkillers. If the cancer doesn't kill me, the pain will. And if the pain doesn't do it, the pain-killers will finish me off. Oxycodone is kicking my tail."

"I'm glad you're sounding so much better, sir."

"Yeah, right. You said it's more complicated than a simple yes. I may not have the energy to hear how. And you all seem to have this under control—good work, Blackshear—so I'm not

248

getting involved any further. But humor me and give me a quick summary of how it's complicated. And I mean quick, Conner. I'm fading fast."

I sigh. How do I condense this down?

"Bobbie got pregnant, was going to have an abortion, changed her mind, put the baby up for adoption, used the proceeds to start her business, and tried to never think about her little girl again."

"She sold her baby?" Martinez says with a whistle.

"I don't think she sold her. She put her up for adoption. I assume she isn't the first person to get some financial assistance."

"You're right on that, Conner," Zaworski says. "What else?"

"Penny showed up on her doorstep. Said she wanted a job. Bobbie gave her a job not knowing it was her daughter. I guess Penny had been hunting her down for some time. She wanted to maximize the emotional revenge and she sure knew how to do it. Bobbie had just found out Penny was her daughter a month or so before this Durham business."

"That's what she says," Martinez says righteously. "Not sure I believe anything that comes out of her mouth."

"Where's the father in all this?" Zaworski asks.

That takes me aback. No mention of the father.

"No clue, sir."

"And she talked to you . . . why?"

"She says her daughter is innocent."

"Okay, folks," he says, "I gotta get some sleep. Great work. Blackshear, you're doing good, so don't bother me unless you have a big problem. You have a little problem, you're on your own."

"Yes, sir."

"Konkade?"

"Yes, Captain?"

"Tell Helen the soup tasted great. Made me feel a lot better too."

"I will, Captain."

Konkade obviously married up. She has a drapery business *and* makes tasty soup.

Martinez, Randall, Konkade, Don, and I are chowing down at Costello's Sandwiches and Sides on Roscoe. I took too big of a bite of my pineapple chicken salad sandwich on whole wheat, and my mouth is too full to answer when Don asked me what's wrong with people. Since I'm going to be chewing for a while, he decides to answer his own question.

"This case was already messed up," he says as he daintily wipes a glop of mayonnaise from the corner of his mouth. "But just when you think people can't get any worse, they do. A mother lets

250

a daughter do that? C'mon. This has to be a sign the apocalypse is on us."

He shakes his head.

"*Sí, señor*, you are right. *Esta situación es un lío*," Martinez adds with his mouth still half filled with corned beef on marbled rye. He doesn't finish the bite before shoving the last of his Reuben down the hatch.

"Not sure if this daughter situation changes anything," Konkade adds. "We made a righteous arrest. Penny lied to us about where she was the night Durham was killed. Now we know she was in Durham's neighborhood at the time of the murder. The car park's surveillance camera has her pulling in an hour ahead of the estimated time of death and then back out seventy-three minutes later. She paid with cash, but even the grainy black-and-white pictures show her and her car. If this guy that owns the car park had been forthcoming with the tapes, we would have been done a lot earlier."

"What can you do when people won't cooperate and get the lawyers involved?" Randall asks defensively.

"Not much," Konkade says. "I'm not busting on you, Randall. I've just never seen anything like that delay on a major murder investigation."

Randall's face is working and he is going to say something but I spare him the effort. "But what if Bobbie is right and she's not guilty?"

"You think that's a possibility?" Don asks me. "That girl is cold."

"You're right," I say. "But why not at least pretend to care if she's really guilty?"

"No one here doesn't care," Don shoots back.

"I never trusted her," Martinez says. "But I didn't think she was the murderer. Just goes to show that women like that are tricky."

"I don't know if she was trying to be tricky," I answer, "but what threw you off, Antonio, was her legs."

"*Unas piernas muy bonitas*," Martinez says.

Konkade ignores us. Then he blurts out, "She's not innocent of killing Durham. Because we're eating lunch, I hate to remind you, but she vomited on the crime scene. It all matches up, Jerome said."

"I just know Bobbie is convinced Penny is innocent," I say.

"Good," Don says. "She's finally acting like a decent mother."

"What I still can't believe," Konkade says, "is her mom was supposed to be helping us catch a killer but had zero ideas on who might have done the deed. But as soon as her daughter gets arrested she suddenly has a couple ideas on who might have killed Durham. Maybe the brother because they didn't get along. Maybe Janzen because Janzen was jealous of Durham. Maybe Granger because Jack cheated him out of money."

"Does sound a little desperate," Randall says.

"She isn't going to persuade anyone that the real killer is still out there," Konkade says. "Most of all the district attorney. I was in the meeting with her and Blackshear. No way is the prosecutor letting us open this thing back up. She's got her motive and means. The surveillance camera is icing on the cake. Penny's alibi is out the window. That girl is going down for this."

"I hope she did it, then," I say.

"Like I said," Don jumps in, "what's not to like? She did it, KC. Don't let your mind start working on something that is plain as day."

I give Don a dirty look.

"The only thing Ferguson did by talking to you," Konkade says, "is jeopardize the conditional immunity she got for cooperating in the investigation. Zaworski said we have too much on our plates and not to do anything yet, but you can bet he'll meet with Legal when he's back in the office. But Kristen, you worked with Ferguson and know what she is. You've never been a Ferguson fan. Don't let her play with your mind now."

We make eye contact and I give him a scowl.

"Just saying," he says and looks down to find the last bite of his sandwich.

I'm the last one eating and I've lost my appetite with half a sandwich to go. Not like me—but I now have dinner. Don was right. This case was messed up from the start. But it looks like we have the thing wrapped up tight. I'm not sure what's bothering me. I don't like Penny or Bobbie. I'm not predisposed to defend them. But something is nagging at the back of my mind.

I flash back to a sleepover when I was in seventh or eighth grade. One of my soccer team friends had us all over for a birthday party. She put on a horror movie called *Candyman*. I doubt it would be considered scary by today's standards, but that movie creeped me out and stayed in my mind for months. Finding out that Bobbie let her daughter work for her definitely creeps me out—no matter that she didn't know Penny was her daughter when she hired her. I think this case is going to stay in my mind for months.

That and the Keshan Brown murder.

"Who's questioning Bobbie?" I ask.

"The DA sent his staff over," Randall answers quickly. "I think Flannigan is the one who is going to prosecute this. Stan Jacobs was there too. I know him from when he was a detective in the Fourth and doing law school at night. He's good."

"Good," Don says, looking at me pointedly. "That means we have nothing to worry about."

"I don't think Flannigan has ever lost a case," Konkade says. "She's smart."

"If you haven't lost a case it means you've done

a lot of plea deals and don't overcharge," Randall says. "No one can stay undefeated in our judicial system otherwise."

"True," Konkade says. "But I bet she goes for murder one with all we gave her."

"Some defense lawyer is going to argue that no one whacks someone in the head with a hammer seventeen times based on premeditation," Don says. "Murder two can still get her life, so that may be the smarter way to go."

"She'll get a conviction either way," Randall says. "The sergeant is right. Flannigan's that good."

"Sounds like my *amigo* has a crush on the DA. Is she married?"

Randall reddens. He plows on. "And with that scummy crowd Martin ran with, her attorney is going to have a hard time getting a jury to feel sorry for her."

"Good point," says Don. "So is she married?"

Randall waves him off.

It is a good point. So why do I feel sorry for her? And Bobbie? And why did Gretchen have to tell me Randall got looked at by IA on his finances? I don't want to work with a guy I have questions about.

"Go over your paperwork, folks," Konkade advises. "Investigation may be done, but you're going to be working your tails off for Flannigan while she builds her case."

Konkade is the epitome of a good manager. He knows how to get things done and make everyone play nicely together. I have a lot of respect for him. He usually eats lunch in his office. I wonder if Zaworski (the two are even tighter than I thought if Helen Konkade is making soup for him) told him to eat with the troops to make sure we're on task—and to make sure I don't try to take off down a rabbit trail. I think he trusts Blackshear, but it doesn't mean he doesn't have his eyes open, despite his protestations that he isn't getting involved.

I know they're right. We have an ironclad case. So why is my mind still roiling with the thought that something isn't right with Penny as the murderer?

I drive the Ford, today's American-made ride, back over to the precinct. I got to the driver's door first. Don didn't have anything smart to say; he just handed me the keys. He's quiet. He's brooding over something too. It's contagious.

"What's up, partner?" I ask, a couple blocks from the parking lot.

He doesn't answer.

"What gives?"

"Did you know I have a sister?" he asks me.

I know he's got a brother who's an attorney or something big out in Southern California. I've never heard anything about a sister. Should I know that? Has he said something when I wasn't paying attention? Klarissa and Mom claim I don't always listen very well—especially for someone who's a detective.

"Don't know how I missed that," I say.

I start to feel guilty. Maybe Mom is right.

"You didn't miss anything."

Okay. I wait him out.

"She was a beautiful girl."

Was? "Did she pass away?"

"Nope. She's alive."

"Where does she live?"

"Chicago."

I have no clue where this is going. I decide to keep my mouth shut. That's about the only time I never go wrong.

"You know Vanessa wants me to quit CPD. After our Dean Woods case I gave it serious thought. Heck, Vanessa is making so much money with her real estate, I don't even have to work. She's wanted me to work with her—but her real motivation is she wants me to stop being a cop. Makes her nervous. She wouldn't care if I decided to be a stay-at-home dad. I could coach Devon in football like I always wanted and she would love that too. Wouldn't matter if I made money doing it."

What's he trying to tell me?

"While you were in the hospital with your sister, Zaworski didn't give us much of anything to work on the first week after we arrested Woods. You know I still feel guilty it was you that got messed up by him in the takedown. I'd have given anything to be the one in the hospital."

"I hope you're joking, partner."

"I'm not. But that's not where I was going with all of this. I think he wanted everyone to have a little breathing room after chasing that nut job for six months. So I did some soul searching. Why did I join the CPD? I was a business major at Ball State. My brother, Rodney, was already making good money as an ambulance chaser in LA and said he'd foot the bill for me to go to law school. Not at Northwestern or University of Chicago—but about anywhere else I wanted to go that didn't cost a fortune. I knew I didn't want to get into personal injury, but he said I could open up any area of law I wanted to. We would be Squires and Squires."

"Your brother does personal injury?"

"Oh, yeah. He's on billboards and does late-night commercials. He's a big shot in LA."

I've parked and turned off the engine. We just sit there. This isn't about his brother or Vanessa. He has a sister he has never mentioned in more than two years of partnering with me.

"I finally figured out why I became a cop."

Another long pause.

"I wanted to help Debbie."

"Your sister?"

"Yep. My sister."

"What happened with her?"

"Local crack dealer got her hooked and put her on the street to pay for her habit. About killed my parents. About killed all of us. I can't count how many times Rodney and I had her in rehab. She's never made it past a week before she bolts to the street again."

"I'm so sorry, Don."

"Well, fifteen years later I'm still a cop and I haven't been able to help Deb. But I see her from time to time. Take her some groceries. Clean her place up. Invite her to come live with Vanessa and me while she gets things sorted. She's never even set eyes on Devon or Veronika. Can you imagine that? Being so messed up you won't meet your niece and nephew?"

I can't. If I ever cried now would be the time. But I don't.

"When you got back you asked me what made me decide not to leave the force. I know when you say your prayers you don't get to negotiate with God—even if my pastor sometimes suggests otherwise. We go along with him but know better. But I can't get rid of the feeling that if I ever quit trying to put bad people away and save maybe a few good people, all hope for Debbie will be lost. Doesn't make sense. Probably not true. I know in my head I'm trying to cut a deal with God. But I can't shake the feeling. So there you have it. Now you know why I couldn't quit.

"I don't know why I'm telling you all this. I guess finding out Penny was Bobbie's daughter —her flesh and blood—punched me in the stomach and got me thinking about Deb."

Don has a sister.

"And just so you know, I don't want anyone else in the department knowing about this."

Not sure he needed to say that, but I'm not saying anything. He's been a great partner. He's had to listen to all my problems surrounding the shelved investigation of the person who shot my dad in the line of duty. Well, not all my problems with it—I'm the only person in the world that knows some things—but he's heard enough that he knows my every complaint. So I'm just listening.

I forget sometimes that there is plenty of sorrow in the world to go around. I think of Tandi Brown and the death of her son Keshan.

God, thanks that the captain is doing better. I want to put in a good word for Tandi. And Debbie.

Is prayer negotiating? If so, I'm negotiating.

36

"But you aren't looking at what happened last week," Martinez says to Don, jabbing a finger in his direction, then settling back into his seat, arms folded, a blank scowl on his face. He stares at what might be a mildew spot on the ceiling tile—a Rorschach ink spot open to everyone's interpretation.

"Gonzolo was only nineteen and he got a beating by the Black Dragons and is dead. That's bad. But he was a drug dealer and probably a murderer. Him getting knocked off doesn't come close to excusing what those evil little *hombres* did to Keshan. Not close."

"Oh, so now they are evil little *hombres*?" Martinez flares back at Don.

Both have their arms folded now. They won't look at each other. Probably a good thing. We're the police. We keep law and order. Problem is, we are humans. We're black, Hispanic, white, Native American, and everything else.

I should know but don't know if Martinez is from Mexico or Puerto Rico or Barcelona, Spain. I'm pretty sure he's not from Barcelona. Don is black as an Ethiopian prince, which probably isn't too far from where his family tree leads.

The point is, we don't care about color. We just get the job done.

Martinez partnered the first month in the Second with Don and it seems they got along fine. They seem like friends to me. Now things are tense. The whole city is smoldering over race. Nothing new in one of America's most segregated cities, but more in the open at the moment.

Keshan was an innocent black kid who got kicked to death by a pack of Hispanic kids. Could have been the other way around or could have been a Muslim kid from Somalia on either side of the equation. A Jewish kid. A skinhead. A rich kid. Most black murders are by blacks. Ditto Hispanics and whites and I assume Eskimos. Sometimes murder spills over racial lines and that makes things a lot more complicated.

I don't believe these guys are racist. I had a sociology professor at NIU that said everyone is a racist. I guess that's true if being a racist is being aware on a superficial level that others look different from you. But Don and Antonio don't like or dislike people for the color of their skin. Still, the tension between them is palpable right now. Crimes that are race motivated and the subsequent mood of the politicians and media have an incredible impact on the whole community. And we are members too.

I'm a white kid of Irish descent. At least in

name. Put Mom and Dad together and it's the typical American Heinz 57 sauce.

"No point arguing," I say. "Doesn't have anything to do with either of you."

"Yeah, time to get back on task," Blackshear says.

He's been careful to let everyone have their say in his fill-in captaincy, but it's probably time to rein things in.

"I know," Don says, blowing out air in a sigh. "Anyone else notice race things are tenser than usual?"

"I haven't," Randall says.

"That's because you're not black," Don says.

"And you sure aren't brown and beautiful, homey," Martinez adds.

I roll my eyes and laugh. Here we go again. But at least the tension in our circle is broken, even if it's just for a moment.

"Everyone just needs to turn off the news," Konkade says. "I listen to Kristen's sister and I'm convinced I and everyone else on the CPD is a raging racist who creates conditions for a murder like Keshan. This isn't on us," he says. *Kristen's sister? Really?* "We work together. We serve everyone who will be served. We did our job. Period. We got the kids who did the killing. We gathered the evidence. We handed it to the DA. She can sort out the politics. You know what Zaworski would say if he was here—no offense,

Bob," he says, looking at Blackshear. "You're doing great. Making all the right moves."

"And I'm green. So what would Zaworski say?"

He clears his throat and lowers his voice into a deep growl: " 'I don't care if it's an election year. I don't care that Mayor Daniels is retiring and has ordered a moratorium on murder. I don't care about anything but identifying, apprehending, and seeing killers convicted. That is Homicide. You want to do social commentary and figure out how to get people to love each other, go get a job in the media. Better yet, go be a professor at UC. Tell the world what and who is to blame. Homicide is going to stick to finding the person that pulled the trigger. Now get busy, ladies.' That's what he'd say."

We all laugh. Konkade does a decent Zaworski imitation.

"Before we break up for the day and before someone else pulls a trigger," Blackshear says, "I need to mention something."

My mind has gone elsewhere until I hear my name mentioned.

"Sorry, Bob—I mean Captain Blackshear—can you repeat what you just said?"

"Yeah. You and Squires have funeral duty."

37

Blackshear called me into his office after the meeting to tell me he had just been with the DA, Angela Flannigan, and she is very happy with the case we have gathered to charge and convict Penny Martin. He told her about Bobbie's Sunday night visit to my place, letting me know she had information that would point to the real murderer. They talked it through thoroughly and decided that anything she said would be looked at to corroborate what we already know, but that regardless of her visit and whatever we find—unless "absolutely extraordinary"—we won't be reopening the case. He repeated that several times and told me Bobbie had already been interviewed by the DA's office and one of Czaka's lieutenants. He said her testimony was high on drama but low on real facts.

I think he was trying to make a point without saying it for me to back down. *Duh.* But I am a detective and figure things like this out. Eventually. Zaworski would not have been so circumspect.

I suspect Konkade made a beeline to Blackshear's office to let him know I had some doubts about our arrest and might cause some trouble. I like Konkade and his bald dome, but even if I can't prove he gave the temporary boss a heads-up on my uncertainties, I am not very happy with him at the moment.

I wonder if Blackshear considered this a big enough deal to call Zaworski.

Blackshear gave me some more details about the funeral for Keshan Brown and asked me to pass them along to Don. Don and I are to be present as official representatives of Homicide but also interested civilians. We are to get as close to Tandi as we can. We are to project the concern and care of the CPD for all citizens of the city—every race, creed, and color.

Mayor Douglas announced his retirement at the end of August. *Was it because he knew I was flying back from DC?* He will step down in January, when a new mayor will be sworn in. He doesn't want his twenty-four-year tenure remembered for race riots and has ordered Commissioner Fergosi to have blue uniforms and un-uniformed out in force. The line between the black and Hispanic neighborhoods in Garfield Park is being treated like the demilitarized zone between North and South Korea. CPD soldiers are to keep either side from visiting the other. Tensions are seething. The night air has been filled with gunshots—though nobody has taken aim beyond hitting streetlights as of yet. A few television crews and some reporters are set up in front of Prince of Peace for the funeral and have been giving hushed, breathless updates every fifteen minutes whether anything has happened or not. When it gets too quiet, they snag anyone passing by who will stop to ask him or her about the mood of whichever respective neighborhood they represent.

I actually think it's reasonable coverage. I'm surprised and not surprised the story hasn't gained great traction in ratings and greater Chicago interest. I don't know if that's good or sad. On the good side we don't need the racial intensity turned up any higher than it already is along the thin asphalt ribbon separating neighborhoods and gang territories—please, no buses delivering protestors. On the sad side, it's amazing that there isn't outrage for the death of a twelve-year-old of any color at the hands of kids his same age.

My sister Klarissa continues to do a nightly segment on the murder of Jack Durham on WCI-TV. In less than thirty-six hours Mayor Daniels has done not one, but two, press releases and a major press conference on the arrest of Penny Martin. I had the option to stand in a line of law enforcement agents behind him as he spoke. I declined. Blackshear was our sole representative from the Second. Czaka and Fergosi took questions along with the major. I don't like Czaka after what he did to my family, but I have to admit he does a good job in front of the camera. I know he was very unhappy that Zaworski was the man in front of the cameras after the Cutter Shark arrest.

The Gangs division has reported that plans are underfoot in the black community to get revenge. A bounty has been placed on the head of Chico Ramirez, the reputed leader of Diablos Santos. On the Hispanic side of the line, the area alderman is claiming that the CPD has practiced racial profiling that led to the arrest of five boys between the ages of eleven and fourteen. They're not going to be tried as adults despite the cries of outrage from the black community, but if convicted—and they will be—the juvenile home they are sent to won't be a picnic in the park. They'll come out angrier and more violent than they go in.

Don said the Durham murder was a mess from the start. It was. But the Brown murder is beyond a mess. It has enflamed every grievance of our two largest minority communities. Not sure Mayor Daniels is going to sail into the night as peacefully as he hoped.

38

"You don't sound like yourself tonight."

"Because I'm not fighting?"

"Maybe," Reynolds says with a chuckle. "I've usually defended my every word, action, and attitude by this point in the conversation. When you're on a roll, my honor and manhood have been called into question as well."

"Am I that bad?"

"I find you delightful."

"Thank you. But that's not what I asked."

"You're complex."

"I think I'm simple. Life is complex."

"It does take some twists and turns."

"I'm sorry for all the grief I've thrown your way, Austin."

Did I just call him Austin?

"Did you just call me Austin?"

"Maybe."

"All is forgiven."

I got to work early today. No way was I going to be late for the funeral. Don and I pulled out of the parking lot ninety minutes early.

I visited church with Don and Vanessa once. It was a two-and-a-half-hour service. Call me a Philistine, but one hour and fifteen minutes, with a strict ending time of noon, is what I like. I like church. I believe in going to church. I think I'd go to church even if my brother-in-law wasn't a preacher and my mom didn't call me every Saturday night to make sure I didn't have any plans to play hooky. The Methodists and Catholics can take a week or two off without getting in too much trouble. Mom lets me know good Baptists never miss. The emphasis is always on *good,* and I'm not sure I always measure up in her eyes.

We got to Prince of Peace an hour early and were taken into a back room to meet with Keshan's mother, Tandi. She looked calm enough. In fact, too calm. I was pretty certain someone had given her a little blue pill. Or two. She is pretty but looks a little worn to be just thirty. My age. Already the mother of a deceased twelve-year-old son and two younger daughters.

Based on everything we know, Tandi is the perfect mom. No criminal record. Works night shift at a small candy factory. Her mom lives with them and is there at night while the kids sleep and she works. The place is a dump on the outside but not too bad inside. Clean. Organized. Kids go to school every day and get good grades. Keshan was an honor student. He was going to be the first in the family to go to college. He was only in eighth grade but held the dreams of the family, whether he knew it or not.

I can hear Billy Joel singing, "Only the good die young." It's not true, of course, but seems poignant at the moment. *Oh, man. Life is tough.*

The service was scheduled to start at ten. It started at ten-thirty-three, my second hand told me. I look down at my watch again. It is almost one-thirty. I press my hands against my abs so that the police and media outside the church don't hear my stomach growl again. Don gives me a sideways dirty look. *What am I supposed to do?* We've heard from a long line of politicians, ministers, and friends of the family. We sang for an hour. A large woman with an even larger voice sang "His Eye Is on the Sparrow." I've never heard a woman's voice go as low as hers when she ended the song with ". . . and I know He watches me." Mine might have been the only dry eyes in the church. A kid that couldn't have been more than sixteen sang a soulful version of the old Andre Crouch song "Through It All," and I thought the place would erupt. If that doesn't move you, you can't be moved.

After all the speeches were done, Rev. James Wilson Cleveland gave a forty-five-minute sermon on heaven. It was good. He was good. If someone taped the service I'm going to give a copy to Jimmy. Might give him some ideas about moving around and mixing up his tone a little more when he preaches.

Kristen, you are so bad.

I watch as he nods to one of the pallbearers, who steps forward and closes the coffin. The auditorium is silent. A slow murmur begins throughout the congregation and then Tandi bolts to her feet, a look of terror in her eyes as she stares at the coffin lid moving down. Now fully awake after a near stupor throughout the service, she screams with the same soul-piercing wail I heard seven nights ago when I held her against my chest in front of the broken body of her dead son. My impatience evaporates. Even I know that a moment like this takes as long as it needs.

Tandi's friends and family surrounding her in the pew gather as tightly around her as they can. Those closest hug her, and the others reach out and lay hands on her. Her wail has been joined with a chorus of crying, praying, and screaming. I just close my eyes and shake my head back and forth. I pray for a mom who has looked at her son's body for the last time.

After five minutes Rev. Cleveland begins to pray with a humming tone I have never heard before. Sometimes I can make out his words, sometimes I think he is just humming notes and tones. I am looking at him when I see his head jerk up. His eyes narrow as he looks at the back of the church. Then a thousand heads turn. At the very back of the center aisle is a Hispanic man in a black suit. He is being held by two CPD uniforms.

"Let me speak. I pray, let me speak, *señor*," he calls to Wilson.

I think everyone in the church service has collectively held their breath.

"I come in the name of the Lord. Please let me speak," he calls out, his voice rising with urgency.

Heads turn slowly from front to back and to front again.

"Step forward," Cleveland says with a nod. "Let him go," he says, and I can't help but hear a note of hostility toward the police officers. No matter what you do . . . Nah, it's not the time to let my mind go there.

They release him. He squares his shoulders and walks down the center aisle with every eye on him. I look around and see hatred in the eyes of some and curiosity with others. He nods in respect to Cleveland and slowly passes the closed casket. He kisses two of his fingers and touches the casket, then steps up the four risers to the platform and stands next to Cleveland. He nods at the microphone as if to ask permission. Cleveland nods in assent.

"My name is Rodrigo Espinoza. I was born in La Playa Ortes, the Dominican Republic. My family come to this country to flee from the hideous dictatorship of Rafael Trujillo three years after I was born."

No one is stirring. Where is he going with this?

"We came here for a better life. For safety. For prosperity. We did not come here to continue the hatred and violence of my native land."

No one is restless or stirring. Except for me. I've had to go the bathroom for the past hour.

Focus.

"I come before you today because we love one God and one *Jesú Cristo*. We are brothers and sisters in Christ."

He puts his head down and begins to sob. Amazingly, Cleveland puts an arm around him to comfort him. Espinoza raises his head and looks to heaven and then directly at Keshan's mom, Tandi.

"My nephew Tito was one of the boys who have done this evil thing in sight of God and man. I wish to apologize from the deepness of my heart for what my family has done. My heart is broken. My words cannot bring back your son. I don't ask you to forgive me, to forgive us, for what we have done to you. I ask you to pray in your heart that you can forgive us, forgive me someday. I ask everyone here and I will ask everyone where I live to shed no more blood. I don't want my family to cause no more bloodshed.

"My name is Rodrigo Espinoza, born in La Playa Ortes, the Dominican Republic, where the stones of the land still cry out for justice. Sometimes you can't get no justice, so I ask for forgiveness. That is all I came to say."

He turns and embraces Cleveland and begins the slow walk to retrace his steps.

We are in the conference room at the Second. Don has just told everyone what happened at the funeral.

"Rodrigo Espinoza?" Martinez asks again.

"Yes," I answer for Don.

"If he's who I think he is, he's a longtime gangbanger. Drugs and violence. Just like his old man. We need to watch that cat."

"He looked sincere," Don says. "If that was an acting job, he should be nominated for an Academy Award."

"People do change," Blackshear says. "Just not often."

"Well, if that's the Espinoza I think it is and he got religion, then I better start going to mass and confessing my sins more often."

Eight of us sit around the table silently for what feels like five minutes. Konkade smoothes the nonexistent hair on his bald dome. Martinez blows in and out as if he wants to say something but then decides not to. Blackshear picks nothing off his spotless tie. Randall moves a pencil around his knuckles and between his fingers in a practiced routine. I close my eyes and sigh. I look up at the broken tiles of the drop ceiling.

I'm glad Don told the story for us. He's much better at presentations than I am. I'm also a little mad. I know I'm mad because of foolish pride. I still can't fathom what Tandi Brown is feeling right now. But on the way out of Prince of Peace someone spit on me. It took every ounce of self-control I had to keep looking and moving forward. I know who did it and still want to pop him in the mouth.

I pray for a forgiving spirit. I pray that I can keep things in perspective. And I keep my mouth shut.

Yep. Five minutes. I think that's a record for one of our meetings going without a word spoken.

39

"Don't tell me. You're still at the office and you haven't had dinner yet."

"Good guess, Austin."

"Ah, my given name from the lips of Kristen Conner. Music to my ears."

I was actually about to turn off my computer and head home. It's after eight o'clock and between the six hours I spent at the Prince of Peace Church for the funeral, a staff meeting, and rereading my notebook so I could write summary file reports on the Keshan Brown funeral and the time I spent with Bobbie Ferguson, which are past due, I am beat. When the phone chirped I picked it up and swiped the screen without looking to see who was calling. Major Austin Reynolds of the FBI. An ex-boyfriend? Still a person of interest in my seemingly nonexistent love life?

I'm not sure what the three or four meals we had together meant. At least two of them were officially recognized as dates. Then I found out he had an ex-spouse he hadn't mentioned. She was assigned to Chicago to work on the Cutter Shark case as well. I felt betrayed that he didn't give me a heads-up. On the other hand, I made him fight for every inch of ground just to have dinner together. So what did he owe me in terms of his background? Nada.

"I was only partially guessing that you were still at the office. I have my sources, you know."

"You're my favorite stalker."

"There are others?" he asks with mock hurt.

"Come to think of it, there might be one. Either that or someone keeps texting love and yearning to the wrong number."

"You are a magnet, Detective Conner."

"That's what scares me. So what have your sources told you about what's happening with me?"

"I've been told it took you about fifteen minutes back in Chicago to get real busy again with another intense case. So much for your plans to ease back into things."

"Your sources are good . . . or you have me under electronic surveillance?"

"I confess to nothing but would note that electronic surveillance is for sissies. Just don't look behind the potted plant next to Shelly's desk or you'll find my hiding place."

"Now's your chance to clear out. I'm getting ready to water that with the burnt sludge we call coffee here."

"I only tried Homicide's coffee once—and it is toxic. I'm already out the door. But the good news is I'm parked in front of your building and I'm ready to whisk you off for dinner. I'm in the mood for steak and the Morton's on State Avenue has a table with my name on it awaiting us."

"You're in Chicago?"

Duh.

"Indeed. And I'm starved. And more to the point, I'd like to see you."

"I'm not sure I'm dressed for Morton's."

"Two things. First, the lighting is low. Second, you look fabulous whatever you are wearing."

"That means you have to bring me back here to get my car."

"That's not a problem. Or I could drive you home."

"But then I have to take the bus in the morning."

"I can drive you to work too. My day starts late."

"So you're gonna drive me home, go back to wherever you're staying, then come back and get me in the morning."

"If necessary," he says flirtatiously.

"It is. Or would be. Just bring me back here tonight."

"I can't change your mind?"

"Nope. And I wouldn't push it if I was you."

"I somehow knew you were going to say that," he laughs.

"And Austin, if you want to go somewhere quicker and cheaper, that's fine with me too."

"I told you, I'm starving for a Chicago steak."

"You really out front?"

"I am. Would I lie to you?"

No. But you have been known to leave a few details out.

I hang up and power down my computer. I can print my reports in the morning; I need to do a final edit on the Ferguson report. I put things away and lock my desk drawers and file cabinet. Then I unlock the top desk drawer and pull out a compact I keep there and take a quick peek. *Ugh.* I actually did my hair this morning with a soft curl. It's fallen flat. I have dark rings under my eyes. Long day. I have on my best skirt suit. Black of course. White blouse. A string of fake black pearls and matching earrings. All under-stated because of the occasion. Well, it is what it is.

I relock the drawer and exit my cubicle.

Sigh.

Back to the cubicle. I unlock the top drawer yet again and pop a couple of Tic Tacs in my mouth. I'm not going to get close enough to Reynolds to need them, but I've drunk enough bad coffee all day that my breath is close to rivaling my sweat socks after a ten-mile run through the Drake Memorial Forest Preserve. I make fun of Don for keeping a toothbrush in his cubicle. I now wish I shared his meticulous planning.

I lock up and head for the elevator. My phone pings. A text.

I think of you all the time. Every breath you take.

Reynolds, are you messing with me? I'll be there in a second. I look again and see a blocked number same as before. Austin wouldn't joke like this, anyway.

Five minutes ago I was telling Reynolds I might have a real stalker—but not really believing it myself or taking it too seriously. Now I'm wondering if something is going on I should be concerned with. Is this my third or fourth text from an unknown admirer? At least I assume it's an admirer. That might be wishful thinking.

I walk through the nearly deserted downstairs lobby and out the front door. The air is crisp. I think fall is Chicago's best season. I look up and see a full moon above our amber glow of smog.

Reynolds has stepped out of his rental car. A Cadillac, of course. It would be a Mercedes, but the FBI requires their officers to select American-made cars.

He is wearing his Reynolds uniform. Navy suit. White French-cuff shirt with black onyx cuff links. I'm not close enough to verify, but I'm sure his initials are monogrammed on sleeve and chest pocket. Red tie with subtle designs I see as I get closer.

We give each other a quick hug and he places a small kiss on my cheek, as close to the corner of my mouth as you can get without touching it. No doubt, he is a good-looking man.

He walks me around to the passenger door and opens it for me. He doesn't even walk back around until my legs are tucked in and he can shut the door for me. What a gentleman, especially when you consider we were yelling at each other a month or so ago.

I think I like that he yelled back.

I need to shower off the remains of a long day. All I want to do is stumble into my bedroom and fall on my bed and go to sleep. I force myself to spend two minutes under a steaming hot spray of water. Can my teeth wait until morning? I run my tongue over the front of my barnacle-encrusted top teeth. Not a chance. I fire up the Braun after loading it with enough

AquaFresh to caulk a log cabin and let it do its thing.

I put on some face lotion and head to the bedroom. I look at the phone on my nightstand. The red message light is flashing. I should listen, but I'm too tired and ignore it.

Dinner was marvelous. I've never eaten at Morton's. They don't have a printed menu. I thought every restaurant had a menu. The server brought a shiny silver tray with the various cuts of meat that old Mort offers. He also showed us fresh asparagus and a baked potato. Both looked to have been genetically altered to feed a tribe of giants. I wondered if they had an electric chain-saw to cut through the stalks of the asparagus. Ever the delicate fair maiden, I ordered the sixteen-ounce Kansas City strip. The waiter said it was boneless. I hope he was right because I ate everything on my plate. My mom yells at me to not eat fat. I usually don't. And whoever carved the meat didn't leave much around the edges anyway. But that marbling tasted way too good to leave for the garbage disposal.

We split an order of the asparagus with a hollandaise sauce and an order of creamed spinach. I'm not a huge spinach fan but it tasted so good there had to be a lot of unhealthy things in it. Reynolds polished off most of a bottle of red wine over the course of three hours. I sipped San Pellegrino sparkling water with lime squeezed in it and coffee made at the table in a French press. I like my latte or Americano at JavaStar every morning. But I think this was even better—and the office brew just got a little worse.

After his third glass of wine Reynolds explained why he didn't tell me he had been married before when we went out a few times together. I told him he didn't have to explain. But I ended up mentioning that since his ex-wife, an FBI psychological profiler, was also working the case, it might have been nice to get a heads-up. I agreed with him and he agreed with me, so that is behind us. Unless he was tipsy and I was just too tired to fight.

He might have hinted that I could come to his place or he could come to my place for the night one more time, but if he did, he didn't push hard. He probably knows I have my defenses up and am processing a few things, so bonding isn't on my mind at the moment. If this thing heats up at all, I have to think through the fact that he has different boundaries than me. That's going to bother me. It might be why I don't even give myself a chance to get close to guys—I don't want to hassle with hand-to-hand combat and explaining my position on not sleeping around. I need to give that some thought. But I'm too tired tonight.

I pull back the covers ready to fall into an immediate coma. But even with my eyes closed tight and my head spinning from fatigue, the little red light on my answering machine keeps blinking away. Like the subtle sound of a dripping faucet, it won't leave me alone.

I sit up and let my legs dangle over the edge of the bed. I hit the Play button.

"Kristen, I know you don't like me. And at the moment I don't like me very much either. But you have to talk to me. No one else is listening. I can prove that Penny didn't kill Jack Durham. I can prove it. Sorry to call your home phone, but I don't want your employer knowing that I'm calling you, so I skipped your cell. Please call when you get in. Doesn't matter how late. If not tonight, please call me in the morning. First thing. Please. Someone needs to hear what I have to say. There's something else I should have told you sooner." She pauses. "Kristen, things aren't as they seem. I need your help."

Dinner at Morton's took three hours. I ended up insisting that I take a cab home and that Reynolds take himself back to his hotel. He protested and argued. I think he was on the edge of drunk. I ended up hailing a cab for him too. I hate to think what his parking lot bill is going to be when he finds his car in the morning. Seventy or eighty bucks, I bet. Dinner had to be pushing two hundred bucks. Out of my league.

I look at the red digital letters on my clock. It's after one a.m. That settles it for me. I roll over and decide to call Bobbie back in the morning. First thing.

I do roll on my back long enough to wonder who is sending me texts.

Surely not Dell. Couldn't be; he's engaged. My punching partner? Nah. He's been straight-forward even if I'm not convinced he's *semper fi*. A joke? Did the texts start before I went out with Derrick Jensen twice? After. But it couldn't be him. I'm sure he's already moved on to several pretty young things. Not him. But who could it be?

40

"Quad shot grande Americano, room for cream, extra hot."

"Coming right up," a perky blonde who for some crazy reason seems very happy to be alive before seven o'clock in the morning tells me excitedly. She obviously didn't eat a pound of cow at Morton's late last night. She almost makes me miss the guy with ear studs the size of quarters who used to mess up my order at this location most mornings. Haven't seen him since I got back from DC. Should I ask if he's okay? When my order awaits me at an amoeba-shaped counter less than two minutes later—correctly, I would note—I don't miss my old order taker nearly as much. I can thank him that I stopped using artificial sweeteners. I never knew what I was going to get in my coffee with him at the cash register, so I quit trying.

I sit down in a bright-orange vinyl chair that was obviously designed by someone who flunked or completely ignored the study of ergonomics. I sigh and stifle a yawn. I'm going to fall back asleep if I stay seated, even if the chair is designed to mess up my spine. I get up and head for my Miata. I'm tempted to put the convertible top down but my hair is already a mess this morning, even pulled tight in a braid, so I'm not going to risk further unruliness. I am an officer of the peace.

The engine fires right up. After rolling it backward down an incline to start it by popping the clutch for close to five months, I never get tired of the sound of my engine turning over. I'm tempted to turn it off just to hear the soft rumble again but resist.

I've been listening to light jazz on Watercolors all week, so I figure it's time to crank some eighties. I hit the third preset button for WLLP—"the looooop"—as Sting finishes singing the phrase, "I'll be watching you." I like "Every Breath You Take," but after last night's text I'm a little weirded out.

"That was the Police on 'the loooooop,'" an excited DJ tells me. "Stay tuned for news at the top of the hour after these messages from our sponsoooooors. You won't want to miss first details of last night's killing of the Lincoln Park Madam."

I have bounced out of the parking lot and shifted from second to third to fourth in fast succession as he says that. I gasp and hit the Seek button. A commercial. I hit it again. Another commercial. I have to find a station with news that's not on a commercial break. The Lincoln Park Madam. That's what the press has been calling Barbara Ferguson. Bobbie.

PART THREE

Blood is thicker than water.
GERMAN PROVERB

41

"She left the message on your home answering machine at eleven-thirty. My guess is she was dead within the next hour," Jerome, the techie from the medical examiner's office, says. "So even if you called her back after you got in, she was probably already dead."

I look at him closely. Is he just trying to make me feel better? I've been back in Chicago for twenty-two days now and I'm officially on my third murder case.

Jack Durham was dead before I landed. Keshan Brown was killed a week ago. Barbara Ferguson, my dating consultant and nemesis and almost friend, was killed in the early hours of today.

The Lincoln Park Madam. Mommie Dearest. Mommy Madam. The press has had fun giving her nicknames since the story broke that the woman we arrested, one of Bobbie's contractors, was also her daughter.

In many ways I'm a boring person. I like it that way. I am not looking for drama in life. I get enough drama on the job and through my family. I don't watch reality TV—though I have to admit I flipped channels one night and watched almost an hour of the Kardashians for the first time. But that was a car wreck I stumbled upon. I could not take my eyes from the carnage at the site, but it doesn't mean I went looking for any more wrecks to ogle.

This is my fifth or sixth time in Bobbie's condo. She told me her designer was big into feng shui, the belief that the geometric arrangement of furniture could create energy and peace for the person living there. I don't think I'm buying all that. But it's obvious that furniture, decorations, and basic arrangements say something. In Bobbie's case the eclectic but somehow harmonious blending of styles was elegant and comfortable. When I see nice furniture and stuff I rarely think "comfortable." In fact, I think the opposite. I think of being careful so nothing expensive gets messed up.

I didn't grow up poor, but I grew up in a working-class home. Dad was a detective and mom worked thirty hours a week at the library. Not big-paying jobs. Even when Kaylen turned sixteen we still had one car. We had a Chicago address, so we were connected to both an east-west and a north-south bus line. So we never felt like we were missing anything. The elite soccer team I played for as a teen had some girls from what appeared to be pretty wealthy families. Heck, anyone with a pool in the backyard was rich in my eyes—although I visited some of the homes with a lot more than a pool. I remember one of the girls—Abby, a decent sweeper—could not get over the fact that I was sixteen and didn't have a car. She wasn't trying to make me feel bad, but she yammered on about it one entire night when we stayed in a motel outside of St. Louis for a soccer tournament. That may have been the first time I was aware that how much money you have is a big deal to some people.

But how much is relative. From my perspective Bobbie looked pretty rich. I heard her say a few things that indicated she thought she was pretty poor.

A lot or a little is irrelevant at a crime scene. Dead is dead.

Bobbie's death did not match her surroundings. She was beaten with a blunt object. Why am I guessing it was a Stanley twenty-two-ounce claw-head hammer?

Jerome will let us know. He walks next to the gurney being wheeled out the front door and into the hall with a black bag containing the bodily remains of Barbara Ferguson's earthly life.

We are scouring every square inch of her place—all thirty-five hundred costly square feet with an almost front-row view of Lake Michigan on Chicago's Gold Coast.

"Guys, I found something," a voice calls. Randall, the new guy.

I am not a guy, but join the throng gathered comfortably in her walk-in closet, which is bigger than my bedroom.

"There's a drawer unit here in the back that didn't look quite flush to the wall," he says.

"You a carpenter or something?" Don asks.

"Matter of fact, I am," Randall answers. "I gave it a few pushes and could tell it wasn't anchored. So I found the lever that releases the spring-load latch. It popped out about six inches. It's got a hidden hinge. When it's out, the frame and hinge are far enough out that you can open it."

We are looking at the front door of a safe that is probably three by six feet. Impossible to tell how far back it goes.

"What was her birthday?" Martinez asks.

"What's yours?" a uniform asks him. "And what's your bank. I think I just figured out your password."

Everyone laughs and Martinez reddens and mutters under his breath.

"No one is punching numbers anywhere," Blackshear says. "We're going to get some backup in here. The code isn't her birthday, but even if she was stupid enough to use that, there might be a trick or two that destroys some important evidence."

"Besides, no woman would use her birthday as a code," the uniform says. "Too sensitive a subject."

He thinks that is hilarious but takes his laughter down a couple notches when he realizes no one is laughing with him. I look at his lanyard and see the name *Russ*.

294

We all head back for our assigned areas of the condo, but Russ goes for a laugh one more time as he calls to Martinez, "So what is your bank, Detective? I got the key."

"*¿Qué te parece un puñetazo en la cara?*" Martinez calls back.

I look at Don for a translation. He just shrugs.

I have to pick a new password for all my accounts.

I like my new iPhone. The guy at Verizon told me it was part of a 4G network. I am using more features than I thought I would, like Words with Friends with Kaylen and Klarissa. At the moment, though, my phone keeps vibrating but nothing is happening on my screen. I sweep the screen again. I push the only button on the unit. Nothing. I put it back down. There is another long vibration.

I'm of the age that is supposed to be intuitive in all things technological. We not only didn't have a second car when I was growing up, we didn't have a home computer. We did walk six blocks to where Mom worked and used the public access computers at the library. It was uphill both ways in the snow. Even in the summer.

I downshift to fourth and then third in quick succession to assist my braking and dart off at my exit, then gun into a gap in the traffic, barely slowing down. Reynolds is picking me up in twenty-five minutes. I'm still fifteen minutes from home and have to take a shower.

It's Friday night. We went out last night too. He flies back to DC in the morning. He wanted to pick me up earlier but it's been another overtime day that had Martinez crying about the toll the hours are taking on his love life. I told Reynolds eight o'clock was the best I could do and left the office at seven. The Friday night crowd is already out in force.

I consider running the light at Division, but since I have no suicidal tendencies, I think better of putting my tiny Miata in the path of a giant SUV or dump truck. My phone vibrates again. I look down. Still nothing on my screen. Is it broken?

Then it finally dawns on me. The temporary phone they gave me to use with Derrick Jensen is what's vibrating. My eyes don't leave the road as my right handle fumbles and feels everywhere in my carryall purse, searching for the phone. I growl in frustration. I remove my hand to shift gears numerous times and finally find it as I bounce into my parking lot. Someone near my unit is having a party and I end up parking in another area of my apartment complex.

I start walking briskly and look down at the little Nokia screen. Can that be? Twenty-five texts, eleven missed calls, nine voice messages. All from Derrick. All for me. I scroll down and realize he's never stopped calling and texting me since the night of the president's campaign dinner. I think I was so relieved to be pulled off undercover duty that I blocked him and his crowd out of my mind. That's not possible of course. Most of them know Penny and many will be called in by the prosecutor or defense attorney to say good or bad things about her.

"So are you asking me for a male assessment of this guy or for an investigator's perspective on background for the Durham case? Or are you just trying to make me jealous?" Reynolds calls from the living room. I'm in the bedroom putting the finishing touches on my ensemble.

"I didn't think FBI agents were allowed to have emotions like fear and jealousy. Might divert them from the task at hand."

Reynolds arrived a few minutes after I got out of the shower, and I threw on a pair of jeans and a blouse. When I looked through the peephole of my door, I saw that he had dressed casually. For him that means no dark suit—just a pair of gray slacks, what looks like Italian shoes with black tassels, navy jacket, and white dress shirt. He didn't forget his monograms. My hair was a wet and tangled mess, and I hadn't started putting on next-to-no makeup.

I now have a row of new clothes in my closet from my undercover stint. Problem is everything is tighter and smaller than I like to wear. I'm halfway being modest, but I'm all the way being comfort-conscious. Why would I wear jeans that squeeze my waist like a boa on a baby pig?

"I'm not ready," I said.

He just smiled and pulled me into a big bear hug. I caught his first full-on kiss. I think I kissed him back.

"You look fabulous," he said when I pulled back and motioned him to come in.

"Give me fifteen minutes, Major," I said. "Want something to work on while I make you wait?"

I already told him about the Durham case last night. I got the feeling he already knew everything I told him. I talked about Bobbie a lot. I'm guessing he's up to speed on her murder by now. When he came in the door I gave him a thirty-second synopsis on Derrick Jensen and my newfound discovery that he has been trying to reach out to me.

It took me forty minutes to get ready. What has Bobbie done to me? My hair is down but I got it to flip up at the bottom. Black dress. Three-inch heels. A cascade of five or six necklaces. Dangling earrings. Not as many bracelets as Bobbie would have put on me, but more than I've worn at one time in my entire life.

"Wow," Reynolds says.

My vocabulary is rubbing off on him.

"Thank you," I say awkwardly. "So you're jealous of Derrick's interest?"

"I am. But before we go, there might be a few messages you want to listen to."

I think I might be crazy about Reynolds. He takes work as seriously as I do.

42

You never know what you're going to get for Halloween working Homicide. CPD is always out in force to watch out for the trick-or-treaters, big and small. The old-timers say that the little ones used to be the problem, egging cars and soaping windows. Now it's the grown-up kids in costume that have found yet another date on the calendar to get smashed. When they get smashed, smashed cars and smashed feelings are sure to follow. The latter can get lethal. Maybe being dressed in a devil costume encourages violent behavior.

Seven people shot in the city but only one death. It's the First Precinct's turf. We've been watching Garfield Park since the Keshan Brown murder en masse. Somehow the uneasy truce between the two communities brokered by Rev. James Cleveland and Rodrigo Espinoza has held. If you don't believe in miracles, I can guarantee you that qualifies. I still think about

Tandi Brown late at night before falling asleep. I wonder how she is doing.

Grand Jury saw enough evidence to charge Penny Martin—but that was before Bobbie was killed. Who knows when she is going to trial or if she is going to trial. She is still in Cook County Jail. The DA, Ms. Flannigan, still has her being held without bond as she is a flight risk. Her defense attorney says she has no previous criminal record and her rights are being trampled on. There is another bail battle scheduled on Monday. With the Bobbie murder he's going for charges being dropped as well. I think he has a shot at winning.

Flannigan is digging in her heels. She may be undefeated as a prosecutor but I think she's off base and stubborn on this one. Randall said he heard she still thinks she has a case to convict Penny.

She might be right—if the Stanley hammer has become the weapon of choice in Chicagoland.

My instincts as a detective have been better than my discipline at times. I was the only one who questioned the arrest of Martin—then I was the one who read her her rights—but with another Stanley hammer murder occurring while she was behind bars, I'm not the only one who questions it now. The bandwagon has almost filled up. Except for Flannigan.

I suspect she simply hasn't figured how to backtrack on her dramatic press conference to announce the charges against Penny and save face.

We're in a bit of limbo at the moment, but I'm assuming we're still looking for a killer. Our search of Bobbie's safe once it got popped open was interesting, but I'm not sure helpful.

I think everyone on the case is still in shock. There was almost two hundred grand in cash. No surprise there. Jewels. Two Springfield XDM .45 caliber handguns—a little bit of a surprise. The bottom two rows of her safe held two hundred one-pound gold bullion bars. The day we collected it the value was estimated at 6.6 million dollars. In the time I knew Bobbie she expressed a lot of jealousy of others' wealth. I'm having a hard time figuring that out. She was rich. Period.

We found her little black book with the clients' names and are being sued by various news agencies to turn over the names of the men. (She catered exclusively to men.) Our legal department is fighting on the grounds that Bobbie was never charged for running a prostitution ring.

There were checkbooks. Certificates of deposit. Her yearbooks starting from kindergarten and all the way through her high school graduation in 1979. Other family photo albums, but nothing with pictures taken in the last twenty years or so.

Every driver's license she ever carried was in there. She lived in Arizona for almost five years.

She was a student at Arizona State University for two years, but when she dropped out to get married, she was still a freshman in status. Her marriage lasted three years. Both the marriage and divorce certificates were in the safe. She had a passport in her name and, interestingly, she had a second with her picture but a different name. Her escape plan. But how did she think she was going to carry all that gold? Two hundred and fifty pounds of anything is not easy to smuggle across a border.

"You got that much gold bullion, you got a bunker mentality," Blackshear said. "She wasn't going anywhere."

Our financial forensics team is still going through her estate. It might be worth ten million. Penny is her sole heir. We found Bobbie's Last Will and Testament. Even after some tax restitution and fines, at least half will be waiting for Penny whether or not she gets off on murder charges.

When Flannigan heard Penny was the heir she started working on a theory that Penny had Bobbie killed to get at the money. She's grasping at straws.

The most interesting thing we uncovered in the secret safe was Penny's birth certificate. Bobby's neat handwriting was easy to read. Next to it, under the father's printed name, was the unsteady scrawl of a sixteen-year-old high school junior.

Jack Durham.

43

We had figured that Barbara got her start with the money she got from putting her baby up for adoption. We might have been partially correct, but her real starter capital was she got a cool million dollar check from Robert Durham Sr. to have the pregnancy terminated and to disappear.

She cashed the check—a copy was found in her safe—stuffed it in an investment account and did disappear for a time. Her first stop was downstate in Mansfield, Illinois, where she had Penny and put her into what looked like a warm and happy home. (Penny wasn't the first kid to not like the family she grew up with for no apparent reason.)

Durham Sr. still hasn't agreed to a time when we can question him, so we don't know if he knew of Penny's birth or not. Stanley McGill has been quite adamant that we will hear what he has to say only when he is ready to say whatever it is he decides to say.

From Mansfield, Bobbie moved to Phoenix, had a short marriage, and from there returned to Chicago. Her return coincided with Jack's graduation from college.

We've worked back through all Jack's friends and Bobbie's contractors to try and find out what happened between her and Jack then, if anything, and why both of them—both of Penny Martin's parents—are now dead.

We have spoon-fed the media as little as we can get away with. My sister Klarissa is actually mad at me. Heck, she's just plain mad these days. She and Warren, the sports guy at WCI-TV, have broken up yet again after barely being back together. If I had a gold bullion bar for every one of their breakups and reconciliations, I might be living in a villa overlooking Lake Como in northern Italy. She is also waiting to hear back from Channel 2 in New York City, so that's probably got her on edge too.

In all the interviews so far it was Derrick who probably told us the most and got us closest to the truth on Bobbie and Jack.

"Jack was a bad boy even in high school," he told us in an understatement.

"You can look at him and all of us like we are the scum of the earth, but . . ."

"But what?" Don coaxed.

"But he was a good guy," he said, looking down at his hands. "He was a real good guy. His dad messed him up on Barbara. Jacky thought he loved her. He might have decided for himself that he wasn't going to spend the rest of his life with a woman who was ten years older than him—but he never got that chance. His old man went crazy. They used to be fairly close. They fought, but they had a relationship. Never again. Jack was never the same. I honestly don't know how he graduated from high school. The fact that he got through college and law school while seriously depressed and medicated is pretty amazing. He was a bad boy, but he was more than the press has portrayed."

I didn't know how to respond to that. On one hand I wanted to say something sarcastic and put the guy in his place. Let him know that his buddy wasn't the first person to experience loss and a lot of people cope in a whole lot more positive manner. But I had to admit to myself most of those people don't have a billion-dollar trust fund to hide behind. I kept my mouth shut even when Derrick said to me on his way out the door of the interview room, "I was ready to change."

That's where I really drew the line. No way am I going to let someone play the victim card on me as an excuse for doing absolutely nothing positive with his life.

I still feel guilty. About Bobbie too. I've wondered if there is any connection between Bobbie reaching out to me and her death. But that would mean someone inside the department is feeding the killer information.

Reynolds and I never made it out that Friday night four weeks ago. We listened to Derrick's messages, I made some notes to report on Monday and add to the case file, we ordered a pizza from

Giordano's, we watched a college football game on ESPN—Navy v. BYU. Austin played at Cornell and while he was there Navy beat them by fifty points. He wanted to cheer for whoever was playing the Midshipmen.

I booted him at midnight. I think he knew for sure already, but if he didn't, he was sold that any courtship with me is going to be a long, twisting, and tortuous journey.

Maybe I gave him a little hope at the door with a long kiss, but I would have thought the Giordano's garlic festival would put a damper on his spirits. He flew out a couple hours later, called me every day for a week, then slowed down to every couple days.

I think we are both a little relieved. I like him. A lot. He says he wants a real relationship with me. I've responded that I am interested but I have to think about that some. The reality is, we do have a relationship. I can't deny I have feelings for him. But I don't know him well enough to come to any conclusions in my mind, and I'm not ready to crash headlong into something that has as many questions as this one does. I suspect my defenses have been down with him to some degree because we live so far apart; that makes things a little safer. He can't make claims on my time and space very easily.

I think he was ready to make a mad dash in my direction and has realized it's best for both of us to slow down. Something as simple as a daily phone call with me, often ending up in some sort of juvenile skirmish, has sobered him a bit.

Good. I think.

It's the first Saturday in November. Got a game in two hours and thirty minutes. Big game. We play the X-FORCE. We have identical 7-1 records.

I'm sipping a soy latte at JavaStar, waiting for Klarissa. She's not usually late. I look at my cheap watch. Ten-ten. I need to be out the door in fifty minutes now. She needs to hurry.

I check my phone in case she's tried to call. Nothing from her, but there's a number I don't recognize. I listen to the voice message. It's from Gretchen at city hall.

"I hate to leave this on voice mail, Kristen. I know I said too much already. But I was filing some work away and took another look at Randall. Not sure how he got cleared. Just consider this a friendly warning. Keep an eye on him. Something's not right. Okay . . . I've said it, and my conscience is clear. You don't have to call back."

What did Randall do? And why call me? This is information for Zaworski or Blackshear. And I don't want to be the snitch to bring it up. No time to think about it. We have bigger fish to fry.

I fidget. Where is Klarissa? *Just relax and enjoy the moment, Kristen.* After all we've had going on, it's nice sipping a cup of coffee and being ignored by everyone else. That'll change when my sister gets here. When she walks through the door, white doves will flutter in the air. A Broadway soundtrack will drown out the awful retro rap song JavaStar is playing and promoting. (They have to get a new music director in Seattle.) Once the Broadway showtune starts, customers and JavaStar employees alike will break into song and dance to rival *Glee*. The barista will lift her into the air and twirl with her.

That's how things go with Klarissa.

I look down at my iPhone again. Kaylen just made a move with Words with Friends. I touch the yellow letter tile and groan. I played a double-double that got me over fifty points. But it left a triple play open and she hammered me—I have got to stop referencing hammers in my word pictures—and scored 108 by getting a triple letter on the *Z* to go along with the triple word. Rats.

I look up. Klarissa is looking down at me, her lips quivering. She didn't set off a Broadway musical today. A tear falls on the table by my latte. I instinctively move it over a couple inches.

"What's up, sis?"

"I am so ticked. Life isn't fair."

44

I'm trying to understand. I want to be sympathetic. I want to be a good sister.

Klarissa and I are rollerblading along the concrete walkway that ribbons along Lake Michigan from Navy Pier to somewhere near Evanston. I haven't rollerbladed in years. I didn't really want to go—after the soccer game I was planning on some long-overdue cleaning—and I'm surprised by how much I'm enjoying it. I had to go to the cage in the basement of my apartment building to find my blades, but there they were.

November has started unseasonably warm in Chicago. When we left it was low sixties. I'm guessing it's low fifties now. I look over at Klarissa and her nose is bright red. I'm sure I match her. At least she has gloves on. I didn't think I'd need them. The wind has picked up and my hands are freezing.

We hopped on the path across from the Drake Hotel at the top of the Magnificent Mile. We cruised five miles up to Lincoln Park Zoo. Klarissa ranted and raved the whole way. We stopped at one of the marinas and talked some more. Now the sun is dropping fast in a seasonal Chicago fall. I bet the temperature is in the forties when we get back. We're pushing hard on the return trip, and she's too winded to talk. Good.

She and Warren broke up. No big biggie. She's fine with that. But *Chicago* magazine just came out with their list of Chicago's ten most eligible bachelorettes. She's not on the bachelorette list. One of her tri-Delta sorority sisters from the University of Illinois is editor of that feature and told her she would be on it—especially after her ordeal this summer. Her sorority sister was obviously wrong and has been called some choice names by Klarissa.

My problem is, I'm not feeling her pain. I don't think this qualifies in the *Life isn't fair* department. If Tandi Brown calls me to tell me life isn't fair, I'll listen to her all day and night and agree with her 100 percent.

I'm just glad I've held my tongue. What Klarissa is feeling—insecure, betrayed, left out— is real for Klarissa. Doesn't mean I get it and can fully sympathize. Of course she isn't sharing my euphoria over the Snowflakes' victory today—an unbelievably wild game that we snatched with two goals in the final minutes.

How can sisters be so different? Maybe it was the piano lessons she took.

The Drake, the Hancock, the Standard Oil Building, the Bloomingdale Towers are looming closer and closer. Maybe a mile to go. Now the wind is gusting off the lake. I come close to taking a spill when I get knocked off balance. I look over. Klarissa is really struggling. I need to slow down. But she does have a fierce determination on her face.

I about pee my pants when a dog charges us from the middle of a group of teenagers sitting on a blanket in the sand and smoking something that I'm pretty sure isn't legal. Klarissa does a 360 but keeps her feet. She grabs my arm halfway through her circle and I end up in a tuck and roll and sitting on my butt facing our spectators. They are pointing and laughing. The dog is about two feet from my face and snarling. Maybe a lab and shepherd mix.

I'm not crazy about dogs. We had a mutt when I was a kid and I remember yard scooping duty too well. Our dog knew I didn't like him, so he didn't like me back. I was the only kid that got snapped at.

This thing weighs more than seventy pounds, I bet. I also bet he doesn't stop at a snap. He darts in closer and my heart about bursts out of my chest. Klarissa has absolutely frozen in place. I hear one kid yelling, "Down, Monster, down," but other voices are still laughing. I'm up on my knees and facing him with a snarl of my own. No way I can get a foothold and gain balance if that thing decides to transition from feints and snarls to a full-on assault.

I guarantee the meatheads on the blanket won't

be laughing when I do what I have to do to defend myself from Monster. If Monster charges, my left arm will go up to take the teeth. Instinctively he'll go for the throat, and that's the attack trajectory I'll anticipate. I'll push forward with everything I can muster from knee level and my right arm will close on the back of his neck. I'll use his momentum and the opposite motion of my two arms to snap his neck. If he clamps on my left arm with his teeth it will hurt like crazy, but it will seal his death sentence.

I don't know if it was the kid calling Monster's name or Monster's survival instinct buried somewhere in a brain about the size of a meatball at Carmine's, but he backs off. No blood lost today. I struggle to my feet and about fall again.

"You ever hear of a leash law?" I storm at the kid.

He snaps a leather leash on Monster's collar and pulls him back and farther away from me.

"I should have let him mess you up," he says and flips me off as he strides back to the blanket, Monster fighting him all the way.

I'm about to say something back at him when I see one of the group members sauntering up the short hill to the sidewalk beside Lake Shore Drive. Unless my eyes deceive me—and they don't—it's a punk I arrested last April. Jared Incaviglia. The kid had beat up and robbed some senior citizens. He was looking at eight to twelve in the state pen when he got cut loose from the Cook County correctional center due to an administrative error.

He glances down and sees I'm focused on him. "She's a cop," he yells to his young friends and they immediately scramble to their feet and follow him to street level.

Can I get these darn skates off and catch someone running in just my socks? I wonder. Incaviglia reads my mind and laughs. He blows me a kiss and takes off.

Finally home. Klarissa surprised me. Instead of getting weepy and declaring she was traumatized, she was excited about our run-in with Monster. She got a second wind and flew the last mile back to the top of Michigan Avenue, where we pulled off our skates and put on walking shoes before separating and heading to our cars. She showed me a canister of pepper spray she carries for self-defense. I asked why that stayed in her pocket when Monster was considering where to take a hunk out of my flesh.

"You had it all under control," she said.

I called Reynolds on the way home and spent twenty-five minutes giving every detail, including my plans for Monster.

"So where'd you learn to kill an attack dog?" Austin asks.

"Gym class in college," I answer.

"Judo or Krav Maga?"

"Krav with a little judo thrown in," I answer.

"It would have worked," he said. "But can I suggest something?"

"Sure."

I was expecting some feedback from his training as an Army Ranger.

"Don't tell people how you were going to break the neck of the dog. They'll think you're a killer and turn him into a martyr. People are funny about dogs."

"Are you?"

"My lifestyle doesn't support having a dog. But to some degree I'll admit to having an irrational affection for the creatures. Make a movie and kill a bunch of humans and no one will complain. Kill a pet and you'll have picketers."

"Not quite what I was expecting from you. I thought you'd have a better defense model that didn't include teeth marks in my forearm."

"Nah. You had it right. You had it under control."

I wonder if he knew I was a little peeved when I got off the phone in a hurry?

I shower and pad into the kitchen. I open the refrigerator door hoping something good to eat has magically appeared. No such luck. I open the half-gallon milk carton and don't even have to raise it to my nose to get a whiff. Didn't I buy that earlier in the week?

Out for dinner? I really don't want to eat by myself in a restaurant. Go over to Mom's or Kaylen's? I think I've had enough family interaction for the day. I jab the phone number from a magnet on my refrigerator door into my iPhone and order Chinese takeout from Friendship Restaurant. It's a little more expensive and will take longer than the shop a mile from my place, but I'm in the mood for something really good. I like chop suey and theirs is the best. I was outside most of the day and have built up an appetite. Mushroom consommé for starters and then flaming Szechuan pork tenderloin. I throw in an order of creamy crab rangoon for good measure. It comes up to about thirty bucks for just me. I've been hanging around too many rich people.

I watch football while I eat—Northwestern is getting hammered by Michigan. Unless I'm hungry at midnight, there is enough pork and noodles left over for breakfast. I put another load of laundry in the washing machine, transfer a load to the dryer, and fold warm clothes, then spend an hour organizing my closet.

I try to read my Bible—there might be a little dust on it—but my mind is too busy on too many things. I prefer to keep it simple. What's the name of the book that was such a big seller? Eat and pray? I'm leaving something out. I pray for Tandi.

I get in bed with a new Daniel Silva novel. He's got an Israeli assassin as his hero. I wonder why he doesn't talk about Krav Maga. The book holds my attention for an hour, but I get up at midnight and finish the Szechuan pork.

I realize I am lonely. That's a strange feeling for me. I never get lonely. I have plenty of friends at work and a family that is really close even if we suffocate each other at times.

Is it having a boyfriend? One that lives in another city? Does having someone you want to spend some time with make you feel lonely when you're not together?

45

"Can't do it, Kristen."

"I know. But how can this be right?"

" 'Right' has nothing to do with it. The file is sealed. Your name and rank don't give you access."

Dad was shot four years ago. He passed away in February of this year. Two weeks later Dad's former partner and then-captain closed the case and sealed the files. Czaka. Commander Czaka.

I know I went too far in protesting that decision. Especially showing up at his office after he wouldn't return my phone calls or answer my e-mails. I made my case. I felt disrespected when he said, "You're not changing my mind." So I yelled to the point that I was escorted from his office and put on a one-week administrative leave. With pay.

My dad and Big Tony, Anthony Scalia, brought down a hit man who had Mayor Daniels in his crosshairs. That was back in '94. He and Scalia were given the Commissioner's Award of Valor and the department's highest honor, the Police Medal. My family sat at a front table at a Sheraton ballroom overlooking the Chicago River. Daniels always attended, but for the first and only time, asked for the privilege of presenting the awards to Scalia and Dad. I was a sophomore in high school. I remember feeling a lot of pride when Big Tony and Dad got a standing ovation from a crowd made up of their peers. I've wondered if that was the moment I decided to be a cop.

Dad's relationship with the mayor is what kept me from getting canned. As mad as I still am, I know I deserved it.

Daniels leaves office in less than three months. This is not a good time to push the envelope. It's not fair for me to ask friends of my dad for favors. Margaret Zelwin runs the massive labyrinth of case files. She is close to retirement age. What am I thinking?

When Czaka first sealed the files and personally ordered me to stay away from the case—even if it was on my own time—I was so angry I was about out of my mind. Which is why I went off on the commissioner of homicide detectives, my boss's big boss. I thought I had things under control. But today I was pushing to get a couple hours alone with the cardboard file box with every interview, theory, and scant piece of evidence drawn from the night my dad was shot and subsequent investigation.

"I'm sorry, Ms. Margaret."

"All you did is ask. No sin in that."

I'm not so sure on that.

"How did the humongous soccer game of the century go on Saturday?" Don asks.

"You didn't watch it on TV?"

"I don't get satellite," he says with a laugh.

"Well, my Snowflakes are now 8-1. The one-time juggernaut known as the X-FORCE is 7-2. A tie or victory on Saturday gives us the regular season crown."

"Not bad, not bad," he says. "You all didn't win a game last year, did you?"

I sigh. "We won three games."

"But that was only the games when you didn't coach, wasn't it," he says with a straight face.

He's pulling my chain. Not always very hard to do. I'm not taking the bait today. I like joking around, but after my visit to Records, I'm feeling somber.

"What's wrong with you? Your FBI boyfriend not talking to you?"

I'm still not taking the bait. He looks disappointed.

"Notice anything new?"

"Yes, Don. Nice tie."

"It's not a new tie," he says with a frown.

"Shoes?"

"Nope."

"I give."

"How could you miss this new suit? It's a Hugo Boss."

"Did it cost more than two hundred dollars?" I ask.

Now he frowns. I just returned the favor and tugged his chain. It wouldn't surprise me if the thing cost more than a thousand. Heck, the Dolce & Gabbana jeans that are one or two sizes too small for me cost over a thousand. The suit might have cost even more.

We are driving over to see Penny Martin. She made bail this morning and was on her way home shortly after noon. Despite Flannigan's ongoing objections, the judge agreed with the defense attorney that with a lack of criminal record, she merited release on bail. He did relent under Flannigan's attack and ordered her to remain under house arrest. She is wearing an ankle monitor that sends a transmission with her exact whereabouts every five minutes. There's a small strip shopping center next to her apartment with a few restaurants and shops. That's as far as her tether will let her travel.

She has exercised her right to remain silent throughout the five weeks of her incarceration at the Cook County Jail. She answered no official questions from CPD or the DA's office and spoke to no other prisoners. We know because we rotated a couple plants to get close to her and hear what she might have to say. Nothing. Even when Flannigan herself dropped the bomb that Bobbie was dead and we knew Durham was her father. I watched and rewatched the video. She barely batted an eye.

She was raised by a nice family in Madison, Illinois. They drove in to visit her once a week but she refused to see them each time. What is going through the mind of someone who has not only lost both parents, but who is being accused of murdering one of them?

As she was being checked out of Cook County detention center she told the dispatch officer that she would like to talk to Detectives Squires and Conner.

"You sure she didn't ask for me?" Martinez asked in our quick meeting to go over what we should ask and—more to the point—what we should answer.

No one laughed. I think Antonio is wondering if he made a good decision to move from the Third over to the Second.

Don is driving. I hear a *ping* and look down at my phone and give the screen a swipe. A new text.

How was the food? I hear Friendship's crab rangoon is the best in town. I miss you.

Yep. I have a stalker. I told Blackshear informally. Time to turn in a formal report. I should have sooner. But I know that I'll get a hard time over this.

"Come in," Penny says.

I haven't seen her face-to-face for five weeks. She was slim and trim before. She's lost fifteen pounds at least and looks anorexic. She's still beautiful but now with the waifish model look.

She points to the living room. "It's a mess, but you already knew that. You should have at least cleaned up after yourself a little."

It is a wreck.

"Let's go to the kitchen," she says.

She's been busy. It's clean and tidy. The dishwasher is running.

"Coffee?"

"Yes," I say immediately. Don nods in agreement.

"I think the filter is still good," she says and fills the coffee carafe about two-thirds of the way full with water from a side tap. She pours it into the water holder.

She then opens a canister and puts three scoops of whole beans into an electric grinder.

She holds the button down for fifteen seconds—I counted. She opens a cabinet and puts a brown filter in the basket. She pours the ground coffee into the basket, shuts it, then hits a button that turns green. Even before water hits the grounds the kitchen is filled with a rich aroma that is great.

She puts three ceramic mugs on the table, then fills up a matching ceramic pourer with half-and-half. She puts it on a tray that has packets of raw sugar and several varieties of sweeteners. She makes it all seem so effortless. Good hostess. I should take notes.

I might save on my JavaStar bill if I went to this much trouble every morning.

The three of us sit silently while the carafe fills up one drip at a time.

"Put what you want in your cup and I'll pour," she says. "All the flatware is in the dishwasher."

I think Don has lost another five pounds this week. He's been coming into the Precinct workout room most mornings. But his weight loss has nothing to do with sugar intake. He rips the tops off four sugars and dumps the contents in the bottom of the cup. No cream. I do the opposite. Plenty of half-and-half, nothing sweet. I wonder if our coffee fixings are symbolic of our personalities.

We settle in. I sip my coffee. I think it's better than JavaStar. I need to check out what brand of beans she uses.

She hits it. "The prosecutor is very motivated to prove I killed Jack Durham."

"That's what they do," I say.

"I have no problem with that."

Okay.

"But I do want to know if Chicago Police is equally as intent on seeing me put away for life. Specifically, I want to know if the fact that Barbara was killed in the same fashion as Jack—while I was in jail and despite the fact that it is well documented I saw no visitors and talked to no one other than my attorney—has raised doubts with anyone as to my guilt." She pauses, then continues, "I'm sorry, I'm rambling. I haven't spoken much in the past month and I'm out of practice. I have a couple of simple questions. Are you actively investigating the deaths of my mother and father? And if you find anything that points to my father being murdered by someone other than me, can I count on that becoming a matter for the court to consider?"

She may be out of practice, but she's laid her cards on the table clearly and concisely. Don and I look at each other.

"The answer to both questions is an unequivocal yes," Don answers.

"Why am I not convinced?" she asks after a pause.

"What would we have to say or do to convince you?" I respond, going with the tried-and-true gambit of answering a question with a question.

She ignores me and says to Don, "You appear to me to be a man of honor. Will you promise me that if you find something that points to another murderer, you will personally present it to the prosecutor?"

"I don't know if I can do that," he says. "I can promise you that anything Conner and I find that helps or hurts your defense will be submitted to the prosecution. Whether Flannigan will accept our request for a personal appointment is another matter."

"I think you're making my decision easier," she says through pursed lips.

After a couple more sips of coffee and a long pause I ask, "What decision is that?"

"I wasn't sure whether to spend money on a private investigator. I don't doubt that you two will do the right thing, but I still think I better."

"Your call," Don says.

"Yes, it is."

My cup of coffee is two-thirds empty. I wonder if I will get the offer of a refill.

"If you will excuse me," Penny says curtly, "I have a lot to do to get this place back in shape."

Nope. No refill.

Don and I leave our business cards with her as we exit and tell her to call us if she finds any-thing that will help us apprehend the killer of Barbara Ferguson. She takes the cards but her mind has moved on to other things. She's smart. Very focused. And she makes a great cup of coffee.

Barbara and Jack. Mom and Dad. Same killer? Two killers?

46

"Conner! What in the heck are you doing?"

What's he mad about? I hold up a finger to let him know I need a sec. The motorized chain finishes delivering the metal brace with the target to me. I let up on the return button so it doesn't bang into the stopper. That's what usually gets him worked up.

I pull the target off. I went through four clips with my Sig Sauer P2022—the .40 caliber barrel. I've gotten to where I can discharge and reload a clip as slick and fast as anyone. I fired twenty-eight rounds at 120 feet. I count holes. Eleven on the body, another seven on the sheet, so there were ten complete misses. Not good. Not horrible. Better than my last two twenty-eight-round blast sessions at 120 feet, the farthest the target slides back on the static range.

There are twenty-five lanes. Nine others are in use. Pretty busy day.

"Conner!"

I can hear Peterson banging on the observation window. Peterson was chief instructor for CPD for years. Semi-retired, he still comes in two or three days a week to do training. He's been trying to help me with my handgun scores. He motions for me to come out of the range area.

I grab a broom and sweep my shell cases. I reload all four clips, put one in the Sig Sauer and the other three in custom slots on my worn leather holster. I pick up my targets and exit the range into a small transfer room. Once that door closes I open the second door and exit into the observation area. TV and movies are very inaccurate in how they portray handgun usage in many ways, but perhaps most of all is noise volume. I know you can't have a theater juice the volume of handgun blasts to blow out moviegoers' ears, but they could be a little more realistic. The reports of a handgun truly are deafening. I take off my goggles and headset.

"Would you like to tell me what you're doing?" Peterson demands.

He's very easygoing and I'm not sure I've seen him this impatient with me before. I can have that effect on people, even if they were buddies with my dad.

"I know it's not great, but I'm doing the best I can."

"What are you talking about?" he asks.

"You asked what I'm doing and I told you. I'm doing the best I can. In fact I'm not done. I was going to do a couple more rounds."

Hands on hips, he asks, "How many rounds have you gone through so far?"

"I've reloaded about ten times, so not quite three hundred rounds."

He rolls his eyes. "So you've emptied four clips of seven rounds ten or eleven times. No one's score improves after one hundred rounds, so save the armory some budget money and call it a day. But I'm asking what you're doing for two reasons. First, why didn't you wait for me to get here? And second, what in the heck are you shooting from 120 feet for?"

"I just thought I'd get started before you got here. I shoot by myself a lot of times."

"And that's why your scores are mediocre. Practice doesn't make perfect if you're doing things wrong. And you are. Still."

What a downer. I really thought I was improving.

"Your shoulders still aren't relaxed. You end up hunched forward and tight. Until you relax your shoulders and get your hands working together you'll always push right when you pull the trigger. Plus you end up bending both elbows instead of keeping the left straight. I know you're an athlete. Your dad used to tell us about your soccer. If you can control your feet like that, you can get your shoulders, arms, and hands in sync."

"That's what I was trying to do."

"Listen, Conner, you want help or not?"

"Of course I do."

"Then stop shooting by yourself until I give you the green light. We've got to break some bad habits or it's doing you no good. You shoot with me. *Capiche*?"

"Yes, sir." I salute.

"And while you're being a smart aleck, let me add you don't need to be practicing from 120 feet. You shoot somebody from 120 feet, you'll lose your badge and go to jail. You don't know who they are. Your life isn't in imminent danger. And your chance of hitting them if they are on the move isn't very likely. Best shooters hit a moving target at that distance less than 28 percent of the time on their first shot."

"I just figure if you can hit a target from 120 you can hit it from ninety."

"How about you worry about hitting a target where you want to hit it from twenty and forty? That's what handguns are for. Unless you got someone blasting at you from 120 feet, your gun never comes up."

I know he's right but this still makes me mad.

"Conner, you like what you do for a living?"

"Absolutely."

"What's your job?"

"Being a detective."

"You know what I wanted to do when I joined CPD?"

"What?"

"I wanted to be a detective."

"Why didn't you become one?"

"I was too busy shooting at targets. I actually got good at it. Instead of putting me in the field, they moved me to the range to teach others."

"You have all the CPD records."

"I still do. I got a room filled with trophies and ribbons from all sorts of competitions. But I didn't sign up to represent CPD at national shooting comps. I signed up to be a detective. Don't get me wrong—I want you to get better with a handgun, and you can. But don't forget what your job is. You listening to me?"

"Yes."

"Good. Now get out of here. Come back next week and don't take that pretty little Sig out of your holster until I get here."

"Like it?"

"I do. But there was nothing wrong with the Glock. I wasn't crazy about that Beretta someone sold you—but it does have its raving fans. But I like my good old standard-issue Glock just fine. You got to have a good gun, but you got to get rid of some bad habits, starting with them shoulders."

Don't forget your job. Find who killed Barbara Ferguson. Make sure it was Penny Martin that killed Jack Durham. Get rid of some bad habits.

47

"Anything else, Conner?"

Is he amused or not amused? Can't always tell. Zaworski is in the office for a half day. He said he was driving his wife crazy lying around the house and was fearful for his life if he didn't get out some. It turned into quite the brouhaha, but he insisted that Blackshear keep his office. He has reserved one of our smaller interview rooms for the days and times he comes in.

He decided to run today's staff and case meeting but told us about twenty times it was still Blackshear's show. Blackshear has done great but he is definitely uncomfortable taking the lead with Zaworski around.

Don reported our meeting with Penny Martin. The Barbara Ferguson murder is still front burner. Flannigan, is turning up the heat. She sees her case against Martin jeopardized by a similar unsolved murder. *You think?*

"You all have turned over every stone, but it feels too restricted by the original murder. You've visited and revisited Durham's friends and all of Ferguson's contractors. You need to think of some other stones to look under."

"Flannigan is right to be worried," Don said. "The autopsy doesn't prove the same killer did both Ferguson and Durham, but Jerome told me off record he doesn't think Flannigan can prove it wasn't the same person. He said flip a coin. That's all the defense needs for reasonable doubt."

I dreaded it, but as the meeting wound down I submitted not one, not two, but three official reports as required by CPD policy to let my supervisor know about personal interactions that might be job related. I asked if I could have a separate meeting with Zaworski or Blackshear and he said we'd handle it in regular briefing so we don't have to repeat everything later.

First, I reported on my texting stalker.

"But no direct contact with you?" Zaworski asked.

"Well, he or she seems to know where I am, including when I'm home."

He gave a half whistle. "Not good."

I then reported on seeing the punk, Jared Incaviglia. That led to a series of questions from everyone on Monster. I think Martinez and Randall were concerned for his safety. Maybe Reynolds is right.

"Blackshear, I think you should issue an APB with the escapee's last known whereabouts. You should have called this in last night, Conner," Zaworski said.

He was right.

Third, and my most embarrassing report of all,

Derrick Jensen has started calling me again. I already turned in the temp phone, but he got my real number. Fifteen calls the last week. I tried to be nonchalant, but my face was still burning.

"I'm just getting caught up. Let me make sure I understand. All this calling from him since the Ferguson murder?"

"Since five days ago, sir."

"And what is he calling you about?" he barked.

He might be feeling more like himself.

"He called late last night and asked me out on a date."

"Did you say yes or no?" Martinez asked with a smirk.

Antonio might get knocked off my Christmas card list this year if he's not careful.

"You haven't answered," Zaworski says. "Is there anything else?"

"Seems like enough at the moment," I answer.

This gets a laugh from everyone—and for once I think it's not because they're laughing at me but because I said something funny. I am legendary for my ability to butcher a joke.

"Yeah, it is," Zaworski says. "Anyone else feel like their life is pretty boring next to Conner's?"

Everyone laughs even harder this time. I don't think he was funnier. He just got the extra enthusiasm bosses always do.

"Can we exploit this?" Blackshear asks.

The laughter dies quickly.

"What do you mean?" Zaworski asks.

"What if she goes out with him? I know you said we need to find some new rocks to turn over and I agree with that 100 percent. But it still seems to me like we've already talked to the murderer—or murderers. This was a cozy little club. The customers are rich, spoiled, and bored. Not always a good combination for staying out of trouble. The contractors were part of the aspirational class, making more money than they ever had in their lives, but knowing that their prime earnings window wouldn't last forever. So I'm guessing the smarter ones aren't just looking for a fast buck. Some are looking for a husband or maybe even a way to get their hooks in someone through some kind of black-mail scheme."

Everything he is saying makes sense. But I don't think I'm a good enough actress to pull off a dating scheme. Check that. I know I'm not a good enough actress to pretend to enjoy a night on the town with Jensen.

"What do you think, Conner?"

"I am kind of what I am, sir."

Is that stupid or profound?

"I did three dates for the department and two were certified disasters. The middle one, the Bears game, might have been too. I don't think I can pretend to be interested in the guy. He actually gives me the creeps. So I doubt I'd be able to draw anything from him that we haven't already heard through traditional interviews."

"Fair enough," Zaworski says. "I tend to agree, but your call, Bob."

"Wishful thinking on my part," he says. "Anyone else have ideas?"

That's the problem. No one does.

"One time," I say. "But that's it."

Friday night it is. James Taylor concert at the Odeum. That should help—can't talk during a concert. But the point of doing this is to talk.

I talked to Reynolds earlier. Told him what was going on. He didn't like the idea and didn't seem very happy about it. Was he jealous?

I've got my Silva book open and am halfway through. It's only eleven o'clock so I might knock out sixty or seventy pages before I fall into bed and turn out the light. I decide to send Reynolds a text. He's a big boy and probably isn't jealous. But he is divorced because his wife cheated on him, so you never know.

I'm sprawled on the couch in my living room. I pick my phone up off the coffee table. Before I can start my text, I get sonar pinged. Someone is texting me. Maybe Reynolds had the same idea as me. Wouldn't prove true love, but it would be sweet.

I swipe the screen and read: *What page are you on? Still on my mind with every breath you take.*

I'm off the couch like a shot. I storm into my bedroom, open my nightstand drawer, snag the key taped underneath, and open my lockbox. I pull out the Sig Sauer and check the clip. Locked and loaded. I release the safety.

I leave the lights out, head into my living room, and look out the window that overlooks a narrow ribbon of grass that is the backyard of my complex. Beyond that is an eight-foot cyclone fence—an eyesore—and then the back parking lot of Van Buren High School.

My apartment has no side windows but three in the back—the one in my bedroom, a double-wide in my living room, and a third in my guest bedroom. All have the same view. The front of my apartment has a small window over the kitchen sink that looks out an open-air landing with a staircase to the right that leads up and down. Can't see much from there. I walk into my entry hall and open the door. Turn the deadbolt so it doesn't latch shut on me. I look over the railing into the parking lot. No movement.

There really is no vantage point to look in my apartment. What is going on?

I have a sudden flash and storm back in, locking the door behind me. I turn on every light and get a flashlight for good measure. I start in my bedroom. Nothing. Kitchen. Ditto. Spare bedroom. Nada. I find it hidden in some fake plants on top of my TV-stereo cabinet. I don't touch or move it.

My face flushes angrily as I try to remember if I walked through here without any clothes on. I don't usually parade around naked, but I live alone, so I don't worry about modesty when taking a load of laundry to the closet where I have a stacked washer and dryer.

My stalker is an electronic Peeping Tom.

"I can come over, but it isn't my specialty," Jerome, the ME techie, says.

I remembered him telling me he lives close to me, so I buzzed him after calling it in to Dispatch. A couple of uniformed investigators are on their way over. Do I call Konkade? He coordinates action plans in Homicide. There's a good chance this isn't connected to the Durham-Ferguson murders. But you never know. I decide to let him sleep and leave a message for him on his office phone. Nothing to do tonight but make a report.

"Don't worry about it, Jerome."

"No problem. I'm on my way," he says. "The uniforms won't know what to do with it. I'll at least make sure it gets sorted and bagged right."

"Thanks, Jerome. You're my hero."

"Here to serve. And by the way, after what you did to that psycho this summer, you really are my hero. And I'm smart enough to know I'll never start a fight with you."

Three in the morning. My place is finally empty. I'm too wired to sleep. I remember I was going to send Reynolds a text.

Sweet dreams.

I try to read but I think I was secretly hoping he'd wake up and text something back. I'm too distracted to follow the storyline and I don't want to get things mixed up. I snap the book shut, put my head on the pillow, and stare at the ceiling for thirty minutes. Finally, I get up, shower, dress, and head for the office. JavaStar isn't open yet. Wish I could make coffee like Penny Martin does at home.

48

We both look at our hands. The conversation is strained. I don't know who feels more uncomfortable.

"It was nice of you to stop by. But I have to get back to work."

"You okay?"

"No. But I'll be okay."

We're in the cafeteria of Aunt Maple's Candy Company down in Calumet City. While I was waiting for Tandi Brown to get a break from the packaging line I wondered again why I had come. Was it for her or for me?

I don't know what I was expecting, and the fact that I'm wondering what I might have expected confuses the question of personal motive in my head even more. Our inability to connect wasn't so surprising. But in my mind I still don't want to have done this for me. I wanted my coming to somehow be for her.

What do you say to someone who has lost a son? Just being there and saying nothing is usually best. But Tandi doesn't know me, so my visit hasn't brought the comfort of a familiar face and friend. I hand her my card.

"Call me if I can do anything or you just want to talk sometime."

She nods.

It sounds like such a cliché that it almost sticks in my throat but I get it out anyway. And it's true. "I'm praying for you."

"Thanks. I can use all that I can get."

Hug? Doesn't seem quite right with our lack of connection. Handshake? Too formal. I just nod back to her and head out the door.

Who really killed Jack Durham? I'm willing to bet it's the same person who killed Barbara Ferguson, which means it wasn't Penny Martin. I'm driving the Skyline Express from Calumet City back to the office. I'll jump on the Dan Ryan Expressway for a couple miles, merge on to 90 West, and then exit to the precinct west of the Loop.

I urge my mind to race through interviews and reports. Pictures.

An idea pops into my mind. I don't think it gets us any closer to the killer, but it's probably something we should have thought of before.

49

Thursday, November 8
11:25 p.m.

Men. They think they rule the world. But as long as you let them think they're in control, they are so easy to manipulate.

Barbara did it with Jack from his sixteenth birthday on. Some role model you were, Mom. I still can't believe his dad hired a hooker for him as a birthday present. He loves his image. If people only knew. Grandpa, what were you thinking? Although I can't protest too much—if it hadn't happened, I wouldn't exist.

I do need to pay the old man a visit. Will he claim me? Sure. As long as I sign a confidentiality contract to protect him and the family interests. We'll see how that goes.

And to think I almost lost my nerve and bolted.

Not sure Barbara always knew what she was doing, but she learned. She basically controlled Jack's pathetic life. She kept the threat of my presence dangling over his head. So he checked out—but not without taking his friends down the rabbit hole with him.

It's funny. Mom didn't mind using me to get what she wanted but, despite her crocodile tears about not knowing it was me and not wanting me to get in her line of work, I think it bothered Jack more than her that I was working for her.

When I got my hooks in Jack for some monthly cash, she about flipped out. Why would she have cared? It was a drop in the bucket to him. And it made him feel like a loving dad to pay me more than I could make being with his friends. He made them think we had an exclusive relationship.

Bobbie put an end to that, so I found another source. I'm afraid I've made a deal with the devil. I can't prove it, but it had to be him. He was supposed to scare him. He bashed his head in with a hammer. And he'd do the same to me. But as long as he thinks I know more than I really do, he can't move against me. So we'll work together. Mutually assured destruction. My high school history teacher didn't think I was paying attention but I was.

I wish I could turn the spotlight on him, but that's way too dangerous. The downside of mutually assured destruction.

At least he finally decided to communicate

before I was put in a cage. I was afraid he would go quiet on me, but he kept in touch. Thank God my attorney knew better than to ask questions and that the police were barred from checking what he brought in and out.

But no doubt, my partner is crazy.

Now he wants to kill a cop. I hope he listens to reason.

50

"Conner," I said, answering a late-night call on my home phone.

"I wanted to say thanks for working things out for me to see my brother."

"Dell?"

"The one and only."

"Why are you calling me after eleven on a work night?"

I have to change my home number. Or drop it.

"Did I wake you?"

"That's beside the point. You could have."

"You're right. I probably just wanted to hear your voice."

Ugh.

"Would your fiancée feel comfortable with you calling to hear my voice?"

"We split up."

"I'm sorry to hear that."

"I'm sure you are. That made it even easier to avoid talking to me."

"I don't need to have a reason to not talk to you. I've told you I don't want to talk to you. For you to not respect that is the problem, not following through with my wishes."

"You know we were together for six months. I think I deserve the courtesy of civil conversation. Even if you didn't reciprocate my feelings."

Oh, boy, oh, boy. Is Dell my stalker? No way would he put a video camera in my home. Would he?

"You're making my point for me. It's precisely because I didn't reciprocate your feelings that I have every right to expect and demand you not contact me. I think we might be heading for an official restraining order."

"Because of two calls?"

I pause. I'm not going to even hint that someone has invaded my privacy. But he will be a person of interest for the tech team that has taken apart the camera and has been trying to triangulate where the signal was transmitting to. No luck so far, but a suspected destination and a search warrant might be all they need to bust the creep that has been spying on me.

"Dell, I'm not engaging. I have a big day tomorrow. I'm glad it worked out for you to see your brother."

"He's been here the whole time. Smack-dab

in the middle of downtown Chicago at the Metropolitan Correctional Center at Clark and Van Buren. I guess the FBI uses the facility for federal cases. And they have a hospital wing."

I'm actually curious now. I think he knows that.

"Well, I'm sure he's happy to see you and know someone cares."

"You know better than that. He hasn't spoken to anyone, including the public attorney assigned to him."

"But he saw you."

"Yes. I go in once a week. They give us five minutes to look at each other through a glass partition. I do all the talking. He just stares at me. Might be hatred. Might be disinterest."

"Well, I'm sorry to hear that, Dell. You know, there might come a point when you have to let him go so you can move on with your life."

"I know. I think that's why I asked Morgan to marry me. We'd only gone out on a few dates."

No surprise to me. He told me he loved me after a very casual second date. Heck, we just hung out some in group settings. I'm not sure I even knew we were dating. Dell's a good-looking guy. And successful. But I knew he was a lost soul. We definitely were not together for six months. I don't think we were ever together. But my family reached out to him and he clung to us like a drowning man thrown a life preserver.

Time to cut this off. He's like the proverbial

camel. Let him get his nose under the tent flap and the next thing you know he's standing next to you in the tent.

"Dell, I've got a big day. Time for me to sign off."

"Talk again sometime?"

Here we go again. The nose is under the tent flap.

"No."

"Just no?"

"That's all that's required."

"Interesting you stayed on long enough to find out what's happening with Dean but aren't willing to show a little concern for a fellow traveler."

"Dell. You've been through a lot. I know you let your guard down with me and got help from my family. But that's over. It was over before your brother tried to kill me and my sister. But that should put the nail in the coffin on any level of relationship between us even in your mind. You need to find help elsewhere. Talk to your pastor. Talk to your counselor. But not me. And not my family. I wish you well."

"Okay. I hear you. As always, loud and clear. And I wish you well too. I really do. Hope everything works out for you and your FBI agent boyfriend."

The line goes dead. How would he know about Reynolds and me? Was he guessing? Very possible. But it's also a possibility he is my stalker. He may live like a Boy Scout, but he did grow up in the same home that produced a serial killer. Time to have CPD investigators handling my home invasion take a look at him.

Also time to get some sleep. No messages, no texts.

Which reminds me: I haven't talked to Reynolds for a couple days. What's up with that? I know he didn't like the idea of me going out with Derrick Jensen, but surely he can't be jealous. He knows that's on the clock.

51

"Okay, okay, I'm sold," Blackshear says. "I'll take what you got to Legal. But that doesn't mean we'll get your search warrant, Conner."

"Do we even need a warrant?" Don asks. "She's still under arrest for murder even if the judge did grant bail. He did put the tether on her and designate her release as house arrest. I would think we have free access."

"You might be right," Blackshear says. "But we aren't doing anything that jeopardizes evidence if in fact you are right. I think this is a procedural nuance and I don't want to make any assumptions on it. She's not been convicted of a crime and she has rights."

"She also has a steady stream of visitors now,"

I say. "I think we're late as it is. She's not a dummy. If she has anything hanging around that might incriminate her, we need to get our hands on it before she makes it disappear."

"So now you think she's guilty?" Blackshear asks. "I thought you were the one that questioned her arrest even before the Ferguson murder."

"I don't know," I answer. "I go back and forth. But I know she is her mother's daughter. Smart. Savvy. Strategic. If Bobbie had a hidden safe behind built-in drawers in her closet, it wouldn't surprise me if Penny does too. And there may be something in there that helps us nail her or whoever murdered both Durham and Bobbie. Even if she didn't do it, she knows something. She's in the middle of every aspect of this case. Or these cases."

"Like I said, I'm sold," Blackshear repeats. "But the basis of the warrant is highly speculative. I'm just letting you know it may not be granted."

We all nod and stand.

"By the way," Konkade says as I head for the door, "we are going to look into the Dell Woods angle on your home situation. After what happened in June, you should have told us sooner that he has attempted to resume communication with you. I, for one, was never convinced he was as innocent in conjunction with his brother as he looked."

"It was just two calls."

"Two too many," he says.

I've been a little peeved at Konkade during this murder case. I still think he went to the boss a couple times to rein me in on my suspicions. But his concern and follow-up on Woods means he is officially forgiven in my book.

This is impossible. I have no Barbara Ferguson to direct operations and no Tracy to follow orders getting me ready for a date. I don't know what you wear to a James Taylor concert. Sounds casual to me. But it's at the Odeum and that's fancy. I've decided on the spray-on jeans, a silk blouse, and every piece of jewelry I've ever bought. (It's all cheap.) Who knows, it might actually work.

I've been working on my makeup for an hour. I can't remember how Tracy did it. I don't think it's looking right. But it's the best I can do. I crane forward and look at my eyelashes. I run the brush through again; I've got a couple clumps I can't get smoothed out.

My phone vibrates and falls off the toilet tank again. I'm going to crack that screen if I put it back up there again. That's five straight calls. Only my mom hits the green Call button as many times as necessary to get me to answer it. Pick up? Explain I can't talk and get off immediately? Call her in the morning to tell her I'm sorry but I was working? She won't be happy either way.

The vibration stops. And begins again. My phone is sliding across the bathroom floor. I scoop it up and swipe the screen. Klarissa. That's strange. Something must be up, particularly since she's on air tonight.

I hit the Missed Call line and after a pause her number starts ringing.

"Where are you, Kristen?"

"I'm at home, Klarissa, but getting ready to go out. I'm working tonight."

She pauses. I hear a sniffle.

"You got to get off right now. Kaylen fell. Her water broke. They don't know if the baby is okay. She just got picked up by an ambulance. Jimmy is with her. She's on her way to West Suburban Medical Center in Oak Park."

Oh, dear God. "I'm on my way."

"No. I told Jimmy you would head to their house and pick up Kendra and James. I need to confirm you're on the way. He's worried sick and pulled in two directions. I've been on the phone with Kendra and she has everything under control at the moment, but it's just the two kids."

"Where are you?"

"I'm stuck in traffic driving to the hospital. I've been up in Evanston taping a story. It'll take me an hour to get there but at least ninety minutes to get to their house."

"Okay. I'll be out the door in five minutes or less. Where's Mom?"

"She did one of her field trips with the senior adults from church. She's in a van driving back from some conference downstate. I said too much to her and she's nearly hysterical. I'll call her back and keep trying to calm her down. Just go get the kids and call me back."

I can pick up Kendra for a soccer game in twenty minutes on a Saturday morning. Friday night traffic is already a mess. It'll take at least forty-five. I took a minute to scrub my face clean, change to jeans I can breathe in with a cotton pullover, grab my duck boots, and put on a medium-weight coat. My Miata fired right up and I was weaving through traffic in six minutes. I called Kendra and told her I was on my way and to sit tight.

"Aunt Kristen, are Mommy and baby Kelsey okay?"

"They're going to be fine, honey," I told her.

They are.

I hit Derrick's number. No answer. I push one and leave a message. "I have a family emergency, Derrick. No time to explain. But I have to cancel on tonight. I'll call tomorrow and explain."

I hit Don's number and Vanessa answers. "Sorry to bother you on a Friday night, Vanessa, but is Don available?"

"You never bother me, girlfriend. Everything okay?"

"Not really. Kaylen fell and her water broke. She's with Jimmy in an ambulance. I'm on my way to pick up the kids. I was supposed to be working an assignment tonight. I wanted to let Don know so he could pass the message along the phone chain."

"He's in the shower. Hold on and let me get him."

"Just have him call me when he's done. I have a couple more calls to make and I'll pick up when his number pops up."

"I am so sorry, Kristen. We'll be praying. And you know everything is going to be okay. We women are indestructible when we're carrying a little one."

"Thanks for the prayers, Vanessa. I'm sure you're right."

I check back in with Kendra and she's fine but lets me know James isn't obeying her and she's in charge.

"Tell him to behave or he's in big trouble with Aunt Kristen."

She laughs at that. Good. She's handling things fine.

I hit Mom's number.

"What's happening? Any news?" she says the second she picks up.

"Plenty of people praying, and it's all going to be fine, Mom. I'm just making sure you are okay."

"I'm breathing. But a semi turned over on 57 and we've come to a complete standstill."

"Well, relax and keep praying. There's nothing you could do here anyway. Klarissa is meeting Jimmy and Kaylen at Western Suburban. I'm picking up Kendra and James. We've got everything under control. Just relax and I'll call you when I have some news."

She starts to cry as Derrick's number pops up.

"Mom, I'm going to take this call. I'll call back when I have something. I promise."

I feel rotten hitting the button to transfer to Derrick's call. "Conner."

"I didn't think you wanted to go out with me."

"Listen, Derrick, I am so sorry to cancel on you. But my sister is on the way to the hospital and I've got to pick up the kids and get over there."

"Really?"

"Would I make up something like this?"

I think there is strain in my voice. Things are happening too fast.

"I suppose not. I'm in the back of a limo on my way over to your place. I was going to let you know we're running late. Traffic is a mess."

He doesn't sound too stressed. He sounds like he's been drinking.

"Call a friend and tell them it's their lucky night. I can't believe I'm missing James Taylor. I was looking forward to it. But I got to go. I have another call coming in and it might be news on my sister."

"You were really looking forward to tonight?"

"Absolutely, Derrick. But I have to get off and take this call. Talk to you tomorrow."

I'm on another call before he can answer. "Conner."

"Everything okay?" Don asks.

"Yeah, Don. Thanks for calling back."

"You sure everything's okay?"

"I keep telling everyone things are fine. I don't know anything. Klarissa said Kaylen fell and they're not sure the baby is okay."

"Oh, man. Tell everyone we're praying."

"I will. I just got off the phone with Derrick. I let him know I had to cancel tonight. If you could let Blackshear, Konkade, and everyone else know what's going on, I'd appreciate it. Sorry to mess with your Friday night. I know you haven't had many nights home lately."

"No problem. We're staying in and watching a family movie."

"Thanks, Don. I owe you. I have to get off. Kendra is calling me."

"Go—and tell everyone we're praying."

"I will."

I hit the Transfer button again. "Hey, Miss Kendra—what's shaking?"

"James still isn't listening."

"I'm not very far away," I say. "Tell him to get

his soccer stuff, some pajamas, and his pillow. You all are going to spend the night with me."

"Can we see Mommy and baby Kelsey at the hospital?"

"We'll see. We don't know when baby Kelsey is going to pop out. So it might be tomorrow."

"Okay," she says with a sniffle. "Should I get my pajamas and soccer stuff too?"

"You better. I'm not leaving your house unless you're spending the night with me too."

"I am!"

She sounds better already.

"And Kendra?"

"Yes, Aunt Kristen?"

"Tell James to pack a toothbrush or he'll have stinky breath."

She laughs and is already yelling at James when we hang up.

"She's beautiful," Klarissa says when I answer my phone in a stupor.

I look at my clock. It's three in the morning. I am on the far edge of my bed. I can feel Kendra's warm breath against my neck. I let both kids sleep in my bed with me. James has kicked and squirmed his way sideways and has claimed most of the bed for himself.

"How's Kay?"

"Still in a lot of pain. She wrenched her back twisting sideways to protect the baby when she fell. The doctor is going to x-ray her tomorrow, but he thinks she chipped her hipbone. But she's a champion. She's all smiles."

"How many times did Jimmy faint?"

"He kept his feet all evening and is holding Kelsey now. I've lost count, but I think he's cried at least four times."

"That's our Jimmy. Mom still there?"

"Just left. I put her in a cab."

"What time can Aunt Kristen come by with the kiddos?"

"I wouldn't make it too early. After ten."

"Okay, I'll take the kids to soccer and be there at one."

"Soccer?"

"Uh, yeah. Last week of the regular season."

She laughs. "That's our Kristen."

Before I go back to sleep I say a short prayer.

Thanks, God, that baby Kelsey and Kaylen are okay.

52

I'm not sure he's up to the task. Unless it's with a hammer. We just need the police looking in another direction. With all the enemies Jack had, is that so difficult?

I never signed up for murder, even if I wouldn't mind that detective disappearing forever. I don't know how she puts everyone under her spell. I don't see the attraction. She is querulous. She has lousy taste. I don't care how much lipstick Mom put on her, she is rude, difficult, awkward. Maybe that's her appeal.

Derrick? I figured he'd be the last to fall for a woman. Too cynical. Maybe it shouldn't surprise me. He's thirty-seven years old but has the emotional maturity of a middle schooler. Entirely different from Jack. Jack was at least aware of his surroundings. Derrick's so repressed he doesn't know it. No wonder he's captivated by her. I think she's got the emotional maturity of a middle schooler too.

But it's still a problem. Derrick knows things. And he wants to be with her. Who knows what would get said if he succeeds in landing her. With his money, how could she resist?

My partner thinks it's easier to get rid of a cop than Derrick.

It might be easier, but what creates more heat? I don't know how somebody so smart can be so stupid.

Everyone I've met since finding my mom is a case study in arrested development. Mom wanted to keep it that way. The only one who could have stepped in and said enough was Dad, but Jack didn't have the inner strength to fight it. Women and booze, no money worries— all helped medicate any desire for change. I could have helped him.

I thought Flannigan had me for a while. Now I don't think there is any way they can convict me. Even if he wanted to point a finger in my direction, he won't. He knows by now that if the heat turns back up on me, I can point everything back to him.

So why is he thinking crazy things? He's afraid of her because of that other big case she solved this year. Am I the only one who has the ability to reason? All we have to do is nothing and they will never figure out who killed Jack and Barbara.

I think she's clueless. His insider says she's clueless but lucky. That gets him wound up.

To think I almost bolted. I would have left with a lot more than I had when I arrived. But now I'm closer than I ever dreamed I could be to the real river of gold.

She lifted the rim of the large round cup with half a skinny latte left in it and took her last sip. It had passed from lukewarm to tepid. Her granola with fruit and yogurt was only half eaten too. It was delicious but she didn't want to put on weight in this period of confinement.

She rose gracefully from the table. Black ankle-high boots. Sweater dress that was probably too short for the temperature outside. But she'd had only a one-block walk; she was near the edge of her electronic tether. She put on the fitted version of a pea jacket with a thin fringe of mink around the collar.

Every eye having brunch with her in the Third Coast Café and Wine Bar at the corner of Dearborn and Goethe followed her steps out the front door and into the cold.

The two CPD watchers across the street saw her enter the used bookshop next door and resumed their argument on whether the Bears' offensive line couldn't provide pass protection or Jay Cutler held the ball too long.

53

"I never get to hold her," James says, pouting.

"Yeah, but you scored a hundred goals today," I say.

"He did not," Kendra says.

"Did too," James says and sticks his tongue out at her.

"Quiet, you two," Kaylen says sweetly. "James, you need to use your soft voice around Kelsey."

My turn to hold her. Bright blue eyes. Pink chubby cheeks. Soft downy blond fuzz. Her lips move in and out; I think she's hungry. She's wrapped up like a papoose, but I've loosened the blanket up top so I can touch those tiny little fingers. What is more amazing than a baby's fingers?

"How'd you do?" Kaylen asks Kendra.

"We won," she says, ho hum.

"And she scored two goals," I say.

"I did too," James says with a loud, hissing whisper.

"And I went to James's game and he was incredible."

"He kept knocking people down," Kendra says.

She didn't mean it as a compliment but he's beaming anyway. He's a one-man wrecking crew.

"Okay, baby sis, give me back my baby. She's ready to eat and both of us need a nap."

We made Kendra sit down when she held Kelsey. We made James sit down too, and none of us moved more than a foot away from him. But he was gentle. No one has said I have to sit down, but holding a baby makes me nervous so I've kept my butt on the chair. I stand carefully and place the pink bundle into her mother's arms.

I'm not liberated enough to be an advocate for public breastfeeding, so I give a nod of my head toward the door. Kendra and James make a beeline for Kaylen and each get a hug. They both plant careful kisses on Kelsey's forehead. I give mom and baby a kiss too and join the rest of the family in the waiting room. Jimmy went home for a couple hours to prepare his sermon. Klarissa is going to take James and Kendra with her to my mom's house. Mom will stay with Kaylen and leave when Jimmy gets back.

Usually insurance covers only a one-night stay in the hospital for newborns. Because of Kaylen's fall, the two will stay at least another two days. She does have a stress fracture in her right hip bone. Nothing too serious, and there's no real therapy other than rest and pain meds. But she's nursing, so she's having to bite the proverbial bullet.

"I didn't even know you two were together," Klarissa says.

We are at McDonald's. James wolfed his meal and is somewhere in a maze of tubes with a slide that sends him down into a pit filled with bright-colored plastic balls. One of Kendra's school friends is there and the two are talking intently at their own table. Do eight-year-olds talk about boys yet? They are giggling. I suspect maybe they do.

I chowed a Big Mac value meal. Klarissa watched me eat with thinly concealed disdain. She got some sort of salad with mandarin oranges and chicken on it. I think she's taken two bites in the last twenty minutes.

"Never seemed like the right time to tell you about it," I say.

"Well, it all sounds very romantic. Dinner on the town and then phone calls every night when he flew back home."

"Until this week. About the time I'm finally getting comfortable with the idea that we're in a relationship, he goes AWOL on me."

"That's men."

"Since my younger sister is much more experienced in the world of romance than me, explain to me what that means."

"It all goes back to the Melville novel. *Moby Dick*."

"*Now* I understand."

"Didn't you have to read that in high school?"

"It was an option in English Lit. I went with a

lighthearted comedy called *Lord of the Flies*."

She rolls her eyes. "Captain Ahab was obsessed with the hunt for the whale."

"Moby?"

"Yes, Moby. That's how men are. They are obsessed with the hunt. But when they catch us, they get bored. Catching isn't as fun as chasing."

"So Austin has buyer's remorse?"

"No, not buyer's remorse. He's crazy about you. Probably since the first day he blew into town. But you played hard to get. That made him crazier."

"I wasn't playing hard to get or anything else."

"Even better. That makes you innocent too. But no matter what your motives, you were hard to get. You always have been. You were a challenge. So when he caught you, he . . ."

She hesitates long enough for me to finish for her: "He got bored and had buyer's remorse."

She sighs.

"Hey, I'm not arguing with you," I say. "I agree. I've always confessed to being boring."

"You're not boring."

"I'm thirty. All I do is go to work, coach my niece's soccer team, go to church with my family, run the steps at my local high school, read the paper and do the crossword, and repeat the following week."

"And you do have a knack for catching bad people. That makes you interesting."

"True. But that's covered with my statement that I go to work."

"I think it's sweet you're calling him Austin."

"I haven't talked to him for five days, so I'm actually not calling him anything."

"Are you hurt?"

"I don't know. Maybe a little confused. It was kind of interesting to get a little closer to someone. On purpose. I kind of like it. But I wasn't looking for a relationship and I have some pretty big questions on getting serious with him. Little things like religion."

"What is he?"

"I'm not sure. I seem to remember him saying Episcopal."

"Have you explained that Conner girls are Baptist?"

"Not yet."

"Well, next time he's in town, invite him to Sunday dinner at Kaylen's. Mom will set things straight for you."

"That she will."

I'm not sure I'm setting my alarm. I'm exhausted. If I wake up by eight-thirty, I'll go to church. If I sleep later, can I assume God wanted me to catch up on my sleep? Does he approve of me attending Bedside Baptist?

54

Not sure why, but I woke early and read the *Chicago Trib* at JavaStar. The reviewer said the James Taylor concert Friday night was incredible.

After church I took the kids out for pizza and back over to the hospital. I held the baby again. A bunch of people have come through and apparently Jimmy has been loaded with more casseroles than the refrigerator and freezer can hold. He's now subletting half his neighbor's freezer. Kaylen is sleeping again, which is good, since no pain pills. Jimmy, Klarissa, and Mom look tired but have everything under control. Time for me to take my leave.

The temperature dropped below freezing overnight. It's a little warmer than that now but cold. Weather guy on WCI Radio said the first snow could hit by tomorrow. Time to get out my tarp and cover my car.

I decide to get at least one more outdoor run in and drive west to River Forest and park at the Thatcher Woods Forest Preserve. I take off on a seven-mile course I've done before. I've switched my Sig to a sport holster under my Under Armour cold-weather gear. I need to think. I put in earbuds from my iPod but turn the volume way down low.

Someone set up a surveillance camera in my home. Lots of times people have to go to counseling after their home has been burglarized. They feel a sense of personal violation even if they weren't there, which is usually the case. What am I feeling? Definite concern over what images someone got of me and what they might do with them. Once something goes up on the Internet there is no calling it back. It can run off to a million different sites and a million different personal computers. But heck, I didn't go to counseling after a fight to the death with a serial killer, so I doubt I'm going for this. Do I feel violated? Yes. But I think what I feel most strongly is anger.

We now know my stalker was both texting me and spying on me. Was it Dell? He definitely needs some counseling, but it doesn't feel like him.

My mind switches gears. I'm not sure what Flannigan is going to do with Martin. Unless we deliver some new piece of evidence, how can she try to prosecute her when the exact same killing method was used while she was sitting in jail?

I can faintly hear Foreigner in my earbuds. I reach down and turn up the volume and hear Kelly Hansen wailing, "You're as cold as ice . . ."

I need to keep thinking about the Martin case but my mind jumps to Reynolds. I don't think he's done anything to "sacrifice our love," since neither of us has said anything to the other about love, future, and all those other mushy things people in love talk about. Klarissa asked if I was hurt. I'm still not sure. I might be feeling a little relief. In the Middle Ages I might be a grandma. But even though I've got the number three in front of my age I think there are a lot of teen girls more ready to have a steady boyfriend than me.

I look at my watch. It's four o'clock. I do a quick estimate and calculation in my mind. Seven-minute miles, give or take. Not that bad. The sun is dropping real early these days. Thanksgiving is less than three weeks away. I have a lot to be thankful for.

Back to you, Penny. You really are cold as ice. I know it must be tough to find out you're adopted and then discover your parents are both rich and creeps. I know that the curiosity to know your blood relatives had to have been great. But from everything I saw, you didn't have too bad of an upbringing in Madison. Do you regret leaving that behind for the big city and all the junk you've gotten into?

I am still breathing heavy. Glad I remembered to charge my iPhone last night. I had to call a tow truck. I can't believe it. Someone slashed all four of my tires.

"So whose heart did you break?" the tow driver asks me while I bounce along in the passenger seat of a Mack truck that may have lost its springs on one side.

"Not guilty," I say.

"Well, you made someone real mad. Any ideas?"

"I wouldn't even know where to begin," I answer.

"Yeah, I figured you for the sort that gets along with everybody."

"*Au contraire.* The reason I don't know where to begin is the list is so long."

The driver says the tires can't be fixed—"He cut through sidewalls, so you're getting four new tires"—and the cheapest place he knows is Wrigleyville's Discount Debbie's Tire Store.

Discount Debbie?

He senses my concern about Debbie. "Same tires, same service, but about 15 to 20 percent less."

Does he do Discount Debbie's Tire commercials when he's not loading broken-down cars on his flatbed?

"And nobody does this on a Sunday night?"

"No one is open. You need to let me know if we're dropping your ride off at Debbie's or somewhere else."

"Debbie it is."

I call Klarissa and she gets online and finds a rental car place still open other than at Midway or O'Hare. I take the cheapest deal they have.

It's seven o'clock when I get home. Two hours later than I planned. I kept trying to shift gears with an automatic transmission the whole drive. I don't mind a manual transmission, but it would be nice to keep two hands on the wheel—or if something else needs attention, at least one hand. Is it time to look at getting a new car? I'm guessing four new tires is going to run me six to eight hundred bucks. Not sure I can afford to take on new payments again. And with what I'll have left after the tires, I probably couldn't buy anything better than what I have.

Two phone calls to make. Jensen and Reynolds. I'm not looking forward to either.

Tomorrow I'll report the tires.

55

"Slow down, slow down," Officer Long says.

All-white hair but a young face. Forty? He's in charge of my stalker case. After telling him on the phone about my tires being slashed, he popped right on up to interview me and get some background.

"So you're saying in the last year someone has sent you Hallmark cards with cryptic messages? But not since the Cutter Shark case ended."

"Right."

"And someone put yellow Post-it Notes on your desk?"

"Correct. But that stopped about then too. I think I know who did it but can't prove it."

"Think it was the same person doing the Hallmark cards?"

"No. I think someone who works here did the Post-it Notes as a joke. I've suspected the Hallmark cards were from someone I arrested."

"So two people. And both open investigations."

"I don't think the Post-it Notes are a big deal and we can just leave that alone."

He scratches out *Post-it Notes* on his interview pad. "Then there's the text messages. Same guy that's doing the cards?"

"I don't think so. And the cards stopped. But the guy who I suspect sent the cards got cut loose from Cook County Correctional back in May or June. And I'm wondering if it's him who slashed my tires."

He looks at his interview pad perplexed and finally writes a note.

"So that's three with the text-message guy."

"Or woman."

He nods and writes that down.

"Then we have the Peeping Tom with the video camera and your ex-boyfriend who's made contact with you and who was material to a case. Are we looking at a fourth and a fifth?"

"I may be wrong, but I don't think whoever

slashed my tires is the same one who's doing the text messages—who I know is the Peeping Tom. We're talking about two people. The tires was either someone totally unrelated to me and the case—or it could be Incaviglia, the guy I arrested," I say, pointing to his name on the interview pad. "But we aren't pursuing the Post-it Note poster, so I think that's one less to worry about. And Woods isn't involved in this. I think we can leave him alone too."

"That's not what Squires said about Woods."

I'm confused now.

"Listen, Kristen, we'll look at Woods because we know where he is. Maybe lean on him to eliminate him. The guy that got cut loose is still roaming the city somewhere, but we've got his picture out there. If we find him he's got a lot bigger problems than slashing your tires. But we'll make sure you and Squires get some time alone with him.

"This camera in your house is another matter."

"What's that mean?"

"That was a high-end piece of equipment. It's not common in the market yet."

"What does that mean?"

"Well, that's why I was doubling back on previous things that may have had to do with the department."

He is chewing on his lower lip, hesitating.

"So?" I finally ask.

"Only people using that model I know of right now are law enforcement."

"How'd it go?" Don asks.

I roll my eyes.

"What?"

"It's just such a mess sorting things out."

"Who's got your case?"

"Long."

"White hair?"

"Yes."

"I know him a little. He's a good guy. Want me to talk to him?"

"Don, I know you already have. You don't have to fight my battles."

"That's my point you keep missing: I'm not sure if any of these are just your battles. If CPD cut Incaviglia loose due to an administrative error and he's involved in any of this, then anything he directs at you is directed at all of us. Ditto on the camera, which is probably connected to the Durham case."

"Possibly."

"Even if it's only *possibly,* you have to communicate."

"I hear and obey."

He snorts and we move on.

Two calls I didn't want to make. Two strikeouts.

I left a message for Derrick: "Everything

worked out here. My sister and the baby are fine. I read the review in the *Trib* this morning and it sounds like it was a great show. Hope you enjoyed yourself."

If he never calls back will I be unhappy? Probably not. Do I think he knows something about both murders? I don't know anything for sure, but I think he knows more than he is saying on Jack Durham's murder. Do I think Derrick is a suspect in either murder? He and Durham fought. But their friendship goes back furthest. He and Kelly Granger are the two friends that go all the way back to kindergarten with Durham. Would he kill his lifelong friend? I'm not sure I see the clarity of thought in his alcohol haze to do something like that.

It's not that he's dumb. Between his education and sarcasm, he shows evidence of being intelligent. But there is such a lack of focus the few times I've been around him. He's there but not there. It's obviously alcohol, but I think it's more a bad habit of avoiding thought in case it forces a commitment of any kind at any level. With most of Durham's friends that was the common denominator. No commitment to a job, a woman, or anything noble.

I called Reynolds next. When it went into voice mail I hesitated just a second and then hung up.

Jerk. Maybe I've been smarter than I've given myself credit for. Is this what happens in relationships? Maybe I've been the smart one to keep guys at a distance. I thought there might be something wrong with me, but maybe I have a refined gut instinct that tells me when someone is just playing games. I was reluctant to let Reynolds get close. Then all of a sudden I wasn't, but I still had an uneasiness.

I suppose I should check to see if he's okay. It's always possible he got hurt in the line of duty. He's a former Army Ranger and I'm not sure he has a job description with the FBI even if he is a major. I think he has some violence in him and would gladly accept dangerous assignments. But who would I call? Willingham?

Hey, Bob, sorry to bug you, but what's up with Austin?

I'm not going to do that. I think Klarissa might be right—even if I am a white whale in her narrative. He liked the hunt more than the catch. Not sure I can blame him. I think I've got a good heart but I'm still not easy to be around. I'm definitely not politically correct. At the time I thought his advice about how I described what I was going to do with Monster was humorous. He delivered it with a light touch. But I think he was serious. I think he was trying to socialize me a bit. I admit I need to do some refining and fine-tuning—*Mom, your work is not in vain; I might be growing up a little*—but I'm not sure I would do well in that kind of relationship anyway.

I'm a mile from my house and downshift into third as I turn onto my street. I dropped off the Kia rental car and picked up my oldie-but-goody Miata at six o'clock. Putting almost seven hundred dollars on my credit card was painful. I considered skipping the extra sixty bucks for alignment, but Don overheard my conversation and poked his fat head in my cubicle and said, "Get the alignment." I did.

I downshift into second and pull into the Gas & Grub. I push the button beside my seat to release the lock on the gas tank door. The first snow decided not to show up but it's freezing. Low twenties. I'm not dressed for it yet.

I reach in to get my credit card out of my wallet and glance up at the front of the convenience store. Someone is huddled close to a pay phone with a small aluminum roof and sloped sides to provide cover for head and shoulders. Someone very familiar. The punk. Jared Incaviglia. Coincidence he is blocks from my place? I think not.

I sit down in my car, grab my iPhone off the passenger seat, swipe the screen, bring up the dial pad on the phone, and hold down the number six until it starts ringing in to CPD dispatch.

"This is Detective Kristen Conner. I need immediate backup at the Gas & Grub on Ravenswood Avenue, east side of the street, just north of Foster. I am moving in to arrest Jared

Incaviglia. I-N-C-A-V-I-G-L-I-A. He should be considered armed and dangerous. There is an outstanding warrant for his arrest. I am moving in to make contact now. Send any squad car you got in the area. Doesn't matter if you send them silent or with siren."

Gun out or holstered? Last time I faced off with him he gave me a half-inch scar on my left wrist. No big biggie. Unholstered. I hear a siren that's within a mile. He is too engrossed in his conversation to look up. I'm sure he's arguing with someone. He never hears me come up behind him. Then he reaches back and scratches the back of his head. He turns right. It's Incaviglia, all right. He spies me in his peripheral vision, flings the handset against the wall with a sharp crack, and bull-rushes me. I sidestep him easily and put out a leg to trip him. He sprawls on the concrete and barely gets his hands down to break the fall. Before he can push up on his knees to run for it, I am on top of him. I wrench an arm up behind his back as far as it will go and plant my knee in the small of his back to keep him from wriggling forward.

The manager of the Gas & Grub has run out into the parking lot. Everyone outside has run in or gotten in their cars and driven off fast. A couple people across the street and on the corner are looking over with jaws hanging. I keep Incaviglia's arm shoved up high, put my gun in its holster, reach in my pocket, and flip open my leather case that holds my gold shield.

"CPD. Back off, pal."

He does as a squad car races in next to us, siren blaring and blue lights circling the night air. It's getting dark way too early these days. I hold my shield up high so they don't shoot the good guy. I remember the last time I arrested Jared. He got a lawyer to press charges of excessive force against me. I wonder if he will try that tactic again. Either way, he's in big trouble.

"He's armed and likes to fight," I say to the officer closest to me. "Careful when you cuff him."

Two more squad cars pull up in the next few minutes. We like to socialize when we make arrests. Incaviglia has been cuffed and is in the back of the first black-and-white cruiser. He looks sullen. He has been read his rights. I've given my statement. The owner and a couple customers are being asked questions and statements are being taken now. I still need to put gas in my car.

I look over at Incaviglia. The door has been opened and the officer is saying something to him. He looks past the officer and winks at me. Typical of him.

"Hey, Conner," he calls out.

I just look at him and say nothing.

"We'll talk again, but better be nice if you want to learn anything about who shot your old man."

I am speechless.

The door slams and the officer circles the car to the passenger side. They pull out of the lot toward the Second Precinct, where Incaviglia will be booked for the second time this year. He and I stare at each other as long as we can make eye contact.

Yes, Jared, we'll be talking again. Soon.

As I get in my car I wonder again when we are going to get the warrant to re-search Penny's condo. Blackshear assigned it to Randall. Randall seems like a good enough guy, but everything he works on takes forever.

56

Monday, November 12
7:43 p.m.

It's a problem when two people who don't trust each other have to trust each other.

He said to cut all communication for a couple days. That was fine. We needed to.

But that means I have no way to know what's going on and anticipate things. And I was right.

So he suddenly contacted me again just two days later. They want to take another look at me. He said if I've got anything hidden, to get rid of it. That's a problem. I need everything I have hidden to prove I didn't do it.

I didn't think he could do it, but he killed Jack. Then he killed Bobbie. If I get rid of what I have, why would I not be next?

Even if I wanted to move things out of my place, how would I do it? My attorney could do it—but who's to say he wouldn't go with a better offer? And he would get a better offer than what I pay him. One thing I've learned is that these people know how to use money as a weapon.

Let's hope my backup hiding place is as good as I think it is.

Sometimes it's better to leave things alone and let them sort themselves out. The way things are isn't such a bad thing. It might be better for the investigation to stay stuck on me. That attorney is arrogant and stubborn. That's a good combination for me. If she keeps the focus on me, less chance they'll look at him. And that increases the chances both of us get off free and clear. If he gets nailed, he's going to try taking me with him as an accomplice. That's not true with Jack's murder for sure. If you look at things a certain way, it could be construed as true on Bobbie's murder.

A jury isn't going to be sympathetic to someone who might possibly have contributed to her mom's death, even if she had nothing to do with her dad's.

If I let him think he can just quit on me and go on living like he was, that's probably the only short-term solution. But it's not a long-term fix. It's obvious he can't be trusted. He'll screw it up either way.

He will need to be taken care of. I can't believe I just thought that.

Then there's her. She just doesn't impress me, but if his source is right and she's the one behind the warrant, then she does seem to have a sixth sense. I guess she is lucky.

Maybe his plan to make her disappear is the way to go. That wouldn't have anything to do with me.

But if he screws that up and ends up under the spotlight, that will probably be what topples me.

That would be a disaster.

She dipped a toe in the bath steaming with scented ginger bath oil. Might still be too hot for comfort, but heat is what cleanses you inside and out, she thought. She flinched as she stepped in but refused to budge an inch and pull her foot free. She pushed the button on the side of her Jacuzzi tub and jets of water began to shoot from various levels and angles.

She slid her second foot into the water. She was feeling better already.

57

I didn't even feel my phone buzz.

I missed four calls while arresting Incaviglia. Mom—a short message telling me to call her. Kaylen's home phone. Then a short message from Kendra to say thanks for letting her stay at my house. *Hope you feel that way forever about Aunt Kristen—even when you are a snotty teenager.*

Next up was Derrick. Long message.

"Okay, Detective."

His voice slurs. Pretty sure he's drunk. I am a detective after all.

"I'm going to put you out of your misery."

A pause. Is that a threat?

"I know I'm not a very good guy, but I'm not as dumb as I look. Not even when I drink too much. I know you can't stand me. Can't say I blame you. I can't stand me either."

I hear the sound of him taking a swallow of something. I can picture him drinking whiskey straight from a bottle. Then again, it might be fresh apple and carrot juice. Not.

"I know you were willing to go out with me so you could take notes for the good old Chicago Police Department. Plus I guess you like James Taylor. Maybe you would have let me nibble on your ear and then blurt out a confession or the clue to who did it."

He laughs and then starts a hacking cough. Takes him ten seconds to cough out whatever went down his throat the wrong way.

"Sorry 'bout that. Hope I didn't blow your eardrum out. I do have a confession to make. I kind of liked you. No. Scratch that. I mean I really liked you. You actually made me a little nervous and tongue-tied at the Bears game. I watched you all afternoon. I probably already knew then you weren't one of Bobbie's girls.

"I was kind of back on my game at the president's fundraiser. Sarcastic. Sardonic—and I do know the difference between the two. Even after you got busted because of your sister I still liked you. You got me thinking it might be a good time to change. But there's been a lot of water over the dam. And a lot of it was polluted.

"So I'm calling to put you out of your misery. I'm not going to ask you out again, so you don't have to pretend to be interested in me. Have a good life, Kristen."

His voice goes down to a whisper and he says, "And I really mean that."

I want to think about what he said—especially the part about polluted water over the dam and wanting to change, but my phone beeps over to the next message. Reynolds.

"Hi, Kristen. Was hoping you could pick up.

Miss me? I sure missed you. Sorry all I had time to do was leave a message on your office voice mail. And yes, as I predicted, I'm wiped out. China is always a grind. But the meetings were good. Don't know if our presentation on the amount of pirated software and music we have coming in from their country will do any good. But we served them fair notice that there will be repercussions if they don't crack down. That didn't come from the FBI, obviously; that was State Department. But I was, as they say, proud to be an American.

"Hey, you have me rambling. Call back when you can. I got to type up reports at the office tomorrow, but hopefully I can fly to Chicago a little later in the week. Talk soon."

I'm mediocre at best on responding to e-mail. I might as well not have a Facebook account—not hard to keep up with my ten friends in person. And I'm still not sure I know what Twitter is. There's only six others like me in America, and the seven of us hold a convention every year.

I do pick up texts and fire back immediately, if so inclined. I'm also very good about checking all phone messages and returning calls in a timely fashion. I don't like it when my voice messages back up.

Reynolds has been out of the country. Says he left me a message. I can check Records tomorrow morning—and believe me, I will. Maybe I'm not the great white whale.

I'm going to give him the benefit of the doubt tonight. Innocent until proven guilty. But if I find out he didn't really leave me a message . . .

Okay, Kristen, cool it. Why would he lie to you about something so easy to check on? Why would he lie about anything? He seems to be a stand-up guy.

58

"I was right."

We knocked on Penny's front door at ten this morning and Konkade served her the search warrant. She just shrugged and said, "Well, come on in, but please wipe your feet on the mat—and pick up after yourself this time."

The place is immaculate. Just like I remember it. Very stylish. Contemporary. Great taste. Very different from her mother's vibe, but she could still be featured in a style magazine.

Randall and I led the way to her bedroom and into the closet. He got on one knee and reached under the bottom shelf. We all heard the sound of a latch releasing. And there was the built-in safe. Like mother, like daughter.

"Okay, let's call in the mechanic and get this bad boy opened," Don says.

"Why?" Penny asks. She has followed us and is behind us in the doorway of the closet. "I can open it for you if you'd like."

Martinez was supposed to keep her segregated from our search. I think Martinez's brains turn to mashed potatoes when he's around a pretty girl.

Don looks at me. I shrug and nod yes.

"Make room," he says.

Penny looks at each of us with a pleasant smile as she squeezes through the gauntlet to the electronic keypad. *Uh-oh.* That is not a good sign.

She keys in the necessary numbers and pushes the green lock button. There is a hiss and the door pushes open.

"Step back, please," Don says to her.

She obliges and he steps forward. Twelve eyes peer intently as he opens the door. There is no sound of an explosion, but Geraldo Rivera would be proud. I had to watch *The Mystery of Al Capone's Vaults*, a show he produced and hosted back in the mid-eighties, for a class on law enforcement and the media. Not sure why the prof picked that one, but it was fairly interesting until the vault was opened and found to be empty except for some trash.

Penny's vault is almost as empty as Al's. She has no trash.

I'm driving back to the station. Don is on the phone with Blackshear.

"Conner was right, but someone emptied the contents."

He listens.

"Yeah, we think someone tipped her off. Maybe her attorney has a source in the DA's office. Maybe we have a leak in Homicide—though I doubt it. We looked her place over thoroughly, but we didn't turn it inside out like the first search. No one has that nice of a safe and keeps nothing in it."

I can hear Blackshear's voice droning in the background but can't pick out very many words.

"Randall said the same thing. This actually makes her look suspicious. She should have left some stuff in there. Made it look more natural."

They both laugh at something Blackshear says and then Blackshear speaks for at least a minute.

"Taken care of. Bruce was with us. He swiped the entire inside of the safe. If there's any DNA from Jack Durham in there, he'll find it."

"Do you think Penny is innocent?" asks Robert Durham Sr.

Don and I are in his palatial office along with his son, Robert Jr., and my football buddy Stanley McGill, Durham Jr. and Sr.'s personal attorney.

Don and I look at each other.

"There are still a lot of reasons to think that Ms. Martin committed the act or was involved in the act against your son," I say. "But with the striking similarities in how Barbara Ferguson was murdered while Ms. Martin was in the Cook County Correctional Center, there are serious doubts."

Durham Sr. considers this. He licks his lips. He looks at Robert Jr. and at Stanley, then looks me straight in the face. Don is playing the role of the Invisible Detective this time around.

"I believe that Barbara Ferguson told you of the possibility Ms. Martin is Jack's daughter and my granddaughter."

McGill clears his throat.

"Don't worry, Stanley, I'm not confessing to a crime. Robert Jr. and I have talked it over. If the girl is innocent and proves to be who Ferguson and she claim she is, we are happy to welcome her into the family and she'll be added to my will. If she decides to live up to family standards, she can be included to whatever degree she wishes in family functions."

"That's good, sir," I say.

Now is definitely not the right time and I won't let myself smile. But the thought of Robert Sr. and his long-lost granddaughter Penny locking horns is something I would pay to see.

"You're younger than I thought you would be," he says to me. "You've had quite a lot of success at an early point in your career."

"Luck and being in the right place at the right time," I say, a little embarrassed.

"I don't believe that and neither do you," Robert Sr. says. "I know a lot of successful people, and many of them have a sixth sense. Let me know if you ever want to make a switch to private investigation. Durham and Durham could make room for a person of your obvious talents."

I nod but have the feeling I am being set up for the kill.

"The reason Dad asked if you thought Penny was innocent is not something he's comfortable bringing up," Robert Jr. says. "None of us are. But there is the matter of Jack's share in the Durham family trust. We have provisions on how to divide and assign it, but want to know if Martin will be in a position to contest it."

Ahhh. Now we know the purpose of this polite get-together on the sixty-eighth floor of the Standard Oil Building.

"It wouldn't be appropriate for us to share any particulars of the case," I say.

Did I say too much already? I think Senior and Junior have the good-cop, bad-cop routine worked out.

On cue Senior says, "We wouldn't want you to do anything that would hinder your investigation. Robert, I think we could have brought that up in another more appropriate time and place," he says in a slightly scolding tone.

Yep. They have the good-cop, bad-cop thing down to a T.

"We are sorry for your loss, sir," Don says, now visible again. "We will continue to do everything in our power to seek justice in your son's death. Unless there's anything else we might answer—"

"No, no," Robert Sr. says, rising to his feet. "We've taken valuable time from you and don't want to be a burden to the system."

We all give polite nods, smiles, and handshakes. As Don and I exit the office, Robert Sr. calls to my back, "Don't forget what I said, Detective Conner. Consider that an official offer to join the firm of Durham and Durham."

On the drive back to the Second I yawn.

"Forgot to mention, nice job on busting Incaviglia," Don says as he turns left onto Western Avenue. "Long night?"

"Not really," I say. "I didn't even have to drive down to Precinct. I made my statement at the Gas & Grub."

"Same place we arrested him first time?"

"No. Different one. The one on Ravenswood, close to my place."

"I wonder why I didn't get a job offer," he says. I laugh.

"Wasn't because I'm African American?"

"McGill is African American."

"True. So either they've filled their quota or I'm just being sensitive."

I punch him. "This time, yes, you are being

sensitive. And by the way, if I show up at his office tomorrow at eight a.m., what are the odds Durham will explain his offer wasn't really an offer?"

"I'm not betting on that one, but I wouldn't trust anyone in that room as far as I could throw them."

"No doubt. I think Junior might have played the real reason for the meeting a bit too hard."

"All planned and rehearsed," Don says.

"You read my mind, partner."

Don applies the brakes hard and I wake up wild-eyed with a snort. I suspect he stopped harder than he needed to, and I give him a dirty look. We are in the parking lot of the Second. I look at my watch; I fell asleep for twenty-five minutes on the drive from Durham and Durham. I am tired. I talked with Reynolds until one in the morning. That's two in the morning for him. He's got to be dragging today too. Not sure I even remember what we talked about. Reminds me that I need to check and see if he actually left me a phone message that he would be out of the country with little to no cell phone access for six days.

Don and I cover the meeting with the Durhams with Blackshear, Czaka, and Zaworski, who joins us by phone. He says he'll keep working half days, then get back to full-time after New Year's.

Czaka is impatient and pushes us to stay on

task. When the senior Durham—a billionaire and big political donor—is involved, everyone in authority wants to know what happened and exactly what was said. My guess is Czaka won't leave the office until he's done writing a report for Fergosi and Daniels.

It takes me five minutes I don't have, but I found the unplayed message from Reynolds. Don't know how I missed it and I feel stupid for getting dramatic that he didn't call or pick up his phone when I called. Klarissa will love every minute of this. She puts the drama in drama queen.

I make another hour-long visit to the Jack Durham contact-and-event board. Kelly Granger. One of the inner circle. He and Jack had a fist-fight five years ago on a yacht in the Mediterranean. Sounds like the kind of thing that Granger might have harbored in his heart. But he won the fight and everyone present said the two were drinking together all night. Granger was divorced two years ago. Someone thought Jack was the cause. Granger's ex said no. Granger said no. Who knows?

My mind traces over every face. The only face that jumps out is the only one that didn't have an alibi that held up, the only one caught on security camera in the near vicinity of Durham's condo, the one that seemed most sincere in her disdain for Durham—the others spoke horribly about him but it was always mixed with amusement. Penny Martin. Abandoned daughter. Has to be her.

But then who killed Ferguson? Derrick? Maybe the most lost of all Jack's lost boys. Another member of the circle. Someday a psychiatrist will have a field day writing about this group of grown men with full-blown Peter Pan syndrome.

I look slowly and carefully at the faces of Ferguson's contractors. We've gone back five years to interview anyone who worked for her in the past that we could find. They come and go. Some return to wherever they came from to start a normal life and hope their time with Bobbie doesn't come back to haunt them. Jack's crew weren't Bobbie's only clients, but they were the most lucrative part of her business. None of them established a real relationship with any of the girls. But a few of her clients not tied to Durham ended up marrying women they had previously paid to sleep with. I'm not going to even joke about which period of the relationship cost them most. I do wonder how they put that kind of history aside.

Penny. Derrick. Could those two have worked together the whole time? When I was looking at the board it kind of felt right. Now I'm not so sure.

I finally head home by way of Planet Fitness. Gary called and invited me to a boxing workout with him and several friends. It's great, though one of Gary's punches slips the paddle I'm holding and clips me on the chin. I look at it in the mirror next to the mat where we were sparring. The chin doesn't bruise much, but I might have the smudge of a blue-black contusion by morning.

A couple of his other buddies want to see if a "girl" can punch, so I hit a total of four rounds, which has my arms as wobbly as Jell-O. When I take my turns with the paddles, Gary's definitely the best. One guy hits harder, but none of them can combine his speed and power. Gary's fiancée shows up at the end of the workout and he introduces us. Heather. He's definitely all *semper fi* today. *Good.* No cheater is going to have a chance with me anyway.

There I am being judgmental again. I agree it's not up to us humans to separate the sheep and the goats in eternity. But I still can't shake the feeling that when you see a goat, you gotta call it what it is.

I'm sure I'm missing something. I doubt I'm going to get nominated for theologian of the year. Do they have awards for theologians?

I arrive home after eight. I stop at my mail slot and carry it up along with a takeout bag containing a plastic carton filled with a grilled chicken Caesar. It's been in the car for ninety minutes but shouldn't be too soggy. The question is whether the twenty-degree temperature ruined the lettuce.

59

Thursday, November 15
4:30 p.m.

What is wrong with him? Does he want to get caught? Does he want both of us to spend the rest of our lives behind bars? I had a taste of that. No, thank you.

I know he was bitter, especially when it came to Jack. But he has jumped the shark. Kill Derrick. Kill the detective. Then kill another cop to tie up loose ends.

Why doesn't he just come out and say it? Then kill me.

To think, when he introduced himself to me I thought I was lucky beyond belief. Barbara was putting barriers up between Jack and me. He was one of the few people who could knock them down.

He was charming, even if I could see the anger and resentment bubbling just below the surface. He was at least under control. Not anymore.

Why did he have to kill Jack? I wonder if I could have controlled him like Barbara controlled Jack. Obviously not.

Even after he killed Jack, he was never in

danger. I never wanted Barbara dead, but in reality, it was a stroke of genius that cleared me and protected himself at the same time.

It's time I start thinking about loose ends. Namely, him. I've never killed anyone in my life, much less considered it. But I am considering it.

I have to step carefully. I don't think I can move against him now—and he certainly can't move against me without killing off the perfect diversion for his crimes.

One day one of us will act.

She sighed. A bell rang. The masseuse said the ninety minutes were up. *The end of a massage is always a sad thing,* she thought. But she hadn't eaten yet today and was ready to travel 250 yards, the outer limit of her electronic tether, to have a salad and glass of wine. She watched him fold up his table, which had been set up in her living room. She handed him three one-hundred-dollar bills. Two for the massage, one for the tip.

It felt a whole lot better to give tips than to receive tips. Giving meant you had something to give. Receiving meant you were depending on others to get by.

She wondered why her attorney couldn't seem to get the order for house arrest rescinded. He told her to be patient and he might have even better news for her. He felt the DA was finally wavering and might drop charges completely. She could be off house arrest and a free person within days.

Only one person could mess up things now. *Why can't I act against him now?*

60

"I forgot to ask," Reynolds says. "Did Dell Woods ever let you know I got it worked out for him to visit his brother?"

"Yes, he did," I say. I roll my eyes. "True to form, he asked if we could meet to talk and tried again to put a guilt trip on me that I have cut him off completely, including any contact with my family."

"Smart to do. He seems okay in so many ways, but not when it comes to his brother."

"Or me."

"True dat."

"So what took so long for him to get to see his brother?"

"His brother didn't want to see him or anyone else. He asked for solitary confinement and invoked his right of privacy."

"So the FBI wasn't hiding him?"

"Not at all. Not sure we're still so glad we insisted on being the custodial agency. I think

Dr. Van Guten and Willingham thought they could mine a treasure trove of psychological data from him to help on profiling psychopaths. But he isn't talking to anyone."

"That's what Dell told me. Have you seen him?"

"I have. But not face-to-face. From behind a one-way viewing mirror. After what you did to him, he's never going to be handsome again."

That brings up a flood of bad memories and emotions. I look down at my plate and poke at the last of the ribs. We are tucked in the back of Chicago Q. When I go out with Reynolds it's always a new restaurant for me and usually one I've never heard of. He said the reviews for here were great if you wanted a bistro approach to a barbecue joint. I don't know about the bistro part of that equation, but I do like barbecue.

We split two appetizers, the fried green tomatoes, and an order of shrimp and grits. I held my own. I went with the full slab of baby back ribs and he ordered prime rib. I know he is on some fitness program that alternates weights and running throughout the week. He better keep it up. He might have a bigger appetite than me, and that's saying something.

The snow outside has begun to fall. The TV and radio stations have been announcing it was upon us like an alien invasion and the street traffic is light. So the snow is accumulating as a beautiful white instead of a dirty gray. That will change tomorrow.

"I probably shouldn't have brought that up," he says.

"No big biggie," I say back to him. "It happened. Not the last time it will come up."

"What did the psych doc say to you when you were debriefed on the whole case?"

I clear my throat and take a long drink of water. My mind whirls, figuring out how to say I skipped the mandatory psychological sessions.

"Don't tell me . . ." he says.

I smile.

"I love that smile, but I'm not sure it's going to work this time."

I stand halfway up and kiss him. Not quite full on the lips but pretty close.

"That, however, might get you off the hook and delay this conversation for a couple months."

I don't care who is watching. I stand up, bend over, and give him a long, hard kiss. Might be the most kiss I've delivered since my boyfriend in college. I sit back down and smile again.

"So what are we going to do with you, Detective Conner?"

"I don't want to be a downer, but the last person who asked me that very question is now dead."

He laughs. "Good thing I'm not superstitious, but that is a downer."

I told him about my first experience with Barbara Ferguson, my blatant dislike of her, and how I think we ended up being friends at some level. He just listened. He never looked bored. He kept eye contact the whole time. He didn't say anything until I was all talked out.

"Let's look at this thing from the heart," he said. "When identifying the motive for a murder, what motivations top the list?"

"Jealousy and money usually top the list. Revenge is up there."

"Well, if it's Penny, you could cite revenge, like the DA is doing. Her dad abandoned her. I guess you could add jealousy if you wanted to argue that she resented growing up in a nice middle-class home while her dad lived like a Saudi prince. But on the money, if it was daddy dearest sending her the monthly stipend, she would actually be killing the cash cow. Now it sounds like grandpa and uncle are going to shower a lot more wealth on her than the stipend, but unless she knew them, she wouldn't know that. She would probably assume she was going to have to go to court to get anything from her dad's estate. And rich people like that always have wills. If he didn't know about her, she might not be in it."

"A lot to think about," I say.

"But even if you sort out Penny's hypothetical motives for hypothetically killing her dad, you haven't started on assimilating that into the Ferguson murder."

"Correct. That's where the DA is stuck."

"So ignore Penny. Doesn't mean she wasn't involved. But go with the obvious. One murderer. And then throw out love and jealousy and revenge and everything else. Make it simple. Follow the money. Who would most profit from the deaths of Jack Durham and Barbara Ferguson?"

"I think we've talked ourselves all around that question, but I think you've put that in much sharper focus than we've achieved. I guess that's why you're FBI and we're local law enforcement."

We talked until midnight when Chicago Q shut down. I think he wanted an invite over to my place. We haven't hit expectations head-on. I'm still trying to wrap my mind around the idea that I have a steady in my life. It's been a long time and I still have a lot of other things on my mind. He's got a room in the O'Hare Hilton, which is connected to the airport—and a six a.m. flight. So it wasn't hard for me to prevail in sending him on his way. I slipped and slid through empty streets back to my apartment. I hate to admit but I'm kind of glad he lives in a faraway city. I like alone. I need some space. I have to think through what he means to me and what that might look like if we tried to create a future. He's not said it, but he's done a little hinting that we should perhaps talk about us. I agree. But not tonight.

I need to sleep. And I need to ponder the question: *Who has the most to profit from the deaths of Jack Durham and Barbara Ferguson?*

When I was on the Cutter Shark case I prayed that God would help me find a killer. Usually when we pray like that and we get the answer we asked for, we have already moved on in our minds and don't give thanks where thanks is due. I think I said thanks to God. I do so now in case I forgot. And I ask him to help me find a killer.

61

We pulled Tedford into a meeting with the principal investigation team on Jack Durham. Blackshear had me pose the money question to him.

"So when you ask who has the most to profit, are you defining that in terms of raw dollar increase or relative dollar increase?"

"What's that mean?" Martinez asked.

"Amount versus percentage," Randall said.

"Like I said, what does that mean?" Martinez repeated.

After a few minutes of back-and-forth, I said, "We want both."

Tedford nodded. "Easy enough."

"So do we try to guess how people thought they might be benefitting at the time of the murder?" Don asked.

"Not necessary," I said. "Really, the only person whose point of view might have changed over time is Penny. She was in jail when the second murder occurred. So this exercise doesn't include her. It's always possible she will be implicated as an accomplice, but let's find the person who would benefit from Jack's death and who had the freedom to kill both him and Barbara."

Everyone nodded. Tedford accepted the invite to go to lunch with Martinez, Randall, Don, and me.

"What if money isn't the motivation?" Tedford asks.

"Then we're no closer to or further from the murderer," I say.

We're eating at Portillo's Hot Dogs on Ontario off the Magnificent Mile. No surprise, Martinez has mustard in his beard. I'm not a big hot dog eater, but I probably like Ed Debevic's over on Wells the best. If I'm in the mood for a hole-in-the-wall, it's hard to beat Devil Dawgs. But Portillo's is great. I got Don to split a chopped salad with me. I should have stayed healthy—or at least healthier—and gotten their chicken salad. But I do like a chili dog. Good thing Reynolds flew to DC this morning. I asked for extra onion.

"Well, what you're asking for is straight-forward. I'll put everyone on your board in a spreadsheet and run both formulas. But based on the last will and testament, I already know who stands to gain the most dollars. Probably the most percentage-wise too."

"Who?" Don, Martinez, Randall, and I ask in unison.

I'm sure four mouths stuffed with hot dogs is not a pretty picture for Tedford, but he just smiles.

"I should have said 'I think,' so give me the weekend. If money is the motive, you'll have your murderer on Monday by noon."

"Conner."

"This is . . . this is Tandi Brown. Is the offer to talk still on the table?"

"You bet. When and where?"

"How about tonight at my house? I'm home from work now but I don't want to take public transportation after dark."

"Have you all eaten?"

"I'm getting ready to fix something."

"Why don't I bring a Gino's pizza and a salad over?"

"You don't have to."

"But I want to. Your girls eat pizza?"

"Not sure they eat anything else."

"Give me your address and I'll see you in about an hour and a half."

I had just arrived home. I shed my work clothes and put on jeans with a heavy cable-knit sweater. I look at tonight's weather forecast on my iPhone. It got up to forty today but it will drop into the low thirties overnight. Then it's going to move up to the low fifties tomorrow. That's great. My Snowflakes are in the championship game of our league tournament at six. Our first-ever night game.

"I told you my story, but what about you? Why isn't a pretty girl like you married?"

"I haven't found Mr. Right."

"Well then, don't settle until you do," Tandi says with a laugh. "Nothing good happened to me from hoping I could turn Mr. Wrong into Mr. Right. I really did love Keshan's dad, but he really did love the drugs he sold."

"How'd he take the news?"

"I don't know if he knows. No one has seen him around for a couple months. When I told his mom she said she'd pass the word on to him when she heard from him next. Thought he might be in New Orleans."

"How'd he get hooked?"

"Same as a lot of people. He did some merchandise runs when he was a kid and suddenly had pocket money. Then he tried the merchandise. End of story."

"Sad."

"Very sad."

We talk until eleven and I head home. I don't know how you survive what she's been through. But I think she's going to. She has her mom, her daughters, and her faith. She wants a man. She feels lonely even with a full house. But she reminded me not to settle for the wrong guy at least ten more times. I told her to make sure she followed her own advice.

When I got up to leave she grabbed me by both hands and said she was going to pray for me. It was beautiful. I don't know exactly what I felt, but it was strong.

I don't cry but my eyes were moist the whole drive home. I wanted to meet with Tandi Brown to give her some kind of encouragement. It ended up being the other way around. We're going to get together again in a couple weeks. I have a feeling I'll need it by then.

62

Saturday, November 17
7:45 p.m.

Freedom is glorious!

No house arrest. Charges not dropped but suspended. Not ideal, but it's a start.

I caused a lot of my own problems by going over to Jack's house the night of his death. But it looks like I'm in the clear.

I know I'm still in danger. But what can he do to me? I've done nothing but think about what I can do to him, and I can't find an answer. We are officially in a stalemate. We both need the other to stay alive.

At least he sounded normal again this morning. Maybe he's coming back to reality.

I'm supposed to meet Grandpa tomorrow. It feels weird to call him that. But he's reached out to me and supposedly is going to publicly acknowledge me as his granddaughter and put me on the family dole. I've also been told I have to pass the interview test with good old Grandpa tomorrow night and then sign some papers.

I told dear Grandfather's messenger boy I wouldn't sign anything until my attorney had time to review the paperwork and make appropriate counterproposals if necessary. He said fine.

Just two years ago I was living in a one-story ranch in Madison, Illinois. Now I'm negotiating my piece of the pie with a billionaire.

The Chicago police technician took off the ankle bracelet this morning. My attorney was furious they didn't do it yesterday when the judge lifted the house arrest order at the DA's request. I actually didn't care. Tonight I'm going out on the town to celebrate.

She looked herself over in the full-length mirror again and gave a twirl. She looked at her diamond-encrusted watch. The cab should be down front in less than five. She was so ready to cut loose on a Saturday night on Rush Street.

She walked out the front doors of her apartment house—she wouldn't live here much longer; her attorney had already filed a motion for her to be the beneficiary of Barbara Ferguson's estate, including the incredible condo—and saw a chauffeured limo. She looked left and right for a cab, but the limo driver got out, opened the back door, and beckoned her.

"Ms. Martin?"

"I am."

"I'll be your driver tonight."

63

We are the champions of the world! From the cellar to the penthouse. From worst to first.

I'm trying to think of other trite sports clichés. The fact that this feels so good to me probably says something about my overall maturation in life.

The whole team came to the Pizza Palace to celebrate after winning our first-ever game under the lights. I need to eat something besides pizza tomorrow. We put the girls at three tables we scooted together. Parents formed groups of four and six around them. I am sitting with Jimmy, Klarissa, and Tiffany's dad. I finally remember his first name: Steven. A single dad who has custody of his two kids, he is acting more attentive than I am comfortable with. I definitely didn't like him last season after he had a few too many coaching recommendations for my taste and ego, but I've grown to admire his commitment to his kids. Even if he does want to become co-coach instead of assistant coach—something I don't intend to let happen—I have to admit he is great with the girls. He does want Tiffany to score more. I would kind of like her and Kendra to score less if we want to keep improving. But it is great to have two star players on the team.

The girls are still in uniform and each is wearing a gold medal. Based on the price of gold—and I actually know what it is from when we got Bobbie's safe open—I'm guessing they are made of a cheaper metal and painted gold.

Jimmy looks frayed. Neither Kacey nor Kaylen can sleep and that means he can't sleep either. Kendra is easy and maintenance-free. James will keep you running after him all day. He's a great kid with enough energy to light up Peoria, Illinois, for a night. He has enough volume to be a roadie for Bruce Springsteen. He is currently perched on a video game in the arcade trying to figure out how to kill alien invaders without putting a quarter in the slot.

My phone vibrates. I've still got an open case, so I stick a finger in my ear and pick up.

"Conner."

"Hi, Detective, this is Byron Tedford."

"Hi, Byron. What's up?"

"Are you at a club or bar or something?"

"Nope. I'm at Pizza Palace with my niece's soccer team. We just won the championship and we're celebrating."

"Very nice. I don't want to interrupt you, but I've been in the office all day. I found out something interesting."

"The name of who had the most to gain?"

"Yes. That was no surprise. But I got online

and started sifting through his finances. I discovered he's the one who's been making a monthly payment to Penny Martin through an account in Switzerland."

"And?"

I'm expecting the name.

"I also found his name on an account at Electronic Express."

I guess that's supposed to mean something to me.

"He buys at least one new prepaid phone every week. No name on the phone number, but his name on the credit card purchase."

My mind is whirling.

"Then it gets real interesting. The only other person authorized to pick up purchases for him is a Ms. Penny Martin."

"Are you going to give me the name or do I have to come down there and beat it out of you?"

We glanced his direction early in the investigation, but he was never really a person of interest in this case. He wasn't close to Jack Durham. He was the opposite of Jack and his cronies. Hard worker. Apparently a family man. His father's right-hand man in business.

Robert Durham Jr. The younger brother.

I am driving to the office on a Saturday evening so I can sort through the evidence and put Junior under the microscope. The first recorded murder in history was Cain killing Abel. We still talk about being close as brothers and blood being thicker than water. But that's not always the case.

Before I arrive at the office Konkade calls me.

"Yes, Sergeant?"

"You're not going to believe this."

"I don't know about that. My day has turned very surreal on the Durham murder case. Nothing you tell me should come as a surprise."

"You got something too?"

"I do."

"How soon can you get down here?"

"Is five minutes fast enough?"

"Perfect. I'll give you something to chew on, then you give me something to chew on."

"Deal."

"I just got a call patched through to me from the doorman at Penny Martin's apartment."

"Yeah?" I'm all ears.

"He says someone just dragged her into a limo and drove off."

The evening started with a sense of euphoria—*We're going to arrest a killer tonight!*—but slowly faded to frustration.

Konkade worked the phones to get everyone involved on the case into the office no matter what they were doing. He found everyone but

Randall. He also pulled together a small army of officers to help with legwork. Zaworski came in. Czaka was there when I finished sprinting up four flights of stairs. Someone said Fergosi was on his way in.

Naming a new official suspect is a very tricky part of any investigation. Durham's status made this one even trickier. Do we arrest a prominent Chicago businessman, the heir to a multibillion-dollar empire, based on what Tedford discovered? If he's not the murderer, this is going to blow up in our face. The DA is still furious and the media is merciless. I can hear Klarissa on WCI's late report saying something to the effect of "A beleaguered Chicago Police Department, led by my older sister Kristen, arrested billionaire Robert Durham Jr. on the basis of his account with Electronics Express." This one won't end well.

We can go visit him in his home, but not search it, without his clear permission—and he's not compelled to come to the precinct without a warrant for his arrest. Either way, the Fifth Amendment clearly states he doesn't have to say anything.

But with a warrant for his arrest we can get a search warrant. If he's holding Penny in his home—doubtful—we could look for her.

"Am I in trouble?" Tedford asked, sneaking into my cubicle before we made final plans for the evening in the larger battleship-gray conference room.

"What for?" I asked.

"Someone said I might not have had the right to look at Durham Jr.'s numbers and anything I found might be inadmissible in a court of law."

"But he volunteered his information at the beginning of the case. So did Senior and most of Jack's friends. Those that didn't, we issued injunctions on."

"Correct," he said. "But apparently the injunctions expired November 16. Today is November 17. With Martin behind bars, nothing was renewed."

That didn't sound good and it wasn't.

It's after eleven-thirty. I might not get home until the eighteenth. I don't care how guilty I feel, I'm sleeping in and not going to church tomorrow morning. I haven't had more than six hours' sleep in a week. Closer to five most nights. I need about seven to feel good.

After a quick burst of enthusiasm, saber rattling, and congratulating of Tedford and me that this thing might be solved, by the end of the evening we decided to do exactly . . . nothing. When I say *we* decided, what I really mean is Czaka and Fergosi decided.

I'm almost numb, but I have just enough feeling to be seething with anger.

We ended up all dressed up with nowhere to go. The decision was made to renew the injunctions to study Junior's financial records on Monday—and to wait before moving against him until Tedford crunches his numbers and looks through materials again, but this time legally. Yes, he was in trouble. Fergosi was mad.

"But what about Martin?" I ask.

"The doorman didn't get a license number. Do you know how many black limos there are in the city?" Czaka answers back with a question. "We can't tie whatever happened in front of her apartment to Durham Jr. And we don't know if anything illegal happened anyway. We've sent officers over to question the doorman. He was not absolutely certain she was forced into the back of the limo. He said he was watching her walk over to the vehicle, she stopped at the last minute, and then a hand shot out and pulled her in. It's possible she and her date were playing a game."

"*Me gustaría jugar con ella,*" Martinez mutters under his breath to me.

I just look at him. I don't know what he said, but I can guess.

"So we're not even going to try and locate the whereabouts of or question Junior tonight?"

I wonder again why I was the only one questioning the decision to back off on Durham until Monday at the earliest. Was that so obviously the right thing to do that I'm the only one who doesn't get it? Or am I the only one dumb enough to squawk and put up a fight when the big brass makes a political decision? And for CPD, the big brass doesn't get any bigger than Commissioner Fergosi.

From my lowly vantage point this appears to have politics written all over it. *Wealth has its privileges.*

I'm glad I didn't say what I was thinking on that out loud. Zaworski and Blackshear kept their heads down while I was pushing Fergosi and Czaka. The fact that Zaworski didn't make eye contact was significant, I thought. If he had disagreed with me I would have been given the stink eye the whole time.

I wonder if the offer to work for the FBI is still on the table.

Don't complain. Focus. Respect your bosses. Work with the team. Be patient. Think. Pray. Do your job.

I slam my fist on the steering wheel, which really hurt.

I have an idea. I hit Konkade's number.

64

Saturday, November 17
11:51 p.m.

So this is how it ends.

Did I always know I was destined to fail? I can't believe how close I got to the prize. Maybe I was never as close as I thought.

When I saw Jack's head—Dad's head—beat in with a hammer, I should have known there was something seriously wrong with him and he could never be trusted under any circumstances.

I thought I was protected by a pact of MAD—mutually assured destruction—if either of us betrayed the other.

I'm sure I would be fully exposed if anything suspicious happened to him. I've let him know that the same thing will happen to him. He doesn't seem to care. He's not right in the head. I knew he was angry and that he resented Jack and his lifestyle. But I didn't know how deep the hatred ran.

First, he set up my mom in business as a silent partner to spite Jack. Then, when she tried to defend me for the first time in her life, he killed her.

I thought I was smart, but I obviously wasn't smart enough to stay clear of him.

So it ends here. The same place life started anew for me. Mom's place.

I finally figured out where I had seen the driver before. He is a detective for Chicago Police. When Robert bragged about having a source in the CPD, he wasn't joking.

It's ironic. All I've ever really wanted in life was for my family to acknowledge me. My adoptive father used to tell me, "Be careful what you wish for." I guess he was right on at least one thing.

She strained against her constraints. He had gone to another room. The two men were conferring quietly. She couldn't hear the words, but she knew that how her life was to end was being discussed.

She tugged at the ropes on her arms and legs again. Her movements didn't loosen them but instead seemed to tighten them. He'd been sailing on Lake Michigan and around the world his entire life. He knew how to tie a knot with no loose ends.

I can't believe he acted. He'll burn for this. Doesn't do anything to help me, though.

65

"Just stop talking for a second," Konkade says. "I'm with Blackshear right now and I can't do two conversations at once."

We're all feeling frayed tonight.

"We're the last two in the office. And that's the problem. He's not going to approve of you checking anything out without backup."

I hear Blackshear call toward the phone, "No way, Conner."

"Just send a patrol car over behind me."

"You are technically correct—we have unfettered access to her residence," he says. "I've got paper-work in front of me. Nothing has changed. She is a murder victim and her home is still officially the scene of a crime."

"And since you believe there is little to no chance Junior took Penny there, we don't have a problem."

"We don't know if he took her anywhere."

"Maybe *we* don't, but I do."

"Your instincts are legendary, Conner, but you haven't always been right."

"And I agree with you that my instincts are probably wrong on Durham taking Martin to Ferguson's condo. I have no proof, but I know they aren't wrong that he took her—but I have no sense of where he would have gone. It was just a thought. So since they aren't going to be there, what would it hurt for me to take a look?"

He sighs.

66

"You all are busy here tonight."

My detective antennas go up. "What do you mean?"

"The other cop arrived a couple hours ago. I figured you were meeting him."

I laugh to cover my confusion.

"You know us. Always falling all over each other because no one knows what the other is doing. Did he have anyone with him?"

"I assume just one other person. But I didn't see him. I let someone in through the garage entrance. That's what the other detective said to do."

"Makes sense," I say while nodding.

None of this makes sense. I look out the large plate-glass windows from the lobby to the street. I'm waiting for a patrol car as backup. Two officers are going to accompany me into the condo. But something might be happening up there now.

"Did you get the other detective's name?"

"I wasn't paying as good attention as I should have," he says sheepishly.

Who from CPD is already up there? And why? And why don't I know? And where is my backup?

"Listen, uh—"

"Frank."

"Thank you. I'm lousy with names. Listen, Frank. Two more police officers will be here in the next little while. Can you buzz them up when they get here?"

"Sure."

"I'm going to go on up now."

"Sure. I'll key you up."

"Speaking of keys, do you have an extra one to the apartment?"

"I do, but I don't mind going up and opening the door for you. But if you have a colleague already up there, can't you just knock on the door?"

I don't know who's up there. What do I say now?

"Based on a new lead, I know we're running new tests up there so I don't want to disturb anything that's in progress. And I don't want to disturb you from keeping an eye on the lobby. So just give me the key to Ms. Ferguson's unit and I'll bring it back. Work for you?"

"I'm really not supposed to."

"I'll bring it back before I leave. Scout's

honor," I say, holding up two fingers and crossing my heart.

I was never a Scout, so I'm not sure if it's two fingers or three.

"Just be sure you bring it back to me so I can sign it in."

"Will do."

"And, Detective?"

"Yes, Frank?"

"The press said a lot of horrible things about Ms. Ferguson, but she was always good to me and the others that work here. I hope you nail whoever killed her."

"I do too, Frank."

The situation has changed. Junior isn't alone. Someone claiming to be a CPD detective is with him.

I begin thinking through attack and defense strategies and tactics on my ride up the elevator. I know the layout of Ferguson's condo very well. That helps. But it's big. A lot of space to account for with Junior, a pretend cop, and a hostage. Will Junior be armed? Even if the other guy isn't a real cop, he will be. Penny will be in the apartment too. No clue if she's dead or alive. I'm hoping alive, but alive gives them leverage. So dead is easier. But I'm not thinking that way. I want her alive.

It's always possible she is on their team. Doubtful, but possible.

I arrive on Ferguson's floor and it sounds to me like the elevator bell rings louder than an air-raid siren. I wonder if they could hear it in Green Bay, Wisconsin.

I am thankful the tiled hallways (looks like marble) are striped by a long carpet runner. Red, of course. I'm wearing a pair of Asics running shoes and could have kept my footsteps quiet anyway, but this makes things even easier.

I turn left out of the elevator, walk twenty feet to a corner, and turn left. Hers is in the large northeast corner unit.

Forget the sound of footsteps, my heart is pounding so hard I think it can be heard down in the lobby. I wonder how far behind my backup crew is. *Where are you, boys?*

I get to Ferguson's door. I can see a tiny full moon of light behind the peephole. I press my eye and see exactly what I expected to see. Nothing but the distorted shapes of furniture in an empty room.

I have drawn my Sig. If I end up using it, everyone in a square mile will hear it. No one in the building who is asleep will be once the explosive charge of a handgun sounds.

I pause. It's now after midnight but the sounds of the city are still wide awake. Tires squeal. Horns blare. Motors rev. The *swoop-swoop-swoop* of traffic on Lake Shore Drive is constant. I can feel the beat of music. Must be a club on this street. Might be my imagination, but I hear what I think is the faint trace of voices and laughter.

Last night was pizza with Tandi and her mom and girls. Comfortable. Intimate. A graceful moment with a survivor of violence. Earlier today —I guess it's yesterday now—I ate pizza again. The Snowflake invasion of Pizza Palace was much noisier and more boisterous than Tandi Brown's home, but it was still sweet and innocent in its own way.

What awaits behind the door is much different. It's evil and malignant. It's a force of destruction. Greed? Jealousy? A warped psyche?

Unless no one is in there.

Time to go in and find out. I raise the electronic key to the keypad over the door handle. A security chain will probably stop the door after five inches. I'm going to put my legs, shoulder, and all 120 pounds of me into that gap and break it. I'll keep my Sig Sauer held high and my head on a swivel. I will be ready to deal with whatever awaits me. I'll enter the living room, sprint to the dining room—with a tuck and roll if necessary—drive into the kitchen, zigzag into the sunroom, and finish my orbit in the back hall that leads into the bedrooms. The key will be to keep moving.

"The Lord shall preserve thy going out and thy coming in from this time forth." I breathe a phrase from a psalm I learned when I was a kid. I

don't know which one. But I know I need some preserving where I'm going to—particularly if I want to come out.

I lift the card to the electronic pad. Before it gets there, the door opens. I'm standing face-to-face with Bob Randall.

Both our jaws drop. Either he's changed into a chauffeur's uniform or there are three men inside. I'm almost disoriented.

"It's about time you got here," he says. "I've got them secured in the back room."

I'm disoriented. But not stupid. My gun is up and pointing at his chest at the same time his gun magically appears.

"Drop the gun, Conner. Do not think I will hesitate to blow your brains out," he says with a snarl.

"Your trigger finger so much as twitches, you are a dead man," I snarl back.

"Then how about my gun?" Junior asks. The barrel is pointed at my face. He is hidden by the side of the doorway. Yep, he's armed. "Drop the weapon, Detective."

My mind runs through percentages and options. None of them favor me.

"Now."

My only prayer is that he doesn't have a silencer in his pocket and doesn't want to wake up the whole building with a blast from his handgun. He's got a Beretta 9mm. My old model. I actually still have one in my lockbox at home.

I see him tense and I immediately point the barrel of my Sig Sauer at the ground. I've watched cop dramas on TV, so I know the routine. I remove my finger from the trigger and hold the weapon by the handle between my thumb and forefinger.

Junior laughs.

"If you would be so kind as to hand that to my colleague—carefully, I would add—I would be most appreciative."

"How many pieces of silver did you get, Bob?" I ask as I hand him the gun.

"Shut up, Conner," he says. "Your shtick gets old real quick."

"Let's go back where you can join an old friend and get more comfortable," Junior says.

"You know he's tying up loose ends and you'll soon be one of them," I say to Randall.

"Shut up, Conner," he says again.

Quiet, unassuming Randall is dirty. Oh, man, oh, man.

"I think Detective Randall can take care of himself," Junior says. "Unlike others, which should be very obvious to you at this particular moment. That's why I selected him for my team. You should have accepted my dad's job offer; you could have been on the team too. He was serious, you know. I'm going to recommend Detective Randall to work for us full-time instead. I think he might enjoy his pay raise and bonus."

I look behind me at Randall and he smiles. He

gives me another poke in the back with his standard-issue Glock. Where is my backup? New shift. Tell me they didn't stop for a cup of coffee already.

The gun nudges me again. I'm sure Randall scores better than I do on the firing range. But I'm positive he hasn't studied the tactical moves of capturing or being held captive to the degree I have. The three of us are walking into the sun-room, where Penny is gagged and tied up on the floor in the corner. Alive. We are in a single-file line. That basically neutralizes the second person's weapon. Durham is a civilian and doesn't know anything, but Randall has at least gone through classes on basic coverage concepts and should know better.

I take a second step into the room and slow down. He nudges me yet again. *Bob, you may not like my shtick, but you have poked me in the back with that Glock for the last time.*

When I feel him pull back the weapon, I stomp on his instep with all my strength and weight. At the same time I snap my head back and catch him on the nose. I've thrown both elbows down and back in a blind attempt to hit the tops of his forearms as viciously as possible. His left was already down and I make no contact. But his right arm was up with the gun and I can feel my elbow drill into his ulna. Not sure I snapped it but I got it good.

He roars in pain as he staggers back. But he keeps his senses and ignores his broken nose—no easy task—and begins to bring the Glock up to shoot me. Before he can reach firing position, I whirl and grab the wrist of his gun hand and push it back down. I hear bones grind and note with satisfaction that I did break his ulna—thinner than the radius, but not bad.

He is in trouble and knows it. I know his instinct will be to ignore the searing pain in his forearm and to push against my downward force. Things are moving in slow motion and I am fully ready for the move. What I'm not ready for is what Junior is up to behind Bob.

I take my hat off to him; I know how bad the move hurts. But Bob launches his arm forward with his weight behind it. Instead of resisting, I go with it and yank his arm over his head and out of shooting range in a nanosecond. Then I wrench it down and back and pull it up tight behind his back, turning him face-to-face with a stunned Robert Durham Jr. I taste bile at the sound of bones grinding another direction—and Randall buys me another second as he lets out an earsplitting scream. The Glock clatters noisily to the floor and I'm levering Randall's arm even further up to drive him straight into Durham. He is no longer fighting back and is actually bull-rushing Junior with me.

Durham's eyes widen and he gets the gun up,

but we are knocking him backward one staggered step at a time. The explosion from the barrel of his Beretta is deafening. I feel Randall's body convulse but keep pushing forward to crowd Durham from getting a clean shot off at me. A 9mm gun is a killing machine, but thankfully the ammo gauge is just small enough to carom around inside Randall's internal organs rather than coming through his body and hitting me.

I push hard and we are back in the living room.

Please show up now, backup officers. Please.

Durham tries to get the gun around Randall's dead body, but I push Randall into him as he squeezes the trigger again. The bullet misses me, but I'm showered with shaved bone and brain matter from the side of Randall's head.

With my fatigue, Randall's body is getting heavier as he turns to dead weight, but my adrenaline rush keeps me driving at Durham with his body as a shield. I'm gasping as we reach the center of the living room and tumble to the floor. Durham falls flat on his back and his arm flies over his head, but he keeps hold of the Beretta and is immediately struggling to sit up and pulling his arm forward to shoot me.

I plant a foot on Randall's chest and launch myself at Durham. The gun is arcing down and forward. I am flying through the air at him like Superman—or Superwoman. My eyes are fixed on the arc of the gun. I stretch and strain in midair as if time has stood still. I doubt it looks as good as the fight scenes in *The Matrix* but I'm sure it would still be impressive on film.

The mind is an amazing thing in its capacity to compute incredible amounts of data and thought. I wonder again when my backup will arrive. I wonder again if I get to keep the clothes that Barbara Ferguson bought me—and if I can trade in the size 0 Dolce & Gabbana jeans for a size that allows me to walk and breathe.

My hand connects with his right wrist, pushing the gun up and out. The Beretta explodes again. The bullet doesn't part my hair, but I'm pretty certain I felt it scream within inches of my temple. The gun was less than a foot from my head and the sound was deafening. Literally. My head is buzzing and I can't hear anything. I might have lost an eardrum on that.

I keep my hand on Durham's wrist and push forward on top of him. The fight now feels surreal with no sound. I've got his right hand clutched in my left. Our faces are six inches apart. He gasps as he tries to bring his arm forward. I feel the spray of his spittle and am repulsed.

He wrenches his body hard left and right trying to throw me off him. I hold on for dear life. I may have better tactical position, but he has a gun.

He thrusts his head forward with teeth bared and tries to bite me. I snap my head back, then forward. He dodges and I barely clip his jaw. Not enough force to do any damage.

He bucks to throw me off and tries to bite me again. I'm riding a rowboat in a thunderstorm but stay on top of the raging sea.

I feel him flatten beneath me, undoubtedly to marshal his strength in another attempt to free his arms. I go back to my in-close combat training with Krav Maga. In a timed maneuver, I twist my shoulders hard to the left, throwing my right elbow up and forward as hard as I can from that range. I catch him flush in the temple . . . and I see the lights go out. A one-punch knockout. The gun clatters harmlessly away.

I can't wait to tell Soto.

I breathe in and out. The world is silent. I begin to relax.

His eyes pop open wide. Like lightning his hands are on my neck to choke me.

I push up and away but his hands fumble to keep a hold. Halfway up I fall toward him, my arms rotating up and down and catching his wrists to break the hold. I roll away and see his hand shoot for the gun. Mine gets there first and I send it soundlessly skidding across the narrow-plank oak floor.

Two arms grab me from behind and pull me backward. I see navy slacks and polished black work shoes step past me. I look up and see an officer with his Glock pointed at Durham. He is giving him orders. He might be yelling. I still can't hear anything.

But I am alive.

"I think you've got a perforated tympanic membrane," the paramedic says to me an hour later. I hear him in my right ear but not in my left.

"In English," I say.

"Ruptured eardrum. You need to go to the hospital."

I shake my head, which is aching. The ten bass drum players residing in my brain are awakened from the movement and start to pound out the beat for a Sousa march.

"What will they do?" I ask.

"Not much. There's really no treatment for a ruptured eardrum. It will heal itself in a couple weeks."

"So why go to the hospital?"

"I said I think it's a ruptured eardrum. So they need to look at it. But if it is a perforated tympanic membrane, this does make you susceptible to middle ear infections and I promise you, you don't want that. They'll put you on an antibiotic and might want to apply something topical as well."

"Okay."

67

I can't believe CPD brass agreed to it. I can't believe I agreed to it. My sister will be interviewing me for a thirty-minute WCI-TV special on the Jack Durham murder.

One of Commissioner Fergosi's aides met with me to review what I could and could not answer.

Why did Robert Durham Jr. kill his brother? *"Frustration that Jack was squandering the family fortune as fast as he could help create it."*

Was there anything in his past to indicate he was violent? *Leave it alone*—"Not that we are aware of."

Did Robert Durham Sr. have any role in this? *"No. He was a loving father." I'm not saying that one.*

Did Detective Randall impede the investigation? Did he help Durham Jr. the whole time? *"Sadly and apparently, yes." Don't talk about his gambling problem and financial woes, which the CPD was aware of.*

Why did Durham kill Ms. Ferguson? *"According to Penny, her mom was maybe the only person in the world other than Jack who knew how much Robert Jr. hated his brother. She was going to present that to the police—to me—to get her daughter out of jail."*

How did you know he would take Ms. Martin, his niece, to Ms. Ferguson's home? *Answer that however you want. "Hmm. I don't know. A gut feeling. Maybe a prayer."*

So far Penny hasn't been charged as a coconspirator. How involved do you think she was? *"That's part of an ongoing investigation and I'm not at liberty to say."*

Did Barbara or Jack ever love Penny? *"Maybe. But not very well."*

What was Penny looking for? *Say whatever you want. Not sure how to answer if Klarissa asks. "At least at the beginning she was looking for what we all are: the love of the significant people in our life."*

My last answer got lots of airplay. To my horror, I've started getting marriage proposals sent to my attention at CPD. And I thought the stalker jokes at my expense were bad. It's brutal.

When Channel 2 in New York City called to offer Klarissa a job, they said her interview of me was over the top. She's getting nominated for awards.

68

"I might have seen something but I might not have. I have to think and remember. Just depends how nice you are to me."

"You've told me a bunch of times I have to be nice to you. Tell me what that means."

"What do you think it means? I want a deal on the other charges. Basically, I tell you what I might have seen the night your old man was shot, and I don't do any jail time."

"I'll get back to you," I say, rising.

Could this be the break I'm looking for?

"Oh, one other thing," he says.

"Just one?"

"Yeah. You hated me the day you first laid eyes on me. You're a very judgmental person, you know. I said I wanted an apology for the way you smashed my face in the gravel when you arrested me. I still haven't heard that apology."

I sigh.

"I'm sorry you were hurt during the arrest, Jared."

"That's not an apology. That's sympathy for something that just happened to have happened. You're not apologizing for what you did."

Do I go over the table after him or be a

grown-up? Why is someone this smart in so much trouble?

"I'll get back to you on that too, Jared."

"Can't just say it, can you?" he asks, a look of triumph on his face.

"I need to discuss that with my attorney. I'll get back with you."

"Don't wait too long or it won't count and the deal is off," he says with a smirk.

I'd like to wipe that smirk off his face. But I'm gonna be a grown-up inside and out. So I don't let my attitude and anger go there. Did Incaviglia see something that would help catch my dad's shooter? I'm skeptical. Would CPD brass give him a free pass if he did? I'm skeptical on that too.

A week ago I tried to sneak behind Czaka's back and get another look at my dad's case file. This time I'll set up a meeting and enter calm, cool, collected—professional. I pray I will leave the same way. I think I can do it. I think I'm changing. Maybe growing up a little—but I hope not too much.

I'm thirty. I think that's adult in anyone's book. Even my sociology professor at NIU who lectured us on extended adolescence seemed to draw the new line of adulthood at no later than that. Why have I not felt very grown up, even while doing serious grown-up work? And why do I feel more mature now?

Is it because I have someone in my life? At least I think I do. I think Austin and I are both trying to figure this relationship thing out. There are a lot of issues. Two people that are both focused on their individual careers. Distance—701 miles, according to Google Maps. Personality differences and similarities. He has to look at how his marriage to Van Guten ended and what that means to his sense of trust. Then there's that little matter of values. I'm a church girl. I think he goes a couple times a year when he sees his parents. Christmas and maybe Easter.

We've got a few things to think and talk about before this gets real.

If I was in business, I think I would rather start companies than run them. At least that's the way I am with murder investigations. The hunt often feels futile. Much of the work is numbingly boring. But it's exhilarating. I think it's my calling. Finding killers.

But writing reports and working with the district attorney's office is not nearly as fun.

Jack Durham and Barbara Ferguson are dead and I had a big part in finding their killer. Blocking my way was Bob Randall. Now he's dead too. Call me judgmental, but nothing makes me angrier than a dirty cop. And the only thing worse than a dirty cop is a dirty cop that set up surveillance equipment in your house. I still feel like someone is watching me in my own home.

Even after all he did—and yes, he sent the text messages too—Bob's death is still a tough pill to swallow. He was a colleague. He was someone we trusted and thought was working with us, not against us. I think it's been hardest on Martinez. As Randall's partner, he feels responsible for not seeing something. Watching Martinez flail is painful. His machismo might drive me crazy, but it is missing in action and I miss it.

Then there's Robert Durham Sr. His oldest son is dead at the hands of his youngest son. What must be going through his head? McGill is handling all the details of Junior's defense. He has brought in an attorney from Boston, Massachusetts. Apparently the best criminal defense attorney in the country. Isn't going to do Junior any good, though. We have so much evidence on him, he is going to prison for the rest of his life.

His hatred for his brother blinded him. He kept the hammer he used to kill Barbara Ferguson in the trunk of his car. His attorney is claiming Martin planted it there. He spoke too soon. She was in jail at the time. So they'll have to come up with something better than that. And they will. I hear they are submitting evidence that Randall was the mastermind behind all this and was using Robert. Will it matter that they are simultaneously submitting that Penny was the puppet master pulling Bob's strings? Probably not. The judicial system at work.

Flannigan is in heaven with Junior. Penny Martin is another matter. She has been charged as a coconspirator in a capital crime and faces all the charges that Junior does. But the fact that she was already indicted as the one who wielded the hammer has her attorney filing motions and appeals of double indemnity almost every day. She's guilty as sin. But she might walk. Stranger things have happened. I've done my part. It's up to Flannigan to finish the job now.

69

Thanksgiving dinner was always at my parents' house, but now is at Jimmy and Kaylen's house—not sure we could all fit in Mom's tiny dining room with another King kid and guests. I took a nap during the first half of the Cowboys-Redskins game. I think Mom took that opportunity to move in for the kill with Reynolds. She's going to find out where he stands on religion. I would be mad at her but she is actually making things easier for me. At least the topic will be on the table.

Dinner was great. I did feel a little bad for Klarissa. She was the only one without a significant other. Well, except for Mom; I guess it's a bit unfeeling for me to presume she doesn't count. I watched Klarissa throughout dinner. She is much more serious than me, but she wasn't herself. *Are she and Warren really broken up this time?*

Reynolds was given the seat to my left. Across from me were Jeff and Patricia Williams. Jeff and Austin hit it off. Makes sense to me. A mergers and acquisitions attorney and an FBI operative have a lot in common, I'm sure.

Mom had a lot to say about the recent election and the state of the country.

Before James was allowed to leave the table he wanted to know if Austin had a gun with him. Austin told him yes. Then James wanted to know who would win in a fight: him or me.

"Better ask your Aunt Kristen," Austin, ever the diplomat, answered.

"My Aunt Kristen can beat up anybody," he yelled as he started throwing karate chops everywhere.

Smart kid—but James is a handful. Butkus, Singletary, Urlacher, maybe somebody else, but then the King. Da Bears.

I stop in the kitchen for coffee and Mom's blueberry pie, still groggy from my nap. Kaylen has finished feeding Kacey and I volunteer to burp her and then put her in her crib. Her little blue eyes are able to focus now and she looks at me sweetly and then yawns. My life story. I put a cloth diaper on my shoulder, lay her head gently on it, and then start patting her back. I sing a song Dad used to sing to us at bedtime when we were little girls.

Then through the woods there came,
A dragon breathing fire and flame,
He melted a path through the ice and snow,
And brought the princess down below.

I remember the tune and some of the words, but mess up and forget some stanzas. She won't notice. Before I finish she delivers a tremendous burp and is asleep as I lay her down.

I cut a half of a half piece of pie—someone was already into portion control ahead of me—and after making an attempt to take a normal-size bite, put the whole thing in my mouth. I fill up my coffee cup and head to the back bonus room to watch the fourth quarter. It's just the guys. Jimmy, Jeff, and Austin. If anyone asks me for the secret "guy" handshake for admittance, I'll probably cuff them.

I plop down next to Reynolds and lean in. He puts an arm around me. I lean back and give him a kiss on the neck. Jeff and Jimmy politely look away; this is raging public affection for me. He pulls me close and gives me a hug. I turn the top half of my body back for another quick kiss—it's a commercial break so I'm not missing any more of the game—and reach my hand around the side of his chest. It is bandaged. I feel him flinch. Not much but it is there.

I immediately sit up straight and turn completely to him.

"Unbutton your shirt right now."

"Get a room, you two," Jeff says with a barking laugh.

Jimmy clears his throat.

Austin has blushed.

"I can explain," he says.

"Uh-huh," I answer, "but I bet not very well."

"It was just a scratch."

"I didn't realize those negotiations on intellectual property rights with the Chinese got so rough."

"I wasn't exactly in China."

"So you lied to me."

"I just didn't tell you everything."

"Because I'm on a 'need to know' basis—and yes, you did lie to me. If you weren't in China with the State Department, you lied."

I'm on my feet and heading back toward the kitchen. Forget half of a half. If I want, I'll eat the whole pumpkin pie that hasn't been cut yet.

"Kristen! I can explain!"

70

I open the refrigerator and take out a half-gallon milk carton that is mostly finished. I take off the plastic blue lid and sniff. Bad idea. If I'd waited a second longer the rancid smell of spoiled milk would have attacked my sinuses without any assistance. Not sure there's anything edible in there.

It's the day after Thanksgiving. Black Friday. The roads were snarled with eager shoppers on the way to malls, mass-market superstores, and any other retail environment. With Reynolds in town I made sure to have the day off. I thought about going home after I discovered he had hid a serious injury from me. I don't know what made me maddest: him not including me in a significant moment or the fact that he had me wondering why he was distant when what he was really doing was convalescing.

Still a lot to think about.

Vanessa called me at seven a.m. If she had apologized for calling so early one more time, I would have screamed. She explained Don's brother, Rodney, had flown in from Los Angeles for Thanksgiving. The brothers spent the day before Thanksgiving looking for their sister, Debbie. They found her working tricks near

McCormick Place. It was an ugly confrontation. She called them every name in the book. She threw rocks at Rodney's rental car and broke a windshield. She refused an invite to Don's house for Thanksgiving dinner. She told them to never talk to her again.

Then she called Don at six-forty-five this morning. She gave him the address of a run-down extended-stay motel she calls home. She said she would go to a rehab center. Don and Rod were already out the door.

"Girlfriend, I am so sorry to ask, but would you meet them over there? They care and hope so much, they have tried so hard, but they don't see straight when it comes to Deb. She is sneaky. She is mean. She is a master manipulator. She makes them feel so guilty for the good lives they live—well, I'm not sure Rodney is living quite as good as he should be, but he is rich and successful—they can't see straight. Someone else needs to be there. Someone who might understand and see the situation better. If you can go, I owe you so big-time."

I know Vanessa didn't mean what she said the way it sounded, but I was still tempted to ask if she thought I could relate better to the mean or sneaky or manipulative part.

Don's late-model Buick was the nicest car in the parking lot despite the tarp taped over half the broken windshield. I climbed two flights of chipped concrete steps flanked by rusted hand-rails to the third floor. I found the number I was looking for. The door was ajar.

Rodney was sitting on a beat-up armchair with as much stuffing as cover fabric showing. Don slouched on the edge of the bed. They were sitting in silence. No sign of Debbie.

"Night manager saw her leave an hour ago. Probably within fifteen minutes of when she called me," Don said.

He officially introduced me to Rodney, who seemed to perk up when I arrived and held my hand a little longer than I was comfortable with when we shook. I think Don gave him a dirty look.

"Did she leave anything behind?" I asked. "Could she be coming right back?"

"Nothing," Don said.

"I know men don't always look very well, so I scoured the place myself. Even the refrigerator. They were right. She's gone. Not only am I judgmental, but I might be sexist too."

"Vanessa said you were on your way," Don said. "You didn't have to do that."

"That's what partners are for."

"Looks like a wasted trip," he said.

"You're missing the sales at the mall," Rod added.

This time I gave him a dirty look. He held his

hands up in surrender. Don was right. He is a smart man.

"She might call back," Rod said to Don as they headed out the door into the freezing-cold Chicago morning.

When we parted ways in the parking lot, Don simply said, "Thanks, KC."

I didn't have the heart to get on his case about the nickname.

"Nice to meet the superstar detective I've heard so much about," Rodney said. "You ever get out to Hollywood, look me up," he added as he handed me his card.

As I walked around to my driver's door I heard him asking Don, "Still want to try and do a little hunting today?"

I never heard Don's answer.

I move the gear shift between third and fourth on my way to meet Reynolds for breakfast at Café Selmarie on Lincoln Park Square. I've already got my heart—and stomach—set on the brioche French toast. I don't know all the flavors they have in it but there's lots of orange and cinnamon. I've met Klarissa there a couple times and love it. I like my JavaStar, but they serve Intelligentsia coffee, and that's a nice change of pace. Still nice and bold. Cream, not half-and-half, in a silver server.

I think back on Debbie's refrigerator and the

squalid hovel she was living in, the dirt and stains and odors. I need to think about something else or I'll lose my appetite completely.

"Why do you keep running from those that love you?" I ask Debbie wherever she is.

Dear God, help Debbie find her way home.

71

It's eight o'clock on Monday morning. The calendar now says December. I made it to work on time—by one minute—despite another over-night snow. Last winter was proof of global warming. This winter has brought back the phrase *global climate change*. It's been as cold as January in November and now December.

It's quiet. Where is everybody?

I had no time to stop at JavaStar. I'm thinking of buying a Christmas present for myself this year. If so it will be a grinder and space-age coffeemaker like Penny Martin had. I haven't priced her brand yet, but looked it up and saw it was only available at Williams-Sonoma. Probably not going to happen on my budget. The windfall from drawing a paycheck from CPD and FBI at the same time for a month is gone.

I stumble down the hall to get my first cup of the wretched sludge we call coffee in Homicide. I open the door and everyone screams, "Surprise!"

I was surprised enough I about wet my pants. I know it's not my birthday.

A smiling Zaworski steps forward with a cake that says *Welcome Back Conner!*

"None of us can remember why we missed you when you were gone—you've been back too long," he says and everyone laughs. "But we meant to welcome you back before another little murder took place and we got too busy. We also have a little present for you."

Czaka steps out of the crowd, shakes my hand, and places a small black box in it. I open it and am stunned. The Award of Valor. Same thing my dad got from Mayor Daniels. My eyes mist up and I am speechless.

Czaka turns to face my friends, my family in the CPD. Even Big Tony is here, hiding in the back, which is nearly impossible when you are six feet and four or five inches and weigh at least 260 pounds. He's beaming.

I can't remember exactly what Czaka said, but he's good at speeches. When he was done he whispered to me, "Well deserved. Time for us to talk."

Yes, sir, it is. Time to open the file on who shot my dad.

I take it all in and feel gratitude with every breath I take.

M. K. Gilroy has helped create hundreds of projects and launch dozens of authors, working in every area of the publishing industry. Gilroy's debut novel, *Cuts Like a Knife*, quickly garnered critical acclaim and introduced one of the most unique, fresh, and compelling lead characters in Detective Kristen Conner. Gilroy resides in Brentwood, Tennessee. Visit www.mkgilroy.com.

www.mkgilroy.com

facebook.com/MKGilroy.Author

Center Point Large Print

600 Brooks Road / PO Box 1
Thorndike ME 04986-0001 USA

(207) 568-3717

US & Canada:
1 800 929-9108
www.centerpointlargeprint.com